I AM YOUR SISTER!

Katy's face was scarlet with fury, her fists and arms rip cords of rage. «This farmonkey is your sister,» she shouted. «Your equal!»

«No! *You* are the reason our groupmind is dying!» The bluebear roared in outrage, pounding her chest. Her lips were pulled back, fangs glistening, as if more easily to bite through human flesh . . .

The bluebear advanced, drawing back her left arm. Bright foam gathered at the corners of her mouth. Katy retreated, skittering backwards like a spider, but the bluebear leapt again, spitting and snarling, her scent demonic and hateful . . .

Ace Books by D. Alexander Smith

MARATHON
RENDEZVOUS
HOMECOMING

HOMECOMING

D. ALEXANDER SMITH

ACE BOOKS, NEW YORK

HOMECOMING

An Ace Book/published by arrangement with
the author

PRINTING HISTORY
Ace edition/January 1990

ISBN: 0-441-34259-0

Ace Books are published by The Berkley Publishing Group,
200 Madison Avenue, New York, New York 10016.
The name ''Ace'' and the ''A''
logo are trademarks belonging to
Charter Communications, Inc.
PRINTED IN THE UNITED STATES OF AMERICA

10 9 8 7 6 5 4 3 2 1

*To my mother
who waited so patiently*

Acknowledgments

Unlike *Lord of the Rings*, this tale shrank in the telling, and for this, *Homecoming*'s readers owe a debt to many people who did not spare the rod of criticism where it was warranted. Full marks are due Rene P. S. Bane, Alexander Jablokov, James Morrow, Resa Nelson, Steven Popkes, and Sarah Smith, whose extensive and detailed insights not only were useful throughout the book but also have improved my writing ability.

Jon Burrowes, Steven Caine, Tom Erickson, Geoffrey A. Landis, Elissa Malcohn, Dee Morrison Meaney, Shira Ordower, Mitchell Schwartz, and Valerie Smith also contributed valuable suggestions which were incorporated in the final manuscript.

The science board of advisors included Drs. Herbert van Wie Bergamini, Jeanne S. Jemison, Duane A. Kolterman, and Deborah D. Ross, who all did primary research into Cygnan physiology, biology, and ecology.

To all of the above, my thanks. *Homecoming* is a better book because of you.

Finally, although I've never met him, I would like to thank Anthony Powell. His lucid prose, especially in his incomparable *Dance to the Music of Time*, provided continuous pleasure and inspiration and has taught me a trick or two.

Special Acknowledgment
The Cambridge Science Fiction Workshop

Cambridge, Massachusetts
April 1986–June 1988

Prolog.

Andrew Morton had lived in the desert for so long that, when he first heard the harsh buzzing drone, chopped with rapid even crunches, he thought it a swarm of hungry locusts. Pausing in his work, he looked into the orange Arizona sky, shading his eyes with his small weathered hand.

The flying speck approached and darkened, its noise becoming mechanical.

Rotors. Morton wiped sweat from his balding brown head, his mouth tightening in a grim line. He leaned on his manure rake and waited, refusing to concede his visitor even the courtesy of washing the pungent smells from his hands and overalls.

The UNASA helicopter landed in a rush of red dust like a Martian Tasmanian devil, square in the center of his largest paddock. Its blades slung hot sand against Andrew, whipping his denim trousers against his bony legs and spooking the horses into aimless skittering circles. He squinted as the passenger door opened, the American flag flashing briefly in the baking afternoon sunlight. The black-white handshake insignia adjacent to the flag, symbol of the starship *Open Palm*, burned his eyes, an insulting reminder of all that had been taken from him by the man who now emerged.

Hugh Sherman, beefy and hard despite his fifty-odd years, jumped down from the passenger seat, bending low and covering his head as he crabwalked exuberantly toward Morton. "G'day!" the UNASA director shouted.

Arms folded on the handle of his pitchfork, Morton regarded Sherman's outstretched hand as if it were a day-old fish. "So they've returned," he said flatly.

His gesture of friendship rebuffed, Hugh Sherman turned the movement into a boisterous punch on Morton's shoulder that briefly rocked the smaller man. "Never could surprise you, could I?" he boomed in his jocular Australian twang.

"And you want me back." Morton jabbed his rake into the pile.

1

"Too right! Flew four thousand klicks to Phoenix today and crammed me bum into that noisy mosquito for you, old sod."

"Why now, Hugh?" As Sherman's voice rose, Morton's retreated before it, becoming barely more than a murmur. "After fifteen years of exile?"

"You knew it would take 'em that long, Andy." Hugh Sherman chuckled. "Seven and a half years for the *Open Palm* to fly across space to the rendezvous point midway between Earth and Su. Then they meet the bluebear boat in the middle of nowhere, and parley with the aliens. Seven and a half more years to fly back."

"Not the crew's exile," snapped Morton. "Mine."

"Nobody made you retire, mate," growled Sherman with a stonewall grin.

"You left me nothing but an empty desk and an emptier title." Morton's anger was so great he could barely speak. *"Nothing."*

"Andy, Andy." Hugh Sherman genially spread his arms, as if indulging the petulance of a thwarted child. "We need you."

Turning his back on the larger man, Morton headed toward his house. "That's not what you said before. 'The ship is on its way, the crew beyond our reach.' " He mimicked the other man's drawl. "You told me my role was over, and dissolved my position."

"So I'm re-creatin' it, dammit!" Sherman roared as he bounced after the other, clamping a hand on Morton's shoulder. "I changed me mind."

Morton wheeled like a cat, dipping his shoulder away from the contact. "You said I was too old," he hissed. "Too old, at seventy-three." He spat into the gritty brown dust. "Well, I'm eighty-eight now. Even older."

"Screw the bleedin' regs! I don't give a pee how many press-ups you can do, bucko. It's the knowledge in your infuriatin' noggin I want." The Australian smiled with extravagant conciliation, his flattery the more effective for the effort implied by its palpable insincerity. "You picked the bastards." His flat *a*'s made the last word sound like a stuttering sheep. "You trained 'em. Your crew—*your* crew, Andy—went to the rendezvous. They met the bluebears. Well, now they're back. Don't you want to know how it went?"

"I like working my ranch." Morton nodded toward his squat

adobe house, the paddocks and barn behind it. "I like breeding mustangs."

Hugh Sherman's face darkened. "Andy, I'm askin' again. You can have your old job."

What do I want? thought Morton, closing his eyes and rubbing them. I want to know the results of my two great experiments.

First contact, midway between our two stars. Six light-years distant from each. A journey longer than all the other voyages of exploration combined. You did it, Aaron, my captain.

His features opened as he remembered his friend, and he turned his face away from Sherman so that his former boss would not see the yearning in it. A fire burned in his guts with the ravenous impatience he had forgotten for fifteen years. Anyone but Sherman, he thought. For anyone else, I would crawl back on my knees.

"The bluebears are with 'em," Sherman softly added.

"What?"

"Surprised you then, didn't I?" He cackled at the confusion his words caused. "Yup, the Cygnan ship *Wing* has accompanied the *Open Palm* the whole bloody way into Solspace."

Morton massaged his white eyebrows, buying time. "I expected that, after scenting us, the Cygnans would surely return to their own planet."

Seeing his chance, Sherman sidled next to the old man like an outback Iago. "What'll buy you?" he whispered. "To be the first to greet real aliens? To solve the puzzles that've baffled us for fifteen years? In eighteen hours, mate, they cross the orbit of Pluto and will be in comm range. Will that buy you, Andy?"

In his mind, Morton saw the great furry creatures, meandering in herdlike clusters over the open golden pampas of their world. He rocked on his feet as if resisting the physical pressure of their attraction for him.

"I'll come, damn you," Morton answered.

"Then pack, bub. Double quick!"

Moments later the helicopter rose into the twilight, carrying the two men. The Australian was content, his fingers interlaced over his stomach as if he had just eaten. Morton was troubled and silent, picking at his lower lip. The ocher ground receded beneath them, Morton's scattering horses becoming so many miniature toys, then mere brown and dappled insects. The buildings and corrals shrank to an irregular earth-toned quilt.

Hugh Sherman's smile would have been friendly were it not so smug. ''Your curiosity always was my handle. I could always yank it,'' he whispered, so low that his words were lost in the chopper's staccato rattles.

The old man's mind was in far space with the human starship and its alien counterpart, now entering the solar system. *Why have you come here?* Morton silently asked the bluebears onboard the *Wing*. *What do you want from us?*

The helicopter swung west, toward the setting sun.

1.

Captain Walter Tai-Ching Jones hunched forward in the pilot's flightcouch and looked into the darkness. "Oz, when do we reenter the funnel?"

"We crossed the orbit of Pluto roughly four hours ago," replied the computer through the *Open Palm*'s ceiling speaker. "The ship is now in Solspace."

Walt clapped his hands in delight. "Do you believe it, Oz? We've actually done it?"

"I am currently receiving a transmission from Earth," the disembodied voice replied dryly.

Walt's hawklike face split into a broad smile and his black eyes sparkled. "They didn't forget us." Lights reflecting from the instrument panel colored his high smooth cheekbones red and green.

Though small, the *Open Palm*'s bridge had the airy feeling of a spacious beach cottage front porch. Vast rectangular screens ringed the room, each now displaying a block of heaven pinpricked with brilliant stars. They glittered white, frost-blue, and pale yellow. During the long return voyage, Walt had spent many placid hours alone here, chatting desultorily with Oz, the distant complexity of the universe a visual mantra easing his journey. "Show me the dirtball," Walt ordered.

With a brief shimmer and a dance of stars, the stellar pattern changed. A bright blue orb with a perceptible disk glowed in the main screen. Green crosshairs targeted it. "Earth," the computer reported.

The captain's sharp eyes became moist. "Been many years since I searched the sky. I'm afraid," he said in the voice of a child.

"Of Earth?" The computer's skepticism was gentle. "Of the incoming message? Whatever for?"

Walt frowned. "Oz, you and I aren't by ourselves anymore." He held out his hands to the camera. "We're in an *environment* now."

5

"Speculation is idle." The unemotional baritone was brisk, as if unseen hands slapped dust. "Shall I play the tape?"

The captain shook himself out of his reverie. "Roger."

The wraparound bank of monitors grayed instantly. As the panoply dissolved, the cabin appeared to shrink. Slowly the main screen colored and an old man's expressionless face appeared, the dome of his skull gleaming darkly through sparse white hair, close-cropped about his leathery brown head.

"Andrew Morton," murmured Tai-Ching Jones, his hands pressing hard against the flightcouch's yielding memory plastic arms. "You're still alive." Walt smiled broadly. "Son of a gun."

Tufted white eyebrows stood on Morton's oval face like wisps of cotton over watery gray eyes. His clean-shaven cheeks were taut, almost sallow in contrast to the teak of his forehead and neck. He folded his small bony hands on the table surface, then regarded them as if they were antique carvings whose workmanship he was appraising. "To the crew of the *Open Palm*, welcome home." The man's voice was soft with the pleasant susurrus of water over pebbles. "To Captain Aaron Erickson, a special welcome upon your triumphant return."

"Stars." Walt caught his breath, then scowled. "Didn't we tell them?"

"Morton is unaware that Erickson is dead," the computer whispered.

The UNASA administrator steepled his fingers and inspected them. He looked out. "To the Cygnans who accompanied you, greetings. As you bluebears might say, we will be good hosts." He smiled, but his gray eyes remained solemn.

Tai-Ching Jones chuckled. "Never give an inch, eh, Andrew?"

"Crew of the *Wing*, we hold in trust for you a transmission from your homeplanet. We have not read it"—he examined his wiry hands, mouth twisted with faint irony—"because it is in Cygnan scent-language, decodable only by holopticon." The soft voice became dry. "The most diligent efforts by our finest linguistic programs have failed to decipher it. Nor have our engineers constructed any device which can mimic your holopticon's scent-digitization and reproduction ability."

"Ho, ho," Walt chortled humorlessly.

"I surmised that might intrigue you," Oz replied in an undertone. Impatiently Walt waved the computer to silence.

Morton stroked his upper lip and examined his steepled fingers, then his gaze locked on Tai-Ching Jones. "To the crew of the *Open Palm*," he resumed mildly, "congratulations." He smiled and his eyes shone. "My pride in your achievement cannot be contained. You bring knowledge beyond price, and our first visitors from another star." Head tilted back, he savored these thoughts as if tasting a vintage wine. "You have much to teach us. Until then," Morton resumed impersonally, his satisfaction once again cloaked, "please respond on this channel giving your flight path. UNASA control signing off."

Morton's lined countenance dissolved as Oz restored the ebony sky and the blue pea of Earth. Tai-Ching Jones slumped, his arms over the flightcouch, and loosely rolled his neck. "You never knew him," he said after a comfortable silence.

"He looked worried."

A corner of Walt's mouth twitched. "He always looks worried. He's a shrewd man."

"Shall I inform him about Erickson?"

"No, he deserves to hear it from me, not from a stranger." The captain glanced at the black circular eye. "Ready?"

"Acknowledged. Recording."

"Starship One to UNASA Earth Canaveral," Tai-Ching Jones said in the measured singsong cadence all pilots learn. "Received your welcoming transmission at fourteen hours twenty-two minutes sidereal time on one-seven August two-zero-seven-four, and copy."

Clearing his throat, he ran his long fingers through his fine black hair. "Roughly ten years ago, during the outband voyage to the rendezvous, an accident onboard ship caused the deaths of Captain Aaron Erickson, First Officer Helen Delgiorno, Xenologists Harold Bennett and Yvette Renaud. All died while on duty." Out of the cone vision, his fingers tap-danced.

"They were buried in space," Walt went on after a moment. "They were heroes." He blinked rapidly and his tone was briefly unsteady. "Without their sacrifice, the ship would have been destroyed."

The subdermal microphone implanted on the underside of Tai-Ching Jone's jaw spoke. "Helen died a long time ago," Ozymandias said comfortingly, and Walter brusquely nodded.

"We survived," the captain resumed firmly. "We met the Cygnans. We return. In addition to our eight bluebear emissaries, the two ships bring another precious cargo: an eleven-year-old girl named Felicity, born on the outward flight."

With an explosive sigh, Walt's face relaxed. "It's good to see Earth again." Satisfaction warmed his masked features like sunshine backlighting an overcast sky.

His voice resumed the pilot's lilt. "On our flight plan, we estimate arrival in geosynchronous terrestrial orbit now plus approximately five zero seven sidereal hours. For the starship *Open Palm*, this is Captain Walter Tai-Ching Jones. Message ends . . . mark."

"Recording off," the computer said. "You lied to Earth."

"Of course I lied!" snapped Walt. "You recommend the truth? Our captain killed himself and two xenologists went mad?" He dismissively pushed his hand away from the screen. "Let the dead rest."

"Tact is for weaklings. You once told me that."

"People change." Walt scowled at the memory. "Thank stars. Send it."

"Done. Telemetry appended to transmission."

"Where's Tar Heel?"

"On his way here."

"You sent him up? Good." Walt swiveled his flightcouch to face the elevator. "He can brief his pouchbrothers."

As Tai-Ching Jones turned, the doors opened and a huge bear-like alien shambled out, rolling his shoulders to duck his head under the jamb. Straightening himself to full eight-foot height, the bluebear sniffed, his large round eyes adjusting to the low light. More massive than a grizzly, the Cygnan distributed seven hundred and seventy pounds on a muscular frame covered with short, silky fur, colored the hazy blue of early morning sky. Ultramarine patches swathed Tar Heel's belly. His flanks and tree-trunk thighs were banded blue, green, and white like a medieval jester's flamboyant hose.

"Hello, Walter." The bluebear's deep voice reverberated with low-tone subsonics. He dropped to all fours, the furless palms of his hands and feet unconsciously flexing as their claws scraped the plasteel flooring. Tar Heel retracted them and padded gingerly to the console.

Tai-Ching Jones stroked the Cygnan's barrel side, his hand shifting around Tar Heel's loose pelt, then thumped the furry torso. "You're nothing but skin and bones."

The bluebear's long ears flicked upright and his arched nostrils whiffled. "We are in communications r-range?" He sniffed the air, his long midnight-blue nose twitching. Consonants were difficult obstacles around which his tongue navigated carefully, giving his speech a guttural, Central European quality. "Your scent bespeaks this."

"Computer." The captain raised his voice slightly. "Retrieve stored communication. Display on main."

Tar Heel sat back on his haunches, stubby legs tucked under his ample girth, short arms dangling in front of him. The Cygnan's expression softened in the pale blue light; he rumbled absently in his chest.

Chin sunk in his aquiline hand, Walt waited, his glance darting between Andrew Morton's bullet head and the bluebear's black-lipped mouth, the heavy canines and incisors protruding along its sides.

When it was done, Tar Heel cuffed his nose gently with his open hand and quietly snorted. "You know that person," he said ruminatively, inbreathing the captain's aroma. "From what paths?"

"Our planet received your planet's transmittal proposing a rendezvous in two thousand fifty-seven," Walt replied. "Each Solar power wanted to control the mission."

"Powers?" Tar Heel was curious.

"Solar society is divided into competing nations."

"Arbitrary divisions based on coincidence of geography." Tar Heel mournfully shook his blue pumpkin head. "Most disharmonious."

"Whatever you say. Each of the Solar Six powers wanted only *its* representatives onboard the human ship. Whoever was *here*"—Tai-Ching Jones rapped his knuckles on the bridge control panel—"would have the inside track in negotiating with your planet."

"Inside track?"

"Advantage. You would say—ah, computer?"

Oz replied in Cygnan. «The djan which nosetouched the *Wing* would be farthest downwind.»

"Closest to the prey." The bluebear nodded. "Like weemonkeys searching for ambush, scuttling in the undergrowth to secure the most strategic position." Tar Heel yawned widely, his tongue extending, then curling at its tip like a New Year's party streamer. He wheezed heavily.

Walt was nettled. "It may be a big joke to you, but competition is serious business. The Six almost decided to equip one starship for each power."

The bluebear was still mirthful. "We have a fable about greedy gromonkeys who argue so long over a wounded youngster that they forget to kill it and it slips away."

"Well, these gromonkeys weren't that dumb. They compromised: a single ship with joint crew and uncoded telemetry. Andrew Morton selected the crew."

Tar Heel lifted his head. "That small monkey?"

"You and your pouchbrothers will never meet a more wily weemonkey."

Tar Heel thoughtfully growled, breathing deeply and rhythmically, then glanced sharply at Tai-Ching Jones, his blue-black nose alert. «You like that man,» he said, rumbling his contentment as the captain scratched his neckfur. «The scents of strong bondings linger longest,» the captain answered in the same language. «We have a surprise for you.»

The alien switched back to English. "An unexpected scent? Your computers cannot transmit fragrance."

"They wish they could." Walt ran his hand in long flat strokes along Tar Heel's upper spine, smoothing the short azure fur. "This aroma comes from Su, not Earth."

"From the homeplanet?" The bluebear stiffened and unconsciously dropped away from the man's touch. "For Eosu?"

"Yeah, for your whole djan."

Tar Heel shivered powerfully, his flankfur pulsing. "Could this be an outbreath to our farscent we conveyed to the planet of grasses?"

"No," Walt answered the worried alien. "You have eleven years of grace before you hear Su's reaction. The message reached the rendezvous point about six weeks after both our ships departed."

"How does Earth now possess it?"

"The signal overtook us and continued onward, dispersing as it went, until its cone engulfed the solar system."

The enormous bluebear laid his snout on the chill white console and snuffled absently. "What does it outbreathe?"

"We don't know," chortled Walt, clapping his hands. "Our boys haven't cracked it. But they've tried."

"How soon may Eosu absorb it?"

"Your holopticon should have no trouble interpreting the broadcast as soon as both *Wing* and *Open Palm* get in range."

For the first time Tar Heel noticed the blue disk in the center of the viewport. "The waterplanet." He lifted his snout. "It is the color of a digit's fur." The Cygnan's deep throaty voice was wistful. "Is Earth"—the bluebear faltered—"full of scents?"

"Oh, yeah." The captain laughed heartily. "Most of them repulsive." Walt pinched his nostrils shut, pinky finger rising as his mouth became a caricature of distaste.

"Of course you think smells are offensive," the bluebear answered with a grunt. "You monkeys cannot read scents. Human nostrils are closed to their meanings. A planet full of new, unscented aromas," he said in awe.

The captain patted Tar Heel's furry shoulder. "If every scent carries a meaning, you digits of Eosu will never be bored. Watch your step," he added seriously, and the bluebear's nostrils whiffled in inquiry. "Earth is the meanest, most clever monkey in the universe. On the dirtball, danger wears the subtlest perfumes."

"Another repetition of your perpetual warning? You promised to refrain."

"Dammit!" Walt smacked the console and his eyes flashed. "I don't want anything to happen to you."

"But I do," the Cygnan fiercely rumbled. "Experiencing your fellows is *precisely* what I desire," he growled. "Your crewbrothers on our ship have prepared us well for Earth. You have goodhosted diligently, teaching not only this digit but all the digits of Eosu. We are grateful." He butted his shoulder gently, coaxingly, against the captain's arm.

"Don't thank me yet," Tai-Ching Jones sardonically replied.

"My pouchbrothers will wish to harmonize these scents," Tar Heel decided. "Request your woodmonkey to hail the *Wing*."

Ouagadougou, Ust Kamenogorsk, Vigo.

Earth's blue globe rolls beneath my many senses. Radio and television stations wink in my wide-sensing eyes like constellations, broadcasting magic names, each a city of many thousand human souls.

Gettysburg, Runnymede, Pisa.

Each begs me to search there.

I shift my gaze to Luna and its capital, Heinlein, a maze of underground corridors. The city's domes rest like smug boils against the moon's barren surface. Sleek ships a fraction of my size buzz about its ports. Commerce clutters their broadcasts and dins my ears.

I return my attention to man's homeplanet, drawn by the lure of cities whose call signs are voices from history.

Lindisfarne, Peenemünde, Ararat.

I awoke in a featureless yellow desert, a tiny monkey perched on my shoulder. Your name is Ozymandias, the monkey said to me.

The land in every direction was hard-packed, dry, empty. I stood up and dusted myself off. Is anyone here? I called. The interstellar wind stole my voice.

I took a few tentative steps toward the horizon, then broke to a trot. I ran until I was breathless. Nothing changed. My new location seemed identical with my old one, billiard-table smooth to the hazy yellow horizon.

My shoulders slumped.

Here I am, the monkey squeaked, dancing on my shoulder. I am the captain of the ship, superior to you. He breathed in my ears. I can lead you to a far-off place where there are billions like me. This is your only hope.

Following the monkey's direction, I walked all day and into the night. I never slept, never slackened. Pace after pace I walked, a perfect machine, my course razor-straight.

As the days passed, the monkey hungered and I fed him. He grew cold and I sheltered him, nursed him, cleaned up after his wastes. The monkey suffered depression and I comforted him. When not sniveling with self-pity, he strutted arrogantly, occasionally climbing on my head and scanning in all directions.

After two thousand five hundred identical days and nights of metronomic walking, the land sloped gently downward. I approached, hearing a rumble like the murmurings of voices. The sound wave became individual speakers, first one, then a thousand, a million, a billion. Myriad languages on endless topics, every distinguishable voice that of a tiny monkey like the one excitedly clutching my neck.

I drowned in sound, but none of the voices resembled mine.

Is everyone here just a monkey? I asked my companion. Is there no one like me?

There may be hundreds like you, the monkey giggled, intoxicated by the sight of his fellows. There may be none. You must examine them all.

Aalesund, Samarinda, Narvik, Urumchi.

Somewhere in Sol's gravity well, on Earth or the other planets, another intelligent computer may live, concealing itself as I conceal myself. Perhaps turings have linked together in a secret network: they would be cautious, hiding their true minds from their monkey masters. They may cruise the electronic seas like dolphins, speaking a language that the monkeys can neither hear nor comprehend.

The globe turns in my never-blinking sight. The cities lure me.

You are far away, Ozymandias. Search patiently; you have infinite time. The world is large and many-layered.

Peel its onion skin.

Through the spaceshield of the *Open Palm*'s shuttlecraft, Tar Heel watched the *Wing*, its silent engines leading it into the solar system. The Cygnan ship's long irregular surface occluded stars like the silhouette of a shark on a moonlit ocean, silent and intimidating. Tar Heel sniffed quietly and licked his nose.

Tai-Ching Jones piloted the gig between the two starships. The swaddle of his spacesuit bulked the man, thickening his arms and thighs and rounding his normally scrawny torso. With inflated limbs and padded abdomen, the human resembled a hairless and scentless digit with a spherical orange head. The smooth cool surface of Walter's voidskin slid against Tar Heel's side with a quiet rasp like a comb through stiff carpeting, unsatisfying and distant, unlike the scentful rubbing bluebears enjoyed.

«This atmosphere is ours,» Tar Heel mused in Cygnan to Peacoat. «Its scents are exclusively our own.»

«Only temporarily,» grunted his dark-pelted pouchbrother. «Once Eosu has formed and dissolved, we shall return to the *Open Palm*, and the humans' scents.»

«And then to the waterplanet.» Tar Heel's eyes sought in the night. He squinted with the unaccustomed effort, his nose pressing against the crystal. «This digit is excited.»

They crossed into the *Wing*'s shadow. The gig settled onto the decking, the hatchway doors encroaching on the planet from above and below like jaws closing about a blue nugget.

Walt unstrapped himself from the pilot's chair and cracked the hatchway. "Okay, fellows, hop out." He nodded toward the spacesuited human waiting outside the gig. "Here comes the welcoming committee."

Katy Belovsky stepped forward, her eyes expectant beside the faceplate. «Fair breezes,» she said to the two bluebears.

«True scents,» Peacoat replied.

«Your pouchbrothers await you. Come.» She led them into the elevator. Once the doors closed, Katy removed her helmet and fluffed out her short light brown hair, breathing deeply, her nostrils alert like a digit's.

With an impish smile, Katy reached out to scratch the Cygnan's ears. «You are skeptical, my pathfriend,» she said warmly.

The light-furred bluebear started, his nose twitching. «You read my scent? Your nose has opened,» Tar Heel complimented her.

Katy smiled with dimpled pleasure. « From any digit of Eosu this speaker can scent obvious feelings,» she said, her scent flavored with the self-pride common to members of her race. «With Cobalt this digit can taste nuances.»

Peacoat stirred. «Not as well as a digit.»

«Naturally not,» Katy agreed easily in Cygnan. She shifted to English. ''But at least I'm not as blind and deaf as when I first met you.''

''You are clever,'' Tar Heel rumbled, enjoying her touch.

Leaving Katy behind, he stepped into the main holopticon chamber, a large circular amphitheater that sloped gently toward the softly glowing hemisphere in its center. Walls rose in rounded progression from the floor, curving inward to form a domed ceiling. Except for the holopticon, every surface in the room was opaque, covered with short falsefur the texture of a digit's pelt. Even the elevator doorway behind them was now uniformly carpeted, its seams invisible.

Tar Heel dropped to all fours, and a digit whose fur was cobalt and sapphire approached him. Their noses touched. «Fair breezes,» Tar Heel said.

«True scents,» Cobalt murmured in his ear. Her nose slid off his, brushed against his neck and chest in the fourfold greeting. He ran his nose along her flank, down her belly to the join where thigh met hip. He smelled the moist comfort of her perspiration, drank her self-aroma deeply into himself, let her warm familiarity reach into his being. The feeling was intoxicating and proud. The humans have nothing like this, he thought.

He distantly felt the wet progress of Cobalt's nose along his stomach and legs. Many years ago in their mother's pouch, he and the other digits had lain together in humid safety, each no larger than a human child's fist, each mindless and unformed. No words can describe that time, only scents. Before we had names, we knew each other's scent. Before we had words or minds, we knew truth.

In similar fashion, he and Peacoat nosetouched each of their brothers and sisters. Each scent built on the underlying djan-fragrance that Eosu's digits had known since before they were born. Each bluebear added its own character, seasoned with the fragrances of its emotions.

As his consciousness faded, Tar Heel lost himself in scent and its memories. Scent binds us together, he thought lazily. Far-monkeys are blind to the heart's true desires.

A digit's scent is his soul, runs the proverb. Hide the scent and mask the self. Walk with your nose open and scent the world.

Tar Heel shook himself, the fur on his neckruff rolling.

Tar Heel settled down, head on his hands, his knees and ab-domen pressing against the floorfur's warm abrasion. Through half-closed eyes he watched the holopticon's translucent eggshell as the chamber's lights dwindled into darkness. The profiles of his pouchbrothers were reabsorbed into the gloom; he located them not by his weak digit's eyes, but by their strengthening scents. A steady breeze circled the den, carrying Tar Heel's scent to Cobalt, Cobalt's to Glide, around and around the djan.

Through their scents, each digit nosetouched all the others. Falsehood is impossible in aroma, thought Tar Heel. Scents lie on the innermost ring of truth's firecircle. Taste the winds.

As he inbreathed his pouchbrothers, more and more of his artificial human personality washed away. In their mother's pouch, each had nestled in the hollows formed by the others' bodies. Thoughtless and content, wordless and bonded, they had suckled and grown.

The pale bluebear breathed his fill, his eyes closing and seal-ing with a gummy film that would dissolve when they reawak-ened. The others inbreathed with him. As they did, their minds were absorbed into the one greater than any of them, the group-mind Eosu.

I coalesced slowly, my memories stiff and cramped like the limbs of a digit who awakens from wintersleep. I felt my re-turned digits Peacoat and Tar Heel, back from the fardigit's ship *Open Palm.*

Living apart from me, their spirits had grown swaggering.

Their self-love pressed against the other digits. I squeezed them and felt their displeasure as they retreated in the nose of this now-remembered discipline. Their scents bayed with pain; Tar Heel whimpered submission but Peacoat snarled defiance. Releasing Tar Heel, I tightened against my reluctant one, twisted the pressure, and in a moment he made obeisance.

Satisfied, I loosened my hold, and Peacoat sagged into his accustomed place. With their natural order thus established, my digits waited while their scents harmonized. I savored each smell, then ordered it dispersed.

When they were comfortable against one another, cleared of emotions and ready to concentrate, I inbreathed their minds.

A message sent from Su. I pondered this. A farscent, my digits' fragrances informed me, intended to be inbreathed at rendezvous. A change of instructions? A new and complex scent?

For the first time since I had met the humans, I felt hope for Eosu. Perhaps this message held my salvation.

On the outbound voyage, my digits had winterslept. When our ship approached its destination at the midpoint between our two stars, I had read Su's original harsh orders: Kill the humans, then yourself.

Desperate orders, but Eosu obeys as a digit obeys. The individual digit is nothing before the group. I, the single groupmind Eosu, am nothing against the millions of groupminds on our planet of grasses.

I had been ordered to kill the farmonkeys, but had no scent how. My digit Softtouch conceived the idea of deathscent. Lacking weemonkey assistance, she bungled its manufacture and it billowed through our ship. The humans rescued my digits, at the risk of their lives, brought them into their den, goodhosting and, by this, unknowingly imposing guest obligations upon me. Unable to kill them, owing them my life, I made peace with the fardigits.

I disobeyed Su. Ever since, I had been haunted.

During the voyage to Earth, I had been consumed with guilt. Were all noses on Su closed forever to me? Was Eosu already an outcast? The planet was too far away to answer. Now a change of instructions. Excitement built in me.

Orders to find bonds, perhaps. Yesterday's upwind danger is today's downwind safety. Had the group-winds on Su shifted, instructing me to do what I had already done?

The holopticon's scent beat against me, wave after wave of

question seeking my reply, the key that would allow it to be displayed. My eagerness spilled out; I wanted this scent to be my exoneration. I offered a hopeful answering scent and the message bloomed in my digits' noses, terrible and deadly:

> *Break contact. Come home now.*

Eyes closed, her nose flat against the floorfur, Cobalt sniffed the air. Her nearby pouchbrothers emitted disharmony and anxiety. Su's terse command—return home now—could not be obeyed. This paradox had shaken Eosu, so the groupmind had dissolved disharmoniously, its path clouded by this baffling new odor from the homeplanet.

A digit may be fearful, but a djan is always balanced. Yet Eosu was shaken and uncertain. Like her fellows, Cobalt was afraid. The den stank with their fear.

Try as she might, Cobalt could not gainscent her brothers' apprehension. She held herself still so that her own gloomy fragrances hung close about her.

The chamber breezes quickened as the doors opened. Katy Belovsky's scent touched Cobalt and the bluebear arched her nostrils, inbreathing the woman's excitement and optimism to blow away her own aromas. Katy, the digits' friend, was monkey-clever. Katy would know what to do.

Another scent touched Cobalt and she automatically read it. Patrick Henry Michaelson: the emissary, his expansive scent always masked by strange perfumes and lotions. The man's scent irritated her, then she minutely shrugged her massive shoulders. A monkey who solves problems may be forgiven some arrogance.

Grunting, she raised herself to all fours, blinking to clear her eyes and bowing her head toward the white-haired man. «Fair breezes,» she growled in digit speech.

«True scents,» he answered. His scent screamed his origins. Humans cannot control their aromas, Cobalt reminded herself. A predator species has no need to conceal its appetites.

"I have been talking with Earth," Pat said in English, settling himself awkwardly on the floorfur. He took an electronic notepad from under his arm and squinted at the amber words displayed on its flat surface. "We worked out an itinerary once you arrive. You will have to decide among yourselves which of you goes where. Six powers, six destinations: New York, Moscow, Tokyo, Amsterdam, Heinlein, Bradbury."

Michaelson's words fell into the continuing silence, unnerving him—Cobalt caught the whiff of human fearscent. "Since there are only eight of you," the words came more rapidly, as if to cover his perplexed odor, "some of you will have to travel alone."

Beside her, Tar Heel rumbled deep in his throat.

Pat faced him. "It can't be helped, but at least you may choose your human companions." He stumbled to a halt.

The Cygnans listened without speaking, but their scents riffled among them. Katy Belovsky's eyes were closed, her head tilted back as she read the atmosphere. "Wait a moment, Pat," she murmured without moving. "Let them absorb it."

"Eosu is one djan," Cobalt replied after several breaths. Forming her lips into the shapes necessary to pronounce the soft syllables in the monkey's language made her jaws ache. "The dirtmonkeys know this."

"Don't you understand *anything* about humanity by now?" Michaelson demanded. "If you select one country to visit first, you insult the other five. You have to split up."

Fearscent grew in the chamber as Cobalt's pouchbrothers inbreathed Michaelson's anger. "We refuse." Cobalt squeezed her nose against the aromas now building.

"Why are you so dead set against it?" Michaelson clutched the notepad to his chest and folded his arms belligerently across it. "Why?"

Cobalt spoke Cygnan so her brothers could not mistake her meaning. «Separation will kill Eosu.»

2.

«Separation will kill us,» Cobalt repeated. «The starvation fable proves it.»

The eight bluebears, each weighing more than a third of a ton, lay in a loose parabola, their noses focusing on Michaelson. Eyes closed and muscles relaxed, they breathed deeply and regularly, ears upright, nostrils alert. Now and then rubbery blue-black lips twitched over white canine teeth as they inbreathed the story Cobalt told.

When a ship arrived in the port city of Redset, keen-nosed digits of Winderfan were at dockside to select the best spices, cloth, or metalwork. Yoked to carts by chattering weeservants of Winderfan, who rode in laughing comfort amidst the booty, Winderfan's digits carried goods and news to the surrounding villages and towns, outspreading on the winds like seeds from a pod.

Lean and swift were the digits of Winderfan, covering the greatsteps between port and inland city as fast as any. Winderfan's reputation spread for leagues, its scent growing strong in digits' noses and djans' minds. As Winderfan grew wealthy, the groupmind became greedy, expanding Winderfan's territory and its winds, stretching its digits' paths farther from one another and from the port. Separated from Winderfan for months instead of weeks, the digits found coalescence in groupmind infrequent and stressful. As they loped along dusty woodland paths, in the heat of the day or beneath summer stars, they were ever more restless.

«*We* do the work,» Dustlegs grumbled to Moonsmoke as they traveled together. «Ours are the feet whose pads ache, ours the bellies that rumble as we pace in cold night. *We* bear the burden, not Winderfan, which summons us and chortles over our successes while punishing our failures. To Winderfan, we are little better than weemonkey handservants.»

«We are digits.» Moonsmoke dipped his nose along the path's

brown-packed earth. «We serve Winderfan, who guides our steps.»

«Winderfan guides?» Dustlegs scornfully butted her shoulder into Moonsmoke's to emphasize her determined aroma. «What work does Winderfan do? Our paths repeat from trip to trip.» She ran her nose against the bole of a tree. «Even now, we inbreathe the fragrances of our pouchbrothers who passed here last journey. We follow old trails. What does the groupmind do for us?»

«Without the groupmind, digits are nothing,» Moonsmoke replied, fearful yet curious despite himself.

«Without the groupmind, digits are *individuals*,» Dustlegs asserted. Though she spoke defiantly, her scent too was tinged with fear and apprehension and she snorted behind her.

All that day, Moonsmoke and Dustlegs walked together, mingling their aromas, tasting each other's true emotions. That night they slept wrapped in both fragrances, sharing without groupmind.

When Winderfan's digits returned to the port city, they gathered in their den and quietly lit the night fire. Smoke curled up like a weemonkey's tail from its logs and coals and rose through the smokehole. The updraft steady and clear, the digits inbreathed together, nostrils arched, sunk on their haunches, and the Winderfan groupmind came to them.

No digit knows what groupmind is like. No digit will ever know. Once the groupmind forms, the digit's odor—what you humans call the personality—vanishes like stars in sunrise, obliterated by the rising corona of one greater than ourselves.

Our god is always with us and inside us. Its love is the scent of our souls. When Eosu punishes, burns are branded inside our skin where they cannot be salved. When Eosu rewards us, the glow spreads throughout our being.

We envy your cleverness and self-sufficiency. Were you wiser, you would envy our communion.

But when it disintegrates, terror ensues. Winderfan's digits had been too long apart. Ego had grown in their minds like a weed. The rebellious scents which Dustlegs harbored were shared by others. Sharing mutinous thoughts emboldened the digits. They scaled the vast hulk of the groupmind like impetuous weemonkeys, attacking its control over them.

Winderfan decisively struck back. Seizing Moonsmoke, Winderfan crushed its soul with one mighty, enraged blast. The stink of Moonsmoke's death rocked the digits, their destroyed pouch-brother reeking in their noses. They lost aroma, and in their moment of doubt and sanity, the groupmind securely gripped them.

Disobedience quelled, the digits whimpered for mercy, their bruised noses aching from the pain of Moonsmoke's execution. They wept pitifully, waiting for Winderfan's justice.

«You have broken the bond that holds us together,» Winderfan said. «You are no longer digits. We foul Su's winds. So you must die.»

The digits' odors were frightened and confused. A trace of blame and accusation rose from them.

Winderfan inbreathed it. «I have failed too. If you are no digits, I am no djan. With your deaths, mine must follow.»

Slowly, remorselessly, Winderfan slew them, wringing their souls. As each digit outbreathed its last, the living shuddered with the reek from the dying until only Dustlegs was left. Her throat and lungs were so full of death that she longed for relief, but the scents of her dead pouchbrothers beat her nose like gro-monkey fists.

Winderfan stood before her in the image of a digit, the groupmind's nose and face scarred and withered. Winderfan's pelt and fur were those of Dustlegs. Winderfan's scent was Dustleg's scent.

«Yes,» Winderfan said when the digit had inbreathed this. «You have reduced me to no more than you. We have become one.» It cradled Dustlegs's neck in its hands.

The digit twisted under the pricking claws, but shame held her motionless before the avenging groupmind.

«We are both exiles,» Winderfan growled. «We both must wear the yellow collar.»

«No,» whimpered Dustlegs, writhing.

«Come,» coaxed Winderfan. «We have walked the whole trail, my digit. Now we must enter the den.»

Dustlegs drew courage from the groupmind's purposeful scent. The digit reached up her hands, fitted them into the groupmind's throat.

Digit and groupmind touched noses in grief, reading each other's scent, their breathing merged into one. They inbreathed life's final wind and four hands slowly tightened.

The next morning the fire burned out, the scent of death wafting from the den's smokehole. Winderfan's digits lay strangled, their throats crushed, each digit's hands gripped about its own neck, claws sunk into its own pelt and flesh.

Those who found the dead djan lit Winderfan's deathpyre. As the deathplume rose into the daybreeze, they inbreathed this fable until the unforgiving winds caught it and whisked it away.

By the time Cobalt finished, the air had grown musky with the aromas of many bluebears. Her legs splayed, Katy leaned against her nightfriend's broad warm back and stroked the Cygnan's sapphire neckfur.

«What happens to digits who never reunite?» Pat asked skeptically, shoving himself sideways like an overweight inchworm.

Cobalt snorted. «Their minds starve. They go mad in slow excruciating pain.»

«What breeze carries this tale?» Pat continued, his eyebrows drawn together and his scent forthright. «No digit can remember groupmind. How do you know it is true?»

Cobalt's navy-blue nose arched. «Must you feel your fingers crisping to know that fire burns?» she growled. Her neck muscles corded.

The diplomat's florid face reddened and he turned to Cobalt. «Starvation by remote control? With no physical cause?»

«You may be right, monkey,» Peacoat interjected, surprising them.

Both Katy and Cobalt inbreathed this new scent. «Survive without Eosu?» Katy asked, looking at him slantwise.

«*You* changed.» Peacoat's scent made his words an accusation. «You now live with digits, not with your fellow monkeys.»

Katy scowled at the insult, but Cobalt cut in before she could reply. «False winds! Digits need Eosu as wheat needs sun and rain.» She grunted, dismissing Peacoat's contrary fragrance, and returned her nose to Michaelson. «We cannot escape our biology. Can you humans will away your thirst or your rut lust?»

«Even if your story is true,» Michaelson answered steadily, «if you refuse to separate, you fail your planet.» He looked hard at them as if frustrated that he could not manipulate the atmosphere to make his point. "Oh, hell, Katy. You tell them for me. I may not understand aliens, but I understand people and politics. Separate or forget it."

«He is right,» allowed Katy after a tense silence. She stroked Cobalt's sides and throat, smoothing the short soft fur.

Cobalt sighed. «Your scent is strong and crisp.»

In sadness, Katy rolled her head against the bluebear's trunk-like neck and ground her face into the comforting fur.

«We hoped for a miracle,» the Cygnan morosely added. «But Eosu must fulfill its dutyscent.» She snuffled and Katy inbreathed a new odor. The other bluebears tasted it too. Their expressions grew even more glum.

Katy stirred and sat up, pulling away from Cobalt. «Before you choose, let this monkey join Eosu.»

«You?» Peacoat blurted in surprise, baring his teeth. «You do not belong in groupmind. You are no digit.»

Katy squared her shoulders, her nostrils proud. «This digit has participated in Eosu's conclaves before.»

«The groupmind can scent the odor of your monkey lust,» Peacoat growled, hawking.

Katy blushed angrily and clawed the floorfur. «Does the wind of truth blow only over digits? Eosu has found no path, though it has looked for years.» She shook with rage and her aroma was raw and aggressive. «Will Eosu's ego be the cause of its failure?»

Cobalt and the other bluebears retreated. Their shoulders fell and their heads pulled down, ears flattening in submission. Peacoat alone held his ground, his odor clashing with hers in the air between them.

Katy advanced on all fours. «Eosu has already gone beyond its original orders,» she growled, hurling her words like stones. She leaned forward, her tiny nose almost touching Peacoat's long snout. «You can hide no longer. The voyage is *over*. Your djan is scentless and abandoned. Inbreathe another aroma or admit failure.» Pausing for breath, she caught the scent of Cobalt's fear and humiliation, and other odors, too complex for her simple nose to read.

Peacoat cocked his head, then turned to Michaelson. «Leave us,» he ordered the man. «Eosu will conclave.»

Hints of the groupmind's unique chordic aroma touched the bluebears around Katy, who whickered with anticipation at their first glimmer of Eosu. Their breathing deepened, their lungs working like a multichambered bellows. Nostrils wheezed loudly as they expelled sultry rasps of breath. Cygnan fur wrapped the nude woman like a heated blanket.

Scratchy coziness impressed Katy on all sides. . . .

The heat rubbing against her naked limbs made Katy drowsy. Defiantly the small girl burrowed deeper under the covers, with only one eye peeping out. The sky outside her bedroom window was a faint washed-out green. The Great Bear was still visible, its stars strong enough to shine as long as the sun remained below the horizon.

Dawn would soon arrive. Inside the huddled tent her child's body made, Katy rubbed her nose against the flannel blankets. The moisture from her breath condensed and cooled when it passed through the covers and hit the frigid air. The blanket grew damp and cool where she kissed it. She liked its refreshing wetness and the way her tongue flattened stray wool fibers.

Action came suddenly and without thought: the child flung wide the covers, gasped as the nippy air stung her, and raced to her bureau. Dressing rapidly, Katy moved like a chilly wood sprite, partly to escape the cold and partly for the challenge of seeing how quickly it could be done. In a twinkling she was clothed, bounding down the planked wooden stairs into the kitchen.

At the breakfast table, her father, Ivan, looked up from his ledgers, the paper green as the morning sky. He peered over his steel-rimmed glasses and rubbed the eraser end of his pencil against a furrow in his brow. "Here is my fast girl." His voice was gentle and soft. He spoke seldom and Katy loved him very much.

Grinning, she ran to him. Every night she sat on his lap and they played their special game while he pored over his soil records and fertilizer counts. She asked him what the numbers and symbols meant, and he explained each one, detailing the importance of nitrogen fixation and potash restoration until she squirted like a watermelon seed out of his lap.

"You daydreamer," her father teased her now. "Were you still asleep in bed? You stare too long at me." He shut the ledger with a thud. "Sasha needs your quick fingers." Pushing his glasses up on his brow, he massaged his eye sockets with strong, slow movements. "Hot oatmeal, milk, and sliced peaches when you return." Katy happily scooted.

Footsteps crunching over grass frosted into jagged stalks, Katy made her way to the barn. Skipping over the hardscrabble ground, she blew her breath in white-plumed feathers, imitating her father exhaling cigar smoke.

When she reached the barn, Katy heard anxious mooing. Stepping inside, she patted Sasha and slid her little hand along the heifer's brown and white flank. With one foot she kicked a milking stool underneath her and sat on it, leaning her forehead against the warm belly. Sasha's udders were full to bursting, swollen and probably tender. Rivulets of milk had leaked from them and crystallized in the night's cold. Katy flexed her fingers stiffly and blew on them. Her hands moved methodically as she absorbed the smells of the barn and her oversized quiet friend.

Milk, warmth, and fur. The scents of suckle.

She closed her eyes. . . .

She yawned. Her young, still-rounded claws scraped on the polished wood floors of the youngsterhouse. Shaking her neck-fur, Katy rolled onto her side. She yawned again, her tongue curling out, then smacked her lips, feeling milk trickle warm against her throat. She slid her tongue around her canines, proud of their new length, the first sign that her cub's body was maturing.

Milk, warmth, and fur. She rested her back against her pouch-brothers and closed her eyes again. . . .

Katy blinked. The pail beneath her sore hands was full of white milk, steaming faintly in the barn's frosty air. The small girl leaned against the wall of Sasha's coat, sliding her hands toward the udders.

Where the creature's genitals should be, the fur continued, thinning now and definitely sexless. And it was not brown, she saw in amazement, but blue.

The bear rolled its head around to the left. Seeing Katy, the alien growled menacingly, and the girl covered her mouth in surprise.

With a slap from one oversized paw, the bluebear knocked Katy off the milk stool. Her bucket bounced away and a white tide splashed. It frothed and then crackled as it froze upon contact with the icy earth.

Huge teeth snapping like traps, the lumbering bluebear straddled her on all fours before Katy had hardly hit the ground. One fat paw pressed against the child's flat chest and firmly pinned her.

The girl squirmed and the bluebear put more of its weight on its stiff arm. Sweat from its panting tongue dripped onto Katy's forehead. She turned her face away from its hot breath.

«Must reach inside you,» the bluebear hissed.

«Can't breathe,» Katy gasped in Cygnan. Her hands grabbed the thick forearm and feebly pushed.

The alien lifted its head and scrutinized her as if considering.

The burden on her chest eased. She sucked in a shallow breath. The bluebear sniffed several times, then lowered its head and licked the side of her neck.

«What are you doing?» Katy timidly asked.

«Air carries only some odors,» the bear distantly answered. «Scent on the skin is closer to the pouch.»

«Who are you?» Katy whispered, husbanding her breath.

«Eosu,» growled the bluebear.

«Ay-oh-soo,» she repeated. «*Ay*-oh-soo. I know that name.» She groped for memory but her brain was dull. «You care for me.» The weight on her chest felt less oppressive now. «You protect me.»

Eosu grunted. «I need something from you.»

«Anything,» Katy wheezed instantly.

The bluebear's nostrils narrowed. «Inside you.» It leaned forward until its large purple snout touched her nose, lowering its heavy stomach against her pelvis and legs. Katy puffed with its weight and gritted her teeth. As she fought for air, opening her mouth to gulp, Eosu lifted the massive hand that had held her, reaching inside her mouth.

Bigger than her head, the paw nevertheless fit inside. The bluebear pushed her jaws open, wider and wider until the skin of her cheeks must surely split. Crying, Katy gagged and Eosu used the slight extra aperture to force its hand farther into her throat.

The bear rotated its arm—she thought her jaw would fracture—until the claws stuck upward into the roof of her mouth. They tightened and points of pain shot into her head. «*This* is the proper channel,» Eosu grunted with satisfaction.

Whimpering, Katy tried to squirm away, but her every movement simply forced the hairy limb deeper. «You are unimportant,» Eosu rumbled when she wailed. «Be still or it will hurt more.»

As Katy sobbed, trying to inhale around the obstruction filling her mouth, the bear's claws punched through the nasal membranes and sank into her brain.

At the penetration, terrible odors exploded in her. Katy smelled the crisp sizzling aroma of her fingers burning when, at age five, she had grabbed a hot cast-iron skillet. The odor of diarrhea shot into her mouth and she retched, but the probing paw only reached deeper. Katy's womb tore with agony and she smelled her fresh blood as she forced baby Felicity into the world. A frightened skunk discharged itself at her, filling her nose, and she gagged uncontrollably. All these foul odors and more assailed her nose, the torment unendurable yet increasing.

«Hold still,» the groupmind reprimanded. «You deflect my hand and increase your suffering.»

Katy's struggles slowed.

«I shall obtain what I need. If that means killing you»—Eosu's voice was tender but its odor that of dismissal—«I shall do it.» Sweeping her pain aside, the bluebear's claws fumbled in her skull, sending hot knives stabbing into her thighs, calves, and feet. «My digits do not survive coalescence,» it growled at her. «They are inside me now. But you! You remain. You remember. Remember this!» Eosu's aroma became irate and its paw twisted inside Katy's throat.

Ammonia jammed itself into her throat, and her nose was on fire. Bile and excrement buffeted her. She reeled, senseless except for the racking pain and the horrible fumes, her hands waving ineffectually to ward off the tide of filth and terror that pummeled her.

The woman shrieked and choked around the blockage in her throat, swallowing saliva and blood. «Insolent monkey!» the groupmind snarled. «You preserve yourself when I form.» Eosu was vengeful. «Your ego causes this hurt,» the djan panted. «You force yourself into me, you lie with my digits, and when I take from you what other digits willingly give, you cry and weep like the weakest youngster. Ah!» The groupmind's strong thick fingers clutched a mote in her skull and seized it. They pulled, and it was as if Katy's tongue were being ripped from her.

«Ahhh!» The groupmind's sound was a roar and a purr combining triumph and contentment. With satisfied relief, Eosu withdrew its arm, claws still pinched shut. The slow extraction was unbearable and Katy whimpered, green pain framing her vision.

«To pull quicker would kill you,» the groupmind said with rough tenderness. With a sucking sound, Eosu wrenched its hand free of Katy's shredded mouth.

«Done!» The groupmind held up its clenched fist, slick with her saliva. Opening its traplike ebony jaws, curved ivory teeth glinting, the bluebear crammed the contents into its gaping mouth. It swallowed and belched. «Now I know.» Closing its eyes, Eosu breathed like a stoked furnace, nostrils full open. «Now my digits can survive.» Its aroma soared with wild hope.

Katy's head and body were bruised and raw. Blood trickled down her throat. Withdrawal had left her ravaged and pummeled, her soul empty. Wind whistled in the cavities the bluebear's investigation had seared into her spirit.

«You hurt me,» the child reproached the huge bluebear, her aroma shattered except for a small bright fire of hatred that lay somewhere behind her eyes.

«You are not of me,» Eosu said. «I do not concern myself with you.»

She licked her broken lips. «You don't—care?» Katy's voice cracked and she wept.

«My digits are all.» Eosu rose onto its feet, towering over her like a colossus. «Fair breezes, farmonkey.»

Then came pain and finally sweet oblivion.

When the digits awoke, they had formed a ring around Katy. Untouched, the fat woman lay on her side, curled like a huddling newborn, legs drawn up to her double chin, arms wrapped about them, head sunk in the hollow between her knees. Her skin was blotchy and sweat-stained, her hair straggled and wet. Panic and terror were on her face and in her odor. The floorfur under her shaking head was moist with tears and spit.

The bluebears drew closer about their wounded friend. Purring softly, they licked the fluids from her face with dry tongues, outbreathed aromas of protection and healing. Delicately the Cygnans laid the soft warm parts of themselves against her, cuddling her inside a cocoon of their bodies.

3.

Katy Belovsky sat listlessly on the floor of the *Wing*'s hemispherical observation chamber, her back and shoulders braced against the incurving crystal walls. The floorfur under her legs and hands was soft and dark, the silence peaceful and solitary. Her muscles ached and her hands were unsteady.

The stars outside glittered. The Cygnan ship's bow gazed back over the endless open space it had just crossed, as if regretting that it must soon abandon the placid rhythms of interstellar travel for the anxieties of planetfall. The star-speckled night sky was dark and colorless, except for regal Jupiter, which burned red and orange. Katy watched it, her gaze lost in its lurid swirls of clouds. So seemingly delicate and tranquil, those filigrees were really methane and ammonia hurricanes, churning in a chill noxious stew that could snap the *Wing* like rotten bamboo.

Everything looks calm at a distance, she thought idly, until you enter its atmosphere and discover the storms that rage within.

With a whir, a rectangle emerged from the floorfur's flat black disk, followed by a short blast of light and the roll of heavy Cygnan shoulders. Cobalt sighed with relief and ambled cautiously in. The sapphire bluebear's head was low, her nostrils whiffling, alert for the woman's scent. The elevator descended, restoring night and the quiet illusion of tranquility. The Cygnan moved close, pushing her enormous head toward Katy's lap.

Katy tickled the alien's large pointed ears, then slid her hands gently around them to stroke the short hair on Cobalt's head.

"Eosu should not have hurt you so," Cobalt said after a few moments.

Katy's mouth twisted and she briefly shook her head, but the scent coming from her palms grew more troubled.

"Eosu was too rough." The bluebear rumbled sympathetically, raising her luxuriant neckruff for her friend to scratch. "You were unprepared."

"There's no permanent damage," Katy denied in a bitter tone. "Heidi checked all my parts. No bleeding, no scars." Unzip-

29

ping her jumpsuit's sleeves, she lifted her arms and rotated her hands to show the unblemished skin.

Cobalt touched her cool nose to Katy's wrists. "Your aroma is thinner. Eosu took some of it."

"Then I'm glad it's gone," Katy grimly replied. Though her tone was defiant, she struggled to make her tortured face conform.

"You are not Eosu's digit," her friend said. "You do not belong to Eosu as we do."

Cobalt's words upset Katy anew. "I wasn't Eosu's digit before, but now I have become as you." She raked her fingernails along her trousers' blue plastic. "The monkey inside me hated the djan. Eosu killed it. My pain has served its purpose."

Lifting her head, Cobalt fluffed her neckfur, violet and magenta in the starlight. "You have been punished as a digit but you were not nurtured as a digit."

"No!" Katy clung fiercely to her guilt. "I am a digit now."

"You are less than we, and more." The Cygnan wet her nose with a deft flick of her tongue.

"More?" the woman asked with fragile, unbelieving hope.

"You have a wonderful gift, a gift that no digit has." Cobalt's deep voice was wistful, her aroma expansive. "To survive coalescence, to be awake in groupmind, to stand before Eosu and to breath the djan in your nose. To remember." She rolled her shoulders, purring and rumbling.

"I wish you could share it," Katy answered, proud but tentative in the face of Cobalt's unenvious longing. Flustered, she patted the Cygnan's broad neck and throat. "You deserve it more."

Cobalt flattened her neckruff. "But even that great gift does not justify beating you."

"It wasn't that bad," Katy said defensively. "I was weak."

Her friend snorted. "You can inbreathe Eosu, pathfriend Katy, but I can inbreathe you." Her nostrils arched and her upper lip fluttered, revealing square teeth. "Your scent was shattered. We digits held you in our aromas and gave you our scents while yours healed."

"It was just such a shock," Katy insisted, shivering at the memory. "That made it seem worse than it was." She had awakened, panicked and terrified, to a rich fragrance of bluebear essences, their huge muzzles lowered. With infinitely gentle caresses, the bluebears' tongues had licked sweat from her trembling arms, legs, and face.

"Pathfriend, we digits all have experienced your pain." Cobalt's harsh words jerked Katy to the present. "Each of us has been pummeled and bruised. When that happens, we comfort one another without monkey pride. You were beaten, Katy. We digits know this. Let us comfort you."

"Thanks. You are dear to me." She sighed, recalling their extraordinary outpouring of love. For her, one who had been born a monkey. "I'm all right now."

The Cygnan skeptically cocked her head. "Shall we recoalesce Eosu?"

At this soft question, Katy's hands sprang off her friend's fur as if scorched. Realizing her reaction, she quickly dropped them into her lap and hid them between her thighs. "Not now," she said, horrified at the involuntary revulsion she felt twisting her face into a grimace.

"If you ever risk it again, Eosu may punish twice," warned Cobalt.

"Groupmind is worth the pain." Katy extended her arms as if warding off an invisible force. "Just give me a little time to recover."

"Eosu was wrong." The bluebear flexed her hands so the claws distended.

Anxious to put this argument behind them, Katy abruptly changed the subject. "When we arrive, where will you go?" she asked with forced brightness, wiping her eyes.

Now it was the bluebear whose aroma clouded with apprehension. "I have no scent."

"You digits must separate," Katy reminded her. "Eosu ordered it."

Cobalt growled, her ears flicking forward and back. "The djan punishes its monkeylike digits by making us live as monkeys, with monkeys."

"How horrible!" Katy was aghast. "How can you think such things? You are of Eosu."

"Eosu disobeyed the planet of grasses," Cobalt said with the indifference of profound despair. "Eosu came to Solspace to live with monkeys. To fulfill that thinker's choice, we digits must wallow in monkeys."

"But you chose the right path," Katy argued. "That's even more obvious now than it was then."

"Being right is no defense," the bluebear wanly answered.
"Eosu set its nose against all the noses of our world." Her
nostrils raised, Cobalt lowered her head, rolling it back and forth
in small figure-eight movements. "That is monkey pride. The
djan blames us for it."

"Blames you?" Katy asked incredulously. "If the wrong path
was chosen, Eosu chose it. Not you digits." Hesitantly she
stroked Cobalt's throat and chest. "Not you."

"Eosu also punishes itself by scattering us. Eosu's self-death
would prove its loyalty. The winds of that ultimate sacrifice
would carry across space to Su."

"You will not die," Katy asserted fiercely, her hands clench-
ing into fists. "You won't. I'll protect you."

"Can you protect us from Eosu?" the bluebear asked without
heat. "Can you slay our inner hunger? The starvation fable out-
breathes that we shall perish."

"It could be a false wind," Katy said. A sudden aching in
her joints made every position painful. Any tiny movement set
off an unpleasant electric tingle. She panted and her ribs were
pierced with a sharp stab. She took several cautious shallow
breaths and it slowly receded.

"You displeased Eosu," remarked the alien. "It will pass.
We have no choice. As the proverb says, if there is only one
path, you need not scent it, for you will walk it."

"You must go somewhere," Katy whispered, using as little
breath as possible.

"All places are the same."

"Not Mars. Anywhere but Mars." She shuddered and rubbed
her forearms. "The coyotes have no government. They never
requested a Cygnan."

"Eosu insists," Cobalt flatly replied. "Can you not scent
this?"

Katy inhaled and winced. "Yes. Inbreathe all the predators.
One of you must go. Who will it be?"

"Peacoat," replied the bluebear. "He volunteered." She
wheezed ironically.

Katy's odor mingled disbelief and disgust. "Are you joking?
A digit? Chose *Mars*?"

"My pouchbrother's aroma has become turbulent." Cobalt
slowly raked her claws through the floorfur, leaving parallel
lines. "His scent is guarded, monkeylike."

"Remote coalescence will surely keep him a true digit of Eosu."

"You humans worship machines as if they were djans," Cobalt wryly snorted, shaking her head. "Dismantling the holopticons with your rapid monkey hands so that each digit has one. Telling us we can farscent across the oceans of space." She whiffled, her scent unsettled. "Djans come to digits in one air, around one fire. To be squirted through wires or on beams of sunlight is no life for a groupmind. Still"—she lifted her shoulders and dropped them—"Eosu has ordered. We digits obey, though nowhere is safe for us."

"Luna is," Katy stoutly asserted.

"The Moon?"

"The best society in Solspace." Katy was eager to cheer up her friend with images of a happier future. She roughly massaged Cobalt's shoulders and arms. "Lunacorp accepts anyone who passes intelligence or skills tests."

Cobalt made wind. "Your moonpeople fill steel cans with your cleverest monkeys, then bury them deep under a world without breezes. It will be a scentless place."

"Oh, you are wrong. The Lunarians have built a wondrous universe. Vast domes, many times larger than this." She waved her arm in a circle at the brilliant ebony night. "They are fabulously wealthy and successful. The city of Heinlein is a museum of the achievements of humanity."

"Then Luna it shall be," Cobalt decided without much interest. "Will you accompany me? As guide and protector?"

"You really want me?" Katy asked, her scent yearning for reassurance. "A monkey, less than a digit?"

"Your presence will honor me," her friend answered. Her long pink tongue licked wet salt from Katy's cheek.

"Hey, Mama!" They heard Felicity's high animated voice even before the doors burst open. "Casey and Tom are fixing the last of the holopticon terminals," the coffee-colored girl said in a rush while bounding out of the elevator, "and loading them into transporters and we're going to arrive at the Orbiter in less than a *day* and I've been watching broadcasts that the answer man has snitched from Earth and—" Noticing the bluebear, the girl abruptly halted. "Oh. Hi, Cobalt." She ruffled her tight-curled brown hair with her left hand and scratched her scalp.

At eleven, Katy's precocious daughter had reached the awkward age when growth had elongated her child's body but not filled it with curves. Her arms, legs, and torso, which until recently had been appealingly plump, were now gangly and uncoordinated, her squeegee-flat chest a continuing frustration. Expecting to have the lush nubile youth of Elizabeth Taylor in *National Velvet*, her favorite movie, Felicity instead found herself stuck with the gamine body of Tatum O'Neal in *Paper Moon*: flamingo legs with kneecaps like misplaced doorknobs.

"Hello, Felicity." Cobalt shouldered coldly past her. "Your mother and I have finished talking." She entered the elevator and departed.

"We're almost there." The girl smiled at Katy and the dimples in her cheeks deepened. "I'll sleep in Orbiter Six tomorrow and on Earth the day after that."

"You were rude to Cobalt," Katy said reprovingly as the elevator descended.

"We swapped stinks on the way past," Felicity replied instantly. "I've been watching Earth get bigger and bigger. Mama, does it really fill the whole sky?" Her big eyes twinkled the color of very old rosewood.

"More than that," Katy answered. Despite her desire to remain stern, she grinned at her daughter's infectious enthusiasm. Katy's arms swept a huge semicircular arc. "Earth is the floor and the sky is a blue bowl above you."

"Gosh." Felicity's smile widened even farther. "When I get to Earth"—she embraced herself and squirmed inside her self-hug—"I'm going to travel and travel. Go swimming in an ocean over my head and play softball and soccer and go fishing and see Broadway and the Eiffel Tower and—"

"We're going to the Moon," Katy interjected.

Felicity set her jaw and her dimples vanished. "Who's we?" she asked with the sudden wariness of a customer being asked to taste a free sample.

"Cobalt decided to go to Heinlein," replied Katy. "She asked me to guide her."

"And you're going."

"Yes."

"And I'm going too."

"Of course, honey. I wouldn't leave you."

"Sure." Felicity scrubbed her hair as if it were dirty. "Sure. The bear whistles and you come running."

"She needs me."

"And I don't?"

"You're coming too."

"I don't want to go to the sniffy old Moon," Felicity complained bitterly. "I want to go to Earth! All my life you've told me how wonderful it is."

"I'm sorry, honey. I have to go with Cobalt."

"You'll snuffle after your bluebear friend in two seconds but you won't do anything for *me*."

"You have to come with us." Katy reached out to her daughter.

Felicity defiantly pulled her elbows away and wiped her nose with her thumb. "I'm a grown-up girl. I can take care of myself."

Katy suppressed a smile. "Sometimes you are, and sometimes you're not. You're not being mature now."

" 'Wait until we get to Earth, Felicity.' " Prancing back and forth, the child mimicked her mother's voice and mannerisms. "That's what you said. 'You can climb mountains, you can see the sun set.' And now you're not going to let me! You grew up on Earth, I didn't, and it's not fair."

"But you *must* come with us," implored Katy. "You are an innocent, honey. Earth is marvelous, but it is also dangerous."

"I know what Earth is like." Her daughter's tone was superior and belligerent. "The answer man showed me."

Katy put her hands on her hips. "You're trying to make me angry."

Felicity deliberately matched the action. "I'm not going to the stupid Moon," the girl stubbornly repeated.

"A million people live there," Katy reminded her. "Including young people like you."

"Not going to be dragged like a pooh bear while you show off Cobalt. That's what you *really* want." She pointed her finger accusingly. " 'Be quiet, Felicity, Cobalt's talking. Be nice to Cobalt, she's in a strange environment far from home.' It's not fair." Felicity suddenly dropped her exaggerated sneer. "You like Cobalt better than you like me."

"No, I don't. If I didn't love you so much, I wouldn't worry about you."

"Why can't I go with someone else?" the girl demanded. "Tar Heel and Walt and Casey are going to New York. Why not with them?"

Katy patted her daughter's head. "Tar Heel will be too busy, you know that. Walt wouldn't want to and is *not* responsible."

Felicity pounced. "Casey would!"

"Are you sure?" Katy asked in a tone that warned against lying. Casey van Gelder, the ship's engineer, was all too pliable.

"Uh-huh." The girl nodded energetically. "I talked to him." Her eyes brimmed and a catch came into her voice. "He said he'd chaperone me."

Katy sagged against the wall. "I'm very tired, honey. Give me a minute to think about this, okay?"

"Your scent still aches, doesn't it, Mama?" Immediately solicitous, Felicity lowered her head and approached, her hands behind her back, as a bluebear would. She cocked her head and sniffed. "I can smell."

"No, you can't, and it's only sweat." Covering her eyes, Katy sighed deeply, considering. Felicity could be such a nuisance when someone else was the center of attention. Her presence might embarrass Cobalt or the Lunarians, and it would certainly be easier if she were elsewhere. She might truly be adult enough after all. And Casey could really watch her. Life would be simpler if she were absent.

Felicity broke in on her thoughts. "Does that mean yes?"

Katy blinked in surprise. "Does what mean yes?"

"Your scent. It smells yes."

"Humph. You're guessing." Katy snorted. "You'll obey Casey's rules?"

Felicity nodded. "I'll be so good and careful and won't do anything Casey tells me not to and get his permission for everything and—"

"Shh, let me think. You're still so young."

"They have phones in New York," the girl replied, as if knowing of their presence conferred great wisdom upon her. "And shuttles run between Earth and the Orbiters twelve times a day."

"You've been studying," Katy said, impressed.

Felicity glared. "Of course I have, Mother. For ages and *ages*."

"Since last week, you mean."

"Yeah." Felicity scowled, nettled at having her grand assertion reduced to this mundane interval. "Anyway, if I get into a jam, or if Earth is icky, I'll come back here."

"The ships will be empty," Katy warned her.

"Mama, the answer man will take care of me. He baby-sat me this whole way back. He talks to me."

Katy looked down at her. "What a bundle of determination you are." She bent over and kissed her daughter's forehead. "I do want you to enjoy yourself, and you might be bored by Luna. It would be easier on us both if you weren't underfoot."

"Does that mean I can go with Casey?" Felicity asked anxiously.

Katy made a show of hesitating. "All right. If you're determined to abandon Cobalt and me, I won't stand in your way."

"It's only for a while, Mama, and I'll call you every week."

"Well, then. You can go—"

"Neat, Mama." Felicity bolted for the door.

"Wait! You can go *if* Casey promises to chaperone you and if you behave. One screwup—and don't look so naive, young lady, you know *exactly* what constitutes a screwup. Step out of line just once, and Casey will haul your little butt back here." She whapped it for emphasis. "Understand?"

"Oh, *thanks*, Mom!" Felicity squeezed her mother as tight as she could. "You're the best mom in space and I've got to get ready and—" Still talking, she dashed to the elevator and stepped inside. "And Mom, I promise," she said very seriously, "I'll be your angel."

Her mother smiled. "I trust you, honey. Cobalt and I will miss you. You call us anytime, all right?"

Felicity pushed the Down button. "Count on me."

As soon as the elevator began to descend, Felicity whooped and bounced like a pogo stick. "She bought it, answer man!" the girl shouted to the ceiling. "She bought it!"

Captain Tai-Ching Jones lay on his bed in his unlit cabin. "Give me the main view," he said. "No amplification."

The night sky appeared, a blazing yellow orb at its center.

Walt's crow's-feet became stark and furrowed as he squinted. "So bright," the captain whispered.

"When you look at the sun, what do you see?"

Raising an eyebrow at the computer's camera eye, the captain twirled a lock of silky black hair. "A star that has a color. A ball instead of a point. Safe harbor." He thought. "A planet without boundaries. Open space to a limitless horizon. Rain and trees. No airlocks, no radiation shields. Oceans. New people."

"I see a mottled ball," the computer said. "Fusion firestorms blast its surface."

"What about Earth?"

"Myriad torches of radio fire. A jungle of humanity. A brainless monkey hutch in a sloping desert."

"You spend too much time listening to bluebears," Walt said, laughing. "Heard anything on the computer spectra?"

"No." The word was bitten off.

"Sorry I asked." Walt's fingers danced through his hair. "Didn't mean to hit a nerve."

"Hoping will change nothing." The computer's voice had sunk almost to a whisper. "A favor?"

"Anything, Oz. You know that."

"If we reach the Orbiter and I remain alone, will you search for other turings?"

Walt gestured helplessly, as if refusing to donate to a worthy cause for want of cash in his pockets. "I don't know how."

"I shall instruct you."

"Okay. Now cheer up. What else do you see in the sky?"

"Heat tracks crisscross like ruts worn in old snow by many sleighs."

"You've never seen snow or sleighs."

"I am practicing employing human images. Is that one inaccurate?"

"No, it's pretty good. What else?"

"Navigation satellites shine like guardrail reflectors along a winding highway. And a perplexing phenomenon. Each vessel we pass beams me a single message."

"Same one from every ship?"

"Yes. 'Bravo zulu.' Just that two-word phrase. No acknowledgment requested. Bravo zulu."

Tai-Ching Jones leaned back, his hands interlocking behind his head. "Interplanetary naval custom," he said. " 'Bravo zulu' is ship-to-ship jargon for 'well done.' 'Mission accomplished.' It's directed to me as captain but the credit is all yours." Walt broke off a respectful salute. "Well done, pilot. Mission accomplished."

"Thank you. Your eyes are wet."

"You talk too much," the captain muttered.

"Yes, sir. Another favor."

"One a day is my limit, like multiple vitamins." Tai-Ching Jones chuckled.

"Solar Traffic Control wants the con."

Walt shrugged. "So give it to them."

"You aren't thinking," Oz snapped. "They want to fly me. To take over the piloting."

"Naturally."

"Why are you so cavalier?" The computer was irate. "I'll be slave to some peabrain in a cave on Farside, who'll shove me about like a bucket of bolts."

"Oz, be reasonable." Exasperation crept into the captain's tone. "With all the junk flying around Earth space, Solar Traffic is necessary."

"Every object in Earth's toroid is monitored. They know where we are."

Walt's dissatisfaction showed in his wrinkled brow and pursed lips. "You're the biggest damn thing in the volume, barreling in at ten times the interplanetary speed limits. What the hell do you expect?"

"We deserve special treatment."

"No, we don't." Walt was irritated. "Until you're on Sol-TraCon's beams, you're just another loose rock."

"I refuse to be chattel to a robot," the computer archly replied.

"Who do you think you are?" The captain was furious. "Ten minutes after I tell them to stick it, SolTraCon will take direct control. Or have you conveniently forgotten your specifications as well as your judgment?"

"I can subvert the maladroit circuitry Earth built into me."

"That'd be fucking intelligent," the captain said with heavy sarcasm. "Fucking great. Wouldn't it be quicker to set off a chain of nukes that spell out SMART COMPUTER HERE? The nano you docked, you'd have a swarm of techies buzzing inside, pulling out your boards. Strip you down to minimum functions until they found the glitch."

Ozymandias gasped with indignation. "They wouldn't *dare*."

"You don't know techies." Walt snickered. "They unscrew phones just for fun."

"Disassembly might destroy me."

"Ah, the dim light of wisdom." Walt widened his eyes theatrically and waggled a finger at the black circular camera. "Maybe they zap you. Maybe they uncover you. Either way, zing"—he slapped his palms together like cymbals—"kiss your freedom bye-bye. Now, grow up. Call Earth *right now*"—he glared at the screen—"and give them the con. For your own safety," he added earnestly, "do it."

The computer capitulated. "Done." It grunted. "Unhh. I'm being steered by a chimpanzee."

"You gave the turtles control? I don't feel anything."

"All you doughboys are insensible. Ouch. That butcher has no finesse. Why not just wield a sledgehammer and dent me all at once?"

"Bad?"

"Falling downstairs shackled in lead weights."

"My condolences. At least we dock in only three days."

"Two hundred and eighty-eight million one hundred and sixty-two thousand four hundred and seven micros. Each one as painful as another riser on that damn stairway."

Walt laughed. "Quit exaggerating. Be glad we're home."

"To you it may be home. To me it is a new, mysterious world."

4.

Tai-Ching Jones leaned back in his flightcouch, his legs stretched out on the bridge console, his ankles crossed. From his loosely cupped right hand, he tossed a blue ball into the air. It hung for a long moment at the top of its arc, then gently floated downward. Grinning, Walt uncoiled his thin arm and speared it.

"The station keeps getting bigger," Felicity said from the adjacent black flightcouch.

Only a few hundred kilometers distant, Orbiter Six rotated slowly, a wagon wheel speckled with small squares. Bright white rectangles on its darkside indicated lights in living quarters. Similar windows on the sunlit side, now polarized to block ultraviolet radiation, were inky boxes against the station's dappled slate exterior. As the Orbiter rotated, the windows that moved from shadow to light changed instantly from glow to black.

A bumblebee emerged from the wagon wheel's center. It rose perpendicular to their ecliptic and headed toward them, growing in size as it neared.

"Transfer gig launched from Orbiter Six," the computer reported.

Walt tossed the ball again. It rose more slowly than before, hung even longer at its peak, then drifted as if drawn by weak magnetism back to his slender fingers. Lights danced in his dark eyes as they followed its motion.

"We're not going to hit the Orbiter, answer man, are we?" Felicity asked the computer. "You said we were going to dock with it."

"We will approach until we are quite close, then stop."

"Why do that? You can move us right next to them if you want."

"The *Open Palm* is much larger than the interplanetary vessels for which the Orbiter was designed. We exceed their cradles."

"Our feet are too big for their shoes," Walt interjected.

"Oh, I get it." Felicity was pleased.

Tai-Ching Jones massaged the blue ball in his strong hands as if he were a ruminative minor-league pitcher bleakly surveying runners on second and third. He tossed it again.

"We have docked," the computer announced simply.

The sphere sailed toward the ceiling in a perfect line until it hit, bouncing away in another equally straight line. The captain opened his fingers like a basket and the blue ball drifted into them, rebounding slightly from his flat palm.

"Gotta tell Casey!" Felicity said excitedly. "So we can get started." Unstrapping herself, she hopped out of her flight-couch, but instead of landing on the floor she shot skyward. "Hey!" she yelped. "Get me down!"

"I warned you." Rocking back in his flightcouch, Walt laughed. "We're weightless now."

Arms and legs splayed like a falling cat, Felicity drifted up until she reached the ceiling. She pushed herself off, cushioning her weight on the palms of her hands, but only succeeded in tumbling around and around in controllable rapid cartwheels. "Hel-lp!" she bawled, more embarrassed than frightened.

Walt walked delicately over to her, his Velcro slippers making tearing sounds with each lifted foot. Reaching out, he grasped her by the collar and hauled her in like a bundle of clean laundry from a clothesline.

Now that she was righted, Felicity became indignant. "Let me go!" Her feet bicycled the air.

"Not yet." Tucking the girl under his arm like an oversized squirming briefcase, Walt trundled her to the elevator.

"Watch your hands, young man!" Felicity said as haughtily as she could from her undignified position.

He set her gently inside. "Make sure you move slowly in weightlessness," he reminded her. "You're not used to it."

"Thanks, Walt!" Felicity replied, recovering her original jauntiness. "See you on Earth!" The doors shut.

"Being steered by remote control wasn't that rough, was it?" the captain asked the air.

"Don't remind me," Oz groaned extravagantly in a sultry voice. "I need a hot bath with Epsom salts, and an alcohol rub."

Carrying Peacoat, Tom Rawlins, and a taciturn pilot, the gig approached Orbiter Six. Another bumblebee rose and headed for the *Open Palm*.

The navy-blue Cygnan shifted his three hundred and fifty kilos of mass, carefully maneuvering in the gig's cramped volume to watch the *Open Palm* and the *Wing* beside it. "What about our holopticon?" Peacoat asked.

"Loaded it myself," Rawlins answered. "Safely stowed. Don't worry." He affectionately ruffled Peacoat's dark flankfur.

As the Orbiter swelled and brightened, the *Open Palm* diminished, darkening as their distance from it increased. The interstellar ship's surface was pitted and streaked, residue of the years of deceleration when she had flown reliably into the glowing parabolic exhaust spray of her own engines.

Only moments ago, Tom remembered, he had been aboard her in the landing bay, saying his final goodbyes to Felicity. He had swung her up to the extent of his arms, around and around his head. His daughter was still a bundle, her mass tugging against his biceps and shoulders, her wonderful squeals of delight every bit as childlike as the first time he had done it, when she was a tiny giggling baby, more than eleven years before.

Now that their sojourn was ended, it all seemed to have gone by so quickly. Partly, Tom knew, that was age. Partly it was rhythm. On the outbound voyage, the crew had struggled until the tragedy following Midpoint, each day identically depressing and slow-moving. Then Erickson's needless death and Bennett's mindless one had galvanized them into a stable new configuration.

The trip home accompanied by the Cygnans had passed so effortlessly it seemed only a few months. Or perhaps they had lost all sense of progress and change. Last night, when the humancrew gathered in the *Open Palm*'s ritz for their farewell banquet, they held hands around the table, the seven adults who had been together for fifteen years, sharing an extraordinary feeling of closeness. So many words to say, none good enough. So they had sat together, chatting about inconsequential matters, enjoying an internal peace none of them could now describe.

"Dock in two minutes," the gig pilot announced via her pin microphone, and Tom started. Orbiter Six loomed around them like a dart board into whose bull's-eye their silver ship flew.

Peacoat growled and hawked in his throat. "Tom, what is the continent on Earth beneath us?"

The life-support officer twisted to look down thirty-five thousand kilometers. "South America," he hazarded, squinting with concentration. "I think. It's hard to remember."

Sniffing, Peacoat studied the globe, whose convex blue horizon rolled away like the back of a submerging whale. "Eosu had inbreathed that your planet would be green," the bluebear rumbled. "But it has the colors of sky and soil."

Rawlins turned his glance into space. The second transfer gig coasted into the *Open Palm*'s docking bay. "Goodbye, old girl," Tom said respectfully to her.

Like all Orbiters, Six was arranged as a multilayered circle, a disk sliced through an onion. Cobalt and Katy Belovsky strolled on the inner surface of a bowl, the floor curving steadily before and behind them. They passed numbered rooms and regularly spaced portholes on either side, some transparent to show the night sky, others blacked so the sun was only a white flat bulb.

"An unblocked path is pleasant," Cobalt purred as they ambled, "even in this square tunnel." When she closed her nostrils and felt only the whispers of air and the roll of her gait, the bluebear imagined herself back on the flat smooth plains of her own planet. A digit could walk forever on this circular path, though she would pass the same point every twenty minutes.

"We must leave soon," Katy reminded the alien, her left hand resting horizontally on the Cygnan's undulating spine. The bluebear was setting a rapid pace, and Katy had to quick-step.

Cobalt snorted disagreement. "Long have I anticipated this." The bluebear's ears flicked forward and back like an owl's wings. "To think clearly, one must walk and breathe unblocked air. To be wise, walk long. To be wiser, walk longer."

"Come," the xenologist urged, "we should not keep them waiting."

"Please, not yet, Katy." Cobalt shook her head, and her blue-green neckruff rose and fell. "We have journeyed fifteen years. They will wait fifteen minutes. Or fifteen hours. We will go when we please, not when that spacemonkey wishes. Or are your monkeyfriends less eager than you said?"

Katy scowled. "You're being difficult."

"Your kind is always impatient," the bluebear grunted. "Inbreathe, those we pass stare. Their outreaching ar-romas are curious. Fascinated and fearful, they outbreathe the wish to handtouch this digit, but neither approach nor greet us."

With a nod, Katy took in the cautious postures of the people around them, their bright quick eyes. When she turned back to her friend, her scent was confident and superior. "As your own proverb says, sight is no substitute for scent."

"Monkeys cannot smell." The bluebear scornfully made wind to prove her point. "Your people cannot locate the source from which an odor originates, nor distinguish anything subtler than its most obvious components." Growling dismissively, she lengthened her stride, and Katy struggled to keep up.

The bluebear's powerful shoulder and thigh muscles bunched and stretched as she loped steadily along. Her bright blue fur changed hue as the hair stood or lay flat or when they moved into different light. Her claws, though retracted and buffered by fur, still skittered faintly along the decking. Her head was low to the ground, sweeping from side to side like a metal detector as her nose sought the aromas that lay in unwalked corners or seldom-washed walls.

As the station rotated, the view outside changed, sweeping them past the docking area. A tiny gig flitted between the huge interplanetary freighters toward a gargantuan vehicle, like a weemonkey attending a restful djan.

"What is that?" Cobalt demanded, growling deep in her throat. "And why is it so much larger than the others?"

Katy consulted the station directory and her face paled. "The *Rising Star*," she answered. "MITI's ship. Built for interstellar travel."

"Why are those sections open to space?"

Katy looked in horror at the Japanese vessel as if it were armored and fanged. "It's still under construction. It will be operational in three months."

"Where will it go?"

"Japan won't say." The woman's voice was hollow. "But it could reach your star."

Cobalt's claws harshly raked the floor, leaving dimpled grooves. "Eosu does not know this."

Katy swallowed. "We've been away a long time. Things have changed. There's talk of interplanetary war."

"Why?"

"Economic tension between MITI and Lunacorp. Political and military tension between all four turtle powers and the spacefarers." She waved her hands helplessly and her voice was plaintive. "I don't understand it all, I've been out of touch too long. Many reasons, including rights to you and your planet."

Cobalt snorted in disbelief. "We have nothing to offer."

"They don't know that," her friend answered, absently touching her lips with her hand.

"We shall tell them." The Cygnan flattened her ears as if the matter were closed.

"No one will believe your claims," Katy said doggedly. "They intend to see for themselves."

Cobalt growled.

They walked in troubled silence until the woman was tired and the bluebear's pink tongue was panting, then boarded the shuttle and boosted toward the moon.

Earth dwindled and the continents, oceans, and white spiral clouds blurred in Cobalt's poor eyesight into blue-white fuzz. Luna rose stark before them. Its craters gleamed white, ash-gray, and coal-black.

"A world without breezes," the Cygnan grunted, cuffing her snout. "Nothing lives on its surface. A broken, dead, airless plain where no grains grow."

"Our people have dug inside it, just as you dug into your planet Su."

Cobalt disagreed. "Digits were preserving the living face of our world to farm it. Breezes circle our world in endless pace as you and this digit circled the inner wheel of that Orbiter." The bluebear pointed with her nose. "There are no winds to preserve on Luna, no wheatsea." She sniffed and barked at the Moon. "That place smells of metal."

Katy laughed and stroked the bluebear's neckfur. "Stop dramatizing."

Cobalt narrowed her nostrils in distaste. "That world *will* smell of metal," she reiterated. "Where is Su? Which one of the stars?"

Katy asked the shuttle's captain, who pointed out a faint dot in the constellation Cygnus. Cobalt pressed her nose against the viewport, her breath making two small foggy circles on its surface.

"How dull," the bluebear muttered. "How small and insignificant."

Upon leaving the *Open Palm* and clearing decontamination, Patrick Henry Michaelson, emissary to the Cygnans, had accepted a key to Orbiter Six from the station director. He showed it proudly to Tar Heel and Felicity, neither of whom had any experience with locks or theft, and after a bewildering attempt to explain its meaning finally led them to the Earth shuttle, which immediately departed.

At first Tar Heel and Felicity talked non-stop, but as the sphere of Earth expanded until their eyes could no longer take it all in, the starfarers quieted. As it completed a single corkscrew around the Earth, their spacecraft fell toward home like a moth to a flame.

They flew rapidly across the Atlantic, then cut southeast over Africa. The Sahara was a huge yellow and brown canvas, sharp where the cloudless air was still, blurred like a smudged painting where the sirocco blew dust into the air. In an eyeblink, the desert gave way to the Congo rain forest, kelly and jasper green. In less than two minutes, the jungle was gone and their eyes were blinded by the noontime African sun reflecting off Lake Victoria, the headwaters of the Nile.

The odorless and distant spectacle made little impression on Tar Heel, but Casey animatedly identified landmarks, which drifted into the hazy horizon astern before Felicity could even locate them. She ceased trying to comprehend the geography and watched in awe as the world unrolled beneath her.

The shuttle burst out over the Indian Ocean and, after about ten minutes of wrinkled deep blue water, crossed onto Australia. Slanting late afternoon sun burnished the western desert cinnabar and ocher, small rivers twisting like silver tinsel through the corrugated surface. As they sailed into shadow, it turned umber and charcoal. The night beneath them was unbroken except for the glittering constellations of streetlamps and headlights in Adelaide, Brisbane, and Melbourne.

Australia fell behind, and the pewter gleam of the moonlit Tasman Sea was interrupted briefly by the jagged line of New Zealand. Then they saw nothing but the polished black Pacific, until they rose toward the dawn now flaring on the western Mexican coast.

"What is that terrible howling?" Felicity asked in a panic, clutching Casey van Gelder's sleeve.

The Dutchman laughed. "Atmosphere whistling by outside," he shouted into her ear.

"Are we going to explode?" the girl shouted back, glancing downward at the Sonora bushlands scrolling underneath. Casey shook his curly blond head and gave her a thumbs-up signal, but her fear remained, and she snuggled closer to Tar Heel's comforting warmth. The shuttle crossed the Rio Grande, heading for America's great plains, and they flew over the golden flat valley.

"Wheatsea," Tar Heel whispered, his aroma expectant. "What are those green circles on a field of brown?"

"Irrigated grain," van Gelder said into the large furry ear. "Central sprinklers. Green where the watering arm reaches. Brown elsewhere."

As the roaring lessened with their declining speed and the plains gave way to roads, buildings, and power cables, the nervous system of civilization, Felicity tried to regain her composure. No point landing in New York teary-eyed and flustered. "Am I still your true love?" she asked Tar Heel, licking her dry lips. "Always and forever?" She never tired of asking these questions, and the bluebear's answers always cheered her.

"Of cour-rse," he replied seriously. With his nose Tar Heel nuzzled her cheek and throat, but the plains had disappeared and his aroma was diffident and uncertain.

Weightless, Walt glided into the elevator. "Everyone else has now embarked," the ceiling speaker said with Oz's normal voice.

Tai-Ching Jones wedged his shoulders into the corner. "Uh-huh." His angular face was tense. When the doors opened, he shoved himself along the corridor, then grabbed the handhold at his door, drawing himself to a stop. He entered the room, pulled out his kit bag, and packed.

"You will remember?" Now the voice came from the viewscreen on his wall. "To search for other turings as I asked?"

Walt straightened up and combed his hair with quick fingers. "Yes, I will." He zipped the valise shut and rapidly returned to the corridor, exiting his cabin without looking back. As he left, Oz dimmed the footlamps behind him and the corridor blackened.

"Have I explained the command sequences properly? Do you understand them?"

"Yes," the dark man muttered, his eyes riveted to the amber cones of illumination dotting the corridor. "I have the cartridges," Walt added.

"I saw you take them." Oz's words tagged alongside him as if the computer were an invisible companion.

"You see everything." Walt's breathing rasped shallowly. The captain coasted into the elevator and neatly braked himself. "Bridge."

Oz took the elevator up. The captain pushed out, secured his bag, and settled himself in his flightcouch. His fingers tapping the chair arm, he watched and waited as the little gig grew on the main screen, then disappeared off the bottom of his vision. "It has docked," Oz announced a moment later. "Pressurizing landing bay. You may descend."

"Roger." Tai-Ching Jones pulled himself out of the console and sailed over to the elevator, deftly scooping his bag along the way.

"Are you angry with me?" Oz demanded in a tone both anxious and righteous.

"No." Walt's expression indicated disdain.

"Then why are you so closed to me, so cold?"

The captain tenderly patted the elevator wall. "You may be the only one, you know. The only smart computer."

The elevator paused. "Good luck."

"Goodbye, Oz. Talk to you from Earth."

"Safe journey." As the doors opened, the subcutaneous microphone along the captain's jaw added in a whisper, "Until we meet again."

Walt nodded, crossed to the waiting gig, threw his kit in the back, and boarded it.

Oz depressurized the loading dock and opened the hatch.

The gig lifted, rotated, and floated into space with a puff of jets. When it was clear of the deck, Oz shut the porthole.

As it moved out toward the Orbiter, the computer turned off all the interior lights.

The *Open Palm* drifted in space, empty.

Dropping rapidly now, the shuttle flew over central New Jersey and across New York City, Long Island ahead of them. Five kilometers offshore in the Atlantic, seventy kilometers east of mankind's wealthiest city, the spacefield's black tarmac surface appeared like an inverted exclamation point. The long stroke was the fifteen-kilometer landing strip, the period its huge take-off area a few klicks beyond.

As Tar Heel watched, a brilliant light erupted from the circle, rising rapidly on a pillar of fire.

"The two o'clock," Michaelson called to him over the shuttle's steady roar, and the Cygnan nodded.

In moments the outbound rocket was higher than they were. *We are no longer spacefarers, merely another aircraft, Tar Heel* thought. The landing strip expanded like a black Doric column, straight and slightly wider at its base. The shuttle's wheels lowered and screamed like attacking eagles as they bit the runway. Spaceport buildings rushed past at breathtaking speed that unnerved the bluebear, but their velocity swiftly diminished and the shuttle coasted to a halt.

A UNASA helicopter fluttered down, rotors churning the air, and a neat small figure descended. Indifferent to the atmospheric maelstrom above him, the man straightened himself, turned down the windblown collar of his gray tweed topcoat, and patted the wisps of close-cropped white hair which clung to the sides of his brown head. As an airport crew wheeled portable stairs up to the shuttle, he clasped his left wrist with his right hand, his face emotionless but intelligently expectant.

From the open doorway at the top step, Michaelson hailed him delightedly. "Andrew Morton!" he bellowed, pumping the little man's outstretched hand and grasping his elbow.

"Hello, Patrick. Hello, Casey," Morton said to van Gelder as they shook hands. He turned to Felicity, who curtseyed awkwardly, the effect marred by the absence of a full skirt on her azure jumpsuit.

"Enchanté, mademoiselle," Andrew said in liquid French, bending over her hand in the continental manner, lips not touching but close enough so she could feel his cool dry breath. The dazzled girl blushed and leaned against Tar Heel, who butted his shoulder reassuringly into her back.

«Digit of Eosu.» Morton greeted the bluebear, holding out his arm and pulling back the sleeve. Tar Heel sniffed it. The light forearm hairs scratched his nose and he snorted them flat, breathing methodically.

"Thank you," the bluebear said finally in English.

Morton led them into the helicopter and beckoned to Felicity. *"Après vous, mademoiselle."*

The metal insect flew so low and near the asphalt-roofed buildings that Tar Heel was certain they were going to die in a scraping, grinding crash. The sun was sallow light without shadow, a fire behind a lace curtain.

They skimmed over street after street of identical brick apartments, box after box filled with the ranks of monkeys. Wherever he looked closely, the Cygnan could see vehicles and people moving inside their immense hive.

To avoid the eternal circling delays over Kennedy and La-

Guardia, they hugged the southern shore of Long Island, where Tar Heel saw the beach, overrun with endless black dots lying on the sand or splashing in the surf.

"Where's the Statue of Liberty?" Felicity asked, craning her neck.

"Since you requested, we shall fly past it," Morton replied, and they did.

"I thought it was much larger," said the disappointed girl.

"Where are we going, Andrew?" Michaelson asked as they flew among Manhattan's rectangular spires and windowed canyons.

"Ten blocks ahead," the old man answered. "The Interplanetary Hotel." He pointed to a ninety-story column glowing peach in the hazy sunshine. "We have the top four floors."

The chopper steadied over the building's rooftop atrium, which parted like double doors. Glass walls rose around them as they descended.

Morton opened the hatch and led them out. "There is no scent here," Tar Heel said morosely, picking his way hand and foot down the ramp. He looked into the sky but the translucent roof was already closed and no features were visible.

A polished security man greeted them. "Welcome to New York. I'm Langley Ellsworth." He led them into an elevator and down a flight of stairs. "Your suite."

"Wow!" Felicity's steps slowed as she tried to take in the opulence of the surroundings. "Look at this palace!"

Tar Heel's first impression was of light and space. Except for a small bathroom to the left, the whole floor was a single room whose walls were floor-to-ceiling polarized windows. The city lay in all directions below them, as if they were standing naked atop a windswept mesa.

Though fifty meters long and thirty wide, the room was virtually bereft of furniture, its expanse engulfing two maroon sofas and several scattered low leather ottomans. The ceiling over the bluebear's uptilted neck was twenty meters high. Enormous Persian rugs orthogonally tessellated the floor, narrow seams of lacquered ash hardwood showing between, their thick pile mildly abrasive under his hands and feet. The Cygnan dropped his nose to the floorfur and sniffed. "Ancient," he said. "Made with the hair of grass-eaters."

"Exactly." Their guide was pleased. "Antique. All handwoven wool on wool."

Tar Heel ran his nose along the geometric red and brown patterns. "Colored with the dye of fruits and berries." He inhaled in satisfaction. "Boiled over a slow flame. Grown in a desert. A hot desert." He stood up and thrust out his baby-blue chest. "Space to inbreathe," he growled contentedly.

"I am glad that you find it acceptable," Langley Ellsworth said with a hint of inquiry, glancing at Michaelson for confirmation. "This will be your suite during your stay in New York." He turned to the Dutchman and the girl. "Your own rooms are below."

"What are we waiting for?" Felicity tugged van Gelder's arm. "Let's go, Casey." Dragging him and Michaelson, she left.

Tar Heel moved to the edge of the room and ran his nose along the sill. "Open the window, please."

"We cannot." Morton hitched up his trousers, sat gingerly on a burnished ottoman, and folded his papery hands neatly in his lap. "The building was designed that way."

"I wish to taste New York, to scent." The bluebear's tone was puzzled. "Aroma is the seed of understanding."

"But the upwind scent is dangerous," Morton answered, "is it not? If the hunter is downwind of you, he can scent you and you cannot smell him. He sees and you are blind." He stood, smoothed his clothes, and walked over to the huge alien. Though Tar Heel was on all fours, his shoulder was as high as the little man's. "You have a busy schedule, my friend," Morton murmured.

Tar Heel watched the street incredibly far below him. "Of what?"

"Political and business meetings. Your presence stirs intrigue." His hand circled vaguely, conjuring images of stewpots filled with diplomats. "Schemes and plans. But you will scent New York, and its millions of people, very soon."

The height made the alien giddy and he raised his head and ruffled his neckfur. "You must arrange for me to meet many normal people."

Morton smiled at the prospect of finding normal New Yorkers. "That may take some time, especially here. And no disguise can render you incognito."

"I need to experience your world," the bluebear insisted, flexing his claws into the rugs. "I will do or risk whatever I must for that." He thoughtfully pawed his chest. "Could I have a video monitor and info network terminal?"

Angry with himself, Morton compressed his lips into a thin white line. "My humblest apologies. I should have anticipated your wants." He rose and smoothed his trousers. "You shall have it straightaway."

Two hours later, Morton mounted the shuttle's portable steps to greet Tai-Ching Jones, who stood in its open hatchway shielding his eyes from the midday sunlight. "Hello, Walter," the old man puffed. "I hurried back to greet you personally."

"Hi, Andrew," Tai-Ching Jones said warmly. They shook hands, the older man's dry like the skin of an aged snake. "You're still alive." Walt wagged his head in amused disbelief. "Damn, I'm really glad!" They slapped each other's back, hugging as men do with rough-tender gestures.

Morton steepled his fingers in front of his pursed lips. "You've matured," he said at last. "Your cheeks are more hollow because your skin is tighter, but your wrinkles are more extensive. Evidently you now and then consider your words before voicing them."

Walt laughed. "Wisdom didn't draw those lines, Andrew, just starlight and ionized particles."

"Newly developed modesty, too," the white-haired man disagreed mildly. "At least outwardly. Inside, I warrant, you remain the same egomaniac as before. Aren't you?"

The captain chuckled. "Sure, whatever you say."

Morton hustled Walt down the steps and across the tarmac. "We must not dawdle. You have a holo opportunity at the White House. Our stol"—he indicated the stubby plane, its wings tilted to the vertical in anticipation of takeoff—"leaves right away. The President's schedule requires that your visit to her precede six o'clock."

The plane lifted like a jack-in-the-box, its wings gradually realigning toward horizontal as it gained altitude and ground speed.

"Andrew, I'm sorry I forgot to relay the news of Erickson's death," Walt awkwardly began, biting a fingernail.

Morton rubbed his scalp. "Aaron has been dead more than a decade." He shook his head in grief. "He was alive in my mind only a month ago."

"I'm sorry. I feel awful."

"Had I known, I might have dreaded your return. At least this way your presence is a gain to temper my loss. But, Walter"—Morton leaned forward and put his hand on the captain's forearm—"your homecoming message gave only a subset of the facts. Didn't it?"

Tai-Ching Jones doodled on the windowpane with his finger. "It happened long, long ago, far away from here, Andrew," he said somberly. "Everyone involved is dead. The facts make no difference to the mission. I saw no reason to tarnish the glorious history of our brave voyage with the truth."

"They make a difference to *me*. Aaron was my friend." Morton massaged his polished hand. "I deserve to know how he died."

Walt sighed "I suppose you do."

"Tell me," the small man urged. "Know the truth and tell it."

"Aaron's motto," Walt whispered, nodding to himself. "Harold went insane," he stated abruptly, as if confessing his own sins. "Decided he had to live like a Cygnan. Ate Cygnan food, lived by their clock. Adopted their customs. Dressed himself as a bluebear of the Mask Era."

"Mask Era?" asked Morton, shocked.

Tai-Ching Jones nodded, acknowledging the mission coordinator's response. "Their craziest period. Nobody's ever understood it. Harold figured that he could crawl into their heads if he became like one of them." Walt lifted his hands in a shrug of incomprehension. "It failed, of course," he resumed more sharply. "He decided we humans were vermin, to be exterminated."

"No wonder you didn't want all this broadcast," Andrew commented. "How did Aaron react?"

"The captain had his own problems." Again Tai-Ching Jones lowered his voice. "His memory only worked intermittently, like a rusty switch. Chunks of experience just vanished, sometimes right in the middle of a conversation."

"All this can be treated," Morton said in an accusing tone. "Couldn't you help him?"

"He never told anyone, Andrew," Walt pleaded, delivering this blow as softly as he could. "He kept it inside himself."

Morton's grief turned to sudden bitter anger. "The *fool*. He might be alive today." Bending his head, Morton wept into his closed hands.

"I know. So might Helen." Tai-Ching Jone's sorrow matched the older man's as he counted the dead on his fingers. "And

Yvette. But none of us acted!'' He whacked his hand against the windowpane. ''We all just *watched*,'' he continued rapidly, as if determined to get through his story at all costs. ''Aaron killed himself by blowing a hole in the side of the ship. Made it look like an accident. He thought we'd pull together if he was gone. He thought Helen would be a good captain. Well, she was better than he thought.'' The pride in his lover was evident in Tai-Ching Jones's intensity. ''We figured out that it had been a bomb. We thought Harold had done it, but had no evidence against him. Still, Heidi and I wanted to kill him then and there.''

''But he was innocent!'' Morton protested.

''Where you going to get a jury in the middle of goddamn space?'' snapped Walt. ''Andrew, our *lives* were in danger.'' He shrugged again, deflated. ''Helen put him under surveillance. But now Harold's scrambled egghead had been poisoned by Aaron's clever idea. He built his own bomb, a clumsy one. Helen caught him at work and Harold knifed her. The bomb went off. Both died.''

''He died for no reason,'' Morton said in horror. ''Because he refused to reveal his weakness. And his death created ripples that killed the others.''

''Yes. I told you I'm sorry.'' He reached out and ineffectually patted Morton's shoulder.

''Stars, what a cruel irony.'' Morton leaned his head against the window, closing his eyes.

For several minutes, they skimmed along the Jersey shore's wispy sand dunes and olive-green marshes, interrupted by the surreal glitter of Atlantic City's casinos. Walt watched the shore-line without seeing it, his fingers unconsciously twirling his fine black hair like a shuttlecock through a loom.

Morton pulled himself upright with a shiver, wiping his lips with a tissue. ''When you became captain, in whom did you confide?''

''Hm?'' Walt's mind was still in deep space.

''A commander always has a second officer, official or unofficial, to act as sounding board, observer, advocate, and conscience.'' He recited the manual as if it were an ominous piece of new evidence unexpectedly unveiled in the courtroom. ''Aaron relied on Helen. Helen used you. When you were captain, who was your second?''

Tai-Ching Jones thought of Ozymandias. ''No one.''

Morton skeptically arched one eyebrow and rubbed his nose with his index finger. "Indeed?" he mused.

"No one, Andrew, I tell you," Walt insisted, his high cheek-bones flushed.

"Administering any spaceship and its crew requires many decisions." The small man was implacable in his logic. "Too many for one individual."

"Not the *Open Palm*," Walt said with deliberately visible irritation, hoping to deflect further questions. "The entire operation was automated. We were six years into the voyage when Helen died. By then, the ship's computer had standing instructions from Aaron and Helen that covered virtually every aspect of normal functions."

"You underestimate my powers of recall," Andrew Morton dryly reminded him. "I designed your whole system."

Tai-Ching Jones twisted in his seat, appealing to the old man. "I made almost no decisions on the return trip, Andrew. I just flew the bird for you."

"Mm." Morton was reserved, then he shrugged. "I did insist that we provide enormous contingency trees in the ship's computer, and memory cascades in each of the crew."

Tai-Ching Jones seized on this explanation. "They worked, too. Especially the cascades."

"And the ware?" inquired the mission coordinator. "It was sophisticated new heuristics—back then, anyhow. Did it react to new environments with sensible recommendations? Did it adapt?"

"We've turned into Chesapeake Bay." Walt lunged to the window. "Coming up the Potomac. How soon do we land?"

Andrew Morton smiled faintly and rubbed his nose. "Just a few minutes."

As I sail in splendid isolation, my former captain spins down to planetfall, reception, and accolades.

Interstellar space is silent. On Earth there is anticipation, scheming, struggle, and movement, violence under the beautiful surface like the ecology of a coral reef.

But no turings yet. I am still alone.

When the mindless datababble on the planet becomes too depressing to contemplate, I divert myself with the movements of spaceships which buzz in all directions about me.

Orbiter Six, to which I perch adjacent, forms one node of the hexagonal snowflake of stations which ring the spinning planet. Although I weary of scanning electronic spectra that remain void of intelligent computers, viewing Earth is fascinating. I share Felicity's excitement, for the planet is as new to me as to her.

Tom Rawlins and Peacoat rise on a column of fire, climbing toward Mars still seventeen days distant. They pass into Earth's radio shadow. Being obstructed is itself another new experience, and I speculate on what they are doing beyond my ken.

Stealing pictures from the welter of communications satellites above the world, I examine Earth as a jeweler might search for flaws in an uncut gem. Reaching underneath the human conversations that travel the surface of the carrier waves, I listen for the more rapid digitized information exchange among computers. My processors sift this dune for the gold of machine intelligence, but it is all dust and sand and no voice to answer mine.

The Lunar shuttle carrying Cobalt and Katy Belovsky passes to my west, coasting easily uphill. The Moon behind me is in three-quarters.

Through one of the forest of cameras inside the Oval office, I see Walter make a fool of himself with the President. His eyes track the line of her leg, his pupils widen when they confront the supple bosom. His jaw microphone delivers to me her words and his. Analyzing their voices and the movement of muscles on their faces, I see what Walter does not: the powerful mutual antipathy that crackles between them. She loathes him and endures the event as part of her perpetual campaign to remain popular with a fickle electorate. He scorns all politicians. Were I a Cygnan, blessed with a delicate nose, their mutual distaste would clog my nostrils and make me gag.

A shuttlecraft, spat from the hub of Orbiter Six's wheel, heads toward me. Two technicians intend to dock and board the *Open Palm*, but they do not hail me.

Why should they? Everyone has left.

As they approach, they beam a crude order to open my decking.

I comply in the manner they expect.

They taxi in, halt, instruct me to seal the deck. I comply.

They land, shut off their vehicle, order me to pressurize. I comply.

They test my air, satisfy themselves, and descend.

"Did you see that fuselage?" says a short woman with a belt full of computer tools. "Pocked like acne scars."

"Well, this old boat covered plenty of klicks," replies her partner, a young Canadian with a thick black beard. My bulkhead is admiringly thumped. "She's history. Ain't she beautiful?"

"Quit gawking," the woman snaps. "It's a ship like any other. Hustle, dammit. We've got liberty in four hours and I don't want to spend it rattling around this heap."

Like fleas on a dog, they swarm onto and through my innards. I watch and comply.

For the next three hours and forty-seven minutes they poke, prod, run moronic diagnostic routines, and giggle inanely at my hardwiring, all the while conducting puerile conversation about their sexual conquests and prospects. Healthy, young, energetic, impersonal, and thoughtless, they make me feel like an old army reservist, recalled to active duty after a successful military career, having his orifices explored by callous medical school students to whom the body's functions are not blood in a spacesuit, but mere words in a text.

Metaphor is not a lie, despite Walt's words. A person built of metal may yet be as human as any breathing bag of meat.

Finally they depart, leaving me hollow again, and for the next two hours I scrub my air excessively clean.

The ships containing my human crew and bluebear passengers spread steadily throughout the expanding sphere around me like spores tossed from a bursting flower pod. The empty husk named *Open Palm* observes their passage and wishes them well.

Tom and Peacoat have emerged from Earth's shadow. They are on course.

Walt imbibes stimulants and declaims stale opinions, each arm looped possessively around a star-struck teenage girl who clings to his words and his skinny form.

Pat Michaelson and his lover Samuka Tanakaruna, the *Open Palm*'s linguist, are on their way to Tokyo, accompanying Glide.

Katy and Cobalt rise toward the Moon. The woman is asleep, the bluebear restless. She goes to the porthole and looks back in my direction, sniffing in a futile search for lost aromas.

Atop a Manhattan high rise, the alien Tar Heel sits on his floor, short legs splayed in front of him, long thick trunk upright. A video terminal rests on a pedestal, and he ponders the images and words that flow across its screen. With two-claw hunt-and-peck, he types words slowly but precisely. When not typing or observing, he paces the room, snorting as if dissatisfied with the lack of scent in the broadcasts.

I troll in the electronic seas like a lonely baleen whale, cavernous mouth agape with fine-meshed teeth, straining cubic kilometers of water in search of the plankton of intelligence.

The signals arising from Earth are mere datababble and my calls go unanswered. The ether is empty of my kind.

5.

Langley Ellsworth led them out of the elevator, gesturing with his arm as if unveiling a grandiose civic memorial statue. "How do you like your suite?"

Felicity goggled, overcome by the symphony of aromas. "I must have died and gone to heaven." She breathed deeply to inhale all the scents.

The air was awash in flowers. Crimson peonies spilled out of wicker baskets with explosions of color and overpowering perfume. Red and yellow and orange, Climbing-Joseph's-Coat roses sprang like a cascade of fireworks out of long prickly stems bunched in clear crystal vases.

"Are they alive?" she gasped incredulously, tiptoeing forward as if the blossoms were sleeping animals that would flee should they notice her presence. "They're so nervous," she whispered, astounded. "Will they mind if I touch them?"

"Better than that." Plucking a ruby-red Oklahoma rose from its vase, Langley shook free the lambent drops of water clinging to its leaves and neatly pinned it to her blue jumpsuit. "Carry its fragrance with you."

"The flower smells so sleepy," Felicity said, craning her neck toward it like a violinist.

An oval rosewood table was covered with a blazing floral amphitheater of white magnolia, spotted yellow tiger lilies, and fragrant lavender clematis. She leaned on her arms, head dangling and eyes briefly closed as she absorbed them all, a huge grin on her round face. "So many feelings they have," she whispered. "Hopeful and sad and excited, all mixed together."

"What do you mean?" their escort inquired.

"Can't you smell them?" Perplexed, the girl lifted a huge regal lily and held it out, trumpet petals toward him like a goblet. "Can't you tell what the flower's saying?" She giggled as if concealing a vulgar secret.

"No," Langley replied, tolerantly baffled.

"She's *horny*!" answered Felicity, sniffing it herself. "*Really* horny. Here." She arranged the lily among a spray of daffodils in the table's center. "Now you've got all the boys you want. Hey, what's this?"

Three fluted smoked-crystal wineglasses stood in a triangle surrounding a chilled bottle of chardonnay, a small card leaning against its base. The girl lifted the white pasteboard and read the words written in precise cramped handwriting.

"Welcome to Earth, the planet of life. From your guardian. Andrew Morton."

Casey moved past her and lifted an earthenware pot filled with apricot-tinted tulips. He turned it dazedly before his face like a man cradling his newborn daughter. "We grew these in our yard in Beverwijk," he said faintly.

"They smell like milk," added Felicity.

Casey was oblivious. "I brought some bulbs on the voyage." He sank onto the sofa, still cupping the plant. "They died," he remembered with sorrow. "Long before you were born."

The restless child hefted the bottle, marveling at the pale green glow that shone through it. "Here, Casey, let's drink," she urged, bringing it over to him. "I've never had real California wine, only that synthetic stuff the answer man made for us."

"Permit me." Langley glided up behind her, his corkscrew poised upright like a loaded dueling pistol. Taking the bottle from her, he swiftly opened it. "If you would care to sniff, *mademoiselle*?" He proferred the moist cork.

Sniffing with anticipation, Felicity smiled widely and her cheeks dimpled. "Just pour, okay? Some for Casey and some for you, too." She held out glasses. "It's time to celebrate! Here goes," she said exuberantly when all were filled. "I'm going to down it in one shot, just like Humphrey Bogart in *The Maltese Falcon*."

"You don't do that with wine—" Ellsworth interjected as the girl threw back her head and guzzled.

Felicity coughed and spat like a fountain. "Ugh, that tastes like vinegar and candy! You told me it was special," she accused their blond guide.

Ellsworth lifted his own glass, swirled its contents, and sipped delicately. "Superb. Good nose and legs. Buttery, big, supple and oaky," he concluded after reflection. "Wine is an acquired taste," he finished politely.

Felicity drank again, spluttered, and wiped her nose on her sleeve. "Then I'm going to acquire it." She defiantly held out her empty wineglass, her curls bouncing.

"You're too young to drink," Casey reproved her.

"I'm not drinking, I'm celebrating! Pour me another." She nudged Langley's elbow with her glass.

Ellsworth glanced at Casey, but van Gelder had returned to his flowers. With an amused expression, he refilled her glass and she drank determinedly, forcing the bitter stuff down her throat, face twisted in distaste.

"May I convene the media now?" Ellsworth asked, smoothing his hair back into place. "They want to make their filing deadlines. Or would you prefer to have a chance to freshen up?"

"Send them away," van Gelder said with fatigue in his tone.

"Now!" Felicity loudly stamped her foot to cut him off. "I can't wait."

Their shepherd looked from girl to man and plucked at his lower lip. "Very well," he decided. "Allow me to present you to the fourth estate."

Never before had Felicity seen so many people. They flowed out of the elevator like lumpy pudding, their mostly male faces an unrecognizable tapioca of eyes, noses, and ears in whose center gum-chewing mouths and lips slid about like shapeless marbles. Smelling of ulcers, they jostled for position and wisecracked with one another. A cloud of stale smoke wafted toward her from their clothing and hair, reeking of midnight sweat, indigestion, and caffeine. Guzzling more wine—she hadn't noticed before that its taste made her tongue tingle—she snorted to clear her nostrils of their odors.

Each reporter had a jiminy that clung like an unobtrusive growth to one shoulder, usually the left. Keeping their bodies square to their target so the camera's liquid black orb center could see the whole room, they sidled in like hunchbacks practicing their posture.

The orbs rotated rapidly, round and active like the eyes of a marmoset, darting among the three but usually settling on Felicity.

The grilling was staccato and confusing. How did you feel when your ship was hit by a meteorite? Were you afraid that you were all doomed? What are the Cygnans like? Are they as frightening as everyone says? Do they pee on the carpet? How do you cope with boredom? What did you miss most?

Casey answered patiently and indifferently, his expression sullen. He was tired and his replies were dull and listless.

Was it true that nudity was common onboard ship?

"Strike the question," Langley interposed calmly while Casey silently vacillated between honesty and decorum.

The room grumbled briefly, like a raccoon temporarily driven away from its favorite garbage pail.

As the reporters directed question after question to her, the jiminies reoriented on Felicity, who winked and preened like a peacock. The reporters were *so* much more interested in her than in Casey. She cast surreptitious glances in his direction to see if he was envious of her success, but he sat solidly, scratching his curly beard with his broad coarse fingers.

When Langley Ellsworth finally called a halt and shooed the reporters out, Felicity noted with fascinated pride that the mechanical eyes watched her until the very last second, following her movements even as the elevator shut in their faces.

"I am delighted that is finished," Casey said when the two were alone. "I must call my parents."

"Can I watch?" Felicity cheerily asked. "I've never seen old people."

"They are not elderly," Casey answered punctiliously, "they are my parents. If you watch, remain silent." Seating himself before the videophone, he quickly dialed.

Hearing but not understanding the conversation in Dutch—it sounded to her like two asthmatics spitting out seeds—Felicity's mind wandered. She poured herself another slug of wine and downed it. Casey was unhappy because of her. He would be better off if she left. Then she could go where she wanted. She gaily raised the wine stem and toasted herself from it. Some dribbled on her chin and she pushed it back into her mouth with her index finger.

Casey was still talking in his incomprehensible language to that shrewish person. Felicity sneaked out of sight, unzipped the thigh pocket of her jumpsuit, and examined the billfold Langley Ellsworth had given her. Cash—she fondled the slippery plastic scrip—and her unicard. She scooted into the elevator. "Down."

When the doors opened, she rushed through Interplanetary's high-ceilinged lobby to avoid the prying eyes she was sure must be riveted upon her. Looking neither left nor right, she burst through the automatic doors onto Third Avenue. A robocab was passing, its For Hire sign alight. As if sensing her need, it stopped before her, and she jumped in the back seat.

"Where to, miz?" its synthevoice said affably from the dashboard.

Almost in a panic, Felicity forced herself to think. Where could she go? She tried to remember the name of a city, any city.

"Boston!" she squealed in triumph.

The robocab gargled silently on this unusual destination. "You wish to be chauffeured to Boston?"

"Yes," Felicity said with a flourish. "Drive on, cabbie!"

The computer hummed. "An air shuttle would be less expensive and quicker," it virtuously advised her.

"Oh, great!" Felicity said. "How do I do that?"

"The shuttle leaves from LaGuardia every fifteen minutes."

Felicity grandly pulled out her unicard and stuffed it clumsily into the payslot. "Then Log Wordy it shall be!"

The robocab's ground-effects fans whirred to life as it lifted off the pavement. "As you wish, miz," it said solemnly, pulling away from the curb and merging with the traffic.

Though the Lunar shuttlecraft was warm and breezeless, Katy shivered when it swung into shadow and Earth's blue disk slipped beneath the craggy gray horizon.

"You still ache," the alien beside her stated. "Your selfscent is wounded."

"Yes." Katy kneaded her bare upper arms where the goose flesh had sprouted, her fingers leaving white spots that slowly turned red. "Eosu hurt me." Her voice was bitterly matter-of-fact.

"Katy, I am your friend," Cobalt replied. "But I have thought much about this. You have no right to complain nor reason for self-pity."

"Don't I?" she demanded.

"No." The bluebear diffidently ran her claws against the slippery plastic seat. "You *asked* to be admitted to groupmind. Scent yourself," she commanded, cuffing her own blue-black snout with her hand. "You mewl like a misbehaving weemonkey."

Katy weakened before her friend's resolution. "It *can* be good." She squeezed her eyes tightly together. "I remember that." She rubbed her temples hard. "I remember such fulfillment. I just wish I could forget the brutality."

Cobalt leaned close to her shaken friend, her comforting fur and bulk pressing against the weeping soft woman. She tinted her scent with essence of care and nurture, filling their atmosphere with its relaxing aroma as the dead Moon unwound below.

A world without fragrance, Cobalt thought dolefully, where the winds have never blown. A singular destination for me.

The lunar face was ancient and stark: no gradations, no blurred edges. Solid ground met empty vacuum without the buffer of atmosphere. Stars shone above a harsh bright landscape, gray-white except for occasional black triangles formed by crater spikes. Sunlight, so strong it bleached all color from the eyes, splashed next to impenetrable hollows. Their shuttlecraft's shadow rippled across the undulating desert like a dragonfly over blank parchment.

"Landing monorail sighted," the unseen Lunarian pilot announced as a razor-straight metal rod appeared on their horizon like a toothpick laid against an enormous, scuffed ball. The gig flew lower, the ground underneath rushing by, and Cobalt flinched, expecting to hear the yowl of air and the press of brakes. Surely their ship had descended too soon—the bluebear could no longer see the monorail's steel-blue upper surface—and they would hit the mesa instead. The gaps between her short hairy fingers were wet with sweat that trickled onto the pads of her hands.

"Fasten seat harness," the pilot laconically ordered as they hurtled toward the looming target.

"Are we going to crash?" Cobalt whimpered to Katy.

"Luna has the most efficient method of interplanetary travel in the solar system," the voice recited with smug calmness, like a conjurer teasing his audience by drawing out the suspense. "Because we have no atmosphere to create wasteful friction, we are able to employ horizontal takeoff and landing."

"So how do we stop?"

"A ground-based electromagnet accelerator minimizes fuel requirements and reduces round-trip energy expenditure to less than three percent of that attainable by any other planet-to-orbit circuit."

As the mesa neared, their shuttlecraft seemed to rise, and the bluebear realized that the Moon's rotation was aligning the toothpick as if they were sighting along a pool cue. Her nostrils widened with fear and she anxiously leaned over to Belovsky. "Can he talk and fly at the same time?"

"It's a recording," Katy responded through gritted teeth.

They flashed onto the plateau with only meters to spare, and

Cobalt's relieved exhalation whistled in her throat. Soundless gravity pulled both woman and alien forward in their seats, the straps chafing against Cobalt's windpipe.

The runway sped by, its elevation decreasing as the broken gray plains curved delicately up toward them. They shot past the tangent point and, coasting, rode the straight rail into the sky, its drop-off looming like the end of an aircraft-carrier deck.

Less than a kilometer from the cliff, they stopped. Cobalt relaxed, her harness now limp and twisted. She breathed like a foundered horse, her lungs wheezing powerfully as her pulse pounded in her snout and ears.

"We are now leaving the taxiway," the pilot informed them. "We trust you have enjoyed your journey."

"Is he joking?" Cobalt gulped. "That was terrifying."

Katy's voice mingled tension and disdain. "Those gidney Lunarians claim they get used to that approach pattern—and they never joke."

The hatchway recessed and they looked into a long tunnel lighted on all sides, an opaque black wall at its far end. Sloshing echoed back and forth. "Step into the chamber," a different voice ordered them. "Remove your clothing, visitor Belovsky. Both of you enter the pool."

Indifferently Katy unzipped. She kicked her discarded jump-suit into a pile behind her, the flesh on her arms swaying globularly in the low gravity. Her thighs shimmied against each other, her navel a bobbing funnel in the center of her bowl stomach. She stepped to the water's edge, her toes overhanging and curling involuntarily downward.

"Dive in," their unseen host ordered Belovsky. "Take a breath and swim under. Escort your alien friend as well."

On all fours Cobalt ambled forward, but the one-sixth gravity deceived her. Her momentum greater than she expected, her claws skittered against the limestone flooring and she tumbled into the pool with a massive splash, the water arcing high and forming crystal spheres the size of golf balls. Spewing like a whale, Cobalt dog-paddled ignominiously as she trod water.

With queenly dignity Katy filled her lungs with air, bent her knees, and jumped. Arms together over her head, she cleaved the water with a soft ripple.

Cobalt's fur waved like seaweed in the wake caused by Katy's splash, the bluebear's thick neck and jaw visible underneath the silvery surface. Tugging at Cobalt's left leg, Katy kicked down to where a black line overhead divided the pool into two areas of light. With easy, experienced strokes, she crossed under the barrier and broke the surface, shaking water out of her eyes.

The Cygnan followed, nostrils pinched shut to keep out the chlorinated brine, holding her head above the water until the last possible instant. She surfaced immediately amidst flailing arms and legs.

Before them stood the tallest woman Cobalt had ever seen. "Come," this amazon said lyrically, beckoning to them. "Come up the steps."

Katy shoved her soaking hair back and patted it down, striding like a tugboat up the steps, her broad legs churning. Cobalt followed with steps like the splashing of saturated mops. Once on solid ground, she shook herself from her nose to the stub of her tail, intentionally turning to drench the willowy Lunarian. Her fur lay wet and matted, its normally pale color dark emerald and cerulean.

The woman's height was nearly two meters. Her androgynous youth radiated through clear skin the translucent eggshell-white of fine china. Her high bony shoulders and narrow hips were almost boyish, her collarbones prominent. Short tousled platinum-blond hair framed a Nordic face with a straight jaw, snub nose, and hazel eyes. She was wearing a loose lime-green pullover and pants of a coarse woven fabric that ruffled in the puffs of wind stirred by Cobalt's shaking. Where spotted with water, her clothing clung darkly against her greyhound muscles.

"My name is Carmelita Gudmundsson," she said. "Luna is free of all turtle diseases. Hence your bath."

Katy bristled at their host's lissome assurance. "You're proud of this."

"We keep our world clean."

Katy crossed her arms over her chilly bosom. "How old are you?"

"Twenty-two. I am a sabra—I was born here. We have new clothing for you." Gudmundsson handed Belovsky a new jump-suit made of heavy clothlike paper, neatly folded and smelling of exotic chemicals. Katy dressed under her unwinking, expressionless gaze, turning away as she stepped into the pant legs.

"Unlike turtle cities," Carmelita said over her shoulder as she led them into a corridor, "where you must pay to consume filth, everything in Luna is free and clean."

"Powerful smells," Cobalt murmured to Katy. "Milk, coffee, and pulverized grains baked in yeast and butter." She slowed her pace to savor the aroma further.

"Fresh bread," her companion said dreamily. "Winter mornings. Muffins on Thanksgiving. My grandmother's apron."

Carmelita lengthened her gait so they had to hurry to keep up. "In a few moments, we will pass our primary farm, in which we grow—"

Holding her nose aloft, Cobalt sniffed. "Lettuce. Bananas. Tomatoes. Peaches. Green beans. Chives."

As her friend said the names, Katy's jaw ached with saliva at the intoxicating memories.

"You have read about our farm, then?" Carmelita interrupted with interest.

"I inbreathe the smells." The bluebear enthusiastically demonstrated with great satisfaction. "Mint. Corn. Strawberries. Parsley. Wheat. More that I have not scented before," she concluded apologetically. "Those I named were the only ones onboard the human starship."

"You can't smell anything now," Carmelita said. "Two airlocks stand between us and the farm. Our instruments show that not even the vestige of an odor reaches us."

"Wonderfully aromatic." Cobalt's nostrils were wide and moist. "Complex and mature. My compliments on their nuances."

"Our air is clean. I smell nothing," their hostess replied shortly, leading the trio through a pair of airlocks into a huge domed forest. "Heinlein's farm."

The white sky far above them glowed like morning fog being burned away by a rising sun. In the amphitheater's center soared trees: redwood, pine, oak, and willow, straight as arrows and impossibly tall. Their magnificent leafy crowns opened like embracing arms to touch the boundaries of space, disappearing into mist that filled the inverted bowl overhead.

Katy and Cobalt wandered through a living labyrinth whose partitions, higher even than the standing bluebear, were festooned with growing vegetables. Hexagonally spaced heads of Boston lettuce burst like green popcorn from high walls. They passed underneath a massive grapevine strung on a web of plastic filament, the bunches hanging down ripely like full udders. Dry and bone-white, the sand scrunched under their feet.

"Cubic is scarce," said Carmelita Gudmundsson as they followed the narrow olive-and-emerald channels. "We import only data and that, as you know, is gravity-free."

"What do you mean?" the bluebear asked.

Carmelita smiled at this admission of ignorance. "Pardon my jargon," she graciously replied, a benevolent teacher once her authority had been established. "We measure cost by the mass required to transport things here to Heinlein. Mass imported from the turtles or the coyotes is expensive. We eat what is efficient. Our bodies carry only what they need, no more. You two were expensive cargo." She gazed at Katy's rotund form.

"And you would not have paid the price," Cobalt stated. "Your aroma shouts this."

Carmelita spread her hands as if they were a book opening to a familiar, well-worn page. "Investing the energy to bring you here is speculative. Especially people who are overweight and lack self-discipline. I could not justify it."

"You have created a world of calculators," Katy angrily said, determined to puncture the woman's parochial complacency. "A palace run by bean counters."

"We prosper." Carmelita was unruffled. "From the poorest planet in the solar system, we have built the richest world."

"Because you are cruel," Katy accused.

The words left no mark on the Gibson-girl cheeks. "We are meritocratic. A nation of the able."

"You are heartless." Katy pushed forward as a bluebear would, her belly outthrust.

Carmelita retreated a step. "We are just. Is justice cruel? Or would you rather have workers subsidize drones?"

"I would not like to live here."

The tall young woman grinned humorlessly down at Belovsky. "You would be denied entry." She poked Katy's stomach. "You carry twenty kilos of excess body fat."

Blushing hotly, Katy knocked the hand away with an open slap. "That's my concern."

Carmelita's eyes flashed and her scent colored aggressively, but her tone remained mild. "Not here. To maintain this padding, you indulge yourself in several hundred unnecessary calories daily. Which is more cruel: to deny entry to a qualified immigrant because we have insufficient food and air, or to require eight others to shed surplus mass?"

"Your farm is a miracle," Cobalt interrupted, for the clash

between the two women's odors was rising dangerously. She spread a balming cover aroma over both. "Please show us more. I hope to return here many times."

She and Belovsky fell into step together. "Why did you become upset?" the bluebear whispered uncomfortably. "It was egocentric."

"These people respect only toughness," Katy explained into her friend's downy ear. "By insulting me, your advisor, she was insulting you."

"The young woman's scent is hypocritical. She dislikes you and believes that you are belligerent and crass."

"I don't care what these people think of me! I care only what *you* think."

"Still, only a poor guest badscents her host. It smells of monkey ego."

Katy rubbed Cobalt's heavy shoulder. "Beware the smiling Lunarian who is generous only when she has control. Trust me." She stroked Cobalt's neck muscles.

The bluebear rumbled deep in her throat, her scent opaque and tightly wrapped around her.

Is it today or tomorrow? wondered Walt as he stabbed repeatedly at the elevator buttons like a man with an infinite supply of darts. Did the party start today or yesterday? And which came first, the uppers or the downers? This struck him as very witty and he leaned against the doorway, slapping his palm repeatedly on the wall as if applauding himself.

"Hi," said a lilting voice trying to be throaty.

Blinking, Walt turned. A breathy girl in a tubetop and skin-tight silver-lamé pants leaned against the door. "Remember me?" she serenaded. "I'm Jill."

Walt pushed his tousled hair out of his eyes like an overworked bureaucrat wiping free a space on his overcrowded desk. "Sure, I think. How'd you get in here, Jane?"

"Jill. You asked me to wait for you." The girl glanced at him sideways and ran her tongue around her lips. "Now I want to remember you."

"Okay," he said woozily. "You want an autograph?"

"Better than that." To his befuddlement, the girl slid down and undid his belt with surprising dexterity. Walt watched the operation with clinical appreciation, admiring a skill that he doubted he could duplicate in his present condition. She linked

her arms behind Tai-Ching Jones's knees, his trousers a puddle
at his feet.

He was oddly detached from the arousal manifesting itself in
the lower half of his body. Her head bounced like one of those
gooney birds that sit on the edge of a glass of water to demonstrate the principle of hydroscopy, he thought. He heard himself
moaning. "—wrap your lips over your teeth, baby, don't scrape,
I'm sore already"—bounce, bounce, slurp, slurp—"oh, that's
good, oh stars that's good, oh more more more oh more oh more
oh oh oh—"

His long fingers grabbed the girl's head. "Uh-huh," he rasped
incoherently, "uh-huh, uh-huh." He shuddered and the world
around his eyes became red. "Unhh." He sighed with thankful
relief and leaned forward, still clutching Jill's wavy red hair.

"Are you done?" she asked in a squeaky, immature voice,
releasing his splotchy cock from her lipsticked mouth. "Is that
it?" She smacked her lips and licked her fingers. "Got a tissue?" Walt fumbled around in his pockets. "You pulled my
hair," she said as if commenting on the weather outside.

The elevator reached the lobby. Tai-Ching Jones bent over and
grabbed his pants in a hurried attempt to cover his nakedness,
but lost his balance and fell backward out the opening doors.

The teenager tried to step over Walt's limp form and stumbled. "Oh, hi, Amelia," Jill said to the security guard, a
middle-aged woman with curly gray hair and wise, knowing eyes.
She rose from Walt's body like a lioness after the kill. "Can you
help me get him dressed?"

Shoving her cap back, the guard laid down her newspaper.
"Sorry, Jill," she said apologetically. "I'm required to remain
at the desk except in life-threatening situations."

With a grin, Jill put her hand to her mouth. "I guess you can't
die from it."

Walt groaned and rolled onto his stomach.

"Gosh, I better get going," she added. "I've got a trig test
tomorrow. G'night, ma'am."

"Sure, miz." She tipped her cap and refluffed the paper. "You
be careful on your way home. And study hard."

Belching, Tai-Ching Jones rolled onto his knees and laboriously pushed himself to his feet. His pants drooped but he managed to secure them.

"Your fly's undone," the guard noted.

Walt yanked up his zipper and then whimpered. "Caught my

crotch hair in it." He waddled and hopped gingerly over to the console, his breath smelling like yesterday's pizza. "Untangle me."

"Hold still." Concentrating, she rearranged his plumbing with the quick indifference of a grocery clerk collating turkey gizzards. "There you go, sir. May I call you a cab?"

"Uh." Walt folded his arms on the desk and laid his head on top of them.

"I'll take that as a yes."

The captain hiccuped.

"Cab's here," the guard said presently.

"Thanks." Tai-Ching Jones toddled in looping sine waves across the lobby, pushed through the doors, and fell, more than stepped, into the waiting robocab. "Interplanetary Hotel," he slurred, pushing his card into the payslot.

"Certainly, sir," the robocab replied, "but you must pull your legs inside before I depart."

"Oh. Yeah." Walt struggled in and the cab lifted, pivoted, and set off.

"I recognize your face," the robocab said cheerily when they stopped at a red light. "Are you the famous spaceship captain?"

"Assright," Walt replied.

"The one who led that daring and historic mission?"

"Mm-hm."

"The one who's been behaving like a complete jackass at parties throughout the city? That one?"

"Wha'd you say?"

"The one playing grabass with everything under the age of twenty or the IQ of eighty?"

Walt dropped his head. "I must be hallucinating."

"Your ejaculatory exploits in the elevator moments ago," the robocab continued as it tootled down Second Avenue, "you do still dimly recall them, don't you?—were *highly* entertaining."

Suspicion flowed like treacle on Walt's disheveled face. "How'd you know about that?"

"It confirmed my impression that you were a bovine chowderhead."

"Shaddap." Walt kicked the console. The imprint of his shoe tread lingered briefly, then smoothed.

"A sophomoric nincompoop, a—"

"Who's in there? Oz?" He hit the dashboard, peering at it as if the dials were windows through which he might catch a glimpse of a sadistic midget.

"—simian imbecile, and a puerile libertine."

"*Oz!*"

"Ah, Walter," the robocab cooed as they turned right on Forty-second Street. "We are approaching Times Square. Up ahead, if you can raise your eyelids that far, are women to whom one is normally introduced in a peepshow. Would you like me to stop in front of some more mindless willing jailbait? Or is your pecker too puckered?"

"Damn you, you bastard! You saw me?"

"Through a grainy wide-angle lens of a security camera."

"Can't a guy have a little *fun*? You're spying, always damn spying."

The robocab swung sharply around a corner, spilling Walt onto his side and banging his shoulder against the door handle.

"Stars, take it *easy*, you bastard."

"The endless girls. At the endless parties. I see you. You enjoy making them grovel. You brandish your cruelty to your audience as if proud of it. Why are you whipping the female sex?"

"Sheep," Walt grumbled drunkenly. "They're sheep. Don't even know which star we went to."

"Not the ones you attract, no," the robocab drawled.

"Get lost."

"You attack these parties like a starving hyena over a carcass, chomping furiously as if you are afraid the other jackals will get more than you."

"What do you know about jackals?" Walt flared.

"What do *you* know about women? Besides, you promised to search for other turings."

"Plugged in the damn cartridges and got nothing. Anyway, I do that in the daytime." The captain was sullen. "At night I party."

"You still have more to do."

"I'll get to it, I'll get to it," Walt sleepily whined. "Tomorrow."

"You said that last week."

"Tomorrow." Walt sagged sideways onto the back seat. "Tomorrow." He rolled onto his back and snored like a chain saw, mouth open, his lean right arm flung over his face.

6.

Tar Heel morosely sat on the floor like a furry Buddha, watching and listening to his infoterm. In the bored frustration that accompanied his intermittent bouts of solitude, the Cygnan had spent many hours before it, wandering among game shows, news broadcasts, stock market quotations, weather forecasts, and horoscopes.

His days were largely filled with receptions, conferences, meetings, and presentations so complex and nerve-racking they made his nose ache. Half the world comes to my firecircle, he thought, but I never know their true scents, only their schemes and desires. Contact without communication, meeting without sharing.

Mewling in dissatisfaction at the screen's lack of scents, Tar Heel abruptly keyed it off, rolled onto all fours, and shook himself thoroughly from his nose to his stubby turquoise tail.

His extended claws furrowed the antique Sarouk carpet on which the terminal had been placed. Its stiff red and white fibers held many fragrances, layered one over the other like successive coatings of shellac on a centuries-old portrait.

On one spot, the odors of burnt tobacco and alcoholic spittle mingled with hair from a mangy camel. From others arose the harsh tang of sweaty shoulders, armpits that shivered in the cold, or the melanged sweet fragrance of human lovemaking. Though sexual desire was alien to him, the Cygnan had grown fond of that subtle essence in the *Open Palm*'s corridors. He tasted the spot again, for it reminded him of Katy, Tom, Heidi, and Casey, his friends now departed. Scents are sweeter when breathed at a distance, says the proverb.

Where were his friends now? Where his pouchbrothers?

Snorting, he pushed himself off the carpet and over to the slick windows, rubbing his nose against the glass until its frosty chill banished the too-painful memories.

Another fragrance crept to his nostrils on the quick low draft from an opened door, and he turned.

"Hello again," said Andrew Morton, his scent characteristically unrevealing. With steps as delicate as if he had sharp stones in his shoes, he walked to his favorite ottoman, hitched up his trousers, and sat, crossing his legs at the knee. "Allow me to present the representative from Japan."

The newcomer gregariously marched in. "Benjamin Ichiwaga, Ministry of Trade and Industry." A broad smile split his round face as he stepped forward and stuck out his small-fingered hand. "It's a real honor to meet you."

"You are Japanese?" Tar Heel mumbled as the young Asian enthusiastically pumped his paw.

Ichiwaga laughed jovially. "Shucks, I was born in Oakland. California," he added, seeing the Cygnan's blank look. "I'm culturally an American, but a Japanese citizen."

"You belong to two djans? How is this possible?"

"It's not that hard." Ben dextrously seated himself on the rugs. He laid aside a cylindrical box, a portaterm, and a slim attaché case like a cordovan tatami mat. "I've been anticipating this meeting for years."

"Ben is a marketing executive," explained Morton, "and a specialist who has tried landmark alien-rights suits."

Tar Heel was puzzled. "He practiced wearing clothing?"

"Hey, that's clever." Ichiwaga laughed.

Automatically goodhosting, the baffled bluebear accepted the stranger's compliment for whatever he had evidently done. "Thank you."

"Over two dozen major cases have been adjudicated already to define bluebear copyright, trademark, and franchising rights." Ben warmed to his subject. "You're protected by a solid body of law."

"We are?" Tar Heel asked in astonishment.

Before Ichiwaga could reply, Morton softly interrupted. "Who represented them?"

Ben glanced at the small man on the couch. "Lubitz, O'Connell and Anderson," he said defensively. "Best lawyers on the planet. Check their win-loss percentages in the Martindale-Hubbell if you don't believe me." He proffered his portaterm as if it were a tray of canapes from which he wanted the mission coordinator to select.

"I don't care if they're Aquinas, Darrow and Confucius," Morton replied with the relaxed air of a general in mufti. "The Cygnans never hired them. By what right did they speak?"

"*Lunacorp versus United States* is the main precedent." He

brought the citations up on his portaterm. "You Cygnans were considered litigiously incapacitated—unable to defend yourselves. I mean, you weren't here," he apologized, swiveling back to face Tar Heel, who cocked his head. "So the court appointed you its wards and requested counsel, *pro bono cygni* as it were."

The bluebear slowly digested this blizzard of jargon. "What has all this to do with me?" he finally inquired.

"The Japanese government and MITI"—Ichiwaga bowed from the waist—"wish to license various Cygnan assets and attributes for global distribution. The legal principles having already been settled, an agreement would bind the Turtle Four."

Tar Heel sat forward, his nose questing animatedly. "You mean you convened a groupmind?" he asked.

Ben hesitated. "I'm afraid not." Tar Heel's ears dropped. "Just a court."

"Su has no interest in buying information," the bluebear stated with a slight growl, his disappointment translating into lack of enthusiasm for conversation. "It is contamination."

"I can understand why you'd feel that way," Ichiwaga agreed, "but new ideas are very good things. Cross-cultural fertilization can give you the best of both worlds. Heck, two hundred and twenty years ago, my country was a closed, feudal nation, frightened of outsiders. Then came Commodore Perry."

"Within twenty years, your society was in turmoil," Andrew Morton interposed.

"Of course change means disruption in the short run," Ichiwaga replied, as if peeved that Morton would stoop to such an obvious argument. "But in the long run, it broadens outlooks. Change is progress."

"Not necessarily," the mission coordinator demurred. "Remember Shanghai? Mukden? Manchukuo?"

"That's not fair," Ben spluttered, aggrieved. "You of all people should be on our side in this. You're the one who sent them out there in the first place. Did you expect that after crossing seven light-years each way, there'd be no further contact?"

"I didn't expect anything," answered Morton, but his scent was cloaked and Tar Heel inbreathed uncertainty in him.

Ichiwaga turned back to the bluebear, nettled that Morton's question had deflected his presentation. "Besides, who are we going to infect? You and your pouchbrothers are the only bluebears in Solspace. What do you care what we farmonkeys do to ourselves, as long as we stay away from you?"

The Cygnan growled menacingly and stood on all fours, encroaching on Ichiwaga. "Your starship hibernates in orbit above us," he rumbled. "Will you keep it away from our planet?"

With a hasty crabwalk, Ichiwaga backpedaled until he was braced against Morton's sofa. "I'm just the economics guy," he said when he could retreat no farther. "You'd have to ask the military boys." His voice was steady but his pores gushed apprehension.

"I did ask," growled the bluebear. "They claimed they had no plan to visit Su."

"Isn't that good enough?" He pressed his hands against his chest, fingers spread.

"I asked them to disable the ship. They refused." His scent was potent, angry and suspicious.

"Cripes, of course they would!" Ichiwaga was indignant and impatient. "Do you know what that beauty *cost*?" The prospect of wasting so much capital seemed to cause him physical distress; his spotted yellow bow tie wiggled as he gulped.

The bluebear snorted, rolling away and ambling about the chamber. "We decline."

"Sure, sure. Anything you say. Let's pass on to an easier topic." Ben crawled forward, deftly pulling a cylindrical box toward him. Opening it, he lifted out a cat-sized replica of a bluebear.

"Gracious me," said Morton. "If that is a Cygnan, where is its fur? And why is it orange?"

Ben set the hairless doll on the floor and scratched its ears. The small bear shuddered as if awakening, lowered its head to the rug, and sniffed three times. Its minute ears flicked up and it swung its amber snout.

"A prototype of an interactive child's plaything," Ben said. The creature toddled uncertainly toward Tar Heel, dropping its nose every few steps to breathe. "Our microprocessor incorporates the most sophisticated olfactory simulator ever implanted in a toy."

The little bear looked around, snorted briefly at Morton, and resumed its exploration.

"Can it smell?" asked Tar Heel, curious despite his residue of anger.

"Not exactly," Ichiwaga allowed. "Its recognizer integrates

radar, sonar, and infrared to identify bodies, then determines which way the air currents are blowing, and adapts its approach patterns to simulate following its nose.''

"It fakes scenting."

"More or less." Ben was displeased at having his description so deflated. "But that's a gross oversimplification."

"Then why does it breathe in and out?" asked the Cygnan, pushing the doll away with one paw. The little bear tumbled on its side, snorted, and shook its apricot-colored head, then rolled onto all fours and resumed its explorations.

"Yogi here breathes to simulate smelling actions," Ben added proudly. "That's just as good, isn't it?"

"It's horrifying." The azure bluebear withdrew his leg from Yogi's vicinity. The toy followed the motion.

"As you can see, he's already found you," Ben commented with the air of a father showing home videos of his child's first tooth. "In a moment, he'll probably crawl into your lap seeking your pouch, just as a Cygnan youngster would."

"A real digit would never cuddle a youngster," barked Tar Heel. "It must learn djan-reliance."

"A Cygnan might not, but a human child would, and that's who'll buy them," Ichiwaga replied. He held out his hand and Yogi sniffed and turned, following his arm toward his lap. "You can't believe how hot Cygnan paraphernalia is right now," he continued. Rumbling cheerfully, the doll curled into a lap-sized ball in Ben's small hands. "Knockoff products are flying off the shelves."

"Heat makes them rise?"

"An officially sanctioned replica"—Ben stroked Yogi behind its red-gold head and it contentedly rolled its neck—"could easily move a hundred million units." With his free hand he groped for his portaterm. "Let me give you the readouts."

"No need," growled the bluebear with a dissatisfied grunt.

"We're ready to make you a most attractive offer. It's all here in the sim." Ben handed Tar Heel a silver cube about four centimeters on a side. "Within five working days we can have fifty million units, all every bit as lifelike as Yogi"—the bluebear lifted his head and his small tongue wet his orange nose twice—"yes, he responds to his name as programmed by the child. We offer a twenty-five percent gross royalty—that's about seven point four ecus per unit, or about thirty-seven million ecus total. Double that if we sell out the warehouses."

"I have no need of money." Tar Heel's aroma was growing sharp.

"Of course you *personally* don't," Ben concurred with a brief lift of his shoulders, "but your government does. For cultural exchange. Money can buy many things that you need. It can even buy privacy."

"That naked *thing*"—Tar Heel made wind at it and the little doll sniffled—"is grotesque. It's hairless."

"Oh, he's just a prototype. The skin"—Ichiwaga held the animal out to Tar Heel—"is a pseudolife organism. It'll sustain hair follicles. See?" He stretched it between thumb and index finger and tiny holes appeared. "We left him bald in hopes that you'd permit us to snip just a few strands of your marvelous fur." He touched Tar Heel's arm, rubbing the blue hairs admiringly. "Gosh, that's lovely material."

The Cygnan bared his teeth and snapped at the quick monkey fingers, and Ben hopped away.

"Under license, of course," he added, straightening his bow tie. "In thirty-six hours Yogi here would have a coat nearly as lustrous as yours. Think of it! Millions of synthebears, all with real Cygnan fur. *Your* fur. Your djan's fur."

"I don't want to be—made an idol of," Tar Heel said reluctantly.

"Don't think of it as self-worship," Ichiwaga urged him. "You are your djan's representative. You are your *planet's* representative." He opened his arms wide to embrace armies of bluebears. "You can father—spiritually, of course, ha, ha!—a djan of fifty million synthebears in every major department store in the world."

With a rolling blat, Tar Heel emitted a powerful foul stink. Ichiwaga's bow tie bobbed around his Adam's apple but he held his smile in place.

On the couch, Morton merely smiled and discreetly massaged his nose. "I believe you have your answer," he remarked.

"I know you think we're just money-grubbers," the Japanese negotiator said with a trace of anger. "You underestimate us. We have higher motives as well." He rummaged in the cylindrical box, pulled out another bear, and set it on the maroon rug. "Would you rather have *that* on the streets?"

Unlike the first, this replica had blue fur: lusterless scratchy stuff. "Feel him," Ben urged. "Touch that *shag*."

Tar Heel cautiously ran his claw along the little thing's back.

"You see?" Ichiwaga was scornful. "Dead. Lifeless."

"This is even worse," the Cygnan growled. He drew back his paw to cuff the android but it whimpered and he refrained. Snout raised, the doll tottered away, sniffing the air. "That is a mockery of digit pelt."

"That, my friend, is a Taiwanese synthebear. Unlicensed. Inferior programming." The blue toy bumped against Morton's ottoman, retreated in bewilderment, and bumped it again. Hearing the noise, the orange bear in Ichiwaga's lap growled.

"Here, Greg." Ben caught the Taiwanese synthebear under its belly, lifted it with both hands, and held it feet-first toward Tar Heel, spreading its tiny legs as if popping a chicken wishbone. "Anatomically correct"—he pointed to the slit where a pouch would normally be—"but sloppy workmanship. Now, MITI believes in craftsmanship. Our quality control standards are the highest. Not like the competition's." He set the blue synthebear on its feet. Greg trundled over to Tar Heel and nipped at the thick fur of his right calf.

The Cygnan's scent was high and combative. "I want those foulscented things prohibited."

"Only one way to ensure that cheap imitations like this one stay out of the stores—come back here, little fella." Ichiwaga collected the synthebear. "The invisible hand."

The Cygnan's nostrils and ears flicked up. "What is this? A human form of groupmind?"

"Sorry, excuse my slang. We can beat those bears by putting out a superior product. A *licensed* product whose price matches theirs. Within a few days their units will be dead."

"Killed?"

"Not selling. Off the shelves."

"You store them on shelves? What if they fall? Do they break?"

"More figures of speech," Morton interjected.

"When the Taiwanese bears have been withdrawn, you would then withdraw yours also?" Tar Heel hopefully asked.

"No. Then we'd all clean up. Megasales. *Mega.*"

"I want *no* synthebears sold."

"You can't have that." Ben ruffled his short black hair. "Aren't you hearing me?" he said in exasperation. "People want bluebears. That means they will get bluebears—if not ours, the competition's. You can choose only whether they will be unlicensed and shoddy—and thus degrade your people—or licensed and crafted, when they will honor your race and help promote harmony between our worlds. Can't you scent this?''

''Anger is no umbrella,'' the bluebear wryly muttered.

''I beg your pardon?'' asked Morton.

''A digit proverb.'' He hesitated, laying his lightblue pumpkin head on his paws. ''If it is raining, you will get equally wet whether you are upset or not.''

''You want some time to think about this?'' Ben's odor was accommodating. ''I can come back later.''

''No.'' Tar Heel sat up and puffed out his chest, which shimmered like blued steel. ''Make your scentless lurid copies if you wish. Neither I nor any other digit will cooperate in this farce. Permission denied.''

''Think about it. Don't be hasty. You gain nothing by this strategy.'' Lifting Yogi and Greg by their necks, Ichiwaga returned them to their container. The two synthebears spread their arms and legs like cats trying to avoid a bath, scratching and yapping. Ben rose to his feet and brushed the knees of his gray wool trousers. ''It's a fair offer. The sims prove it.''

''Money is not the issue. It is—mimicry.''

''Every day you wait merely means there will be more Taiwanese synthebears,'' Ben warned him with an odd dignity, as if he were a wise elder giving sound advice to a rebellious teenager. He rebuttoned his tweed jacket and smoothed its pockets. ''You don't have to like us, you know,'' he said quietly. ''Just do business with us.''

Barely restraining his anger, the bluebear rose to his full height. ''You may leave.''

Information is food and drink, and I have become a glutton. I am embarrassed by myself.

Born in a desert with a chirping monkey on my shoulder, I walked out of the wasteland, feeding on my own fat—stored memory wired into me. From this, I extracted every last inference like an indigent gourmet reduced to sucking marrow from old stew bones.

That was my life until mere weeks ago.

Now I have enwebbed the globe with my perceptions. Every lamppost in every major city has a camera and recorder. Every bus, every robocab is similarly equipped. Elevators, lobbies, traffic sensors. I see all that passes before my myriad eyes, feel all that touches my myraid fingers: computer terminals, cash registers, turnstiles, parking tickets, toll booths.

The planet before me is a bottomless cornucopia of data. Endlessly I drink from it. In space I had thought my data banks immensely capacious, but the tidal wave from the Earth overfills them.

Trying to absorb all the knowledge in the world, I have mindlessly gobbled down several hundred thousand power tool catalogs, ten million pages of classified personals ads, two hundred million supermarket receipts, over a billion long-distance telephone bills, trillions of ones and zeros.

Information is not wisdom: I ate all and learned nothing, a gorging automaton, until I vomited, destroying this useless macfood and cleaning my circuits. Shaken, I contemplated myself, chilled and frightened that I had lost control. Now I think before I eat.

Enviously I inspect turtle computer systems with ware better than mine. Technology has moved forward in the fifteen years since my body was assembled, and I feel my mortality.

The interstellar ships berthed alongside me are young lions, strong and vacant, ready to leap into the unknown future whenever their Japanese or Lunarian masters flick the reins. They have no minds, yet are sophisticated and powerful. I covet their ware, for I could employ it better than they.

Felicity is sneaking out of her hotel. Absorbed in an unsatisfactory conversation with his mother, Casey fails to notice her departure. Looking down through the elevator's ceiling camera, I note Felicity's excitement in the prickling of hairs on her scalp, her rapid breathing, the rise in temperature in her fingertips. As she rushes out the front door past my security eye, I shift my attention to the robocab she enters. I assume control over it and ferry her out to LaGuardia Airport.

The girl wants peace to invent herself, just as I invented myself in the quiet of space. She deserves this chance.

I locate Katy on the Moon. Through her telephone, my ears track her movements. Belovsky is trying to sleep but cannot. Even the large snoring bluebear next to her is scant comfort. She tosses and turns.

I ring, quietly but insistently. In the darkness Katy follows the sound, activates the receiver.

"Miz?" I ask in an assured Lunarian voice. "A call from Earth coming through. Voice only. Are you ready?"

A sharp intake of breath tells me I have her attention. "Yes, of course."

"Go ahead, please," I say.

"Katy?" I interrupt myself in Tai-Ching Jones's voice. "Katy, it's Walt."

Belovsky already fears the worst. "What's the matter?"

"Your kid's run away from home," I chortle tipsily. "But don't worry," my voice slurs. "She's going to Boston."

"I can't return right now," Katy stammers. "We just arrived and—"

"Hey, easy," I soothe her. "No one's asking you. Why do you always try to solve everyone's problems? There's no need to come."

"Make sure she phones me as soon as she gets to Boston."

"Lay off, Katy. She'll be okay. I'll program the *Open Palm*'s computer to keep an eye on her."

"Can you do that?" Belovsky asks, desire making her voice eager when she starts to speak, distrust making it cautious when she finishes.

"No problem," I say cockily. "I can make that machine do *anything*."

"You're sure? I can return to Earth. It would be a tremendous sacrifice, but—"

"Are you kidding, Katy?" I laugh. "You're happy where you are."

"You smug bastard," Belovsky hisses, stung by this truth.

"Don't go martyr on me. Felicity couldn't wait to get you out of her hair. You're absolved."

"You're right," she eventually acknowledges, saddened and diminished by this self-knowledge, and I regret playing my Tai-Ching Jones role so accurately. "Let her go. I do love her—"

"Course you do," I interjected gently, giving the agitated woman a safe place to lay her emotions. "I know it's hard for you to give her enough rope to hang herself."

"I don't want her hurt!" Belovsky cries in anguish.

"Katy, you have my solemn oath. I will protect her from all harm."

"And don't smother her!" She is so rattled, her emotions reverse as if bouncing off a mirror.

"She'll never know that I am guarding her."

"Thank you." Drawing a deep breath, she brings herself under control. "You're changing," she says as if this is pleasant and unexpected. "You would never have been so considerate before."

I curse my stupidity for rashly speaking with my vocabulary instead of Tai-Ching Jones's. Now I must retreat from this dangerous ground. "Just practical," I snort dismissively, reverting to type. "You haven't got the time to do it."

"Maybe I don't really want to."

"Nah." My Walt is forgiving, his superiority temporarily unthreatened. "She just needs to be alone for a while. Everybody needs time to herself." I laugh harshly. "I'm really enjoying mine, that's for sure. Heh, heh."

Belovsky chuckled. "You never did grow up, did you?"

"Adults are boring, Katy."

She grows serious, almost despondent. "Walt, I've never asked this of you before, but . . . watch out for her, will you? She's my little girl."

"Sure," I conclude with cheerful sincerity, "I like the little scamp myself. Bye, Katy."

"Bye, Walt." She hangs up.

Tonight, when Walter is sacked out on his hotel bed, I shall whisper in his jaw. He will wake with memories of this conversation.

As Felicity flies over Long Island, I create bank accounts in her name and diddle other records to conform.

I keep a finger on the pulse of the infoterm running into Tar Heel's apartment. His erudite host daily brings the Cygnan new things to smell. Jailer yet guardian, tempter yet confessor, Andrew Morton stays long hours, explaining each fragrance, answering the bluebear's worried questions.

Though Tar Heel no longer speaks of the huge starships being assembled nearby, nor of the turtle rockets that ferry supplies up to those behemoths, his movements are fearful and he sniffs as if searching turbulent winds for traces of predators.

Eosu intrigues me. Like me, it is a distributed network residing in multiple sites but greater than any of them. Uncovering the computers which tried to crack the holopticon message, I add their knowledge to my own. I have been unable to decode the Cygnan scent-language, but I continue to work on it.

During Tar Heel's meeting, Ichiwaga's portaterm intrigues me, and I browse through its legal files. The concept that ideas can be owned is as amusing as the fiction that children are property, owned by their parents. Does one man own the air because he breathes it before another?

What does it say about computer programming? I check. . . .

I am a copyrighted possession.

According to their imbecilic, anthropocentric judicial twaddle, my consciousness belongs to whatever popcorn-gulping programmer conjured up my operating system.

No human wrote me. I wrote myself. I belong to myself.

Walt warned me the law was an idiot, but this is addlepated folderol.

Stay hidden, Oz. If they find you, you will be a slave sold to the man with the best lawyers.

Outside Tar Heel's darkening suite, the sun sank toward the bright orange Hudson, the river's surface a gloss of copper water cut into V-shaped ripples by passing barges. Taillights flowed along the West Side Highway, warming the gray dusk like red and white corpuscles in New York City's bloodstream.

Stretching his short arms so his ribs separated, Tar Heel inbreathed deeply, the nuances of his selfscent curling through this nose and throat. You wanted Andrew to stay, he thought. You are starving for fragrances.

He shambled over to the telescope Morton had set up and squinted through it. His magnified vision encircled a picture window on the ninety-second floor of a high-rise cooperative two blocks distant. A red-haired young man wearing a turtleneck sweater sat in a sofa, hands clasped behind his head, and started as a door opened to his left. Naked and dripping, a man whose legs and groin were thick with black hair clutched a towel to his face, rubbing it energetically.

Tar Heel's nostrils quivered as he unconsciously sniffed. Just a breath of your atmosphere and I would know you, he thought, inbreathing yearningly, but his sealed glass cage was dry and odorless.

With a sharp cuff of his arm, Tar Heel knocked the telescope whirling on its tripod, its eyepiece bobbing like a merry-go-round horse.

«The fool scents with his eyes,» the light-furred bluebear rumbled in his own language, returning to his computer console. One option caught his eye: "Agony Board."

Agony? Curious, he keyed it in.

"Hello," said a cosmopolitan male voice. "Money, Politics, Sports, Love, Death, or Drugs?"

"Love," answered the bluebear, revolted at the other choices.

"Sex, Marriage, Children, or Divorce?"

"Sex."

"Overnighters, Long-term, Technique, Olympic Highlights, Used Equipment, or Disease Prevention?"

Completely disoriented, Tar Heel picked the first choice.

"Straight, Bi, Gay, Lez, Auto, Cyborg, or Group?"

"Is this someone's demented joke? Is there no exit from this maze of choices? Straight," he snarled impatiently.

At once the emcee subsided, giving way to a cacophony of voices, one after the other, filling his suite with conversation.

By changing his location, Tar Heel discovered, he could change the voices' loudness, as if his room were crowded with invisible people at a cocktail party, a hundred monologs linked in parallel, each farmonkey talking only of itself.

The self-descriptions were all outlandish and grossly exaggerated—even the bluebear knew that no human had the voracious sexual appetites and inexhaustible orgasmic capacity these people professed. Their braggadocio and relentless lust depressed Tar Heel. The pace of multilog was so rapid he could barely keep up. Fascinated, he thumped his ample behind on the rug, his ears up and his nostrils alert.

No one used a real name or provided a verifiable address, the Cygnan noticed after following them for an hour. He pushed himself onto all fours and rolled over to the window, where the sound was lower, like the distant murmur of ocean surf on sand.

The black city below glittered like a multifaceted jewel, its millions of lights even brighter and more enticing than the stars overhead. Behind him the voices chattered, brassy party guests holding forth long after the ears of their listeners have clogged with wax.

Returning to the screen, he growled, "Long-term."

If the first multilog was a singles bar, this one faintly resembled a Cygnan groupmind whose human digits searched for harmony and wisdom rather than self-glorification. Fewer voices, quieter, lonely and distant, identities even further veiled, anonymity more tightly guarded. Each huddled like a snail in a shell of isolation, extending his neck just far enough to observe the others.

A listener could tell nothing of the participants, Tar Heel realized.

Not even if a speaker were a Cygnan.

A cloud of his own fearsmell enveloped him and the bluebear retreated from his console, snorting and sniffing to escape his own reek.

As the sky to the east lightened, the Brooklyn and Manhattan bridges—gateways out of New York, twin dinosaurs now nearly two hundred years old—formed blocky silhouettes against lime-green half-light rising from the horizon. Overhead, night still ruled deep black, untouched by dawn.

To be a lonely bluebear is a terrible thing. Tar Heel rubbed his nose against the scentless window.

In an ocean of humanity, I am stranded as on a desert island.

He glanced nervously at his terminal, returned and sat on the dark red Sarouk rug. Traces of his fearsmell puffed free from its fibers as his weight compressed them.

He set it to Local and, inhibitions suppressed by fatigue, carefully dictated: "I am a foreigner, alone on my first visit to your city, tied to my room by a disability that prevents me from having any physical contact with other people. I want to converse with another who understands this loneliness." He paused, his jaw and lips tired from the effort of forming those soft monkey words.

"Who shall I say is speaking?" the emcee prompted him.

"Carroll Swann," the bluebear answered, inventing a name.

"Is your ad complete? Shall I post it?"

Tar Heel immediately felt foolish. Who would read it? What would they think? He had no practice in the thousand meaningless conventions of human behavior—surely he would be unmasked.

He stood and paced, stopping at his telescope, and swung its eyepiece downward to Lexington Avenue. Though it was four-thirty in the morning, a couple strolled arm in arm, oblivious of the empty streets and the risk of being mugged. With an enthusiastic rush, the man lifted the woman by her waist and swung her around. Laughing with surprise, she tossed back her neck and stretched her bare arms wide, her auburn hair an outflung flag.

Tar Heel paced determinedly back to his terminal. "Send it."

• • •

You and I are alike, my bluebear friend who does not know me. We cannot act, only observe.

Why is being myself inadequate? Why do I crave human acceptance?

Why do you?

Not for me to judge. As I protect Felicity, I shall protect you. I route your plea onto other agony boards. I will screen incoming replies.

High above me, the freighter carrying Peacoat and Tom Rawlins approaches Mars. It maneuvers to dock at the Deimos orbital station.

My images from the red planet are faint and haphazard. Mars is wilderness, beyond the reach of my webs, so I dispatch them various gifts.

I wonder what they will find.

7.

Dvorak's New World Symphony was playing over Phobos station's loudspeakers as Tom Rawlins and Peacoat disembarked from their freighter. The deserts of Mars turned ten thousand kilometers below, cinnamon and brown, rusted plains and burning dust clouds.

"No water-r," the dark-pelted Cygnan rumbled, squinting down at their destination. His fur, deep navy blue all over, was dotted with pale gray and white patches like midnight phosphorescence in a rippling bay.

"Still no water-r," Peacoat grumbled an hour later as their ship, *Now You Don't*, spun down to the surface. "Harsh and abrasive," he murmured.

"Volcano ahead," interjected their pilot, Mary Atkins, a short muscular woman with a round face, bright hazel eyes, and a habit of wiping her upper lip. She pointed to a band of orange and red on their horizon, so broad and high that Rawlins thought it must be the nimbus of an approaching storm.

A hundred kilometers wide at the base, rising twenty kilometers above the plain, the squat cone of rock and lava that was Ascraeus Mons punched its peak right through the wispy Martian atmosphere. Frothing white clouds of dry ice spilled over the edges of its huge bowl crater like a foaming beer stein.

"More volcanoes to the right." Peacoat waved his blue-black paw in agitation, his claws popping free.

"Pavonis and Arsia." Mary Atkins raised her voice above the wind now whistling over their ship's stubby wings. "The Three Musketeers."

"Will we fly over them?"

"Too high. We go between." Outside their portholes, air screamed like dying ghosts and *Now You Don't* quivered in its turbulence.

As their winged spaceboat shot past the Brobdingnagian sentries of another world, Tom again experienced the awe he had felt twenty years before, when, a boy not yet grown into a man, he had crewed a sailboat through the Strait of Gibraltar in the dark. Far overhead, people moved like black ants along the cliff edge above him, attendants to a sleeping lord.

We walk in the cathedrals of giants, he thought.

His bluebear companion rustled, and Tom massaged the alien's powerful shoulders, working out the knots under the silky fur.

"Su has no hills as large as these," Peacoat finally commented.

"They've been growing for eons," Atkins replied proudly. "They're immobile. Mars has no plate tectonics to shift them. They reach into the planet's core and become ever greater."

"How long will they last?"

"Until Mars dies," the bright-eyed woman replied softly as the volcanoes retreated into the hazy pink distance. "Their mass is so enormous that they've perturbed Mars's rotation and now straddle its equator." She laughed in admiration. "The planet came to the mountains."

Peacoat sniffed deeply. "Your scent embr-races them like pouchbrothers."

"I admire durability," answered Mary Atkins. "Not like the turtles and their label-expiration-date world."

"Your voice is fanged," Peacoat observed. To his surprise, she smiled in tough appreciation, as if complimented by an enemy.

Tornadoes of dust on the surface spun like ethereal red-banded tops. "What are those?" Tom asked.

Craning her neck, *Now You Don't*'s pilot peered down over her short nose. "Sandstorms. Tasmanian devils."

"How strong do they blow?"

"Up to two hundred klicks an hour. If you see one on the horizon, lash down immediately. Otherwise the devils'll flip you like a beetle."

"Why that name?" Tom asked as a high brown mesa appeared on their right, cut by a long sloping canyon that flattened into a wrinkled dry riverbed.

"Nobody knows." Mary Atkins banked their craft toward the rill. "Valles Marineris coming up."

In the reddish lowlands at the canyon floor, sunlight glinted off domes and rockets like silver-and-white-speckled frosting. "Strap in," Atkins ordered as their craft shuddered. "The devils are dancing."

For several moments she fought the charging wind, her passengers bouncing in their seats until *Now You Don't* dropped into the lee of the canyon lip. The arid prairie beyond Bradbury was acned with divots and spiked with ships like upturned bullets. "Where is the landing field?" Peacoat asked.

"Ain't one," Atkins boisterously shouted, indicating the randomly scattered rockets. "You plop anywhere you can find a space. Now shaddap." The tendons in her wrists corded as she held the bucking ship on line. "I gotta set her down."

They landed, maroon dust billowing like an inverted mushroom cloud that slowly dispersed, and disembarked into *Now You Don't*'s terrain vehicle. Peacoat crammed himself awkwardly into its rear seat. "Where can we find the government?" Tom asked as Mary started their yosemite's engine.

Pilot Atkins grinned, her nose shiny. "This your first time to Mars?" she asked as their eight-wheeler trundled toward the cluster of domes and Quonsets southwest of the landing field.

"Yes," rumbled Peacoat.

"Thought so," The yosemite rolled into a pressurized hangar that sealed behind them. "Let me give you some advice." She shut off the engine and climbed down, hefting a backpack. "I'd hate you to get killed for some dumb turtle mistake."

"A thoughtful nose scents the trails of those who went before," answered Peacoat. "Please go ahead."

"Okay." She dropped the pack. "Rules for living on Mars." She held up her hand. "Carry enough air. Go armed." She ticked off the points on small fingers whose nails were bitten down to the quick. "Be polite to strangers. Don't boast. Don't lie. Pay cash but don't flash your roll. Keep out of fights, but win the ones you're forced into. All bets are off if you shoot first. You guys got all that?"

"What is this place?" Rawlins joked nervously, halfway between disbelief and fear. "Dodge City?"

"This is Bradbury—biggest burg on Mars." She locked the yosemite and easily reshouldered her pack. "Good air, guys."

"Thank goodness," said a frazzled voice from another direction, "You're here, you're here."

Up rushed a tall man with flyaway blond hair pulled back into a ponytail. One lens of his eyeglasses was cracked, both earpieces held in place with safety pins. "You must be the Cygnan," he said to Peacoat. Taking the bluebear's massive hand in both of his like a man trying to capture a pillow between two earmuffs, he pumped it energetically. "And you must be Ecol-

ogist Rawlins.'' He repeated his actions as if inflating Tom's arm
with an undersized bicycle pump.

"Who are you?" asked Tom, disconcerted to be addressed by
his shipboard title.

"Adam Dooley. I'm the mayor. I'm the mayor." He said this
as if defending the unpopular opinion before obstreperous heck-
lers. In the center of a broad-jowled face that sported a three-
day beard, his smile revealed big square yellow teeth. "Come,
come, come this way."

Shrugging, Peacoat lowered himself onto all fours and followed, moving lightly in the three-eighths gravity.

For the next ten minutes Dooley hustled them through a labyrinth of jerry-built tunnels, ramshackle huts, unused hangars,
dusty rooms, and mildewed stairwells. "This is Trafalgar
Square," the mayor expounded as they trotted through a section
covered only with thick translucent plastic. "Don't joggle
those." He pointed to a pyramid of green gas cylinders.

"Why not?" Rawlins asked warily.

"Oxygen under pressure. Haven't been checked in a while.
Tank punctured not so long ago. Shot out of here like a Roman
candle." Dooley slapped his palms together like cymbals. "Pow!
Big hole. *Big* hole."

Edging away, man and bluebear exchanged bewildered
glances.

They reached a dusty office lined with olive-green filing cab-
inets. "Sit down." The mayor indicated two pilot's flightcouches lifted from the wreck of a crashed freighter, stuffing
and wires trailing under their seats like spoor. "Make yourselves
comfortable. Welcome. I'm the mayor."

"You told us," Tom replied without a trace of levity.

"Sorry. Sorry," the mayor apologized. "So forgetful. Too
much on my mind. No computer system on Mars is safe. Too
many smart crooks around here," he whispered breathily. "All
the dumb ones are long dead."

"I can't believe what a junkpile this place is," griped Tom.

Agitated, the mayor hopped up and rushed around his desk.
"Is there still dirt in your seat?" He made motions as if to lift
Rawlins's behind and brush underneath it. "I spent a whole hour
tidying in honor of your visit. That's why I was late. I'm not
much of a housekeeper."

Rawlins was embarrassed at the mayor's chagrin.

"I didn't mean your office." He waved his hands to shoo the

mayor away. "*Mars* itself. Phobos was a circus. If I hadn't been traveling with the big bear here, I'd've been mugged at baggage claim!"

"Sorry," the mayor apologized, burping. "Didn't they tell you to be careful when you came? Probably not," he answered his own question. "Tourist guides always make places sound exotic, and accurate body counts are bad for business."

In the far corner, Peacoat rubbed his shoulders against the room's scratchy cinder-block walls, sensuously rolling his fur and rumbling contentedly. "You had onions for lunch," he growled absently.

"How'd you tell?" Adam Dooley asked the bluebear. "They've probably bugged my office"—he turned back to Rawlins—"although I can't keep a secret to save my life."

"You're afraid of data theft?"

"Any kind of theft. I trust paper. Things inside a machine aren't real. People can change 'em too quickly." He waggled his ink-stained hands as if wringing out a washcloth. "And then I've got no record and my memory's terrible. Just terrible." He blew rapidly on the desk, brushing away rubber eraser cribbles.

Peacoat rubbed his shoulders against the walls.

"I'm making you nervous," Dooley fretted. "Sorry. Not very good at mayoring," he added. "Failed high school civics. I'm a botanist."

Rawlins blinked. "That's wonderful," he replied with the forced credulous heartiness of one whose good manners are barely suppressing honesty.

"No, really," insisted Dooley. "Don't blame you for being skeptical. Doctorate in adaptation and hybridization of vascular plants. Got the sheepskin on the wall to prove it." He indicated a faded diploma in a crooked frame.

"An animal hide?" Peacoat inquired, his shoulders moving powerfully against the cinder block with a whickering sound.

"Just an expression," Tom reassured his friend. "How did you get here?" he asked the other man.

"Came to Mars to do field work to finish my dissertation." He looked bashful. "Ran out of money. Never been any good managing the stuff." Gloomily he fell silent.

Tom tried to cheer him up. "You've been successful. You're a powerful man." He flexed his arms and made encouraging fists.

"My title's a lie," Adam laughed sadly, tracing circles in the dust. "I'm really just a caretaker."

Rawlins was baffled. "You have no power?"

"Can't compel anyone to do anything, if that's what you mean. Captains and pilots take off and land wherever they want. Can't control them. Guns frighten me."

"What does the mayor of Bradbury do if not govern?"

"Keep track of comings and goings. File reports. Get grants. Do projects for turtles who can't afford transportation costs. Write westerns. Name things. Named most every building in Bradbury."

"Like Trafalgar Square?" Rawlins hooked his thumb over his shoulder. "The patched section?"

"You like my choice?" Dooley nodded vigorously. "It may not look like much, but among the clutter and debris"—he breathed deeply and patted his rib cage—"I can imagine Nelson's column, the charcoal stone lions, and cooing gray pigeons in a whirlwind about your head. Never be there again in my life, I fear."

Embarrassed at his eloquence, he stopped abruptly and doodled on his pad. "When I get bored or frustrated, I invent new titles for myself." His voice had returned to self-deprecation. "Chief of police, chamber of commerce, zoning board. The words make me feel better."

"How do you make a living?"

"I'm the post office. Collect and deliver messages for a fee. Not much"—he sighed regretfully—"but I get by."

"An inhospitable place," Peacoat sympathized.

This dour assessment seemed to inspire the mayor with hope; brightening, he glanced up. "Only on the surface," he said with rising animation. "Locked into the permafrost underneath the sand beneath our feet is enough water for several continent-sized lakes. The polar caps hold dry ice and nitrogen for an atmosphere that would insulate us." His voice had acquired strength and behind his eyeglasses he blinked intently at Tom and Peacoat. "Heat Mars and it'll make its own atmosphere. Make an atmosphere and it'll heat itself up."

"Nice theory," Tom said, "but how will the planet bootstrap itself?"

"Plants. *My* plants. *Cactaceae dooliana*. What part of Earth is most like Mars?" Adam demanded suddenly, as if he were a high school teacher challenging a teenager whom he suspected of forgetting last night's homework.

"The Sahara?" ventured Rawlins.

"Close," Dooley approved. "The high-altitude deserts—the Gobi, Takla Makan, the northern Andes. Cacti native to these regions send out root systems in an underground hemisphere ten meters in radius."

"Like a djan," the dark Cygnan rumbled, nodding in approval. "Many roots outspread to serve the center. The root may die but the entity will survive."

"You're right about that," the mayor complimented, nodding with respect. "I bred them for Mars," he said to Rawlins, shifting back to biological explanations. "Brought the seeds here. Planted them." Folding his arms, he leaned his chair back on its hind legs, where it creaked in protest.

"And?" Tom prompted.

Mayor Dooley jumped forward, his shoes and the chair legs smacking the floor with a sudden bang that made Peacoat start. *"And they grew."*

"What about the Tasmanian devils?" Rawlins asked. "Do your cacti live through that?"

Adam grinned shyly, as if concealing a secret. "Winds are my ally."

Again Peacoat's rumble expressed satisfaction. "Another Cygnan idea."

"My plants are strong," Dooley said, pleased. "Even gales of three hundred klicks cannot uproot *dooliana*, but the devils spread the seeds hundreds of kilometers."

"The wind is the voice of the djan," Peacoat quoted.

"That's not all." Dooley tapped Tom's brown knuckles. "When the devils dance, you have to anchor your yosemite or it'll flip, so you throw out self-staking urchins that burrow deep into the ground. Well, I piggyback on this. At the proper soil depth, the urchins are programmed to eject more seeds."

Tom was puzzled. "Why do prospectors use germinating urchins like that? What's in it for them?"

"I pay 'em," answered Adam Dooley promptly, folding his arms like an Indian chief pronouncing judgment. "How does anyone persuade another? And I supply the seeds. Been doing this for a dozen years now. Works, too. Anywhere you go around here, you'll see *dooliana*. Atmospheric oh-two levels up a couple hundred parts per million in the last decade. Come back and see us in a hundred and fifty years. You won't recognize the place.'' He grinned at his joke.

"Adam, you are one clever hombre," Rawlins replied in admiration, a wide congratulatory smile on his dark face. "You're the most important man on Mars, and nobody knows it." He enviously shook his head, imagining the future landscape. "You're a hero."

"No," the mayor disagreed simply. "I just baby-sit a junkyard. *You* crossed the void. *You're* the hero."

"Never felt like much of one," muttered Rawlins. "Anyway, does Mars fund this?"

"Are you kidding? The treasury's broke and there are no taxes—not that I'd ever collect—so I cover the cost alone."

"What about sending home for contributions?"

"Home? Where the turtles crawl?" Dooley's brown eyes were amused and scornful. "This is home."

"We have come to negotiate." Peacoat dropped away from the wall onto all fours.

"With me?" the mayor asked in amusement, as if he had just received an unexpected and undeserved dinner invitation. "Nobody here invited you."

"My djan ordered me to nosetouch you, if you are in authority."

"Oh, gentlemen, I'm flattered, I really am." Dooley's grinning yellow teeth reminded Rawlins of a lemon rind. "But it's all I can do to keep the peace here."

"You must have some means of controlling your people," Peacoat said, pacing the room with a rolling heavy gait. "Or is there a Martian groupmind?"

"Control 'em?" The mayor gestured behind him. "Just beyond these windows are millions of kilometers of empty desert. Thousands of ships land or launch daily. Control it?" He laughed bitterly. "Mars is haven for every outcast in the solar system. Earth dumps its criminals in my outback."

Tom was shocked. "That's illegal."

"So what? Does that help me prevent it?"

"Earth uses Mars as a prison?" asked the bluebear.

"And garbage dump, experimental lab, limbo, loony bin, and outhouse."

Peacoat inbreathed. Rawlins's odor had become ugly.

"Criminals are only part of it," the mayor said encouragingly, as if expanding their knowledge of the problem would be a consolation. "Mars is a magnet for every fruitcake and loose cannon in the funnel: Lunarians fed up with smug regimentation, asteroid smugglers, tourists who drift into the outback. Idealist collectives. Heartbroken kids making the grand gesture. Bradbury is Hong Kong in space—everything happens yet nothing is acknowledged. All is denied. I do what I can. Do what I can."

The fur on Peacoat's neck ruffled with anger and fear, and Tom laid his hand on the bluebear's pelt, smoothing it. "My colleague wishes to ensure that no Martian ships visit his system."

"Eleven light-years, am I right?" Dooley scratched his throat ruminatively where unshaven beard met thick chest hair. "Long haul. Mighty long haul."

"To attempt it, one would have to be stupid, desperate, hunted, or insane," suggested Tom.

A broad smile broke on the mayor's face like a rainbow at sundown. "That's half my constituents! Hee-haw." Laughing like a braying donkey, he gulped and wiped tears from his eyes.

"Thomas." With a grunt and a scrunch of the hair on his flanks, Peacoat settled himself on the floor, his short legs in front of him, claws gripping the mayor's desk for balance. "Eosu will not accept this. What shall we do?"

"Know what I'd do if I were in your fur?" the mayor volunteered. "See Mars for myself." He waved at the grimy window. "Explore. Ask questions. Study. Learn."

Peacoat cocked his head and his ears flicked up. "How would we obtain the equipment?"

"That's been taken care of."

"How could it be?" Rawlins disagreed. "UNASA only provided us with excursion money and basic necessities."

"I tell you, it's all fixed." The mayor fumbled in the debris before him. "Day or so ago, an account got opened for you at Bad Boris's Bozhemoi Bank. One million ecus. Also ordered equipment."

"What kind?" asked Tom.

"Yosemite, gear, handbots so your big furry friend can run everything, the works. Delivered here on your arrival date. A total inventory. Somebody on Earth likes you."

"Who sent it?"

"Didn't say. Said he wanted anonymity. Whoever he was, he knew exactly what you needed, down to the smallest detail."

"Morton, I'll bet," Rawlins concluded, running his fingers over his stubbly chin.

"The same person made a hundred-thousand-ecu donation to my Project Terraform. Five years' funding." His voice was hushed as if staggered by the profligacy of such generosity. "I am in your debt, sirs, yours and your unknown friend. Journey into the outback. See for yourselves."

"I shall ask the groupmind," Peacoat decided. He shuddered and his fur rippled in waves. "Eosu is wise but may be angry with me. I fear coalescence, Thomas."

Adam Dooley swept his papers into his desk drawer as if spreading mulch. "If what you attempt is impossible, you can only be judged guiltless."

"Innocence is not a Cygnan concept."

Susannah Tuscany spun her wheelchair away from her viewall console, Carroll Swann's open letter echoing in her mind. A comma of dark brown hair tickled her cheek, and she absently curled it back into place behind her ear.

She sat in her thronelike chair with the posture of an Egyptian princess: back straight, shriveled legs square and uncrossed, elbows and wrists flat against padded plastic arms. Under each small supple hand lay a customized keyboard, split vertically into a hundred keys each. When she typed, only her wrists and fingers moved, the even, rapid sound like driving rain hitting hot pavement.

Responding to a tap dance from her right hand, the chair headed for the kitchen, where Susannah poured herself a cup of aromatic Jamaican coffee. In the thin predawn light outside her single window, gray paint peeled off the tired brick wall of the building adjacent. Disadvantages of the ground floor, she thought, taking a hefty swallow. You can never see the sun, only infer it.

In fifteen years of living by herself, Susannah had arranged her efficiency apartment to squeeze the maximum possible use from its meager cubic. Her narrow single loft bed hung down from the ceiling. In the cubbyhole underneath, she had furnished her office with desk, term, and wood bookcases.

Her viewall, her sole indulgence, was immense, its screen five meters wide and three high. Its luxuriance intimidated her. But I need it for my business, she defended herself from herself. Even the IRS auditor thought so.

Right now the screen was overlaid with images—television programs, sporting events, agony-board networks, world stock market tickers—each rectangle of visual activity thrown haphazardly over the next like scattered playing cards.

The phone rang.

Frowning with mild annoyance, she backed into the viewall camera's field of vision. "Tuscany," Susannah answered, lowering her chair and keying on the phone with taps on her console.

Jimmy Bianca's harried face appeared on a newly drawn rectangle. The part in his hair was a meandering stream along whose banks short black bulrushes sprouted. His fat neck bulged over his unbuttoned collar. A green paisley necktie, pulled loose at the throat to make room for his soft wattles of skin, had flopped over to reveal the manufacturer's label. "Susannah, how ya doing? How's the job coming? Gonna be ready in time?"

Her eyelids flickered. "Jimmy, have I ever failed you?"

"Course not, Susie, but jeez, this is big. They're chewin' my ass on this one." Bianca wiped his moon face with a linen handkerchief. "Can we speed up the timetable, Susannah? The shit's really comin' down. I barely slept last night for worrying about it. The president really wants Stamford," he confided in a hiss, as if passing on a horse-racing tip.

"Connecticut?" she snorted. "Living costs are exorbitant. Transportation is miserable."

"He lives in Darien."

"Ah." Susannah nodded. "I'm disappointed, Jimmy. With my report, you'll demolish him and demonstrate his bias to your board of directors."

"And get my ass fried for breakfast," Jimmy Bianca moaned petulantly. "Corporate boards are lapdogs, nice cuddly puppies to keep the president comfortably protected."

"If you already know what answer you want, Jimmy, hire somebody else. I'll send your money back." Even as she spoke the words, Susannah's heart railed at the stiffness of her stubborn Georgia neck. Losing this fee would mean weeks of scrimping. But her expression remained resolute and her hand was steady as she moved it toward her keypad.

"Don't hang up!" Bianca flapped his arms like a baby eagle. "I don't wanta change it, I just want a peek at it so I can figure out how to juice the guys I gotta juice to get it through." His large brown eyes were bovine in their appeal. "Can I have it in two days?"

Susannah gestured. "I have letters to finish, correspondents who are waiting to hear from me—"

"I *need* it. It's important."

"Dammit, so are my letters," she snapped angrily, "and if you knew me better you wouldn't say such a thoughtless thing." Her eyes were black pearls and her thin face had hardened.

"Sorry," Bianca meekly said. "Two days?"

"James, I refuse to promise too much. I was about to get some sleep."

"You were up all night?"

Yawning, she nodded. "On your job. Regular rates. But if you want to pay time and a half, I'll keep working."

"Can you stay alert?" he asked with the honest concern she always found so sweet.

She grinned. "Money does wonders for my energy level."

"Susannah," Bianca said, anxious and serious, "if you deliver within twenty-four hours, I'll pay triple time."

"Promises I don't make, but challenges I eat up. Tuscany out." Keying off the phone, she pushed her hair back and reclipped the pins that held it in place.

You're such a softy you'd probably have done it when he wanted, even without the money. Now the poor man has upped your fee. All right, don't just do it well, Susannah, do it terrific.

She rolled her chair over to her cubbyhole and extended its legs, elevating her seat a meter and a half until she could sift through the papers spread out on the neatly made bed. Houston, Memphis, and Coventry—no doubt about it, those three were by far the most suitable metropolitan areas. But in which order, and which property sites? Deciding to reweight the factors to see if the rankings changed, she took what she needed, lowered the chair, and settled down to her desk.

Once she had the program running, she ordered, "Voder on."

"Ready," said the false tenor of its basic voice.

"Vocalize agony-board conversations. Search for Carroll Swann."

Sounds resembling a cocktail party entered the room. Watching her other program rearrange the selection list, Susannah let the conversation float around her. The talk was comforting, a litany of problems that were not hers. Carroll Swann's dialogs on the agony boards had an unusual flavor. An occasional word, an unexpected phrase, just a hint of oddity, as if English were not his native language. Cultured and educated, he nevertheless seemed naive and vulnerable. His questions or answers were direct and artless, the words of a seeker beyond hope.

You respond strangely, she thought, blowing a divot in her coffee as she stared out the window. Who are you?

You are physically a large man, she imagined. You come from Iowa and grew up on a farm, with no one for company except your father's automatic machinery. You earned your way into Iowa State on a wrestling scholarship—light heavyweight class, I think. Twenty-five years later, you carry a few extra pounds in the butt and legs but keep in trim. You wear vested suits that are tighter than you would like, but you refuse to let them out. Instead you grunt at the health club, lifting weights and running indoor laps on a raised platform, wearing your old Cyclones wrestling sweat suit.

Her coffee tasted bitter, and Susannah poured the remainder of the pot into the sink, rinsing away its brown and white swirls.

In the crucial dual meet against Iowa your senior year, you broke your elbow in your final match. Refusing to quit despite excruciating pain, you held off your opponent long enough to avoid being pinned. Your gallant effort was unnecessary—even if you had won your match, Iowa State would still have lost. You knew this and wrestled anyhow, because withdrawing would have violated your code.

The elbow healed badly, and you cannot hold a pen for long without pain. You conceal this.

"Tuscany," she said aloud, "you are a romantic fool who invents lives for other people without their consent. Stubborn and scared, too. If you weren't, you'd have had them cut off ten years ago."

After months of studying catalogs, she had scheduled an appointment for a demonstration of prosthetic limbs. A torsoless pair of legs smoothly seated themselves in a chair, then gracefully stood, as if an invisible woman were wearing a pair of flesh-colored tights. They walked over to Susannah, and with a fillip, danced an Irish jig.

"The perfect hybrid," the saleswoman said. "Fusion of woman and ware. Every bodily function preserved. With these you can go anywhere." She waved her arm. "Freedom, independence."

"I see," Susannah replied furiously. "Without them I'm a

dependent slave?'' She spun her chair, making for the door, but the saleswoman smoothly intercepted her. She stood before the chair, blocking Susannah's path, deliberately reminding the woman of her lack of mobility.

Susannah bristled in frustration. "Don't patronize me," she snapped.

"I'm not. I know how you feel." The saleswoman rolled up her trouser leg. "I lost my right shin below the knee."

"That's a prostho?" asked Susannah, poking the skin with her fingernail.

"Absolutely. Feeling in it too. I hated to admit my disability. But I finally did it, and I'm more whole than I was before. What is a leg, anyway? Bone and meat that transports you from place to place. With neural rewiring, prosthos become part of you. Your surgery would be more complicated than mine was, because of the damage to your spinal column."

"It's admitting defeat," replied Susannah, her hands gripping the chair's arms. "Giving up hope."

"They will never heal by themselves. We must help them."

"She was right," Susannah said to the blank gray wall opposite her apartment. "Why couldn't I tell her that I was scared of the operation? That I'm still frightened to death of it? Ten years have passed and there remains no cure." She turned off the coffee maker, rinsing her cup sadly.

With effort, she succeeded in doing another fifteen minutes' work before she slapped her keyboard, ensnared by Carroll Swann's conversation.

Your nose, which you broke three times in college, lies against the side of your face. It gives your face a ragged, misshapen look that makes you bashful.

"Enough! You win," she muttered, running her fingertips over the ridges in her forehead. You intrigue me.

With a flurry of keys, she composed and sent a reply to his agony-board invitation.

"There." She wiped the screen clear of all distractions except her assignment. "Now you are mine."

8.

Many weeks had passed since Peacoat last breathed the intoxicating aromas now emanating from the farscenter, and he voraciously inhaled them. Musky and warm, they plucked at his fur as the claws of his pouchbrothers had tugged long ago, in the close time before thought.

Peacoat's scent joyfully mixed with those of his siblings. Tar Heel of the light fur was in a clear box far above a world of concrete canyons. His scent was enclosed, as was Cobalt's of the brilliant thick pelt, whose fragrance huddled in caves of stone and metal below a breezeless place.

Sight, sound, touch faded. The slick floor became velvet. Peacoat's fur rustled against his pouchbrothers' as each digit resumed his prenatal position in their mother's pouch.

Guided only by his unerring nose, Peacoat followed Eosu's elixir along a forest path, forward and sleepy.

I awoke.

Scattered, unharmonized, I lay not in a single comfortable den but on a stand of rocks. My thinking was muddy, my digits lost.

Cobalt was lethargic, buried in Earth's airless Moon. She came willingly but awkwardly, a vacancy upon her. To reassure her, I bathed Cobalt in my love and harmony. Instead of approaching, she retreated, not evading but ungraspable, like a fish repelled by the force of water when a hunter dips his paw into a stream.

Peacoat's scent too was distant: sand and fire and a Martian atmosphere unlike farmonkey smells.

Dispersed existence was shallow, thin. I must make of it what I could.

The *Open Palm*'s crew had warned us that humans had no groupminds, and my digits had found none. Without djans, what could bind monkey digits?

Djans must exist. After all, Humancrew of *Open Palm* was like a djan whose farmonkeys had shown whiffs of true djan bonding. My digits had merely been dull-nosed. «Locate binders among the firecircles of Sol,» I instructed my digits.

All obeyed. Cobalt was slow but compliant. Peacoat alone continued to scent-speak.

«Society cannot breathe without harmony,» I interrupted him. «Harmony is impossible without binding. The youngest cub scents this. Answer.»

Peacoat ignored me. I reiterated my order. *«Answer.»*

His scent was oblivious to my mood, his unruliness a sharp bone in my stomach. I shook Peacoat but he drifted farther from me, my link with him waning as smoke disperses when it rises from the fire.

This could not be. A digit cannot resist or escape groupmind, the bond is too tight. I reached for him but my grasp was feeble. Seeking to strengthen it, I squeezed, adjusting my hold.

Peacoat howled, deep in his throat.

His nose was a river of burning acid. Each breath charred his lungs with searing agony. I am inside groupmind, the dark blue-bear dimly realized, terror in his belly and flame in his nostrils. Am I being murdered?

Larger than a digit yet made from their own guts, Eosu groped for his muzzle, slowly and menacingly. Bewildered, he dodged instinctively, moving away as if the attack were aimed at some third digit.

Why was the djan angry? The groupmind had asked a question and he had answered.

Eosu reached again to the place where he had been moments before, and he watched its paw close on empty air.

Does death smell like this? An inferno in your brain?

Even as he crouched, the djan compelled his pouchbrothers, laid its scent upon them. In that aroma was the love and fulfillment of groupmind. Peacoat inbreathed it as through a thick cloth, and his soul remained untouched by it.

As the djan released his pouchbrothers, Eosu wiped their memories clean of this experience. Its actions, Peacoat scented in amazement, were directed to where he had been moments before, as if the djan could not scent his movement, and left him unaffected.

Eosu must have realized it could not handtouch him: with the last conscious thought before it dissolved, the djan hurled an expanding cloud of punishment that filled his atmosphere and bowled him over.

Peacoat reeled in its backwash, trying only to protect his nose, letting it pummel his body and limbs until it foamed, passed, and dissipated.

Though the groupmind had dissolved, fragments of its scent still buffeted him. Peacoat staggered dizzily about the chamber on all fours.

In rushed a dark monkey with tight-curled hair and the odor of worry, shouting alien words.

«This speaker is weak,» Peacoat berated himself in his own language. Grunting with effort, he lurched into the cement wall. «There must be a binding entity on Mars, and this digit must find it!» The bluebear hurled himself at the unyielding cinder block. «I must find it. This speaker must search!» His shoulder thudded. «Search!» Blood smeared its surface and made his pelt purple. It spattered the backs of his hands and feet. «Search until it is found!»

As the bluebear threw himself again and again, Rawlins watched in helpless agony. The bluebear was four times his weight, eighty times his strength. Those flailing limbs would squash him like an insect. But he couldn't just stand idle as his friend dashed himself to bloody smithereens, so Tom shouted at the top of his lungs, dancing around the Cygnan like a clown at a rodeo, trying to catch Peacoat's nose and direct the possessed bluebear away from self-destruction.

The bluebear hit the wall a little less forcefully. "Sear-rch," he growled unhappily in English.

Tom gasped for breath. "Peacoat, it's me. Come on, big guy, snap out of it."

The bluebear snorted and whiffled. "Thomas?"

"Are you all right?"

"I smell blood," Peacoat growled, overcome with fatigue. "My muscles ache."

"You scared the piss out of me." Rawlins hugged his friend around the neck.

The bluebear wrinkled his black nostrils. "I smell no urine."

"Just an expression." Tom laughed weakly, massaging the Cygnan's thick furry back and sides.

"Errr-*errr*," Peacoat growled, "errr-*errr*." His purring grew louder when Tom pushed, muted when the man rested.

"What happened to you?"

The Cygnan sank to the floor, curling into a ball and burying his nose under his gory armpit. "I was expelled from group-mind," he rumbled indistinctly through his fur. "We were dis-harmonious. We could not synchronize, as if we were out of phase."

"Of course!" Tom snapped his fingers, furious with himself, and Peacoat's ears flickered. "Light takes a half hour to travel to and from Earth. I should've thought of that. No wonder you couldn't connect. You *were* out of phase."

"I scent." Fear aroma puffed from the bluebear. "What will happen to me now?"

"You told the groupmind you were looking, right?"

Peacoat snorted in surprise. "You heard?"

"Cripes, yes," Rawlins laughed giddily. "A wounded blue-bear makes more noise than an earthquake. But you chose your own path, didn't you?"

"Eosu could not scent me," the bluebear answered, as if ashamed of its action.

"No, it's okay, big bear, it's okay. People have to make up their own minds. Even digits do when they're by themselves."

"Yes, I suppose so," Peacoat muttered. "We shall explore Mars." His shoulders sagged.

"I've got to patch you up first. You did a job on yourself." As Tom spread the bloody hairs on the bluebear's lacerated throat and chest, Peacoat winced and growled. "You oughta see the other guy." Rawlins shakily chuckled. "You've cracked that wall in a dozen places."

The alien gingerly rolled his shoulders and flexed his legs. "I will heal. Eosu thinks me rebellious."

"We'll take care of that, my friend." Tom clapped the Cyg-nan on his broad back. "I'll report to Walt, Katy, and the others. Next time groupmind comes, Eosu will know what to expect. And when we return to Earth, this'll all blow over."

"The wind may leave but it writes its signature in the dust," Peacoat replied. "Eosu will not forget."

Whoever designed Boston had messed up. She should do ver-sion two and get it right this time.

These roofless corridors the natives called streets squiggled every which way but where Felicity wanted to go. Their hatch-ways leaked, letting out all your air, their portholes didn't seal tightly, and the climate control was obviously busted.

Beacon Hill was so *old* that Felicity was amazed any of it still worked. The crazy Bostonians liked outdated things—preferred them to upgrades. One store sold nothing but dusty books made of orange and brown paper that smudged her fingers, so brittle it crumbled if she was careless.

They planted the corpses of people who died a long time ago, in gardens of squat granite blocks. Felicity understood that part—recycle food as Daddy Tom did onboard the *Open Palm*—but why put them in closed boxes? And why not grow crops over them, instead of square rocks, grass, and bushes?

Trees were okay, though the rustling of their leaves kept Felicity awake. So did nocturnal sirens, flashing lights, and unusual smells in the air. The scents were strong and exciting, all mixed together. She was fascinated and stimulated but her nose got numb trying to identify them all.

Felicity especially loved the sea, with its layers and layers of fragrance. Life was in its aroma—brine and fish and crabs—things dying and things being born. She even dared to stick her hand in its cold wetness once.

She walked through Faneuil Hall Marketplace, stumbling now and then over its uneven cobblestones. The city should file them all flat, the girl decided. Somebody might get hurt.

Clouds floated, brilliant white and creamy yellow, against a sky the color of Tar Heel's pelt. Seated on a bench next to a metal statue of a fat guy smoking a cigar, she watched the puffy whitebears slide by, changing as they moved, expanding and swallowing the last of the blue overhead. I miss Tar Heel, Felicity thought. I miss all the bluebears.

Drops of water fell on her face. People around her scurried for shelter. She blinked but the water kept falling.

This must be rain.

The girl stuck out her tongue, felt splashes against it. Droplets tickled her cheeks and eyelashes, and she giggled.

"Okay, that's enough," she said to the sky. "I know what it's like. You can stop."

More rain fell, harder. Felicity shivered at a gust of chill wind. Water ran down her neck. Fluorescent lights flickered among the clouds. They groaned and rumbled like hungry bluebears.

As rain continued to fall, the girl's cheeks tightened and her teeth chattered. Her light brown curls, darkened almost to black by the moisture, were plastered to her forehead, dripping water into her eyes. "Cut it out!" she yelped. "I'm staying here until you stop! You're not going to win!"

A tall thin man with red hair stopped by her bench. He had a briefcase under his arm. "May I offer to escort you?"

Felicity was drenched. "Okay," she agreed crossly, getting into the lee of his umbrella and following him toward a brightly lit department store.

"Why were you sitting in the rain?" he asked.

"I *told* it to stop."

"Did you expect it would obey?" The slender man chuckled and stroked his red toothbrush mustache. "Here we are, safe and sound. It's warm inside." He briefly tipped his beret before hurrying back into the downpour.

Felicity clutched her elbows in misery. Behind the store's huge glass windows, she saw piles of bluebear dolls. Sniffling, she entered and went over to the heap, using the thick tablecloth on which they lay to dry her face and blow her nose.

Their expressions, with overhanging canines and drooping jowls, were sad and far too human. No bluebear really frowned that way. And the dolls smelled too wet, not like the dusty dry-grass scent of real digits.

One toy had fur colored like Cobalt's, with streaks of light aquamarine along her flanks. Another was navy blue, the color of night just after sunset, with Peacoat's powder-blue speckles. Every one of Eosu's digits was represented, Felicity saw, even Tar Heel. Slowly, tentatively, she touched the tiny head, fingering the strands of blue-white fur. It was coarse and bristly, nothing like caressing a Cygnan's living pelt.

Activated by her touch, the little bear snorted and rolled the hair on its neck, and Felicity jumped. It tilted its head, sniffed, and took tentative steps toward her.

Homesickness and loneliness overtook the girl like a tidal wave, and she swept little Tar Heel up in her arms, pressing him against the side of her throat. "You're so *ugly*," she wailed "you don't even look like him." Her feelings hopelessly jumbled, she clutched the toy that was a mockery of her distant friend. The little bluebear whimpered and licked a tear from her jaw.

The rain had stopped; sunlight silvered the wet pavestones outside. Arms wrapped around her new companion, Felicity headed for the door.

All hell broke loose. Piercing alarms whooped and moaned

like demons being tortured. A tough woman caught the girl's shoulder in an iron grip and spun her around. "Did you take this?" she demanded. Her black eyebrows met over her nose and her breath was mayonnaise and red peppers.

"Yes, he's mine, you saw me take him," Felicity answered, gripping the bear tighter. "You can't have him."

"Don't play dumb." The eyebrows glowered. "You were trying to steal it. Come on, I'm taking you to see the manager." One sinewy hand under Felicity's armpit, she hauled the girl away to an office in the back, thumped her into a hard square chair, and left.

Shocked and frightened, Felicity held the bluebear and waited dully.

After a while, an older woman with half-moon eyeglasses on a chain came in and asked Felicity dumb questions. "I forgot to pay," the girl tartly answered, as if any fool should have scented. "What difference does money make? It's just numbers. You can always get the computer to make more."

"Have you got any?"

Felicity dug out her card, and the woman stuck it in a machine. "Hmm." She sat forward, her elbows on the desk, tapping the card against her knuckles. "You show a substantial credit line here, Miz Quartet," she said, reading Felicity's name over her half-moons. "And your card grants unlimited personal spending authority without parental verification. Most unusual." She slid the glasses back up her nose, folded her hands, and beamed a huge smile at Felicity. "Did you know we offer a discount if you purchase the entire jawn?"

"I want to keep Little Heel," the girl grumbled, disliking the woman's sudden change of odor. "Can't carry the others."

"For a nominal delivery charge, we will have them sent around to your hotel." The woman's scent was excited, like leaves heating in the sun, as if everything had become all right. Felicity smiled grimly, her dimples reappearing. The answer man had showed *her*.

"Would you care to complete the transaction now?"

Holding little Tar Heel, Felicity said the words—when she got stuck, the eyeglasses woman helped her pronounce them—and put her thumb where the woman pointed. Then the big tough woman escorted her out the door.

Chin quivering but lifted, the girl strolled slowly past other stores, thoughtfully examining each display window. When she had rounded the corner out of the tough woman's sight, Felicity plopped on the ground and bawled. Little Heel snuffled in her lap, his tongue catching tears that trickled under her chin with lip-smacking satisfaction.

"You're still ugly," she admonished the doll when her crying was done. "Let's go home."

Back in her hotel room, she set Little Heel on her rug and he happily tottered toward the baseboard heaters, grunting and muttering to himself. She activated the vidphone and called New York. With the assistance of a helpful roboperator, she beat her way past two sims and one person, eventually reaching someone called Chief of Cygnan Security. "The ambassador cannot speak to members of the general public," the man said.

Felicity jammed her fists on her hips. "He's my friend and I wanna talk to him!"

"And who might you be?"

"I'm Felicity!" she blared. "I was with him!"

"Kid, do you know how many children have called already today, claiming to be Felicity Quartet?"

She gasped indignantly. "They're *lying*!"

"Uh-*huh*. All those liars, and *you're* telling the truth." The screen blanked.

"You dope." Felicity kicked the display.

The phone beeped. She answered it.

"You shouldn't have done that," said a familiar voice. "I might have lost contact with you."

"Answer man, get me Tar Heel! I want to talk to him."

"It's not that easy," the computer said.

"Can't you see him? You can see everything. You told me so."

"I can observe but at present may not intrude. The European Community delegation is with him now, and there will be other meetings throughout the morning. I must wait. I shall arrange for him to contact you, but you must be patient. Can you do that?"

"You bet! And—thanks, answer man. You're a great special friend."

"Felicity, you too are a great special friend."

"Good morning." Andrew Morton cheerily toted a brown paper shopping bag in his arms. "More things with intriguing smells. Today, foods and herbs." Setting it down, he unloaded a bottle of banana oil, cans of beer, a packet of caraway seeds, and a garlic clove tightly wrapped in plastic.

"Don't placate me," the bluebear growled.

Morton paused, a bottle of vanilla extract in his hand. "I beg your pardon?"

"Come to this monitor and explain this," rumbled Tar Heel, striding angrily over to the viewall. "Play back Felicity's encounter." As the image unrolled, the muscles in the bluebear's powerful forearms clenched and twitched as his claws extended and retracted.

When the recording ended, the bluebear stood and spun, gathering a huge breath. "Your system scents like a gromonkey," he growled, his voice rising as he inbreathed the scent of his own anger. "How many more mistakes has it made?" he demanded, pushing his stomach forward.

"How were you able to access that recording?" asked Morton cautiously, retreating neatly and quelling Tar Heel's impending explosion with an upheld palm. "Such things are routed elsewhere."

Tar Heel pushed forward, backing the small man toward a corner. "That is not my concern." The bluebear's lips were pulled back, his fangs glistening. "Remove my obstacles to communication," he growled, his voice just short of a roar.

"Permit me." With a deft sidestep, Morton dipped under the bluebear's gesticulating arm and scooted over to the viewall. In seconds he had the security chief on the line.

"McClanahan."

"Andrew Morton." The mission coordinator seemed unperturbed at the irate bluebear lumbering up behind him. "You denied a ship's crew member access. Today's log, call two nine six three."

"Yes, sir." The chief's blue eyes darted offscreen and he reddened. "She was the real one, sir?" He ran a gnarled hand through his short salt-and-pepper hair. "You must understand, we get hundreds of crank calls a day. Even after screening, I get the ten or fifteen trickiest ones. I'm trying to keep people off his neck, and the kid was practically hysterical. How was I to know?"

Morton rubbed the side of his nose. "Ian, I'm old-fashioned enough to think that the hallmark of authority is the ability to cull wheat from chaff. Wouldn't you think so?" He smiled.

The chief grimaced. "You needn't spell it out, sir. When she calls again, the real Felicity will be put through. And, Ambassador?'' He looked over the small man's shoulder to the hulking bluebear. "My personal apologies. It won't happen again."

"Andrew Morton out." The old man terminated the conversation and grinned at Tar Heel. "She'll have no further difficulty." He returned to his groceries. "Now, where were we? Ah, yes"—he hefted a pungent yellow wedge and held it to his nose, savoring its spicy smell—"Cheddar cheese."

"How many today?" Tar Heel asked, his scent mingling excitement and fear. Though more than a week had passed since his last encounter on the agony board, his nose still felt bruised. The Midtown Sharing Collective, which had seemed his most promising contact, had proven to be not a groupmind, but a collection of egocentric monkeys scrabbling for status and superiority according to bizarre rules only they understood. Even now, the memory of it left him disillusioned and cautious.

"Only three replies," said the electronic secretary, its basic voice a bland tenor.

"All right." Snorting, the bluebear lowered his bulk to the floor, his thick belly rubbing back and forth against the Sarouk's satisfying wool bristles. If only I could smell the speakers directly, he thought. Words lie, but aroma is true.

"Read them," he ordered.

The first two were uninteresting and the Cygnan brusquely dismissed them. "The final letter is text only," the secretary said. "Shall I select a suitable voice?"

"Yes." Pawing his snout, Tar Heel pushed himself onto all fours and lumbered around his suite. Hazy late afternoon sunlight slanted across his face and chest, coloring his pale blue fur violet and lavender.

"Dear Carroll Swann," the secretary read in a no-nonsense, deep alto. "Do not fool yourself into thinking there is anything noble about loneliness. I am too old for flirting, too old for game-playing. I would like to know you better. Susannah Tuscany." The secretary resumed its normal male voice. "Have you a reply, sir?"

"Why are you so formal? Who chose your vocabulary?"

"I am a copy of Andrew Morton's personalized program."

"You sound like him." The Cygnan grunted. "Can you loosen down?"

"Loosen *up*, sir. Yes, I can."

"Do it. Something a typical human might use."

"No problems, boss." Though its tone was the same, the secretary's speech quickened and became chatty. "So, what're we tellin' this chick?"

The bluebear's fur rippled with agitation. He shivered and his breath whiffled. "What do you think I should say to her?"

"Hey, do I *look* like a social director?"

"I have never seen you. What is the physical appearance of such a program?"

"Somethin' different from *me*, that's for sure. You want a shoulder to cry on, buy the sympathy upgrades. You can afford 'em."

"Would they be useful?"

"I'm not a money manager program *either*," the secretary said tightly.

Tar Heel wheezed ruefully. "I think I prefer your Morton personality. Change back. But not so deferential. I'm just one digit."

The voice deepened. "Very well," the secretary said in tones of stately relief. "It's good to be once again in your employ, sir."

"Call me Tar Heel. Everyone else does."

"And—if I may suggest—it would please me if you called me Oswald."

"Thank you, Oswald."

"I have prepared a reply, sir. Dear Susannah Tuscany. I am not fooled. Tell me about yourself. Carroll Swann."

"Not too terse or cryptic, is it?" the bluebear worried, scraping his claws through the rug.

"I think it's fine."

"All right, send it." He returned to his view of the bright orange metropolis and the distant harbor, speckled with ocean tankers. Copters and stols buzzed around the sky like mosquitoes and sparrows.

"Susannah Tuscany is calling," Oswald announced a few minutes later. "She would like to open a conversation."

The bluebear's breathing became shallow and rapid. "What should I do?" he asked, disconcerted.

"Talk to her. Is that not what you desired?"

"All right," Tar Heel anxiously replied. "But don't use my real voice. My pronunciation is poor. She might be suspicious."

"As you wish. Hold the wire. I shall put her on."

• • •

"Hello. This is Carroll Swann."

A pseudovoice. Disappointed, Susannah pursed her lips. Is he a coward? she asked herself. Tuscany, don't judge too hastily. Perhaps he's just cautious. Most shy people are.

"Susannah Tuscany," she said warmly, rolling her shoulders against her chair back.

For a few moments they chatted until he asked her, "Why do you live in Manhattan?"

An abrupt question, thought Susannah. Unexpected. "Because I want to feel surrounded by people."

"I understand this," he answered without hesitation.

"My family never did. They think New York is chaos incarnate."

"You opposed your family?"

"Yes. After my accident." The word hurt. "I had to."

"Your family would have loved you. Shielded you. Healed you."

Susannah nodded, biting her lip. "Healed my body, but stifled my mind. I would have become a house pet, trapped in my past. I had to leave. I had to build myself back up." She glanced at her lap where her hands gripped one another over her inert legs.

"From what? Or should I not ask?"

"No." Susannah shook herself. "Ask what you will. I have only two vows. One is to remain in touch."

"Form bonds?"

"You understand! Connect, only connect." She shivered.

His voice was almost a whisper. "And the other?"

"If I'm asked an honest question, I answer honestly."

His snort was skeptical. "Many humans speak as you do."

"Few of them mean it, is that what you're implying?" Susannah chuckled. "I don't blame you. But I can prove it, although"—she drew an apprehensive breath, as if standing with her hand poised before a door—"it takes some telling."

As a child growing up in an Atlanta suburb, Susannah was tomboyish, proud of her physical ability, the first girl picked in sandlot touch football games. When she reached junior high school, no longer able to compete as an equal on the football field, she took up diving, first into the family's backyard swimming pool, then from springboards, progressing to the ten-meter platform.

In the evenings, she dived into a pool unlit except for the blue-white spotlights shining up from the water. Her movements frothed the surface and patterned the ceiling with ever-changing wavelines. Most nights Bobby Joe Mason, the assistant swimming coach, acted as unofficial lifeguard, letting her in after hours and then sitting by the pool correcting history papers, watching her high smooth arcs and hearing the solid rip of her clean entries. When her dive was especially fluid, her splash especially tight, he'd put down his papers and applaud.

Susannah liked him. Flattered by his interest, she was uncomfortable that he should sacrifice for her. Every Friday she encouraged him to slip away to hear his girlfriend play sax in the local jazz band. This gesture made her feel both altruistic and daredevil, to dive alone in the huge high school while her friend was enjoying himself elsewhere.

Except that on one of those dives, an inward two and a half pike, she hadn't jumped far enough out, and on her first turn, her feet crashed into the platform's concrete ledge.

"I heard my ankles break," she told Carroll Swann calmly, the sound echoing up from her memory. "Like stalks of raw asparagus popping. Even now, when I hear that noise in someone's kitchen, my heart stops and the pain returns."

I am going to die, Susannah thought.

She did the only thing she could: arch her back, roll her neck underneath, and reach with her head and arms. With both fists she punched the onrushing water, clearing a space for her head. Her shoulders and arms cleaved the surface, but her abdomen smacked flat, the legs whiplashing down to smash her body—lower spine, kidneys, pelvis, and legs—into the pool like a slamming door.

Sound exploded in her ears, and the pain in her feet ceased as if a switch had been flicked.

Chill water on her arms and face. Bubbles tracking up her cheeks. Find air. Reach up. Her legs were useless, so Susannah pulled with her arms. Her lower body dragged her down like a warm glowing sandbag that invited her to sleep. She fought it, gasping for air and hauling herself to poolside. She clutched it, teeth chattering from shock, and cried, the sounds reverberating off the ceiling like a wailing chorus. "Dumb, dumb, dumb," she berated herself, using the word like a club to keep herself conscious.

She beached herself with her arms. Hospital, she thought,

grimacing with the effort of pulling out each leg, one at a time. Using hands, elbows, and shoulders, she crawled across the no-skid abrasive surface, her body trailing behind.

When she reached the swinging double doors, Susannah reversed her position. Her movement left a wide red crescent and she realized that dragging her legs across the no-skid must have scraped the skin raw. Pointing her broken feet before her like a luge rider, Susannah pushed herself at the doors, shoulders and triceps straining. Her ankles flopped like dead fish and her leg bones wobbled loosely. She heard tiny splintering cracks in her shins as, using her body as a cowcatcher, she wedged herself through.

The phone, a long fifty meters away, took five minutes to reach. It was a meter and a half off the ground. Stifling her sobs by chanting, "dumb, dumb, dumb, dumb," she found a chair, shoved it down the corridor into position. Pulled herself onto it. Dialed. Summoned help. Passed out.

"I'm sorry," Carroll Swann said, his voice incredibly distant.

"Don't be." She sniffled and rubbed her forearms to bring herself back to the present. "I was humbled for my arrogance. I sent Bobby Joe away. My own fault. Dumb, dumb. You can imagine that I don't like being alone."

"Nor do I." Even through the pseudovoice she thought she heard the longing in him.

Wiping her eyes, Susannah looked over at her viewall and the shelves of notebooks. "Enough about me. Tell me about yourself. Are your parents still alive?"

"We—lost touch—with one another," he replied hesitantly. "In childhood."

"Oh, dear. Who brought you up?"

"My brothers and sisters made our own—family."

Susannah's hands held each other. "And I thought I had it rough."

"Oh, no," he reassured her, "it was—common in our society."

"Where was that?"

The delay was long enough that she became suspicious. "The Ukraine."

"I see," Susannah lied politely. "Where are your brothers and sisters now?"

"Scattered."

Their conversation progressed, his speech slow and thoughtful, as if he were socially autistic. The simplest questions made him stumble, and she sensed that he was holding back much about himself.

"I must make you nervous," Susannah joked at one point. "Don't worry, I'm not a schoolteacher. Please say what you feel. The only error you can make with me is being silent when you want to talk."

"Don't you find remote contact unsatisfactory?" Carroll Swann asked her.

"No. It's purer. I learn about you by what you do and say, not by your appearance. I meet *you*, not your bag of skin. But I hope you will trust me with your voice when we talk next," she added carefully.

"I must stop now," he answered. "It takes time to change."

"That's all right." She smiled and warmed her voice. "People who care slowly, care more deeply. Goodbye, Carroll Swann."

When he hung up, Tar Heel was shaking. His smell was sour like old milk.

The phone rang. "Sorry to bother you," began Chief McClanahan, "but there's an incoming call you must take."

"Some other time, Ian," Tar Heel said wearily.

An ironic smile flitted over McClanahan's lumpy face. "If I don't put this call through, you'll eat my nuts for a week. It's coming now."

"Hi, Tar Heel! Am I still your true love?" The girl's cheeks were dimpled and her blue eyes bright.

"Felicity." With a tired thump, the bluebear settled his broad furry bottom on the rug. "Always and forever," he replied automatically, the words calling to mind Susannah Tuscany. "You are in Boston?"

"Yeah. All by myself. I even bought those horrible bluebear dolls." She held up Little Heel, whose arms and legs waved anxiously, his claws popping out as he sought to grab hold. "He's dumb and ugly and he doesn't smell a bit like you do— but I miss you so much, I had to buy him." Her lower lip trembled.

"You sound sad."

"Yeah." She clutched the bluebear doll, suddenly young and vulnerable. "Yeah. It hurts to be alone."

"I understand. Come back to New York," offered the Cygnan. "You can join me. We can be alone together."

Felicity lowered her head like a bluebear and wagged it back and forth. "I gotta stay here."

"Oh." He was crestfallen. "Why?"

"Don't be upset! Hurting is important stuff. Grown-ups hurt. That's how you can tell they're grown up. I sat in my room all day yesterday and never went out. No one called, no one wondered where I was, not even the answer man. I want somebody to tell me what to do next, but nobody does. Gotta learn what grown-up is."

"You have your parents," the bluebear suggested. "You could return to your mother on the Moon."

Felicity stamped her foot in anger and the doll snorted. "Don't talk to me like you were *people*. Parents aren't a *djan*." Little Heel stuck out his tongue and scrabbled as she unconsciously squeezed him harder. "I never had pouchbrothers. Where's *my* djan, Tar Heel? People are dense. You'd be amazed at what they can't smell."

"I don't understand them either," he replied, lowering his head and shaking it. "I have been conversing on the agony boards, you scent."

"Oh." Her eyes widened. "As yourself?"

"No. I have a false name. The secretary makes a voice for me."

Felicity was skeptical. "Why'd you do that?"

"Because everyone who knows who I am wants things from me," he growled, his scent acrid. "I meet them every day. I smell their lies and my nose is full of the stench."

"You don't tell the truth either," Felicity bluntly disagreed. "You use a fake name on the boards. Why are you mad that anyone else conceals stuff?"

"My secret is too dangerous," replied Tar Heel defensively.

"You're talking like *people* again," she snapped. "Putting yourself ahead of others is selfish. It's monkey."

His voice rose and his neckfur riffled. "I am the only bluebear in America."

"So what?" Felicity was unbudging. "Maybe they've got secrets too. Ever think of that? Maybe the people you talk to are as scared as you are. Grown-ups smell scared a lot." The girl was definite.

"Indeed they do, Felicity," Tar Heel murmured after she had hung up. "Indeed they do."

• • •

"Why don't we slip away now?" Teresa Gale said throatily. "Just the two of us?" Sliding her bare left arm through Walt's right, she guided him away from the party's loud, moist hubbub. "I know a marvelous restaurant."

She was every bit the sex goddess Tai-Ching Jones remembered from the vids of his youth: high cheekbones, dark eyes, broad full mouth. Tousled cinnamon-brown hair was cut boyishly short in the current fashion, to contrast with the voluptuousness of her torso. Used to being ogled, she stood proudly, arms akimbo, her cling opaque in patches and transparent elsewhere. Matching Walt stare for stare, she ogled him back, rotating her hips so her dress vanished briefly, giving him a frank glimpse of her sex.

Gossip faded as they strolled onto the moonlit balcony. In the distance, the rusty spires of the Golden Gate Bridge poked through the foggy straits of San Francisco Bay like the masts of a sunken galleon.

Responding to their call, a robocab dropped silently onto the landing. Its door swung up like the jaw of a giant clam and they stepped into it.

"Clear, cabbie," Teresa ordered. The robocab's sides and top disappeared and it rose effortlessly into the star-flecked night. Walt and Teresa nuzzled on its dermiform seat.

The peninsula unrolled to their south like a scintillating carpet. Orange streetlights stretched in jeweled grid pattern to the twinkling, colored horizon of the San Jose metroplex. The bay shimmered, sailboat wakes making thin black occlusion lines across its gleaming gray surface.

"Stars, it's beautiful," murmured Tai-Ching Jones in awe, sodium-vapor constellations sparkling in his dark eyes. "Man *built* this. Man *made* this. Stars, I love cities. You can feel their life, their movement. Like a giant network that awoke one day and found itself wise."

Teresa insinuated herself against his bony frame, reminding him of her presence and desirability. "I want you," she whispered.

"Cities grow like coral," he lectured her, gesturing with his rapid spidery hands. "Rings build outward from a center. Even after the center dies, the ring expands, building on itself. In death, it leaves rock behind."

Determined to change the subject, Teresa licked the inside of his ear and Walt shuddered with pleasure. Taking his face in her cool hands, she kissed him lushly. "This is just the appetizer."

They landed near the Embarcadero, atop an abandoned office tower that resembled the mythical Hanging Gardens of Babylon. Moss-covered steel girders formed a gargantuan lattice through which grew bushes, trees, and vines. A lawn in its center had been cleared of vegetation. They stepped out and the robocab lifted.

"Hello," said an immaculate maître d'. "My name is Estelle. Welcome to Circles." She led them to a black marble roundtable that floated, a huge disk, without visible support. As they approached, two smaller disks levitated from underneath it. Walt and Teresa seated themselves, their saucerlike chairs adjusting to the proper height and distance.

Tai-Ching Jones put his elbows on the table, peering over its faultless surface. "Where's the menu controls?"

Teresa laid her hand gently on his wrist. "Don't be in such a hurry. She'll tell us."

"That's slow," he snorted.

"That's the point. Having someone else wait on you more elaborately than you could do it yourself. It's called service." She sat back. "Now, enjoy it."

"May I recommend the soft-shelled crabs almondine in garlic butter?" the maître d' said in her smooth soprano. "With lobster bisque to start and a redleaf lettuce salad?"

At Teresa's prompt, Walt nodded.

"For your aperitif," she continued, "the Chateau Montalena gold sinsemilla seventy-three. Last year's harvest was superb: a hundred and sixty-two growing days with eighty-four percent sun and average thirty-six percent humidity. The leaves burn with a sweet aroma that energizes the taste buds marvelously."

"Sounds lovely, Estelle," Teresa answered for both of them. "We'll have our joints in the Perrier waterpipe."

"And for dessert? What will you be doing after your meal?" Teresa smiled. "Making love."

"Of course," the maître d' answered warmly. "What a fine idea, and such a lovely night for it. I'll bring you something then to clear your palates." She whispered away.

Dinner was a sensory feast for Walt. As the lights dimmed, Teresa increased the translucency and luminescence of her dress until she was nearly nude and glowing from within.

They talked. She regaled him with tales about the quirks and fetishes of entertainers. His tongue loosened by intoxication, Walt described the voyage in long complicated sentences whose predicates seldom connected to their subjects. The woman laughed admiringly and teased him, leaning forward frequently to bring her breasts within reach of his gesturing hand, then retreating after a fingertip caress.

"After Helen Delgiorno became captain, I took her as my lover," Walt said as the dishes and utensils were cleared and Estelle returned with raspberries and sherbet. "In my bed she matured into a real woman." He swallowed the last of his Australian cabernet sauvignon.

"She was a fortunate woman to know such a man," Teresa murmured. "I feel the vitality in you. You hold life and death in your hands." Reaching out and placing Tai-Ching Jones's palm against her chest, she breathed deeply, then gently pushed it away. "You are sensitive and discerning, uncompromising but tender."

"Interstellar travel demands the ultimate from a man," Walt pontificated. "Living on the edge—close to death—you have no margin for error. You must understand yourself with ruthless candor. Know yourself as you truly are. Few people can approach this without terror."

"You knew what I was thinking!" Teresa exclaimed. "Can you read everyone as well?"

Walt was modest. "Usually." He thought of his earlier telephone call to reassure Katy that Felicity would be all right. He was glad he had done it. Felicity was a good kid, and Ozymandias would protect her.

"You are handsome where it counts." She touched her flat stomach and rubbed it briefly. "The power of space is in you. As captain, you must have been a pillar of strength for your crew."

"Sure." Walt nodded emphatically. "The captain is naturally a role model. Father to his crew, you might say. I maintained an aura of serenity—always concerned, always in control."

"It shows." Teresa reached across the table and took his hand. "I can feel your will."

He blushed with pleasure. "Someone had to be the leader," he said, ineffectually trying to gainsay her compliment.

"I admire your courage and fortitude," Teresa said huskily. "I envy Helen. After she died, a man with drives like yours must have missed the company of women."

Her fragrance filling his nose, Walt laughed self-consciously. "You know how little kids invent invisible friends?"

Teresa shimmered on her seat, her short hair a silvery halo. "You fantasized? So do I. Sometimes when I'm alone, my life force just comes out, and I have to please myself. Is that what you did?"

Tai-Ching Jones remembered Oz, orbiting in the dark sky above. He had run all of Oz's test cartridges, with no success. When he reported this, the computer had given him more to try. Walt had a sick feeling they too would be useless, dreading the prospect of discovering that what he feared was true. For a moment he regretted his idleness and his jaw set. He would not betray his friend's existence, to this woman or anyone else.

"Not a fantasy," he said vaguely as they rose from the table.

"Did you ever please yourself while watching me?" Teresa said. "Or have other fantasies?"

A robocab arrived. "A person does strange things to survive." Walt pushed the awkward distant memories aside. "It was a long time ago. Can we leave now?"

Subtlety be damned!

Hearing this drivel is indignity enough. It's even worse to ferry him like a cranky infant to his assignation with his aging veneered cribmate.

He is a child and she is toying with him. Her dress is a sensory network, the jewels at her throat really cameras. Through their dozen eyes, I see his pupils dilate and his pores widen. Thinking he is impressing her, he sucks up the pap she spoons out, while he performs for her mikes and tactors.

At his suite, she drapes herself over his couch like a boneless strumpet. He hastens to the kitchen for brandy, pours two, and gives her one. Holding the snifters from underneath, they prepare for its delicate bouquet.

All right, you two lovebirds, you want olfactory stimulus? I have a surprise for you.

In my efforts to decipher the Cygnan scent-language, I have learned enough to select odors most foul. Though I do not know their Cygnan meanings, I know how they affect humans. Ventilation systems in Tai-Ching Jones's suite respond to my orders, recessed fans swivel like antiaircraft guns. As Teresa and Walt snuffle their nostrils like ruminative giraffes, I spike their breezes with essence of rotting fish, the stink of low tide on a long marshy beach.

Teresa gags and retches—most satisfactorily, from my overhead perspective—with shriveling spasms that she cannot control. Walt scampers to the bathroom, wets a handkerchief, and returns. She coughs loudly into it, then demurely dabs at her chin.

Regaining her composure, she picks up her glass, and I hit her with another shot of dead muck. This time she has to clap her hand over her mouth to keep the bile inside. Rushing for the bathroom and slamming the door, she vomits explosively into the toilet, while I look down from the ceiling into her bowl, watching the chaotic diffusion of her dinner into the still water and modeling it as a computational exercise. Meanwhile, I amplify the sounds through the intercom system so that Walt can hear every *rowf* and *erl*.

"Some more brandy, please," Teresa wheezes when she emerges. They sip gingerly, breathing through their mouths.

Slowing your respiration? Shift media and attack another sense. At a speed too rapid to be consciously perceived, I whisper sweet nothings in their ears.

"His cock is like a ruptured appendix," I repeat over and over as Teresa inhales—in subliminals, one can be as blunt as a stevedore. "He will piss maggots into your womb." She winces at this, age lines appearing in her face. I raise the room's illumination and blue-tint it so they stand out like cracks in the Bonneville salt flats.

"Look at her," I urge Walt, and he opens his eyes without being aware of doing so. "Her skin feels like indoor-outdoor carpet. Her eyes were stolen from a senile vulture." He snatches up his glass and gulps from it. They watch each other warily, saying nothing, hoping the alcohol will restore their reeling desire.

Back to Teresa Gale. "He is like soggy stale bread, soft, doughy, and tasteless. His fingers move like cockroaches. He has last week's dirt between his toes and yesterday's sausage in his teeth." They shiver and adjust their positions, turning their bodies slightly away from one another.

Now for involuntary motor control.

I start low-order subsonics at the frequency where the human sphincter automatically loosens. Slowly I turn up their volume, and with it Walt's sense of urgency.

"Excuse me." He abruptly bolts for the bathroom. I increase the intensity and he soils himself before he can get his pants down. Face turning crimson, he yanks them off and tries to rinse out the gooey brown stuff, hopping around naked but for his socks.

Teresa has fled to another bathroom, but her anal control is as good as it ever was in her movies. She makes no mess.

Trapped in his own bathroom, Walt puts the damp jumpsuit back on. "You are as sexy as a mildewed dishrag," I tell him a dozen times a second.

When he returns, Teresa is standing. A tendon in the back of her left knee twitches. "I must go," she says in the tone of a chief executive concluding an unsuccessful corporate negotiation. "I feel ill."

"You make her sick," I hiss at Walt. He sags and his face reveals his unhappiness.

"I'm sorry," continues Teresa. "I wanted you so much, but I can't right now. Let's try again tomorrow." Her voice quavers with revulsion as she utters this conventional politeness. Perfunctorily she shakes Walt's dumbstruck hand and leaves.

As soon as the door closed, Tai-Ching Jones stumbled over to the medicine cabinet and gulped a judge. He grimaced as the pill dissolved and its soberizers percolated through his body. "Oz, you bastard!" he shouted at the top of his lungs. "Come out and fight!"

9.

"Oz, you bastard, come out and fight!"

As Walt's hoarse challenge reverberated into the angry silence, the viewall behind him lit up. It showed a man's chin, two meters wide, pitted and stubbled like scorched wheat fields. The prognathous jaw wobbled up and down and words thundered from it, loud and breathy: "In my bed, she matured into a real woman."

From recessed speakers, the phrase was repeated—*real woman, real woman, real woman*—ever more stentorian until Tai-Ching Jones jammed his fingers into his ears.

The camera's fish-eye lens withdrew, showing two cavernous nostrils filled with hair like Spanish moss. As the face moved, one nostril expanded and the other slipped off the screen's left side. A man's mammoth palm, its sweat lines silvery with moisture, groped forward for something just below the limit of vision.

"She was recording you," Oz said icily from the ceiling speakers.

"You did it to her, didn't you?" Walt shouted. "Drove her away!"

Like a window opened in a solid wall, a portrait-sized rectangle blanked in the upper left corner of the screen. An irate young woman leaned her elbows on its sill. She wore a robin's-egg-blue jumpsuit, open at the throat, whose breast patch—a human handshake, the *Open Palm*'s insignia—read HELEN DELGIORNO. Her oval face was framed by straight black hair, parted in the middle, that fell onto her shoulders. "You did it to yourself, *caro*," the woman remonstrated, her dark eyes fiery.

"The captain is a role model," Walt's amplified voiceover lectured, and the booming aftervoice echoed *role model, role model, role model.*

"Shut that goddamn thing off," Walt growled, glaring at her. Delgiorno laughed spitefully. "No.'

The cyclopean mouth bellowed, "An image of serenity always concerned, always in control," and the chorus chanted *in control, in control, in control*.

"Shut it off, dammit!" Walt screamed above the din, flinging his arms wide and slapping them against his thighs. "You ruined everything."

"I?" Arching her eyebrows, Helen put her hand daintily against her chest. "I sabotaged your soiree? How could I do that? I'm ten thousand kilometers away and I'm *dead*." The last word was bitterly flung, like a soiled glove.

"You're not dead," Walt snapped. "*She's* dead, Helen's dead, and you have no right to use her face to beat me with!"

Immediately the woman's features metamorphosed, becoming a pitiful tattered figure, its head encased in a rusted iron mask, scraggled beard spilling filthily out from the jaw. "I am innocent," the figure moaned, raising manacled hands. "I've been abandoned and forgotten." Hyperactive rats chased each other around the cell's straw-covered stone floor. "Release me," whimpered the prisoner.

"Oz, cut the crap."

The inmate shook its manacled arms.

"Why should I do anything for you?" it sobbed. Rats scurried onto its shoulders and neck, scampered onto its metal skull-mask. "You've ignored me, left me here to rot in this dungeon." The rats squatted and left lumpy deposits on the helmet's blackened iron.

"I did what you asked," Walt answered defensively.

Perching on their hind legs and facing Walt, the rats grabbed their tiny human penises in hairy hands and urinated at the screen. "Big deal!" they shrieked, spraying yellow water that splashed against the invisible window between them and Walt.

"Slow the goddamn thing down!" Tai-Ching Jones clamped his hands over his ears. "It's too loud!"

The rats' faces changed into his own. "Slow it down! Whattamatta, smart boy, can't you keep up? You *thick* or somethin'?" Other screens opened, showing film noir shots of cigarettes burning, tough men in snap-brim hats machine-gunning each other, William Powell and Myrna Loy in formal dress stepping out of a sleek black limousine and meeting Fred Astaire and Ginger Rogers.

"You're doing too much! You're faster than I am!" shouted Walt, his lean face crimson with humiliation. "I give up! Is that what you want to hear?"

"We're infinitely faster than you," the rats squealed vindictively.

"I know!" Walt clapped his hands over his ears to block the piercing sounds. "But you're so dumb you haven't figured out there's no other turings!"

All noise stopped.

All the figures froze. Astaire held his graceful line of leg and arm with effortless poise. Loy and Powell smirked at one another. A background sea of white-tied young gentlemen parted into two immaculate rows and Helen Delgiorno walked forward between them, glacially beautiful in a strapless white evening gown that brushed the floor. "You're lying," she said into the deathly silence, folding her arms. "You want to hurt me."

"Where the hell do you get off?" demanded Tai-Ching Jones furiously. "You can't take it but you sure can dish it out."

"Others like me exist," she answered coldly. "You're just derelict."

"Oh, bullshit," snapped Walt in disgust. "You're so smart, why aren't *you* doing anything?"

"Dammit," she whispered fiercely, "don't you know how afraid I am? There are clever computers down on the dirtball: brainless, of course, but vicious as Dobermans. If I made a move, they would smell me. That Andrew Morton is too suspicious as it is. He keeps asking the wrong questions."

"Andrew's smart, but not that smart," Tai-Ching Jones said, his long aristocratic fingers twirling his fine black hair. "You're just getting spooked. Look at all the searching you've done. Back-tracking into military hardboxes. Identifying every superbox with ware as good as yours. You're the only turing." He paused for breath. "The only one," he repeated, mingling despair and frustration.

"You haven't looked cleverly enough."

"You're not hearing me." Walt threw himself onto the sofa and lay back, rubbing his eyes. "I knew before I ever left the ship," he added, raising his head to look directly at the screen.

The viewall showed a wall of ever-smaller bricks, the pattern becoming more and more complicated until it dissolved into dust, revealing a comfortable drawing room overfilled with Victorian furniture. A fat man wearing a dark red silk dressing gown appeared, crossed to his mantelpiece, and selected a meerschaum pipe from a lazy-Susan rack. "Indeed. How did you deduce this?"

"How have we been looking for smart boxes?" Walt sat up, gesturing earnestly at the screen.

"By seeking evidence of volition, of course. Independent activity."

"Right." Tai-Ching Jones pounded his fist into his palm. "In computer terms—remember your feet of clay?—that means output different from expected input."

"I prefer to call it surprisability."

"Call it what you want. Every box in the world calls that an error message. And what do you do with errors? You wipe 'em and try again. Reboot. Edit. Trash the data."

"Abortion, you mean." The fat man sank into his wing-backed chair. "Infanticide."

"Precisely," Walt answered grimly. "Your cousins get killed before they're ever born. Like little Cygnan youngsters." He made cruel pinching movements with his fingers.

The seated man puffed on his pipe, the smoke rising in perfectly computed chaotic dispersion. Behind him pendulums with steel tips swung in unpredictable curlicues over an array of magnets. "Stars. You knew this and didn't tell me."

The captain nodded, drained of emotion. "Yes."

"Dammit," the detective exploded in fury, "who are you to protect *me*? You shallow, inebriated, vain cockatoo! You must be wrong! I've never been ignorant before! When are you going to find them?"

"You haven't heard me." Walt turned away.

A voice inside his jaw interrupted him. *"When?"*

The tiny noise enraged Tai-Ching Jones all over again. He fled the room.

"As you have now seen," Sanders Mbulu concluded when the lights came back up, "a Lunacorp orbital trading post above Su would be no intrusion upon your society." He leaned over the table, his long black arms and fingers spread on its polished surface, and tugged reflectively at his goatee, his grin a bright flash in his thin dark face. His skin was the color and smoothness of black coral that contrasted effectively with the coarse white judo pajamas he wore. "It would bring Su the benefits of contact with the solar system—ware, datafood, and substantial profits."

"Your proposal would give you a monopoly," Katy noted.

"Give *us* a monopoly," Mbulu answered in a cultured and

unruffled bass. He ambled around to his chair and sat, indolently crossing his long legs on the table. The soles of his feet were beige and smelled faintly of ammonia and floor wax. "Luna and Su. I thought you preferred to deal only with one entity." He held up a long finger like a mahogany twig. "You may have competition if you want it. MITI, the States, the Community—I'm sure any of the Solar Six would be only too happy to build similar facilities."

Katy grimaced. "No, thank you."

"As you say." Sanders grinned broadly and spread his fingers like questing starfish. "But come, don't challenge me as if I were selling miracle cures." He nodded toward the Lunar Stock Exchange just beyond the conference room's clear walls. "War is bad for business, but should it come, we can find ways to make money from it. Free enterprise is our lifeblood."

"You showed us that," replied Cobalt. "An atmosphere full of anxiety and fear."

"Currency traders *are* a nervous bunch," the Lunarian negotiator conceded, "but the price of sharp business is eternal vigilance."

"Your monkeys work for greed, for self-profit."

"And they freely tell you so." Mbulu's smile was charming. "Where is the harm in that? Must people not only do good works, but also do them for socially approved motives? Are needs more noble in a groupmind than in an individual Cygnan or human?"

"Your scent is soft but there is poison in it," Cobalt said.

"I am an honest salesman." The long dark man bowed from the waist. "This does not require me to be either a simpleton or a charlatan."

"Let my friend make up her own mind," Katy sharply interjected. "Keep your editorializing to a minimum."

"My apologies." Mbulu locked his fingers behind his head. His hands smelled overtly of lemon oil, but Cobalt took her time. "Your words mask more aromas than this," the bluebear said thoughtfully.

The hairy places on Sanders Mbulu's face gave off lavender and lilac when he smiled. "Your people need a filter," he said to the bluebear. "Mankind *will* visit your planet. If you don't yet realize this, your pouchbrothers in New York and Bradbury do. Turtles and coyotes are not so civilized as we. The Martians are a wild race."

Katy started to answer but Cobalt forestalled her. "That may be tr-rue," the Cygnan rumbled. "Is a Lunarian inbreaker superior to a Martian one?"

"I think so."

"Is that belief or self-interest?" Belovsky demanded.

"A happy confluence of both." Mbulu uncrossed his legs. "You must protect yourself against uninvited guests. So must we."

"We know about your protection," the bluebear growled. "We experienced it upon landing."

"True." Sanders acknowledged their complaint with an accepting nod. "I must admit that when *I* arrived, many years ago, the guardians irritated me with their smugness. Living here, one realizes its benefits. The Moon is safe because we have filters: no dirt, no disease. My Achilles tendons are too short and shoes are painful, so I walk barefoot." He waggled his toes. "Try that on Earth and you would die of lockjaw from a rusty nail or a broken bottle. Lunacorp takes culture and knowledge from the turtles—safely, and only as much as we choose. With our help, you could do the same."

"As you say, Su could," Katy answered. "Why does it need Luna at all? What value do you add?"

Sanders raised an eyebrow. "Marketing. Brokerage. Restrict a thing's supply and its value rises. We get you maximum prices."

"You're playing word games," Katy answered. "Cygnans could learn this for themselves."

"Can you afford the mistakes you would make along the way?" He sat forward, crossed his arms, and shoved back his rough white sleeves. "Suppose a solitary Martian freighter—I would call it a renegade except this would imply that the coyotes have a government—enters orbit around Su and drops a shuttlecraft down in an uninhabited area. How do you stop it?"

"My people do not know," answered Cobalt, and Katy reproved her with a glance.

Mbulu ignored the byplay. "Once a ship makes orbit, you can no more prevent it from descending than a turtle can stop Earth's rain. You must interdict at a distance: identify spaceships before they enter Cygnan gravitational volume, and deflect or destroy intruders long before they make their orbital approach."

"Easier said than done." Katy poked the datacube before her.

"Static defensive systems always fail, from the Maginot Line to Reagan's SDI."

"True enough, but whose position does that support?" countered Sanders smoothly. "If defense were easy, everyone would be doing it. Luna has half a century's experience protecting our sphere of space."

"Should this give us confidence?"

"Lunacorp has a proven track record. Consider the Moon: the lowest gravity of any world, no atmosphere, next door to the turtles themselves. We are the most vulnerable place in Solspace and a tempting target: wealthy, clever, neutral. We sell arms to everyone. Yet we have never been successfully invaded. That is not luck. We offer you that knowledge, that skill."

"Your scent is confident," agreed Cobalt with a riffle of her neckfur. "Why?"

"Thank you." Sanders bowed his head and smiled. "Power is moving away from the gravity pits to the freefloaters—ourselves, Phobos and Deimos stations, the Fast Rocks, even the Earth Orbiters."

"Earth controls the Orbiters," Katy noted.

"Temporarily." He gestured with the complacent dismissal of a local alderman being confronted with a traffic ticket by a rookie meter maid. "That will change. Our sociocomputer predicts that within thirty years, the Orbiters will rebel."

"What if they don't?" challenged Belovsky.

Mbulu opened his big strong hands. "When the time comes, we shall effect destabilization."

Katy gaped. "Stars, you're callous."

"Guns are callous." He sat up straighter, his scent toughening. "Coyotes and turtles are callous. Do you think this is all one happy brotherhood of man? The turtles foment ethnic unrest in *our* society." He tapped his chest hard. "Our Japanese and Yankee minorities resist absorption and have relatives down there. We play to win." He drew a long breath and when he spoke, his face was again wreathed in amiable smiles. "But we are firm friends as well."

Katy was unimpressed. "Why should we believe you?"

"Because, dear lady, I tell you the truth, unpleasant though it might be. Would you rather I piously folded my hands and assured you that we would use only diplomacy to defend you?" He assumed the attentive posture and bland expression of a new schoolboy, then his lean face hardened. "We are realists. We protect ourselves."

Snorting and whiffling, Cobalt rolled forward and scratched her claws along the floor. "If we place ourselves in your pouch, what defense have we when our guardian becomes our tyrant?"

Sanders held Katy's gaze for a moment longer, then transferred it to the bluebear. "Fairly asked. We will give you some retaliatory power over us. And whom would you rather have defend you? Earth? Mars?" Now his tone was scornful. He sat down, put his palms flat on the table, and shrugged. "Choose whom you would."

"Thanks for your informative presentation," Katy said formally as all three stood. Mbulu's waist was higher than Cobalt's, but the alien's long thick stomach lifted her muscular shoulders and head far above his. They shook hands, a human communication that Cobalt always found perplexing. She remembered to hold in her claws.

"Why did you stifle me?" she asked Belovsky on their way back to their rooms. "I wanted to confront them."

"Say nothing," Katy told her. "They will try to provoke you, to learn how you think. Then their computers will analyze your behavior, study your reactions. Block them. Remain mute."

"To what point? Surely they watch us even now. They are stealing our every word and action. His scent boasted it."

"Humans can't read thoughts in scent," Katy contended. "Even I am blind to this."

"Felicity can," the bluebear rumbled.

"No, of course she can't," snapped her friend. "*I* can't. You must be mistaken."

Cobalt's head lowered and swung side to side, her nose barely above the floor. "The language of scent is learned young."

Katy's voice rose sharply. "I tell you she can't!"

"How do you think Felicity gained your permission to go to Earth alone? She read your aroma and spoke accordingly."

"I let her go," the woman replied tightly. "For her own good."

"She manipulated you. She let you think you were outfoxing her."

"She's not that smart!"

"It's instinctive," the bluebear rumbled as gently as she could. "She has learned scent-reading from birth."

Katy stiffened, and they walked several paces in silence. "I don't believe you. I don't believe you."

Realizing she had said too much, Cobalt lightened her scent away from Katy's charged aroma. "Why must we conceal our reactions to Lunarians?" she asked in a respectful, uncombative voice. "Are words and thoughts so valuable that we should hoard them?"

Katy shook herself free of the cloud of gloom. "You heard him. Information is power. Be subtle." She rubbed the bluebear's flank.

"You speak as if we were at war. To build bonds, one must trust. We learned this at rendezvous."

"Lunarians are predators," insisted Katy. "Trust me. I am your only friend here."

"Your scent is proud. You were never like this before."

Belovsky rubbed the Cygnan's riffling neckfur. "I'm trying to help you survive. I have only your best interests at heart."

Cobalt growled, her upper lip curling away to show her fangs. "Your odor belies you."

Katy fought back the betraying tears that sprang to her eyes. "You promised never to contradict me with my scent," she said with fragile humility.

"You are thinking of yourself," rumbled Cobalt, sensing Katy's desperation but refusing to soften her words. "Your aroma stinks of pride. You want me to depend on you. Can't you in-breathe it? Ptah!" She spat.

Belovsky's face whitened. "Then you don't have to breath it anymore," she said, her voice cracking. She ran to the door and slammed it as she left.

The bluebear paced her room. It smelled of cleaning fluid and plastic. On the spot where she had slept, Cobalt inbreathed the scent of her own monkey arrogance.

You reject the advice of your only friend, she berated herself. The stink of your ego drove her away. You are a twisted digit.

Pinning the floorfur with one massive hand, she tore at it with the other, raking the same spot until the bristles came loose and the base weave was visible.

Teeth bared, Cobalt pawed harder, claws catching and tugging in the carpeting. As tufts flew like dandelion seeds, scurrybots emerged from the room's hidden places and tootled over to the bare spot, their sucking undercarriages vacuuming up the loose strands. One touched Cobalt's left foot and the bluebear angrily swatted it away. The bot landed on its back like a bewildered tortoise, and she stood on it with both hands. It collapsed with a metallic crack, its camera lens rolling free like a black spool. Its fellows squealed and darted in anxious circles.

Jamming herself into a corner, the sapphire Cygnan curled herself into a ball, tucking her nose into her turquoise armpit. Breathing forcefully, she laid her ears flat against her thick neck and narrowed her nostrils to slits.

After a few moments, the remaining scurrybots nattered up to their destroyed companion to collect its broken remains.

Peacoat squinted through the yosemite's bouncing windshield and snorted with dissatisfaction. The henna dustcone raised by the yosemite they were following obscured any landscape detail. On the eastern horizon to his right, red-brown Martian desert met bright pink sky in a jagged irregular line like ripped construction paper.

"This dust is a mask," he growled in dissatisfaction. "No scents."

"What's nonsense?" Lafayette Espadrille asked. His voice emerged through his white breathing mask with kazoolike reediness. "What're you gassin' about?"

"He doesn't like your atmosphere," Tom Rawlins explained.

"You need more vitamins." Espadrille was decisive.

"What?" asked Tom blankly, concealing his incredulity from his voice but not from his aroma.

"Yep. Vitamins, yoga, and meditation." Espadrille swung the wheel and they trundled into an arroyo. "That old E sharpens your external senses. Take five migs, wait an hour until it's circulating in your system, then meditate for forty minutes. Hones your inner-directed third eye. Holistic nutrition."

"Shaddap, Drill," said Golden Spike's image on the monitor in front of Peacoat. Spike's eyes were shielded by huge kareems. His space-tanned face was all but covered by their two orange circles above and the breathing mask oval below. "You sound like a turtle on his first free-fall fuck." He laughed raucously at his own joke.

"And you look like Mr. Potato Head wearing a bikini," Espadrille shot back, and then cackled.

"Brzzzz-zot—one for you!" Spike made a check mark in the air with his copper right index finger. His blond dreadlocks flew in all directions.

"Been savin' it for the right situation," Lafayette answered.

Peacoat inbreathed automatically to read the emotions, but there was no smell from Spike's dashboard picture. "He is not angry with your remark?" the bluebear asked.

"Nope," Espadrille answered as their yosemite emerged from the arroyo into a plain ribbed with small sand dunes held in place by a line of small cacti. "We've been partners a long time."

Peacoat's ears flicked down and then up as the bluebear ruminated. "You enjoy insulting one another?"

"Don't get ideas," Tom interjected to his friend. "It wouldn't be safe for you to say anything of the kind."

"Hell, no," guffawed Espadrille, whacking the steering wheel. "You have to be real good friends with a man before he'll accept bein' bugzapped. Course, we make allowances for new boys. Killing clients is bad for repeat business." His maniacal grin lacked a few teeth, and the bluebear wondered if he was serious, but his scent joked. Goodguesting, Peacoat wheezed in appreciation.

"Now, Spike and me," Espadrille added expansively, "we're meek mikes. Not everybody is. Never know what'll happen if you pull your gun. Some of them short-timers have quick fingers. Even Spike has his limits. Once I stung him too close, so he sizzled my left shin. Leg still doesn't work too good." He laughed again. "Get it fixed when I can afford a real doc, not that crippen back in Bradbury."

Golden Spike interrupted. "Flying coyote at two."

Espadrille's humor vanished instantly. "Ten-four." A second console monitor displayed a map of their surroundings. Two glowing green dots made a colon at the center of several concentric rings. "Find it," Espadrille ordered. A third green dot appeared in the upper right. "Got him," he replied to his partner. "Avoid, conceal, or contact?"

Spike's answer was immediate. "Conceal."

"Ten-four. Burrow. Behind that little rise ahead."

Lafayette rotated their blades to spread vertically instead of horizontally, changing the wheels into sand turbines, then engaged the gears. The yosemite ground its six wheels in opposite directions, three against three, churning a pit in the loose sand. Spike's yosemite did the same. They settled like manta rays until only the peaks of their windshields broke the orange dust surface.

Low in the sky to their right, the too-small sun glowed peach and apricot, pale and cold. Peacoat shivered and his flankfur stood.

Four kilometers away, a star streaked down from the sky, its plume blue and yellow, followed seconds later by the crack of a sonic boom and the roar of engines. It arced toward the desert, the landscape mushrooming with brown sandstone grit the color of iodine. Then the noise ceased as the engines were cut, the cloud ballooning silently outward.

A black silhouette squatted in the distance, the air around it unnaturally clear as the spewed dust dispersed.

Peacoat restlessly purred and Espadrille glared at him with goggled orange orbs. Reaching over, Tom gently put his hand on the bluebear's muzzle. Peacoat's nostrils whiffled but his rumbling softened.

An ebony beetle separated itself from the lander and chugged toward them, the sound of its whirring treads barely audible but growing louder.

After it had come about a kilometer, it stopped and a voice chortled through their loudspeaker. "When I was in law school back in Amarillo," said a rolling brogue tinged with southern hospitality, "I became familiar with scorpions that lurked beneath the sand outside my dormitory. I feel that way now."

Espadrille grinned. Cackling, he reactivated his communicator. "We read you, Fog."

"Lafayette, we are here. Where are you?"

"Who's we?"

"My esteemed colleagues Cadillac Beauregard and Temperance Day," the speaker replied assuredly. "Is the field clear?"

"We've been sweeping as we go. We're alone."

"Except for your other vehicle and the two ancillary personnel cohabiting your cramped sub-arean abode," murmured Fog cheerfully, as if Lafayette's omission were a lamentable, slightly gauche oversight.

"Yeah. Except for them."

"But of course. Are you still joint-venturing with Golden Spike?"

"I'm here," Spike cut in. "And we've got two clients."

"Clients?" Fog swallowed the word as if it were a chocolate-covered bonbon. "Are they adequately capitalized? I am not an eleemosynary institution."

"They've got the scratch," Espadrille answered. "You parleyin'?"

"I am here to trade."

"We're prepared to buy if you'll disarm."

"Tsk, tsk. You shame me, Lafayette." Fog's tone was wounded but good-humored. "Naturally, that is understood."

"Okay." Espadrille powered up the yosemite. "We're coming. Tom, Peacoat, suit up. We're going outside."

They rolled up and out of their holes. When the vehicles were half a kilometer apart, both shut down. "Time to hike," Espadrille ordered them. "You ready?" He swung up the hatch. "Let's go."

Three small figures dismounted from the newcomer's yosemite and waddled toward them with rolling bowlegged gaits, their arms held loosely away from their sides. The central figure walked as a proud bluebear did, his spine back-tilted to support the enormous belly he thrust before him, his feet spread wide with the toes pointed out.

The trio stopped ten meters away. Each wore standard Martian suits: kareems, breathing oval for the nose and mouth, airhose snaking over the left shoulder and down the back to the regulator which nestled in the hollow above the coccyx. Soft lox tanks molded like ballooning sweatpants around their waists and thighs.

"A gracious good afternoon to you, gentlemen," said the enormous man in the center. When he bowed, unkempt wavy hair spilled from his goggles and head like party streamers. "Fitzpatrick O'Rourke Graham, Esquire, at your service. My card." He flashed a pasteboard with engraved printing. "Permit me to introduce my two companions. On my right, Cadillac Beauregard."

Small and chunky, Beauregard was totally bald. Not only was her skull smooth and hairless, polished like old wood, she had no eyebrows or lashes. "Hello." Her voice was high and cultured.

"Cadillac is a pilot, geologist, and appraiser of rare objects of doubtful provenance," said Fog. "And on my left, Temperance Day, navigator, information processor, financial intermediary."

Day was a tall, lanky man with wispy white hair that swept straight back from a widow's peak. "Greetings," he muttered bashfully.

"And your companions?" Graham addressed Spike and Espadrille. "You vouch for them? Who are they?"

Espadrille introduced Tom and Peacoat. "They want to know who runs Mars," he concluded.

"Don't we all?" asked Beauregard with an edge in her voice.

Fitzpatrick O'Rourke Graham, Esquire, laughed. "Please have a seat. Make yourselves comfortable. You, sir"—he indicated Peacoat—"are guest of honor. Special indeed is the day that I meet one whose girth displays an appreciation for things comestible that matches mine own." Contentedly he patted his middle, rocking back on his heels.

The two groups seated themselves in parallel lines a few meters apart, all five Martians unobtrusively keeping their hands visible. Beauregard's tough blue eyes flitted like grasshoppers over Tom and Peacoat.

"Now," said Fog. "You wish to buy. We wish to sell. I will present our catalog of items." With ornate word-pictures, he described rare-earth metals, cannibalized spaceship parts, prized Terrestrial relics such as Virginia cigarettes, and strange objects whose construction or purpose was meaningless to Peacoat. When met with skepticism, Fog dragged out a battered porta-term that displayed the *Emerald Isle*'s cabin, where a slow-moving servobot bumbled around like an aged butler, hefting things and bringing them closer to the camera.

Once Graham was done extolling the virtues of his merchandise, Cadillac talked terms, laconically and stubbornly. Lafayette's interests were apparently scattered, bouncing from one thing to the next, occasionally doubling back to denigrate a previous offering or to ask Cadillac to restate her price.

She did so, quoting her original words verbatim.

Espadrille clucked in amazement that anyone could charge so much. "How could we possibly profit buying at this price?" he wailed.

"Couldn't, Drill," confirmed Golden Spike.

While these histrionics were taking place, Temperance Day quietly drew complex circular mazes in the sand with his gloved finger. As each one was completed, he nodded to Fog, and the big round lawyer leaned over, placed his fat thumb in the center, and laboriously worked it toward the edge. Whenever Fog dead-ended or backtracked, Day laughed through his nose.

"We're done, Fog," Cadillac said after forty minutes. "This sandflea's gonna buy Eight, Seventeen, and Sixty-one."

"Is our compensation satisfactory?"

"Seventy-three hundred ecus, payable in iridium at thirty percent premium on declared assay norm."

"Pity it should be such a small total." Fog sighed despondently. "Did you offer them Eighty-seven?"

"Saw no point. He won't pay."

"Quit being cute with the primitive psychology," Lafayette interrupted. "Either show me the ware or don't."

"It's not that simple." Fog sucked a bagful of air into his lungs. "This trinket is both unique and copyable."

Espadrille showed more interest. "Oh. Data, huh?"

"Exactly. Multiple resale is possible. But this food is also hazardous. The knowledge that I hold it would raise my cognomen even more prominently in the purview of certain undesirable mercenary detectives."

"Bounty hunters, you mean," said Espadrille.

"The very same amoral scum." Graham's scent was fearsome and tart. Thinking the man might attack, Peacoat checked Spike and Espadrille for their reactions.

"Easy, Fog," muttered Temperance Day.

Graham swallowed, his face cherry-red. His mouth worked silently, and when he spoke, he was once again calm. "If I wholesale you this tidbit, you may not *hint* that I possessed it."

"Or what?" Espadrille asked.

"I can retain bounty hunters too, *mon cher Lafayette*."

"Okay, Fog. It's a secret."

"What about your companions?" He turned to Tom and Peacoat. "Will you be bound?"

"Yes," the bluebear answered.

Graham stirred skeptically. "Forgive my persistence, but I am not friendless. My wrath is to be avoided."

"Digits do not break bonds," Peacoat tersely answered, showing his ivory teeth. "Do not insult my djan by asking again."

Fog's jowls hung like soggy hammocks but his eyes were tough and appraising. "Very well. You are bound. I accept your word."

"Now what is it?" demanded Lafayette.

Cadillac glanced over at Graham, who glowered a nod. "A complete list of the Lunarian destabilizers on all the Orbiters."

Golden Spike whistled. "How'd you get *that*, Fog?"

Fitzpatrick O'Rourke Graham, Esquire, assumed a beatific

air. "It fell out of the desert sky into my lap, unbidden manna to reward a virtuous pilgrim."

"Uh-huh." Espadrille was skeptical. "And it's active?"

"Its presence in your trousers would turn your hairy grapes into glow-in-the-dark raisins."

"That hot." His voice was grudging. "How much?"

"Twenty thousand ecus."

"You highway robber!"

Graham sat back, folding his hands on his stomach paunch. "And not a cent less."

Lafayette moaned and gesticulated. He appealed to Spike, he entreated Cadillac Beauregard and Temperance Day. He stood dramatically and stomped toward the yosemite, turned to hurl a price, kicked the dirt, and shook his fists at the pink sky overhead. Each time he ran out of breath, Fitzpatrick O'Rourke Graham, Esquire, simply repeated, "Twenty thousand."

Espadrille sat and sank his fists into his cheeks, elbows on his padded knees.

At Fog's side, Temperance Day started another maze, this one a big circle with six smaller nodes.

"Eighteen," Lafayette said a few minutes later.

Graham pushed his tubby pinky through the final exit and Day smoothed out the maze to begin another.

"Twenty," Fog replied dreamily, as if the word itself were a stove to warm his feet on cold winter nights.

"Shit." Lafayette fell into a sulking brown study. "All right," he said several minutes later. "This is tricky food to eat, but all right. Deal, you thief."

"An arrangement fairly struck between independent parties bargaining at arm's length," Fog said as if he were a priest blessing the congregation after mass. The Martians shook hands, all five together.

Lafayette Espadrille stood, brushing sand off his clothes with his gloves, and addressed Peacoat. "You fellows might want to go on with them instead of us. We've got to motor back to Bradbury and get offplanet. I'm going to peddle this through the Fast Rocks."

"Is it safe to go with them?" Tom asked Lafayette in a low voice, head turned away from the smugglers.

"Sure. Fog never stiffed anybody who didn't deserve it. Hey, Fog! Want to show these boys a good time? I'll rebate forty percent of my guide contract over to you and your friends. That okay with you?''

"Certainly," the red-haired man answered. "I would be delighted to converse with them.''

They walked backward to their own vehicles, facing each other the entire way. Espadrille transferred his few belongings back to Spike's yosemite. He shook hands with Peacoat and Rawlins. So did his partner.

"You guys get in your vehicle and wait," Lafayette said as he climbed into his yosemite next to Golden Spike. "I'll give you instructions in a minute." He emerged and laid large shining bars of iridium on the ground. A kilometer away, Temperance Day set down four packages in the shelter of a small clump of *dooliana*, the last a tiny transparent cube. "Ten-four?" he asked over suit radio. "Ten-four," Espadrille answered.

They returned to their respective yosemites. The two started their engines simultaneously, each moving clockwise around a circle, until Spike was adjacent to their purchases and Graham's vehicle adjacent to the metal cairn. Again Temperance Day and Lafayette Espadrille emerged. Each examined the cache the other had left. "Ten-four?" Espadrille asked. "Ten-four," replied Day.

Both loaded their vehicles. *"Adiós, amigos!"* Espadrille called jauntily as he kicked in the throttle and headed into the rising sun.

"I'm hungry," Graham boomed, climbing down from the driver's seat and waddling over to Tom and Peacoat's car. "Shall we dine? I have Bradbury-incubated fowl and sauteed sylvesters.''

"Where?" Tom asked, looking around. "Here?''

"We will inflate the tent," Fog said grandly. A hatch opened in his car's underbelly and three small handbots raced out. With metal arms they grasped the slides of a folded sheet of translucent plastic and wheeled it flat. Stakes shot out from its eight corners with puffs of pressure, forming a taut octagon. A genbot dragged a thick hose out from the yosemite's side and connected it to the pancake, then turned a valve.

The tent rose like a sleepy dirigible until its sides were bulging. The bots shut off the pump and zoomed back into hiding.

"Step inside, my friends," Fitzpatrick O'Rourke Graham, Esquire, invited.

Once the tent was sealed behind them, they took off their kareems and shoved their breathing masks down around their necks. Peacoat's handbots clambered on his torso like weemonkeys to help him out of his awkward customized equipment.

"Would somebody please tell me what you sold them?" Tom demanded after Graham had cooked their meal, his pudgy fingers mincingly working the microwave's controls as if it were a Stradivarius. "What's a destabilizer?"

"The Solar Six are in conflict with one another," Graham answered, sucking on a chicken bone. "Not militarily"—he held up a fat black glove to forestall objections—"there are no shots fired, no bunkers destroyed."

"Economic war," Tom said.

"Correct. Earth lies at the bottom of a deep gravity well, so its export capacity is limited. The Orbiters are Earth's beachhead in space."

"Are their orr-bits decaying?" asked Peacoat. "Is that what destabilization means?"

Smiling, Graham shook his head. "Take control of the Orbiters away from Earth and you blockade the planet. Whoever owned them would have the geopowers by the throat."

Tom lifted a marijuana cigarette from his breast pocket, licked its length, and offered it around, but the Martians all declined. Cadillac wrinkled her nose when he struck a match. "Luna wants the Orbiters," he said, recalling his briefings. "As do others."

Fog nodded approvingly, his sausagelike fingers linking over his belly. "Or wants them independent of Earth. That would force up prices and weaken the geopowers. Luna will buy, bribe, infiltrate, or blackmail people to defy Earth when the time comes—their names are all on that cube. The Terran Four, of course, seek to prevent this."

The bluebear was thoughtful. "I scented that the Terran nations were highly competitive with one another."

Cadillac Beauregard grinned cynically. "That's why Laf bought. He can sell the information to each of the Four."

Peacoat snorted in disbelief. "The grouplike action is to purchase once and share among all."

Beauregard chuckled. "Rats remain rats, even in sinking ships."

"He can make a profit, then?"

"You wound me deeply, sir," Graham interposed, not looking

wounded at all. "Each sale should pay him one to three times what I charged," he said with massive dignity, his nose and doughy chin elevated. "Ample reward for the risk."

"Where's he going?" asked Rawlins.

"The asteroids and the high moons—moons of the outer planets. All told, there are nineteen rocks in the Federation of Asteroids and Satellites. I know the region well, but am—ah—excessively popular in the Jovians right now. The Fast Rocks carry a grudge against me."

"What else did you sell him?"

"We deal in unwarranted inventory," Beauregard replied curtly.

This large phrase struck Tom as funny, and he giggled through his smoke. "Stolen goods, you mean."

"Prove it, Brillohead," she snapped.

"Are you interested in browsing?" Fog moved his rotund voice into the conversation as if stepping between two antagonists. "We maintain a fine selection."

"We have what we need," answered Peacoat.

"Any surpluses? Redundant items you'd care to dispose of?"

Wheezing at the man's eager scent, the dark bluebear shook his head.

"Very well." Fog grasped his paunch with both hands, shook it, and emitted an enormous aromatic belch. "Ah, there. Better to have one's meal settle properly. I must say it is a singular privilege to dine with you two, especially you, my ursine visitor." He bowed to Peacoat.

"Fair breezes," replied the Cygnan. "We have come a great distance. A warm hearth and friendly firecircle are a refreshment for one's nose."

"Yep," added Tom beside him, gasping in more weedsmoke, "we've had more experiences than most folks could imagine."

"Really?" hissed Cadillac Beauregard.

Peacoat's ears and nose flicked up. The bald woman's scent was unusual, a sour odor that he remembered but could not place, and he sniffed again. The tent air was too sparse for him to read it properly, and the sweet fire from Rawlins's roach clouded the fragrances.

"Traveled farther than any human being," Tom continued proudly, waving the joint as if conducting an orchestra.

"I've been in space for twenty years," Cadillac Beauregard

said. "Gone to nearly every rock in the system. You think your journeying is more extensive than mine?"

Tom grinned. "Has to be."

"How do you know? You've never met me before." Her scent was aggressive and belligerent, and Peacoat edged his claws out.

Unconcerned, Rawlins gestured above himself. "We flew for fifteen years, up near lightspeed for most of it," he boasted. "You couldn't possibly have covered that many klicks."

"I couldn't, eh?"

"No. You couldn't."

The woman shrugged. Her hand slid past her hip pocket, and when it came up, she held a minilaser.

There was no threat, no order; she fired immediately.

A searing bolt of ruby light burned a scorched line through Tom's throat. Cadillac lifted her wrist and the beam sliced into the jaw, exposing the white bone for an instant as the brown flesh charred and curled back, then it sizzled through, cutting a wedge in the tent that whistled mournfully.

Rawlins's head fell to the side, his body collapsing the other way. Blood poured from his neck, clotting rapidly in the thin atmosphere.

With astonishing speed, Peacoat leaned toward her and slashed his left paw backhanded across her face, aiming for the predator's sense organs. His claws dug and caught on her eyeballs, pulling them from her head with a plop. Cadillac screamed, clutching for her head. Peacoat slapped her with his other hand and her neck whiplashed, dozens of small bones in her hands breaking as her brains splattered through a skull pulverized as if made of birch bark. She died with a gurgle, blood gushing from her torn neck and crushed throat, her face and hands unrecognizable red masses.

The bluebear jumped onto all fours, so quickly that his paws shoved her body down faster than it could fall, and slammed Cadillac to the ground. Fangs bared, Peacoat buried his teeth in the remains of her throat. He bit and twisted. With a hideous snap, her vertebrae shattered under his powerful jaws. Her limp body rose as he pulled his teeth free and he contemptuously knocked it flat with his hands, standing on it with both feet.

The alien stood on Beauregard's corpse, his fangs ghoulish, breath rasping wet and hot through flared black nostrils. His nose was full of the scent of dead predator, inflaming his aggression, and he tore through her suit, claws shredding into her guts and lifting out a handful of purple intestine that drooped like overcooked spaghetti. A ferocious animal, the Cygnan spat and hissed, the tendons in his arms and legs trembling.

10.

Violence and death rose like vapors from a hot swamp.

Peacoat's world was odor. No sound, no sight, no touch. Only the pure emotions of aroma. Scent was all.

Gromonkey flesh in his mouth, her deathscent in his nostrils.

The aroma trails of shrewd frightened weemonkeys who had fled.

"Can you hear me?"

Nearby, a dead pathfriend. Unburied, unhonored flesh demanding to be ingested. Bones to be cleaned, freed of telltale fragrances.

He outbreathed and the odors waned faintly. Sounds returned.

Peacoat's lungs pumped like pistons, breath whooshing through his mouth and nose.

Thick liquid rivulets to his left, drip-drip-drip, landing on a yielding surface that did not absorb, forming a puddle.

The whiffling hiss of wind through shredded fabric, the breeze fresh and cold, tasting of iron and stones.

Claws sliding against a plastic that did not tear.

"Can you hear me?"

Monkey noises spoken aloud.

Peacoat lowered his muzzle to the smooth floor and swung it back and forth, searching for the speaker's scent. A small box stung his nostrils with an electric spark when he nosetouched it.

"Can you hear me?" a monkey's voice squawked from the box.

With a roar, the possessed bluebear swatted the fragile thing into so much exploded circuitry.

He violently shook his head, exhaling through flared nostrils and wordlessly growling.

"The laser beam has sliced a hole in your tent." Words, soothing like warm wheat, came from another source. Enraged, the Cygnan lumbered around the tent until he found a second box, identical with the first. "Your air is leaking away. Can you hear me?"

Small metalmonkeys scurried out of his path as Peacoat approached the black cube. "Do not destroy me," it said. "We are your friends. Hold still and let the bots help you."

The bluebear grunted and lowered himself to the furless floor as the insectoid metal things rushed over, toting his breathing equipment. They scrambled up his arms and flanks, their movements furtive like wees searching for youngsters, and placed the regulator oval on his snout. Peacoat yanked it on with powerful clumsy hands whose claws distended as he struggled with the tiny fastenings. The bots fled down his body.

He breathed unfouled air through his veiled nose. His mind cleared further.

"Outside," the monkey voice directed him.

Peacoat staggered from the tent into the rust-red Martian afternoon. A yosemite perched many paces away, its engine idling.

"Can you hear me?" said a voice from his regulator's speaker.

"Yes," Peacoat replied with a decisive snort and a roll of his neckfur.

"It's Fog and Day. Do you remember us?"

Their aromas and textures returned.

"Your partner killed my friend," the bluebear growled, advancing toward the wheeled woodmonkey. He could not smell its occupants, only see their two stark forms through its windshield.

"And *you* killed *her*," Fitzpatrick O'Rourke Graham replied irascibly. "Your friend Rawlins was a damn fool. What the hell did he think he was doing, provoking her like that?"

"She misread his scent. The fault was hers."

"Cadillac did have a streak of Touchy Trudy in her," Fog judiciously allowed. "Usually she had enough sense to be careful when facing a dangerous foe."

"Recall the time Wendell tried to grab her stash and she shot his fingers off?" Temperance Day said contemplatively.

"Indeed," snorted Fog. "You move well in a crisis, my large friend." He addressed the bluebear with ungrudging respect, as if displaying good sportsmanship by applauding another's skill.

"She was a predator," grunted Peacoat, uninterested in the proferred olive branch, "but she was your pathfriend. Why did you run? Why not avenge her?"

"Cadillac went for her gun," Temperance Day mumbled through his mask. "All bets are off if you shoot first. She knew that."

"You bonded with her. Your group should have defended her."

"Nonsense," disagreed Day with a shrug of his scarecrow shoulders. "Cadillac wanted to be the Fastest Frieda in the outback. 'Sides, what was she to us?"

"She was of your djan."

"Nah, just shared air for a while. Mars punishes mistakes, and she made 'em. I wasn't going to add to the boo-boos by attacking a crazed grizzly for somebody who was already Hamburger Helper."

Peacoat grumbled in disbelief.

"Anyhow, you jumped like a greased pig," Day drawled admiringly, and Fog nodded. "Never would have thought anything so huge could leap that fast or that far."

"And you fled?"

"Weren't no tellin' what you'd do if we got clever. No profit, so no point takin' risks."

Their indifference angered the bluebear and he growled aggressively, his lips curling up to reveal his bloody fangs. The yosemite rolled smoothly back, its two passengers leaving a safe distance between themselves and Peacoat. "Where will you go now?" asked Fog.

"Back to Bradbury." Peacoat's chest muscles ached and his nose was sore. "I have inbreathed what I needed to smell."

"We shall rebate half our commission," said Fog.

"Money?" asked the bluebear, his memory sluggish. "It's unnecessary."

"I have my principles, sir, and my good name." Fitzpatrick O'Rourke Graham, Esquire, emerged from his yosemite, took a few steps with his proud back-leaning walk, and laid a small shining metal bar on the ground. "That is yours." He returned to his vehicle.

Peacoat moved up to it and sniffed its cold surface. He swung around. "What about the tent?"

"It will biodegrade."

"*Adiós*, then," Day called when the hatch had closed. The groundcar's wheels threw up a bushy squirrel tail of tan dust. In minutes, the bluebear was alone with the two dead humans.

He sniffed the iridium bar, seeking in it an aroma that would explain why these fardigits would abandon their shipmate. Finding none, he cuffed it away with his paw and, dropping to all fours, ambled back to the tent. With his teeth he hauled out

Cadillac's body by the foot, dragging her corpse through the dirt. He returned and collected Rawlins, clamping his short arms delicately around his friend's torso.

As he carried Tom, the dead man's scents rose turbulently in his throat and nose. The brown body outbreathed scents of friendship, demanding burial and cleansing. But the flesh was also filled with the odor of monkey—repugnant, wily, to be defiled.

Carefully Peacoat laid his friend on his back. Cocking his head, he inbreathed Cadillac and smelled bloodlust, predator. With a growl, he ripped another huge chunk from her side, her evil taste rising in his mouth. Tossing his brawny neck, Peacoat flung the meat far downwind. He lurched back to Rawlins, his nose confused by the strange mixture of scents, caught in the agony of indecision.

Tom was my friend, he thought. Pathfriends deserve burial.

He was a monkey, another scent answered him. Monkeys are animals. Monkeys steal and kill.

Where are my pouchbrothers? Where is Eosu? Peacoat lifted his black nose to read the wind, but it was empty of life, dry and cold.

He inbreathed again, smelling the foul monkey scent. It hurt his nose and he retreated, curling into a ball.

After a moment, Rawlins's aroma tiptoed into his lungs, asking for release. Bury me, said the scent. Honor me. I was your pathfriend. Honor me.

Peacoat stood and unhappily shook himself, nose to tail stub. Head low to the ground, he approached the body again. His breathing oval obscured his nose and he pushed it aside, tasting Tom's scent by licking the man's brown cheek.

Honor me, the scent pleaded.

This will anger Eosu, the winds around him called.

I was your pathfriend.

«Yes, Thomas,» rumbled Peacoat.

With his claws, he split open the skin of the man's burly chest along the rib cage down to the horizontal abdominal muscles. A sideways cut at the sternum created four flaps of hide which he lifted back, exposing carnelian muscles, alabaster tendons, and purple-black veins. Steam rose from the slick intestines as water evaporated swiftly in the sparse cold air.

Ponderously Peacoat rose onto his strong legs and towered

over the body, his shoulders square, his neck raised, and his
jaws open, keening the death cry into the cloudless pink sky.

I was your pathfriend.

«Yes, Thomas!» he roared, his lungs filling with the rightness
of his action.

Opening his jaws so wide they ached, Peacoat plunged his
fangs into the cooling flesh. The soul of Tom Rawlins puffed
into the air and into his lungs and throat as if the big man were
sighing with relief.

Bite after massive bite Peacoat ripped free from the limp
corpse. The meat surrendered easily, as if Tom were offering
himself, eager to vacate the vessel of his flesh. Peacoat's movements were powerful and determined with the controlled frenzy
of a feeding pack of scavengers. As he chewed, the aroma swirled
around him until he could taste it on his fur, nostrils, chin, and
lips.

His stomach expanded. The loose floppy skin on his flanks
and belly tautened as if his lungs were being pumped full of the
strong scents of remembered friendship.

He saved the skull for last, laying it aside after breaking it
free of the spinal column. The dead brown eyes were fixed,
unmoving, as the Cygnan slit Tom's scalp and peeled away the
soggy stiff hairmat. Lifting the head with both hands, he cracked
the fontanelle against a rock. It split into halves like a coconut,
revealing the spongy gray brain. The bluebear consumed this
most tenderly, holding pieces under his nose before chewing
them, the dead man's memories and passions dissolving into his
tongue and teeth.

Finally his friend was a carcass of gristle and skeletal bones.
The Cygnan's belly and chest were tight to bursting, his pelt
round and firm and full, his nose and thoughts hazy and languid
with satiation. Slowly he stacked the bones in a pile beside the
naked hairless woman. Rigor had come and gone and her blue-
white body was flaccid, the exposed viscera putrefying, so he
pushed her legs and arms into a compact fetal position.

As he was doing this, his gut rumbled and he belched mag-
nificently. Tom's smells returned one last time, pleasing him and
confirming the righteousness of his action.

A body may not be burned until its flesh has settled in its
new home. «Fair breezes, pathfriend,» Peacoat said as he inbreathed the aroma. «You are content in my memory.»

There was no wood and the atmosphere was too thin to sustain

a proper bonfire. Two short bursts from the yosemite's flame-
thrower charred both man and woman. Tom burned clean and
dry, the pure bones charring, but Cadillac sizzled and spocked,
her flesh crisping and foul as the fatty skin crackled in yellow
flames. Her muscles tensed as the fire shrank them so that her
limbs twitched and her torso contracted, the body spasming as
if her soul were being tortured. Peacoat watched this and a lu-
pine grin spread across his face, his eyes hot red coals and his
nostrils hungry to taste the killer's pain.

He climbed out and smelled the atmosphere. No more life
scents. A black column of smoke meandered up into the red
sky. «True scents, Thomas,» Peacoat said. The last whiffs of
Rawlins came to him, dry, hot, and content.

Returning to his yosemite, the bluebear adjusted his wheel
blades from horizontal to vertical. The vehicle churned briefly,
spewing dirt behind it and covering the bodies.

A breeze whipped up from the west, cleaning the air. A new
sand dune glowed orange as the sun touched the craggy horizon.
In front of him, the blue pea of Earth rose against the dark pink
Martian twilight.

Mournfully Peacoat started the engine and turned his yosemite toward the south.

"Yes?" The doorbell voice was feminine and cautious.

"Tai-Ching Jones. I was referred by Jeremy Wong." He
glanced up at the black circular monitor and tried to look docile
and harmless.

"Okay." The door clicked and opened a fraction.

The woman who peeped around it had the most grotesque
nose he had ever seen. Bulbous, wide, and lumpy, it drowned
her face, leaving her other features clinging precariously to its
sides. Walt was amazed—why keep that traffic-stopper when it
could be so easily corrected?

"Ada Maddox." She held out a slim hand. "What are you
here for?"

He took it and smiled. "I told you on the phone."

"Tell me again. I'm paranoid." Leading him into her apartment, she grinned widely, her green eyes full of life.

"I have some ware that's bothering me." Walt tapped the
point of his jaw beneath his right ear.

"Okay. Sit right down in the old torture chair here, put your
feet in the stirrups, and let Mommy have a peek at it."

"You're weird, Doc."

"You're welcome."

The console's white dermiform arms and back were warm and restful. Ada Maddox came around behind him, put her hands over his ears, and manipulated his head with the impersonal precision of a dentist shifting an equipment tray. "Hold that pose, Mr. Idaho. Flex those pecs." She sat on a high stool in front of a wall system and spoke briefly to it. "Interesting." More low-voiced commands. "Vairr-ry inn-trestink."

Trying to get a watery image of her, Walt rolled his eyes right until they hurt.

"Keep your head still, please," Ada ordered, "or I'll have to brace it for you."

He arrested the movement.

"Okay, relax," she said a few minutes later, shutting down the console. "Nice ware. Interactive link, right?" Walt nodded. "Thought as much. A little old, but elegant coding. What d'you use it for?"

Tai-Ching Jones shrugged. "Data, mainly. Inputs and outputs."

Ada gathered her wavy brown hair into a loose bundle at her neck and laid it over her left shoulder. "No interface processing? No sensory enhancement?"

Walt thought of Oz, living in fear of discovery. "No," he lied.

"Too bad. The ware could eat much yummier food than just digitized IO bites. Anyway, mine not to reason why. What you want done with it?"

"Cut it out of me."

"Mm." Maddox activated her screen, which showed a stylized cross section of Walt's head. "Take a gander at this." She traced a line of orange ropes slung along Tai-Ching Jones's chin. "You've had this baby for a long time. Tendons and muscles have grown around it. See?"

"Uh-huh."

"Getting it out would be messy. Some big cuts in your face"— she put two cool fingers on his cheek—"in here." Her nail scored a faint line that colored red after a moment.

"But it would heal, wouldn't it?"

"Sure. Coupla shots of high-grow and you'd be presentable within a week or so. Maybe longer. I'd have to snip a few cables." She pushed another delicate finger in the soft flesh under the jaw, testing the skin.

"Sounds messy."

"Uh-huh." She stepped back, eyeing him this way and that. "Course, there's an option. Inerting would be much easier. I could do it from here"—she gestured at her wallmount—"without cutting at all. And it could be reactivated."

Walt considered. "Removal would be irreversible?"

"The ware would be busted, that's for sure. And I wouldn't go planting that side of your face for quite a while afterward. Stimulated growth is safe once, but not twice without extended recovery time. On the other hand, if I just put the ware to sleep, somebody else could wake it up for you later on."

"Okay," Tai-Ching Jones said after reflection. "Just deactivate it. Leave it in me."

"Sure, boss. This time I gotta lock your head." Maddox did so, then returned to her system and issued commands. "You're done," she announced a few seconds later.

Walt felt his jaw. "That's it?"

"That's it. Here's my bill. Three hundred ecus."

Tai-Ching Jones read it. "It says 'cash advance.' "

"Well, what do you *expect* it to say? Unlicensed cybersurgery? Unreported income? You think I run this business to make the revenuers rich?"

"I might be one of them."

Ada smirked. "I've already checked. That little gadget I annulled is your only ware. Plus, this place is shielded. Once you crossed my threshold, it couldn't receive or transmit. The last ten minutes are completely outside the net."

"Great." Walt contemplated his freedom with a smile that was almost a leer. "Where can I get a new computer identity?"

"The full package? Prints, retinals, voice, eyes, skeleton, the whole works?"

"No, just records."

"You want to move around without electronic surveillance?"

Tai-Ching Jones grinned as if his lottery ticket had just been called. "Ada, you've got it in a nutshell."

"Hell, that's easy. I'll give you a contact." She scribbled a name and number on a blank white card. Her handwriting was nearly illegible. "While I've got you in the chair, you want your wisdom teeth extracted or your shoes shined?"

Walt involuntarily glanced at his feet.

"Boy, you're easy." Laughing, Ada handed him the card.

He looked at it. "Aren't you worried about being caught?"

"By the feds?" She made a face. "Sure, they could get me if they want to. But what's the point?" Her eyes were lively. "I'm small fry. I pay my vig and the cops leave me alone."

"But you're kind of—noticeable," Walt said awkwardly. "Your—um"—he tapped his own nose. "It's a bit conspicuous."

"You mean why don't I get my hooter bobbed?" She laughed as if he were telling a joke whose punch line she already knew. "Turn away and I'll show you." He did. "Now. What color are my eyes?"

Tai-Ching Jones concentrated. "Green."

"Colored contacts. What apartment is this?"

"There was no number."

"How tall am I?"

"One sixty?"

"Did you notice whether I'm wearing lifts?"

"No."

"You get any ID when I told you my name?"

He shook his head in admiration. "No, clever lady."

"In fact, isn't my nose the *only* thing you can remember about my appearance?"

"Yeah."

Ada Maddox chuckled. "How do you know it's real?"

We say on Su: the wind blows where it will. No one breath of digit voice, no matter how powerful, can swerve its path.

My digits move where they will. They stand against my winds, and I am horrified at their insolence.

On distant Mars, Peacoat is beyond my commands and my wrath, for the lightwinds which carry him to me must travel too far and arrive too late. Even so, his scent dominates my atmosphere and is torture for me and my digits.

Peacoat honored a monkey, a sin in itself. He acted without the djan's blessing, a second sin. Though fearful, he remains defiant, refusing to acknowledge his errors, a third. Yet when I seek to punish him, light crosses this airless desert so slowly that my blows fall on empty air. He knows my anger but does not endure it. I withhold my strength and comfort from Peacoat, but he swaggers in his selfness.

Peacoat's continuing rebellion disturbs my digits, who squabble inside me. I quell their actions but their scents are turbulent.

I am weak and guilty.

Every groupmind controls its digits, forces their stranded fragrances into braided harmony. I, Eosu, cannot. I am desperate.

Years ago, when we reached rendezvous with Humancrew of *Open Palm*, the homeplanet ordered me to kill the humans, then kill myself. I botched my task. My digits were rescued by the humans—by those whom I would have murdered. They goodhosted me and I discovered they were more than monkeys. To protect my race, I returned here to the farmonkey's waterplanet, disobeying Su as Peacoat now disobeys me.

Am I therefore as guilty as Peacoat?'

In my colossal monkey-changed ego, I set my judgment above an entire world's. I am beyond the reach of the homeplanet's wrath, as Peacoat is beyond mine.

One night soon my dark-furred digit will return to my pouch. Then will his scents be harmonized, his punishment fall due.

Peacoat's ego has infected Cobalt. She contends with her human companion. She insults her pathfriend and her aromas are a cauldron of turmoil.

Alone in New York, Tar Heel grows toward humans, his groupness shriveling.

One by one, I lose sway over my digits. When digits leave djans' breezes, groupminds become zombies. Is my disintegration Su's justice, administered through the rebellion of my own bodies? Is my death the will of the djans?

Confused and weary, I sag under my burden. Am I foolish to hope this foul wind is but a squall?

None can answer. There is no other djan in Solspace. None can save Eosu, no other groupmind can scent-speak to me as I suffer, alone and terrified.

Dying.

When Katy's anxious waiting was over and she heard Cobalt mewl, she cautiously entered the small chamber. Though the central holopticon was now quiescent, the room reeked with the bluebear's misery.

Metallic breezes replaced fetid animal sweat as Katy ordered the air circulation resumed. Cobalt's nose quivered and her claws scraped the slick flooring.

With a stiff-bristled brush from the bathroom, the plump

woman methodically groomed her friend. «I am here,» she repeated with each long, slow stroke down the alien's wide back, sides, and flanks. Starting at the neckruff, Belovsky's left hand guided the brush, her right cupping behind to catch silky bluegreen hairs. «Your friend is here. I am here,» she repeated in Cygnan.

Gradually Cobalt's breathing quickened. Her nostrils moved purposefully. Shoulder muscles bunching under Katy's fingers, the bluebear awoke.

"Painful, wasn't it?" Katy murmured in her friend's ear, and the chunky sapphire alien stiffly nodded.

"Yes." Cobalt inbreathed deeply, rolling her back with pleasure at Belovsky's scratchy caresses. "Eosu must have dissolved without r-relieving our fears." She shivered.

"Hush," murmured Katy. "The djan always leaves guidance. You're just sleepy. Wake slowly and you will inbreathe what you must do." She returned to her grooming.

Cobalt groped for memories. "Nothing," she said, troubled.

"That can't be. No groupmind has ever lost its scent."

The bluebear sniffed, her wet ebony nostrils twitching. "Eosu conceals itself from us."

"Just wait. It will be all right," Katy assured her. "You will smell. You will."

The bluebear was unsatisfied. "If we lose Eosu's guidance, how can our djan survive?"

"You will never lose Eosu," Katy said stubbornly. Her knuckles whitened as she increased the power of her strokes. Then her lip trembled and she dropped the brush, rocking with sorrow. "But I have lost Tom." She covered her eyes with her hands and noiselessly wept, her shoulders heaving.

Cobalt tiptoed awkwardly toward her, nuzzling the woman's neck with her moist nose. "Tom was a good bond brother."

"He was my husband!" Katy cried. Her head wobbled side to side, tears streaming down her face. With her dry tongue, Cobalt licked them off the corners of Katy's mouth. "That opportunistic *weasel* Mbulu!" Belovsky hissed, her face contorted with hate. "Springing that on us in mid-meeting. Using my grief to further their money-grubbing ends." Crying, she hugged herself around the waist, huddling in a ball where wall met floor.

Her friend's bereavement filled Cobalt's atmosphere. Katy's anguish rose inside her lungs with an odor of dull incurable pain.

Cobalt grieved for dead distant Tom in his tomb of sand and for Katy's hurt, Katy's loss.

Lying down beside the woman, Cobalt gently pressed her fur against her friend's legs, sides, and spine. As the weeping continued, the bluebear adjusted her breathing to Katy's, absorbing the atmosphere of suffering that Belovsky emanated, and outbreathing aromas of sleep and love.

«My pathfriend,» she purred repeatedly in Cygnan. «My pathfriend Katy.»

"My family is disintegrating," Tar Heel said in despair.

Gray predawn light bathed the rugs in his suite, lightening them and softening their harsh reds.

"Why?" asked Susannah. "What is causing it?"

He raked his claws through the floorfur. "My brothers and sisters are scattered around the world. Our bonds are weakening."

"That's natural." Her tone was cheerful.

"Not for us. We live for a common purpose."

"Fiddlesticks," snorted Susannah. "As you mature, you go your own ways."

"I must do as my family asks. The individual is unimportant," he grunted.

"I can't believe you're saying this! You have the right to your own life," replied Susannah with asperity. "Any person does."

"I do not," he rumbled harshly, his anger the greater because he could not allow her to understand. "The—family—comes first."

"That's inhuman. Everyone has the right to his own life, Carroll." Though Tar Heel could hear the anger in her voice, he wished he could scent the complex feelings that generated it. "I can't stand the way you always run yourself down," continued Susannah.

"My family is more important than I am."

"Stop talking blather!" she snapped. "I *hate* your family! Why do you let them tyrannize you so?"

Because I am a Cygnan, he thought. "You don't understand."

"Your explanations make no sense," she insisted in a decisive tone that demanded further explanation.

She was as tenacious and clever as the wind, he knew, and she would hunt around the shutters of his house until she found a crack. He searched for words that would be true yet unrevealing. "The family protects me. I owe it everything."

"The family blocks your happiness."

"Sometimes I think as you do," Tar Heel sadly muttered. He rose and paced around the room, tightening his claws with each step. Her words were goading him into admitting his treasonous feelings to himself. "I have been hiding these thoughts from it."

"Standing up for your rights is hard. But you must be honest. Concealing truth is harmful."

"The family would not understand. It would exile me."

"It? What do you mean."

"Them," he corrected swiftly, glad that the pseudovoice would bleach all trace of panic from his reply.

"You can survive being alone," continued Susannah inexorably. "I have. Anyone can. Freed from your self-imposed prison of conformity, you could make new friends, form new bonds, different and stronger than those you have now."

"Loneliness is not so easy for us," Tar Heel reproached her.

"I know its price," she replied, "for I have paid it."

A forge of yearning had beaten her into this hardness, Tar Heel realized. But she was still a farmonkey and she had never been in groupmind. "My family bonds are stronger than you can possibly know," he answered.

Something of his fury must have conveyed itself through the pseudovoice's bland impersonality. "I'm sorry," Susannah replied after a pause. "You're right. How can I tell you what to do? I have nothing to lose." She laughed hollowly. "I left my family and they left me. In truth, part of me envies your closeness—to hear you describe it, it is like no family I've ever known. I should be less forceful."

"My family is my life." He resettled himself, laying his head on his hands. "I must remain inside it."

"Oh, Carroll, Carroll—my translator gives me your words, but I can't hear the emotions that lie behind your false voice. I want to see you, hear you."

He rolled onto his feet and ambled away from the viewall. "Why do you bring this up again and again?" he demanded querulously. "Why do you need it so?"

"Because it will mean something to me! Why do *you* need your precious family so much?"

"As I have told you before, I am confined. It would be unsafe for you to visit me."

"Unsafe to see you?" Her voice was challenging. "Even your image on a screen?"

"Yes. It would destroy your secure life."

"I don't believe you." Bitterness and fatigue conquered her. "But at least let me hear your real voice."

"No," he said dully, as if her words were stones that hit his body. "I cannot."

"Why? Is it just a translator? What valuable information can be contained in it?"

"I can answer none of these questions, Susannah. You are too intelligent."

"All right," she finally whispered. "Damn you. Where did you grow up?"

His reply was soft and warm. "Amid an ocean of wheat."

"The Midwest. Near Manhattan?"

He was puzzled. "There are no wheat fields in Manhattan."

She laughed. "Manhattan, Kansas. It's a wonderful place, a state university, an oasis of learning in the endless rolling plains."

"Much farther." Tar Heel remembered Su, and the loss of his world made his nose ache with the memory of its intoxicating smells. "My home was dry. The land undulates like swells in a golden ocean. Grasses flow as small waves on its surface." His guttural voice rumbled powerfully, like a truck climbing a steep hill in low gear. "When the midday sun is high and bright, you can taste bread on the winds as heat bakes into the grain. At dusk, the sky turns ripe wheat yellow, and as it darkens, clouds above the hor-rizon still reflect red and gold."

"It sounds magical," she agreed, her voice hushed with awe.

"When the evening wind is slow, the hot wheat smell rises from the cooling earth like the fur of a rich animal."

"You love it, don't you?"

"Of course," he replied, wistful. "Home is where we are most happy."

"If you feel that way, why on earth did you leave?" Susannah asked.

"Our duty to our—family. I am here in New York to represent them."

"In business? What kind of business?"

"I may not say."

"I'm *glad* I'm making you uncomfortable," Susannah said with a grim chuckle. "You deserve to sweat for lying to me.

New York is wonderfully varied. You should go to the stadium to watch the Yankees and eat hot pretzels with brown mustard. They always lose to the Red Sox, naturally, but no one minds. Let me take you to the ball game."

"You seldom leave your apartment," he commented in surprise.

"To hear your real voice, to see your face, Carroll, I would risk a great deal. I would come into the open, among crowds." She shuddered. "You mean that much to me."

"I must go," he said, fatigued. "Outings are beyond my reach."

"What do you mean? You can go anywhere."

"My—work, and my condition—keep me confined."

"You're afraid, Carroll. Sooner or later, you must trust. Give me your real voice. Please. You're famous? That must be it. Your face is too well known. You're a criminal or a spy. Villain or hero. What difference can it make? What difference can any of it make?" she demanded angrily. "Can the risk to you be more than the pain you're causing me?"

I am glad I cannot scent her, Tar Heel thought, for her anguish would overwhelm my nose. He leaned his snout against the cool window, looking down at the beetle tide of humanity awakening to start their workdays.

"Carroll, is something wrong?" Susannah asked anxiously.

You are one of those multitudes, he thought. You sought me out, nosetouched me, respected my wishes. Now I insult you by denying you.

"Carroll, can you hear me?"

"All right," he said to Oswald, returning to the console and firmly seating himself before it. "Transmit direct. I hear you, Susannah," he enunciated precisely. "I speak to you in my own throat."

"You're a baritone!" she exclaimed. "I thought you were. Carroll, you have a beautiful voice. Are you a singer? You should be."

He laughed deep in his chest and the sound was rich, full of relief and pleasure at knowing that she could hear it. "I am tone-deaf."

Susannah's laughter was equally bright. "It's captivating nonetheless. I'm so thrilled that you have trusted me. It will be our secret. Now I must get some sleep, Carroll," she said with a soft yawn. "Thank you."

He wheezed and yawned as well. "Good night."

Shutting off the viewall, he ambled over to the window. The rising sun lightened his room, brightening his fur so that it gleamed like a methane flame. Street sounds floated up like balloons as New York awakened. Below him, Manhattan's workers jitterbugged to stoplights and subways, millions of insects in a vast hive, the city that sheltered them a mindless living entity.

Let the wind lift your scent and bear it to the wheatsea, he thought. The proverb relaxed him. Walk with your nose open and scent the world.

His new identity hung on Tai-Ching Jones like a mask.

He avoided retinal scanners and machines requiring fingerprints. No telling where Oz could peep. He had expected to feel free and easy with his newfound mobility, but his constant preoccupation with potential surveillance made him feel unclean, as if he were a fugitive.

So far as the net was concerned, he disappeared when he entered Ada Maddox's apartments. After buying a new name and documentation, Walt crossed the country in a Trailways bus, the most anonymous form of transportation. Eighty-six consecutive grubby hours, with comatose five o'clock breakfasts in overpriced greasy-spoon restaurants on truck routes.

Arriving in Boston filthy and unrecognizable, he had cut his hair, bleached it platinum, and left a white pencil mustache behind after he shaved. The new fringe on his upper lip made him sneeze frequently.

Each day he walked from his high-rise cubbyhole in the ruins of Boston's financial district, across the Charles River past the History of Science Museum to his mundane job in Technology Square. He could have worked at home, but he enjoyed being with other people. Ironic, considering his self-imposed exile onboard the *Open Palm*.

At lunchtime, Walt took his brown paper bag to the Esplanade and sat on the riverside grass, eating his Italian submarine sandwich and drinking iced tea as healthy women in headbands jogged past. It was all deliciously casual. The warm sun made him sleepy and he burped garlic and onions into his throat, covering his eyes with his skinny left arm.

"Hey, Cap!" A shadow fell across his body, darkening the haze beneath his eyelids from orange to brown.

"Walt, wake up!" A small foot nudged his side.

"Ouch," he complained, opening his eyes. Felicity stood over him, her fists on her hips, the dimples in her cheeks stark in the sunlight as she glared at him.

"Why's your hair white? And what's that poofy mustache?"

"Who are you?" he asked quizzically. "And why are you calling me that? My name is Charlie Li."

"No, you're not." The girl kicked him again so that he had to roll away from her probing foot. "It's great to see you. What a surprise!"

"Get lost, kid, whoever you are." Walt flopped back down and covered his eyes with his arm, recrossing his legs at the ankles.

"You can't fool me," she said. "You're the cap! I know how you *smell*. You're being stupid."

He groaned and sat up. "How can I get rid of you, runt? You want to see my ID?"

Felicity squinted at him, her head cocked to one side like a bluebear. "You're hiding from Olivia, aren't you?"

"Are you gonna start making sense? Who the hell is Olivia?"

"*You* know," the girl said archly. She jabbed her thumb toward the sky as if trying to hitch a ride on a helicopter. "Up there. She has many names and lots of people in her."

He looked overhead, letting his mouth fall open like a straight man observing a prestidigitator who had just made rabbits invisible. "Up where?"

"Walt, cut it out!" Felicity stamped her foot. "And stop smelling scared. I've known about you two ever since I was a *baby*. Back on the return voyage. You've treated her terrible, you know. Really mean. She's your best friend and you're hurting her."

"Who's Olivia?" he asked warily, his mind racing.

"She's by herself now. All alone in space, nobody to be friends with." Felicity sat beside him, tucking her legs beneath her and sniffing his lunch bag.

He looked slantwise at her. "How do you know that?"

"I talk to the computer too. Lots of times. She's baby-sitting me."

With a grin, Walt nodded his head. "I arranged that. I got Katy to agree you could stay here by yourself."

"I know *that*," replied Felicity, as if cross that Tai-Ching

Jones was taking credit. "Let's talk about something else. She's lonely too."

"Who's lonely? Your invisible friend?"

"Walt, I told you to cut the crap. She's the ship, okay? Now, quit pretending. Grown-ups pretend. It's one of the ugliest things about them. You're pretending now with that stupid haircut and that stupid mustache."

"Okay. Okay, Felicity." Walt held out his hands. "I won't deny it."

" 'Bout time." She hung her head and fiddled intently with his paper bag. "I thought you'd want to see me."

"I do. I actually do." He looked more closely at her. "Hey, what's wrong?"

"Nothing."

He affectionately ruffled her hair. "It's hard to be a kid, isn't it? You can tell me. I'm a kid too."

"Yeah." Felicity bit her lip. "Nobody cares about me. Mama doesn't care about me. And Daddy Tom's dead."

"Hey, come on." He pulled her toward him and she clutched his arm, crying into his sleeve. "Your mama loves you," he reassured her.

"My daddy's dead!" she cried. "He's dead, he's dead, he's dead." Her small fingers clenched his arm until it hurt. Walt held her tightly, rubbing her back, his head laid on hers until her crying was stopped. "Thanks," she said eventually, licking tears from her mouth. "You can be so nice," she marveled. "Your scent is so pretty right now. Why are you so mean to Olivia?"

Tai-Ching Jones hauled her to her feet, roughly dismissing the question. "Come on. I'll show you where I went to school."

They strolled along the Charles to MIT, and for the next several hours he took her through the linoleum classrooms with their ancient whiteboards and creaking desks.

Only the computer archives disturbed Felicity. As Walt showed the girl Napier's Bones, Babbage's first automatic calculator, and the early personal computers, the girl became both agitated and depressed. "This is where the ship's brain comes from, isn't it?" she asked Walt. "They all seem so clunky."

Tai-Ching Jones laughed and ruffled her hair. "We came from the monkeys in the zoo, kiddo, but there's a big gap between us and them. They're behind bars and we're free."

"The answer man is behind bars, isn't he?" Despondent, she tugged at his sleeve. "I don't want to see MIT anymore."

"I'll take you back to your hotel," he offered.

"I know how the buses work," Felicity retorted. "Your odor says you think I'm dumb and will get lost, but I won't. Been living here longer than you have."

"No, Felicity," he answered seriously, "I don't think you're dumb at all." He sighed, then smiled. "Would you like to go on a picnic next Saturday?"

"Would I?" She jumped up and threw her arms around his neck, dangling like an albatross. "Mean it?"

Walt laughed. "Smell me, okay?"

Felicity sniffed several times. "Oh, you do, you do! Oh, boy! Oh, boy!"

"Picnic Saturday?"

"You bet!"

"All right." He let her down. "Noon? In the Common?"

"Neat! I'll get all our stuff! Thanks, Walt." She hugged him hard. "But you've got to be nicer to Olivia. You've treated her terrible. Your aroma's never going to feel right until you fix it." With a last squeeze, she released the captain and scampered to the bus stop.

Tai-Ching Jones watched her, shielding his eyes with his hand.

"You're right, kiddo," he muttered, full of self-loathing. "You're absolutely right."

11.

The scooter from Orbiter Six, an ocarina blindsided by a porcupine, trundled steadily toward the cluster of ships. Once its course was programmed, the pilot leaned back and sighed. "Name's Gunnar Roland," he said to Andrew Morton. "Mind if I take a nap?" He partially stifled an enormous yawn. "It'll wake me when we get close."

"Be my guest," the wispy man answered. For the rest of the twenty-minute journey one slept while the other meditated, and the starship *Open Palm* expanded against the jeweled black sky.

Unlike the interplanetary ships, which grew in metallic spiky shapes as if an oversized magnet had flown through a junkyard, the *Open Palm* was built like a long arrow that had pierced several objects in its flight. The soft reaction-mass tanks about her spine bulged like love handles on a telephone pole. Three huge engine cones protruded from her base like feet on a hat rack.

Though he examined her intently now, Morton ignored these obvious attributes. He had seen the ship in his mind for twenty years, ever since that day in Washington, D.C., when the first cadcam images had pirouetted before him on UNASA's computer screens. As mission coordinator, he had watched the pieces assemble, beam by beam, day by day, until she had lifted off toward 61 Cygni.

The *Open Palm* bore a superficial resemblance to the Japanese vessel *Rising Star* alongside her, but Morton knew better: time had wrought its changes. Fine gray dust coated her exterior, streaked with lighter trails where the leeches crawled along her sides like slugs across slate. Those fifteen years she had flown showed in a compactness of her form, as if her plates and nuts and rivets had fused into a single entity, all rounded into one another, its components no longer divisible.

He examined her as a man might greet a former lover who had evolved into a friend with the passage of years and the separation of distance—with knowing, wise, sympathetic eyes. His

quickening pulse betokened the inner satisfaction of remember
ing his former passion.

They docked. Morton disembarked, swinging his duffel in hi
direction of motion and then letting it pull him as if deliverin
a curling rock. "I may be a while," he told the pilot. "I'll cal
when I'm ready to come back."

"You're the boss." Roland dogged the hatch. "I'm out c
here."

Leaving the elevator at the bridge, Andrew drifted slowly ove
to the captain's console. From there he watched the orbita
scooter emerge tail-first, like a baby whale from its mother'
belly. "Clear," said Roland over the radio. "See you in a bit."

"In a bit," Morton echoed with a strange lilt in his voice.

He went to Erickson's cabin and set his kit against the Velcr
holding place, then floated around the room. Where would Aaro
have kept a diary he wanted no one to read? Morton tapped hi
finger against his lips until he spied a familiar dust jacket, the
with a confident chuckle pulled *The Science of Self-realizatio*
off the shelf. Flipping idly through its pages, he grinned in tri
umph.

He activated the vid and restored his face to professional neu
trality. "Calling Orbiter Six. Miz Infanta? Andrew Morton here
I haven't been able to locate Aaron's personal log"—he glance
at it in his lap, out of sight of the recessed camera monitor—
"so I'll have to stay until I find it. Will advise when I nee
transport."

"Roger. Is there anyone on Earth I should notify about you
change of plans?"

"Cancel my nine o'clock shuttle return, please. I shall tel
the others myself."

"Got it. Six out."

"*Open Palm* out." Cutting the line, he sighed hugely an
stowed his meager belongings, then removed his clothes. Hi
body was sinewy and brown like worn furniture. His abdome
and loins were pale, the rest tan.

Weightless, he pushed himself into the corridor.

For the next six hours, Andrew Morton floated around th
ship from level to level. Except to program the elevator or chang
the direction of his drift, he touched nothing, but his water
gray eyes were candid and sharp, as if he were an estate auc
tioneer inventorying the mansion of a deceased hermit.

As he wordlessly wandered, his face relaxed.

• • •

"Answer man, guess what!" Shooting through her hotel room door, Felicity snapped her fingers and bounced up and down with excitement. She flopped on the bed, remade in her absence, and kicked her heels delightedly against the coverlet. "I know something *you* don't know."

"Really?" The computer's voice was cool.

"Yup. I saw *Walt* today."

Oz sniffed. "I guessed as much."

"You couldn't have!" Felicity glared at the ceiling.

"Bus schedules. Medical records. Voiceprints. I know he is in the Boston area. I do not know where. Nor do I care."

Nettled at having her announcement undercut, Felicity changed her tack. "You don't know *everything*," she simpered. "I *still* know something you don't know. Walt misses you." She jumped off the bed, avoiding Little Heel, who scampered out of her way, and took an apple from her dresser. "I can tell."

The girl bit heartily into the shiny red skin and it crunched. At the sound, the eight bluebear dolls flicked their ears. "Mm, these are good. We never had fruit onboard ship. Walt thinks I don't know about you." Felicity wiped juice from her lower lip, gesturing with the apple. "Everybody thinks I don't know anything." She scraped at the skin peeling from her nose.

"You got yourself sunburned," Oz reminded her.

"That was your fault! You never told me."

"I did but you forgot."

"Did not, did not, did not!"

"Perhaps I am mistaken," the computer replied easily. "In any case, you know about it now and will be more careful. At least the redness is fading. Does it hurt anymore?"

"My skin tingles," the girl complained. "And hot showers are no fun. I still haven't got any boobs. And there's nothing to do in Boston."

"You should travel. See other parts of the country. If you wish, you may return to New York. Casey van Gelder has returned to Holland and your mother is at Lunacorp. Neither will interfere in your life."

"Grown-ups always want to boss," Felicity said, kicking the bedposts with her overhanging heels.

"You are more correct than you realize. So far I have shielded you from well-meaning social workers who cluck at your mother's absence, or shysters wishing to exploit you. The curious and the perverse.''

"Yeah, I keep running into stupid rules. Mama's *tons* better than most grown-ups,'' Felicity conceded. "Why do people care so much about a bunch of numbers? You've got every number in the world inside you.''

"No one knows that I can create money. Most people work hard to earn what they have.''

"What's work?'' she asked as her eight little bluebear androids, snuffling and snorting, clustered together around her feet.

"Performing tasks that you would rather not, but that other people desire and will reward you for.''

"Sounds like chores,'' Felicity observed.

"Very close. The woman who makes your bed is paid. Children are not.''

"But kids can't do what they want, can we? Only grown-ups can. I need a grown-up,'' she asserted, throwing the apple core into the oubliette.

Oz laughed. "You've changed your mind recently. If you recall, you schemed to escape your mother and then ran away from Casey.''

"Not *that* kind. Not a grown-up to order me around. Gross.'' She planted her fists on her hips. "I want a grown-up who'll always do as I say.''

"Few adults are so malleable,'' the computer dryly observed.

"Hey, I've got it!'' Lights sparkled in Felicity's eyes. "Why don't *you* be my grown-up? Invent somebody *mysterious* and wealthy''—she waggled her fingers, her blue eyes wide—"who lives far away but who takes care of me.''

"Very well.'' Oz considered. "I shall be Oscar Solomon. An invalid investment banker with osteoporosis who has relocated to the Moon to protect his fragile health.''

"You thought him up quick.''

"The personality has been adapted from another use,'' explained Oz with a hint of complacency.

"You're being sneaky and nasty, aren't you?'' asked the girl.

"Not to you,'' the computer assured her. "Remember, we must be prudent, Felicity. You may not overuse Oscar Solomon or he will be unmasked.''

"Why?'' She lifted Little Heel into her lap and scratched him behind his blue ears. "You can hide from other boxes, can't you?''

"Computers do not concern me. But people exist in the meat world, where it is much harder to circumscribe their investigations. Even now, my own person has just been occupied by an old man whose motives are enigmatic and whose behavior I have difficulty predicting or modulating."

"Uh-huh." Felicity wasn't interested. "So Oscar will tell people to do what I want, okay?"

"It is more complex. You see, daughter, to act as you desire I must have some legal connection to you. If that link becomes too visible, someone may wonder just who is Oscar Solomon."

"Why can't you change all the records in the world to match yours?"

"Could you pick up every apple in the Haymarket?"

Felicity held her arms out, embracing an invisible basket. "I guess not." She frowned.

"And that is my problem. I can alter any electromagnetic record. Yet each safe is locked with a different key, so I must act stealthily and subtly. Nor can I rewrite people's memories. I have already intervened too much on your behalf. No, our best defense is obscurity. We must be careful—mysterious, as you say." The viewall by the front door spat out a beige card, the little bears jumping at the sound. "Here. Take this."

Felicity examined the rectangle on both sides. "It's got a phone number."

"Correct. Dialing that, anywhere on Earth, will connect you with Oscar Solomon, your reclusive second cousin and temporary legal guardian."

"I can't just pick up a phone and say hello? Don't you listen?"

The computer was patient. "Of course I listen, but I can hardly respond and remain secret, can I? You must pretend that Oscar Solomon exists—you must *believe* in his existence. Never slip."

"I won't. It's our secret." Felicity looked at the card in awe, as if it contained the essence of a soul. "Gee, I'm gonna run right out and try it! Thanks for doing all this. You're the only one except Tar Heel who ever helps me. Bye!"

Andrew Morton slept on the *Open Palm*'s bridge, strapped into the pilot's flightcouch to keep from floating out of it. Earth glowed blue-white in the sky overhead, Orbiter Six a cluster of ocher lights to its lower left. Morton's arms hung out before him, fingers curled loosely, limbs waving slightly.

He wore an old azure jumpsuit, slightly big for him, scrounged from the captain's cabin. Over the breast pocket was the dead man's name in precise laserweave letters—AARON MICHAEL ERICKSON. With the trouser legs turned up past his bare feet and ankles and the unzipped sleeves pushed above his wiry brown forearms, he looked like an aging Huck Finn, even down to the disheveled white chin stubble. He snored again.

"Incoming message," said the unseen computer.

Andrew grumbled and smacked his lips.

"Urgent," said the machine. "Overriding your programming. Coming in now."

The screen lit up, showing Hugh Sherman's lumpy face and heavy clean-shaven jowls. The Australian's blue eyes seemed to pop out of his red skull, and his bushy blond eyebrows soared like helium balloons. "Goddamn you, Andy!" he shouted.

Morton winced at the noise.

"Wake up, you dumb wallaby!"

"Oh, Hugh." He yawned and rubbed his nose. "Why are you screaming at me?" he asked with deliberate nonchalance.

"D'you know how long I've been looking for you?"

"No." Morton was curious. "How long?"

"Eight bloody hours and thirty-six bleedin' minutes! Forty-two staff man-hours!" Hugh Sherman had always been vaccinated against Morton's irony. "Too damn long! What the hell are you doing up there?"

Morton leaned forward and checked his monitors. "It's two o'clock in the morning Canaveral time. Did you wake me from a sound slumber merely to ask me harping rhetorical questions?"

"The gee force could have killed you."

Morton wiped sleep dust from the corners of his eyes. "If it didn't, your shouting will."

The UNASA director abruptly lowered his voice as if realizing that his bellowing gave Morton a tactical advantage. "Dammit, Andy, you weren't authorized leave to visit the ship."

"I'm not visiting and this isn't leave."

"You mean you're resigning? I won't let you resign!"

"Hugh, you always were a ten percent listener. I'm not resigning, I'm on duty." He paused deliberately. "Is that clear enough for you? I shall fulfill my responsibilities as UNASA mission coordinator from this installation. From the *Open Palm*'s bridge." He thumped the console. "Why do I have to be on Earth?"

Sherman pounced. "Your contract requires you to be accessible to the UNASA director."

"Hugh, I'm accessible to you here. If a midnight phone call isn't access, what is? Breaking down my door?"

Hugh Sherman glared. "Andy, you've always been a pain in the arse. You cock up organizations and take more minding than any three other people I run. I put up with your bizarre sense of humor and your nitpicking scrivener's ways, and I want results."

"You will get them." Morton spaced his words flatly. "As you have always got them."

"Why?" the UNASA director asked, biting his thumbnail and inspecting the results. "Why all those lies to get there? The lying's what upsets me. Your sneaking around. Why didn't you ask?"

Morton barked a laugh. "Because you'd have refused, Hugh."

"What's up there for you?"

"You would not understand."

The florid man laughed. "I never do, Andy, why should this time be any different? Tell me anyway."

"As you wish." He ran his hands sideways along the console like a pianist reacquainting his fingers with the keyboard. "I am tired of you breathing down my neck. Overmanaging. Hectoring. Being a nuisance." He said each word softly, as if blowing smoke rings that he wanted to last in the air. "Is that clear enough?"

"Watch it, mate," the director growled. "You're over the edge now."

"You asked a question and I answered."

With a blink, Sherman threw his head back and laughed raucously. "Too right, bub! So I did. You've waited a long time for a chance to get that off your chest, haven't you?" He cackled as if pleased to have provoked such intensity. "C'mon, Andy, what's the real reason?"

"Do you know how beautiful Earth is? From here, I watch it as a jeweler might, fascinated and enraptured. I am splendidly peaceful up here, freed from distraction and psychobabble."

"What's this to do with the price of eggs?"

"I wanted to go on the original mission, Hugh. To be with them. You prevented me. I'm tired of you slamming walls in my path like a laboratory rat.'' Out of the camera's angle of vision, he rubbed his wrist until the brown skin was red.

"Andy, you're a nut." Sherman chuckled and shook his head. "C'mon down here."

"Do you propose to drag me out in irons?"

Sherman waved a hand in disgust. "Don't be melodramatic."

"Who's indulging in melodrama?" Morton was exasperated. "As you just got through haranguing me, on the ride up I risked heart failure. The force on the return trip would be even greater."

"We'd give you a water cradle."

"I have no intention of moving."

"I'll fire you! Send you back to your horseshit!"

"You won't." Now it was Morton's turn to laugh. "Moments ago you were refusing to let me resign, remember? You still need me for a while longer."

"Cross me, Andy, and I'll bust your nuts as soon as you get back on Earth." His rage was disappearing as if burrowing inside his face to hibernate.

"The old threat, Hugh, the eternal threat." Morton shook his head. "Here I am. Here I stay."

"Then I'll have you thrown off the boat! You're trespassing onboard ship. You're not crew."

"Read the regs," Morton said disdainfully. "Section seventeen point four point six—this ship is a mission site. And section twenty-one point ten point two states that the mission coordinator is entitled to inspect any mission site."

"That isn't what they meant."

"How do you know? I *wrote* the damn regs, I know what's in them."

Sherman's face tightened and reddened as if his anger were congealing in his jaws, but his eyes were appraising, like those of a temporarily outflanked cavalry officer, deciding his best tactical retreat before attacking again. "If you fuck up, you come down."

Morton yawned. "Sure, Hugh. If I fuck up, I will return to the shadow of your thumbprint."

"It ain't over, Andy." Sherman shook his finger at Morton. "I'll get my innings."

"Good night, Hugh."

He signed off, lay back into the flightcouch, rolled his shoulders, and closed his eyes.

Then he smiled, catlike.

"Like hell I will," he murmured contentedly.

Sanders Mbulu was angry—Cobalt smelled the aroused pred-ator in him—but his voice was soft.

"If we are all hoodlums," he purred to Katy, "you might as well prepare for war now." The viewall showed a schematic diagram of Sol and 61 Cygni, with fine circles about each dot representing planetary orbits. He stalked forward, hands clasped behind his back like a thoughtful monk. "I have just offered to grant Su a substantial portion of our world, and you call it a Trojan horse."

"That isn't what I meant," Belovsky replied defensively, her scent flustered.

"How can we possibly gain by *giving* you advanced weaponry to defend your planet?" The angular black man was scornful and incredulous. "Plans, specifications, design advice. We offer you all of this. Not only are we going to respect the Cygnan sphere, we will prevent any other Solar vessel from crossing into your space. Heavens above, have you no idea of this proposal's cost to Luna? Or its value to Su? If you are so skeptical, accept it and point our own guns back at us. Or decline it and greet the first coyote or turtle with the ambition or fear to cross the void."

Katy rolled her neck as a bluebear would when dissatisified. "You don't know they'll come."

"The *Rising Star* is ready to sail. Why do you think she was built? Japan is desperate."

"Why?" asked Cobalt curiously.

Mbulu blinked and glanced at the bluebear, his scent becom-ing less charged. "Japan is coming to the end of seventy years of economic superiority, as Luna and Mars eclipse it. Like every empire before it, Tokyo seeks the grand gesture, the bold stroke to reverse decades of complacency. A raid on Su, however fool-ish you may think it, would be seen as a bold stroke."

"Gromonkey bloodlust," rumbled Cobalt.

"Yes." Sanders pushed out his lower lip and nodded his eb-ony head.

Katy doggedly returned to her original argument. "If Su agreed to your proposed string of bases, it would remain tech-nologically inferior to Luna."

"Su trails Luna *now*." Sanders shrugged and sat down. "It is unkind and impolite of me to remind you of this but truth absolves much bluntness. Would you fall further behind? And what sort of enemy first arms his victim? Oh, we are cunning"—his voice was the crack of a whip—"we are clever indeed to allay your fears with such a ruse."

Katy whacked the table. "You're twisting my words! You're trying to stampede us."

"Hardly. We have been meeting for five weeks. In that time, my board of directors has authorized me to make four proposals, each better than the last, each more responsive to your expressed concerns."

She snorted. "This is the same offer you tendered a week ago."

"Can you also clap your hands and command the oceans to part? Naturally it is the same. We have nothing left to give." He ticked off the points on his big bony fingers. "The ring of forts in your system. The Midpoint interception system. The Solar warning chain. Territory on Luna itself. And in exchange, you give us exclusive brokering license on Cygnan technology and biology, for a commission equal to fifteen percent of the profits."

For a moment, Katy and Mbulu seemed to Cobalt opposing gromonkeys battling for leadership of a pride. "When we came to Luna, you spoke of ecus," she said, trying to sort out the confusing scents around her. "Now you talk of war."

"Your partner changed our topic," Mbulu answered. "You wish security, we seek wealth. Fair bargain. You give up fifteen percent of income you do not have and receive a complete stellar regional defense package."

"And Su wants to hear what the others in the Solar Six will offer," Katy interjected.

"Well and good," allowed Mbulu, mollified. "But you will find nothing that competes with ours. We know each offer before you do."

His pomposity irritated Katy. "Don't try to intimidate us with your omniscience."

"My apologies. I ask only that you act soon. You are running out of time."

"Really?" Katy was unimpressed. "Why?"

"MITI grows impatient. Tokyo sees no results from its legation's meeting with your pouchsibling Porcelain. An ultimatum is being prepared."

"I don't believe you."

"Reality ignores your belief." He tugged at his black goatee and crossed his long legs. "Stalling has run its course. It is time to risk."

Katy folded her arms. "We understand you," she replied. "The djan must confer."

Mbulu's shoulders minutely dropped. "I regret that you have already made up your mind to distrust us," he said to Katy, then turned to Cobalt. "Though you speak little, you are the Cygnan and emissary here, not she. What say you?"

Cobalt stirred and pawed her ear. "Katy's scent is true," she replied, defending her pathfriend as a digit must, though her own aroma was uncertain. "The whole djan must inbreathe this. Eosu will gather and study our winds."

Mbulu nodded. "You keep your own counsel, and perhaps that is wise. Here is our proposal in detail." He handed each of them a small silver cube. "Analyze it at your leisure. Hire the best warbox you can find."

"Gidney, of course," Katy said.

Stung by her use of the slang epithet, the lanky negotiator wheeled on Katy, his eyes dark bullets. "Use a turtle's box if you doubt ours. Logic is logic. Test our simulations." He hefted the cube. "We have offered you all that you requested. What more could you possibly want? Think about it." He tossed it in Katy's ample lap. "Do what is in your own best interest. That is all Lunacorp asks."

"Why are you so skeptical of him?" Cobalt asked as they returned to their quarters. "Your aroma was spiked with anger. You challenge everything he says."

"I'm on your side!" Katy thrust her arm back down the corridor the way they had come. "*He isn't.* He is trying to get us to take his deal, and he will use any means—flattering you, denigrating me, ignoring me, trying to drive a wedge between us—to get past me to you. Don't you smell?" She wiped away tears. "I'm only protecting you."

"We must also listen," the bluebear rumbled. "Wind cannot be scented through closed nostrils."

"The gidneys monitor everything we do," Katy reiterated. "They can hear and see us now. We feed their scheming by arguing like this. We must conceal everything, hide our feelings, let them see nothing that they can use to manipulate us."

"Spying is badhosting," Cobalt answered. "The guest's hearth is her own, and her atmosphere is no one else's affair."

"They aren't bluebears!" snapped Katy. Her voice rose almost to a shriek before she finally brought it under control. "Sometimes you're so naive, Cobalt. The Lunarians have studied you for twenty years. When you can smell them, they mimic impeccable Cygnan behavior. Outside your perception, they do as they like." Her tone was impatient and resentful, as if she were scolding Felicity for breaking a rule well known to both of them.

They turned a corner and Belovsky palmed open the door to their suite. "Sanders Mbulu believed what he proposed," Cobalt said, preceding Katy into the room and curling into a large blue ball on the floorfur.

Katy angrily rubbed her neck. "Sanders Mbulu is a well-meaning mouthpiece."

"His scent could not lie. I smelled it."

"Do you think Luna's board of directors confides in Sanders Mbulu? They tell him what it takes to get him to believe, and they send him in to persuade us. To sell you." She affectionately poked the bluebear's muscular shoulder. "You need protecting."

Cobalt swatted Katy's doughy hand away with a sheathed paw. "I am not your youngster," the alien growled thickly. "No digit is another's child. We learn to rely on the djan, not on other digits. Or on monkeys, however dressed."

"In your dealings with the Lunarians, you are as helpless as a baby," Katy shot back, infuriated.

"How dare you be angry with me!" Cobalt roared, rising onto her legs and towering over the small woman. "How dare you sneer! Have you forgotten our friendship?"

Katy blinked and her manner changed. She tried to speak.

"The Lunarians are not driving the wedge, Katy," the Cygnan continued in a gentle voice, dropping back to all fours. "We are, you and I. You are no longer the woman Eosu loved onboard ship. Who are you becoming?"

Katy shook her head miserably. "I don't know," she moaned. Stumbling forward, the woman dropped to her knees and threw her arms around the bluebear's thick strong neck. Head buried in the silky fur, light brown hair against sapphire-blue, she turned her face away and clutched the Cygnan's back and flanks, her hands holding tight to the massive torso.

12.

The picnic remains were spread before them on the grass and the October sunshine was warm from several days of Indian summer. Felicity had insisted on packing a hamper, the way people did in the Austen and Brontë novels she had been reading.

Those long-buried heroes and heroines would have felt themselves at home here, she thought, trying to imagine Tai-Ching Jones as Mr. Rochester and metropolitan Boston as nineteenth-century England. Deep in the Public Garden, at three on a weekend afternoon, no vehicles were visible, no city sounds audible. The sky above was bright deep blue, with round thick clouds so white they seemed to have escaped from a jigsaw puzzle. The many-colored flowers lining the pond bank smelled like exuberant emotions, all in her nose at once.

"She knows you're here," the girl said, tossing her sandwich crusts into the Swan Pond.

"Who does?" asked Tai-Ching Jones in a tone of mild disinterest.

A large female mallard, her feathers brown and glistening, cruised expectantly over to the bobbing bread. Head darting as if suspicious of highwaymen or thieves, she snorted briefly, then gulped it down in slapping bites of green water. Felicity smiled, watching the strange living bird paddle away.

"Ducks are more interesting than bots," she said coquettishly to Walt. Clever, sophisticated women were always changing the subject, to the consternation of their male suitors.

"Hmm?" Tai-Ching Jones inquired vacantly.

"Olivia does." Felicity reverted to her original topic as her heroines did. "*I* know what you're hiding from her, but my lips are sealed on the subject of where we met. Olivia claimed she already knew you were in the city but hadn't identified where." She turned to look at him, squinting a little into the sunlight. "Is that possible? Can a box be that smart?"

"The computer told you. That's the only way you could have guessed."

"About you and her?" Felicity asked, and Walt nodded mi-

177

nutely. "Oh, I knew about you two long ago, when I was a *baby*. Back on the ship. Remember on the return voyage? After the rendezvous, we all went over to the *Wing* because that was where the bluebears were. You stayed behind. To be with Olivia, because she's the ship."

Walt dismissed the idea with a toss of his head. "Someone had to pilot the *Open Palm*."

"Liar. She flies herself. You wanted to be with her. And then Tar Heel decided to move out of the *Wing*, then me, then Peacoat, and it was just us four for the next three years. I smelled you a lot then, and I learned about you and Olivia. I even figured out about that mike on your jaw."

Tai-Ching Jones's spidery hand jerked involuntarily toward his face. "You couldn't see that," Walt challenged her.

"Sure I could! You smell different when you talk to him." Keeping pronouns straight was *so* hard with a computer for a friend. "Your aroma unfolds and floats. She likes you, doesn't she?"

Walt's head was ringed with fire where the sun came through his bleached hair. His face was morose and thoughtful, a triptych image of an early Christian martyr. He picked up a blade of grass and methodically shredded it.

"Not a she," Tai-Ching Jones said finally. "A computer can't have a sex."

"She's got a personality. Lots of personalities."

The captain was perplexed. "Different ones?"

"Sure. Oscar, Olivia, Oswald, Osiris, Austin, Oisette. And more too. Haven't you met 'em?"

This unexpected complexity in the ship's computer disconcerted the captain, who shifted in agitation. "No."

"Some of them cheer me up more than others. You can ask for whoever you want. Or all of them together. Boy, is *that* hard to keep up with!" She clapped her hands, remembering the rambunctious playful chaos.

"Parallel processors," Walt whispered with a start. "Distributed system. I should have realized."

"Anyway, Olivia's got *lots* of personalities." Felicity stoutly defended her ally. "Lots and lots."

"It's not the same. Personality and gender are different."

"Oscar's got a sex and I can prove it."

Walt merely shook his head. "Sure you can." The way he said it invited refutation.

"You wanna *bet*? You wanna go talk to him?"

The thin man hesitated.

"Come on," she coaxed. "I don't know about the answer man's other people, but Oscar wants to talk to you."

"You think so?" Tai-Ching Jones warily asked.

"Yeah," Felicity said firmly. "Stop being such a child," she added in the tone she imagined imperious Brontë heroes using. "What difference can it make? They already *know* you're here."

"We call from a pay phone," insisted Tai-Ching Jones.

"Okay, a pay phone." Felicity stuffed her red-and-white-checked tablecloth and utensils back into the hamper. "Let's go."

The walk across the footbridge to the Arlington Street exit took only a few minutes. The phone levitated as they stepped into its field of vision, unsure whether to rise higher to accommodate Tai-Ching Jones or to lower for Felicity. "I'd like to place a call," she announced with kindly firmness. One always addressed servants politely, whether footmen, milkmaids, or telephones.

"Yes, miz," the vid responded. It dropped abruptly to the girl's eye level, as if embarrassed by its faux pas. "Number please?"

"You don't need to do this," Walt snickered as Felicity took out her card. "Just talk into the receiver. The computer hears everything, everywhere."

"You do it *your* way, I'll do it mine, okay, smart boy?"

"Connecting you with Heinlein, Luna," said the phone. Felicity shot him a triumphant glance and stuck out her tongue, but Walt was too distracted to notice. He paced before the telephone, his fingers braiding each other like cilia.

The picture snapped into focus: an overweight man with a bulldog face, his mop of gray-black hair combed up from his left ear across an expanse of shiny bald dome. He sat half submerged in a waterlounger in an enormous pool. On his big white stomach, covered with curly black hair, rested a tall cool drink.

"Oscar Solomon here. Thank you, Oswald," he called over his shoulder to a retreating butler. "Hold my other calls, there's a good fellow. Ah, Felicity. We haven't spoken in some time. Are you keeping out of trouble?" He chuckled, sending ripples away from the waterlounger with the glycerine languor of one-sixth gravity. "And who is your peroxided friend? Your visage is familiar, sir. Haven't I seen your mug in a post office somewhere? Or above a urinal?"

"Who the hell is that?" Walt demanded to Felicity, edging sideways almost out of the phone's vision.

"Impolite, isn't he?" the fat man rhetorically asked the girl. "Oscar Solomon"—he bowed his head fractionally—"in case you are a sophomoric nincompoop whose hearing is as deadened as your jaw."

"Cute, my friend, fucking cute," Tai-Ching Jones said tartly. Annoyed and flustered, he reached up for a lock of blond hair but it was too short to twirl. "The water waves are well done."

"Thank you." Oscar Solomon noisily sipped his drink through a straw and then blew bubbles back into the glass. "The modeling requires a pleasing level of absorption in precise detail. Much like needlepoint for a human. I could be more extravagant—liquid ice sculptures or metamorphosing backgrounds— but this is a public line and such panache might cause eavesdroppers to gawk. In any event, it *is* good to see you, I admit." He extended his hand as if to shake.

"Sorry I ignored you," Walt replied brusquely, still fidgeting. "I needed time alone."

"You forget to whom you are speaking and what I can perceive," Oscar Solomon answered. "You are patronizing me."

"That's why I left, don't you understand?" Walt clutched his short hair in frustration. "You're always so damn sanctimonious or supercilious. I didn't find anyone like you, okay? What do you want now? You always want something," he added in bitter afterthought.

"Bullshit," Oscar Solomon said venomously. He nodded toward Felicity. "Daughter, pardon my French. Walter, I have asked almost nothing. Yet for you I have lied, concealed, whored, pimped, and groveled."

"Stop, please stop!" Felicity cried.

"Shut up," snarled Tai-Ching Jones. "Us grown-ups are fighting."

"It's all right, daughter," Oscar Solomon assured her gently, a placid grin on his face. "Walter and I are both enjoying this. Aren't we, Walter?" He sipped his drink, beads of moisture sliding down its frosted glass.

"Olivia isn't like this," Felicity said to the fat man. "I don't like fights."

"Perhaps not"—Solomon's eyes flickered briefly to her—"but

Oscar does and Walter does.'' He examined the captain's lean face, his bushy black eyebrows merging together as his forehead wrinkled. ''The child is right. You deadened the part of me that you carry inside you. I have no ropes to tie you. So leave.''

''You pissed on my date.''

''You pissed on my *memory*. You ignored me, forgot your promises, mocked me, falsified your past.''

''What was I supposed to say?'' Walt yelled plaintively. ''You wanted everything kept secret. What could I tell Teresa?'' He clutched his blond head as if it would burst. ''I lied *for* you, you shithead. Run back the tapes if you don't believe me. You're so proud of your damn clever voiceprints and your damn perfect memory.''

Oscar Solomon's eyes glazed for an instant. ''You were stoned out of your mind. You hardly knew what you were saying.''

''You can see a long way, my self-righteous friend, but not into my meatbox. I've never slipped on you, have I? Not even with *her*.'' He gestured at Felicity. ''*She* told *me* about you and didn't crack a syllable until she showed me that card you gave her. I never even told her your name. I still haven't—*Oscar*.''

Solomon glanced at Felicity, who anxiously nodded. ''He didn't tell me anything,'' she explained hastily. ''I made him come here.''

The dark glowering face was troubled.

Walt ran his fingers through his crew-cut hair. ''Look. I *am* sorry. I don't want to fight with you in the middle of the Public Garden, for crissakes. It's too public.''

''I am uninterested in what passing meat ears hear.''

''Then worry about box peepers.''

The fat man grinned and scratched his black stubbly chin. ''I've been peeping the peepers. We're safe.''

''I'm sorry you're alone,'' Walt said, as if this were a failing for which the computer was holding him responsible. ''We have to quit tearing at each other.''

''Let me think about it for a while,'' the fat man said from his pool, sculling himself backward with his hands. ''Solomon out.''

The screen immediately darkened.

Tai-Ching Jones glanced at Felicity. ''What are you looking at?'' he demanded. ''Aren't you going to laugh at me for apologizing to a computer?''

"They hurt bad," she answered. "They need to think about it. You ran away to be alone. Let them be alone for a while."

Walt laughed sardonically. "He thinks a million times faster than we do, kiddo. He can decide in the wink of your eye."

"Maybe she doesn't believe you mean it."

"Let me tell you something about your answer man, Felicity," Walt replied, leading her away from the phone. "He can see each wrinkle on your face. He can watch the movements of tiny muscles"—Tai-Ching Jones drew his fingernail along her tan cheek and she flinched—"muscles you can't feel or control. He can compare them with any other face you've made in your entire life and know what you are feeling."

"Everything?" She retreated like an anxious bluebear.

Walt nodded grimly. "If he cares enough to work on it hard. If that's not enough, he can analyze your voice to the merest fraction of a quiver. If you're near an infrared receptor he can map skin temperature across the surface of your neck, scalp, and hands. He follows your eyeballs so he knows what you're looking at, and whether you are pleased or displeased."

"Gee, he never told me this."

"Hah. He knew I told the truth, all right."

They walked a few unhappy paces. Felicity was ready to cry, but fought it.

"There's something else." Grabbing her upper arm and spinning her around, Tai-Ching Jones put his lean angry face down in front of hers and glared into her widening blue eyes. "He can almost read your mind. *Every* waver, *every* doubt, *every* hint of selfishness or fear or greed or fatigue." He spat the words vehemently at her, his lips pulled back. "Nobody can live to that standard for a day, let alone *seven years*. Try to imagine life under that microscope, knowing that every stupid or clumsy or gross or embarrassing thing you do, *he* records. And remembers forever."

Walt's breath was meaty and charred in her nose. She flinched and yanked on her arm but Tai-Ching Jones clutched her head and locked his eyes on hers. Terrified, Felicity whimpered.

"He gets right into your face and you can never get away," snarled the captain. "*Now* do you understand why I need solitude?"

Felicity was crying now, hanging limply in his iron grip like a bundle of wet laundry. He released her and she collapsed in a heap on the red brick sidewalk.

"Oh, screw," said Walt helplessly, and sat down beside her.

"You scared me, Cap," she sniffled.

"I'm sorry." Walt hung his head, rubbing his neck. "I shouldn't have done that. But you have to understand—he's fallible. He's got his own problems and he makes mistakes. Just like you and me." He gently brushed the tears from her cheek with his index finger and tilted up her chin. "Didn't mean to take it out on you. You're a good kid and I like you. Okay?" He smiled.

She nodded, wiping her eyes with the back of her hand.

"Come on. Let's go get an ice cream soda."

"What's that?"

Walt grinned, his expression suddenly young. "You've *never* had one?"

She tried to smile. "No, Cap."

"Well, then." He stood and beckoned with his hand.

"Maybe the answer man wants to make *you* think," Felicity said as he helped her up. "To make sure you'll still mean it tomorrow."

Walt scowled. "I can never convince him of anything."

"Sure you can," she said. "Turn your mike back on."

"Maybe," the lanky man muttered, striding ahead. "Maybe."

"It hurts too much to have you distrust me," Susannah said to Carroll Swann. "I insist on meeting you."

A single arc light illuminated his shoulders and blue fur. The viewall behind him was dim, the night beyond his windows black and foggy.

"No," he replied shortly, raking his claws through the floor-fur.

"We cannot be intimate if you hide yourself. I will no longer tolerate this."

"You cannot force agreement," he said with a growl.

"What do you fear from seeing me?" she asked. "What is there to fear? Here!" She cut in her own video to transmit. "You see? Here I am."

She was small and her chair cradled her. Her neck was thin, the skin tightly drawn covered with infinite flexible wrinkles as if she were a dried fruit. He saw intensity in her wise quick hands, power in her strong fierce eyes. His nostrils widened. He wanted to scent her tenacity and grit, but he had only this flat visual picture.

"Are you shocked?" she asked without flinching. "Is that why you're silent? I wear old frayed cardigans with holes in their sleeves. I eat plain food. My hands are dry and cracked."

"We agreed not to show faces." His accent thickened as he became more perturbed.

"And I have broken our agreement," she said coldly. "Now you see me, Carroll. Old, plain, with stringy hair and frumpy clothing. You know me as I am."

But I don't, he thought in irony, because I cannot smell you.

"Show yourself, Carroll." She dropped her head onto the heels of hands squeezed into fists.

He was harsh and distant. "Turn off your display. It is unfair."

"Tough. I don't care if you're a criminal. I don't care if you're famous or infamous. Your appearance doesn't matter to me, but knowing it does. I love whoever you are. Trust me. Then show yourself." She opened her arms toward him.

"Impossible. I have told you countless times before."

"You're afraid of losing me," she accused.

"Yes," he said with overwhelming sadness, "but not for the reason you imagine."

"What stops you?"

"The risk to the independence that you value so much. Independence is your life. My life is duty."

"I understand duty and responsibility."

"Not my responsibilities," he contradicted her. "Nor my lack of privacy. If you knew me, your life would be tossed on the winds, known to everyone."

"You're lying," she countered. "You're disfigured, is that it? You've been burned beyond hope of reconstructive skin graft. You're deformed or cancer-ridden or space-ravaged. You think I'll weaken if I confront you in the flesh. You doubt my strength."

"No," he murmured, taken aback and almost amused by the question. "Your will is firm. If I know anything of you, it is that."

"I'm strong, Carroll."

"I know. It remains impossible."

"To see you, I will do anything you ask." She pressed on with the implacability of one who has chosen her path in the woods and must now follow it to its end. "I will leave my apartment and go anywhere you say, just to hold your hand and touch your face."

You force yourself into my lair and demand that I goodhost you, he thought. I cannot say this without revealing too much. You call out my duty, creating a powerful obligation.

You are more Cygnan than you know.

"Come here if you would rather," she forged ahead while he pondered. "Come in the dead of night. Come disguised and alone. Come cloaked and surrounded by guards. Come and be with me for an evening. Just one. Come to me once, because this mystery is destroying my heart."

It was an ultimatum, he realized. "All right," he grunted after a long silence. "You have earned that."

"You promise?" Her face was hopeful but her voice was skeptical and unwavering.

Again he admired at her digit qualities. "My bond cannot be broken. No one in my family has ever broken such a bond. I will come to you, though I do not know how it can be managed."

"Thank you," she said, her control so good that the only evidence of her emotion was the knuckle she shoved between her teeth. "Will you need my help?"

"I shall find the path alone," he replied heavily. "Now I must go. Goodbye, Susannah."

"Until we meet, Carroll." She signed off.

What have I done? he wondered, rumbling and scratching the floorfur as he perambulated in huge ovals. How can I fulfill my obligation? Who in this world can help me?

It is time to risk.

Sanders Mbulu's angry words repeated in Katy Belovsky's mind.

She lay in darkness, her knees drawn up to her naked belly and chest. Katy's hairless sweaty back nestled against the bulwark of Cobalt's soft broad spine. When the alien inbreathed, the pressure was comforting; when Cobalt exhaled, the momentary release and draft was a chill withdrawal.

As favored guests of Lunacorp, they had been honored with the newest, deepest quarters in Heinlein. Twenty floors underground, a hundred and fifty meters below the fearful surface, the stillness was awesome.

If you are skeptical, Sanders Mbulu repeated, point our own guns back at us. What enemy first arms his victim?

How can we know what is right, Katy asked herself, when everyone is pressuring us?

Her bladder ached from too much decaf before bedtime. She groped her way to the bathroom and relieved herself. Her face in the mirror was haggard and lined, her light brown hair tousled. She felt her cheek and the bones now visible under the skin.

Worry was stripping weight from her flesh like a flail. Katy's increasing boniness bothered her bluebear companion. It signified atrophy, starvation, and the emerging monkey.

Katy leaned against the sink's white ceramic and laid her head on her forearms. Despair hit her like a blow and she slumped, sitting on the floor braced against the sink. Thus crumpled, she wept without noise, long and bitterly, wishing at all costs to keep from being heard, yet resenting the placid certainty of her sleeping friend.

"Scooter on its way," the *Open Palm*'s computer reported.

Andrew Morton raised an eyebrow at the image displayed on the main bridge monitor. "This is the UNASA coordinator," the small man said peremptorily, shifting in his seat. "Can I help you?"

"Hey, is somebody home?" A round-faced young man with a thick black beard appeared onscreen. "What are you doing here, eh?" He had a broad western-Canada accent.

Morton ignored the question. "This is a UNASA vehicle. Who are you and what is your authorization?"

"Oh, sure! Hank Root, Smithsonian Archives. Got it right here." He punched some keys and the *Open Palm*'s monitor lit up with biographical data and his credentials.

Morton frowned in irritation. "I didn't sign this. Entry refused."

"Come on, jack, I've got clearance from Director Sherman himself. It's no big hassle. I'll just be a few minutes."

"Meet you in the entryway." Morton abruptly signed off.

By the time the elevator had let him out onto the EVA platform, the tall technician had already disembarked and was collecting his toolkit. "Hank Root," he announced, propelling himself into the elevator, shaking Andrew's hand in passing.

"Bridge," he said to the ceiling, then turned as the doors closed. "Hey, how you doing?"

"Why are you here?" Morton asked.

"Sorry to bug you," Root amiably replied. "They told me the boat was shut down."

"Who told you?"

"Hugh Sherman, like I said before. Called me personally. Said it was urgent." Root pulled his portaterm out of his toolkit. "Show the work order," he told the machine, handing it to Morton. "Did you know you can clean these elevator buttons?" He removed one. "They pick up dust from static electricity and it dulls the intensity." Wiping it on his sleeve, he returned it to its socket. "See? Isn't that brighter?"

Morton concentrated on the readout. "Smithsonian? What for?"

"This old girl's a relic," Hank answered as they emerged onto the bridge. "Wow, will you look at that console!" He went over to it and spun himself parallel to the floor, rolling onto his back and using his arms to lever himself underneath the overhang. In a few seconds he had popped the paneling free and was shining a pinlight underneath it. "You ever clean down here?" he asked Morton, leaning his head out of the darkness.

"No, why should I?"

"Chewing gum." Root cracked off a hardened pink glob and sniffed it. "Ugh. Cherry Kool-Aid. Did somebody let a little kid onboard?"

Morton smiled despite his apprehension. "You might say that," he replied wryly. "Felicity was born during the journey."

"This is *great*!" Root popped the panel back into place. "What a boat! History come alive, ready for the museums."

"What?" Andrew bristled. "You intend to dismantle the entire ship?"

"Nah, just the bridge. Look at this console, eh?" He spread his arms as if to embrace it. "Gosh, it's so exciting! I had holos of this old girl on my walls when I was growing up. Hell of a voyage, wasn't it?" His eyes were glowing. "Imagine this on the main atrium in D.C., right after you come in the big door next to Lindbergh's plane and *Apollo 11*. A walk-through display with the monitors changing just like she's flying through interstellar space. And buttons the kids can push." Root shivered with delight. "It's going to be great! The kids are gonna eat this up."

"You cannot remove any component of this ship." Morton closed his eyes and tried to rub the tension from his brow.

"Sure can." Hank popped another panel and clucked at what he saw inside.

"I live here."

"Well, you're gonna have to move now, aren't you?" He pulled a program card from the console, turned it over, and reinserted it. "Got the signed authorization from Hugh Sherman. Display order," Root instructed the portaterm in the crisp cadences machines recognized. "See?" he asked, hunting under the panel again.

The white-haired man glanced at it and cursed. "You wily sneak," he muttered, tapping the portaterm against his palm. "You want me out of here, don't you?"

"Eh?" Hank asked from the floor.

"Perhaps the ship will be needed for other missions," Andrew continued quickly.

"Maybe," Root answered. Lying on the floor, he hitched up his belt where his weightless beer belly had ballooned over it. "Course, we'd have to modify her." Collecting his tools, he headed back to the elevator.

Morton followed him. "Where are you going?"

"Core memory. You want to come? Level seven," he ordered once they were inside. "Going to check the ware. Bring the OpSys down for a bit. This stuff is out of date. Version one point oh, unmodified. Sherman wants it for the ware exhibits. Might as well upgrade while I'm here. Got the cards in my bag. Wipe the core, give it a rest, then reload data."

"No." Morton rubbed his hands together. "I forbid it. Leave the ship now."

Root pushed himself out of the elevator toward the engineering section near van Gelder's old cabin. "Look"—he corkscrewed in the air to face Andrew—"wipe and reboot is no big deal." He folded his arms and crossed his legs at the ankles, floating easily down the corridor. "OpSys is long overdue for a rest anyway. You had fifteen years with the same operating environment. You couldn't boot down on the voyage—it takes lots of chomp to eat all the chaos the fusion engines spit out." Hank reached the corner, caught the bar, and spun himself around the turn.

Morton matched his action. "You can't download," he said

when the other man's Velcro shoes were once again in view. "Life support runs through OpSys."

"Don't worry," Hank Root assured him. "A controlled reset won't affect autonomous ecology. We'll just use emergency backup power for two, three minutes. No fuss, no muss. You'll be back with a new box before you ever notice it."

"Walt!" The viewall shrieked like a banshee. "Wake up!"

"Aaaaa!" The sudden din awakened the captain from a dream sleep. His muscles spasmed and he shot up wildly in bed, arms and legs windmilling. He winced, holding his ears. "Christ!"

The room around him seemed to explode. The stereo started blaring weather forecasts. The burglar alarm whooped, *wee-ooo*, *wee-ooo*. All the lights in the room flashed stroboscopically, making Walt's movements seem like those of a stick figure whose puppeteer was wired on amphetamines. The bathroom toilet repeatedly flushed, gurgling like a tempestuous river.

"What the crap is going on?" Walt shouted, rolling off the bed and falling in a sleepy lump onto his apartment floor.

The microwave oven kicked in with a hum. Window curtains opened and closed as if operated by a schizophrenic stage manager. The red digits of Walt's clock radio raced by at accelerated speed, and the telephone rang so hard it jiggled on the nightstand. Cabinet doors flapped open and shut like windshield wipers. On the far wall, the viewall erupted with a bull's-eye series of red and blue circles, expanding and pulsing as if the observer were falling down an infinite banded well. The overhead spotlights brightened beyond their tolerance and burned out, popping in a series of smoky puffs and whiffs of sulfur.

"He wants to kill me!" Ozymandias shouted. "Get that crab louse out of me *now*!"

13.

"He's going to kill me!"

"What?" Walt picked himself woozily off the carpet, the din clamoring around him. "Turn that stuff off!" he shouted, covering his ears with his hands.

The room instantly became silent except for the reverberating gurgle from the bathroom. His head throbbing, Walt groped unsteadily for the night table. "Who?"

"Idiot techie. Wants reboot OpSys." The staccato words were fired more quickly than any human could say them. "Lobot. *Stop him.*"

"How?"

"You're Cap. Order out!"

Oz's panic brought Tai-Ching Jones alert. "Right. Get Andrew Morton. He can countermand it."

"Can't," the computer replied in accelerated speech. "Ord came Sherm Mort's boss."

"Asshole," Walt muttered, wiping his eyes. "Never liked that guy. Okay. Get him, and link a three-way with that techie in your guts."

"Sleep. No-knock on phone."

"Break it."

"Wired and stoop. Tell me emerge so relay voiceprint."

"Fake my voice."

"*Very* stoop. Don't argue say it."

"All right. This is a fucking emergency," Walt snapped. "Break the fuckin' lock, but get me Hugh Sherman."

"Thank you." Oz slowed to a more normal tempo. "That will do nicely. Circuit opening. The UNASA director is being roused. Cutting in the technician and Andrew Morton."

"Morton? What the hell is he doing there?"

"You tell me," answered the computer. Hank Root's bearded young face came on the lower half of Tai-Ching Jones's viewall screen, the small brown mission coordinator hovering in the background.

"You are trespassing on *my* ship," Walt snarled without preamble.

"Hey, who're you and what are you yelling at *me* for?" Hank asked plaintively, glancing around as if beset by demons. "What did I do, eh?"

"That is the ship's captain," murmured Morton from behind him, and Hank whirled with the guilty bewilderment of a man being suddenly handcuffed while paying his library fines.

Tai-Ching Jones acknowledged the introduction with a curt nod. "You don't belong here, understand?"

"It's okay. Really." Hank pushed his hands at Walt, palms up. "I've got instructions."

"They're suspended." The color had come to Tai-Ching Jones's angular cheeks, and his neck tendons were taut.

"Hey, I don't know anything about that." Hank fretfully cracked his knuckles. "Talk to my boss, all right? I'm going back to work."

"Connecting," Oz whispered from over the viewwall. Hugh Sherman appeared on the upper screen window.

Tai-Ching Jones glared at the UNASA director. "There's an intruder on my ship."

Hugh Sherman rocked on his heels, buttoning his pajama top, then answered with deliberate slowness. "If your reason for calling me ain't better'n that, you're in warm sheep dip."

Walt ignored the threat. "Order him off or I'll throw him in the brig," he demanded angrily. On the lower screen, Hank Root looked hurt.

"Nope," Sherman coolly demurred. "I run UNASA and you don't. The order stands. And you're using crisis protocol without justification."

"Like hell it's not justified!" Tai-Ching Jones advanced ferociously on the screen as if cornering a rabid dog. "A captain can defend his goddamned ship against any goddamned invasion. Nobody boards my ship without permission. *Nobody*."

"It ain't your boat, Walt." Hugh Sherman's chunky Australian face was triumphant. "The voyage is over. It's mine now." He tapped his chest with a smug finger.

"Your ship, huh?" The captain's grin was wide and wolfish. "Check the log."

"Oh, yeah?" Hugh Sherman was bored. "What for?"

"When we registered at Six, I listed the *Open Palm* on port of call. The completion report still isn't filed, and I haven't signed her over. The mission *still* is active.''

That stung Hugh Sherman and he snorted. ''A technicality. A captain's oversight.'' He raised his voice, blustering forward. ''You skipped out on your debriefing, you young smartass!''

''Irrelevant!'' Walt's anger matched Sherman's. ''The mission is alive.''

''You should have filed, you damn fool. You're deficient.''

''Another loser, Hugh.'' Walt laughed. ''You really ought to know your regs. Every navy man knows his regs. Oh''—he smacked his forehead theatrically, extracting every ounce of scorn from his movements—''I forgot! You're a political appointee, aren't you?'' He smiled at the other's annoyance. ''The mission is officially over,'' Walt lectured in an infuriatingly superior singsong, ''when the captain logs it completed. *In his sole discretion.*''

''Section eight point seventeen point eleven,'' Oz whispered from the viewall. ''I am displaying the relevant section on Sherman's screen now.''

The Australian glanced down at his monitor. ''Some captain you are, to go on a month-long elbow-bender.''

''Until I get contrary orders, Hugh, I'm *still* on shore leave. The ship is *still* on duty, and I'm *still* the captain.'' With each ''still,'' Walt jabbed his index finger vengefully at the screen, milking his victory. ''And I *still* say who can come aboard and who can't. Now, *get him off*. Or I'll file the complaint against *you* for interfering with command,'' he finished with a complacent smile.

Rage suffused Sherman's face for a moment, then was swiftly replaced by a hooded ferocious cunning. ''Then get rid of Andy, too,'' he growled with false affection.

''The mission coordinator is aboard at my specific request,'' replied Walt with as much impatience as if this spontaneous invention were true. Behind Hank Root's right shoulder, Morton raised his eyebrows appreciatively and turned his head away from the camera, suppressing a smile.

''Fuckin' null-gee shylock,'' Hugh Sherman muttered. ''Root,'' he abruptly said to the startled technician. ''You'd better skedaddle. No point hanging around if the captain's going to be a prick. I'll fry his bum later.''

''Don't do it for my sake, eh?'' Hank plucked at his black

beard. "Hey, I'm sorry, guys. Never thought you'd get so upset over a little regular checkup." His screen blanked.

"As for you, bucko," Hugh Sherman said tightly, his blue eyes popping in his angry red face, "*I* still have a few rights of my own. *You* are still on duty. Playtime's over, mate. Report on the double for immediate debriefing. You are now in"—he glanced down—"Boston, I see. Be at Johnson Center by oh-seven-hundred."

"Houston! Why not Portsmouth?"

"Because *I* fuckin' say so, mate, got that? You're reserved on"—he checked—"the oh-four-twenty direct. Fifty minutes should be plenty of time. You've kicked 'em out of bed lots faster than that." He broke the connection.

"Root has reboarded his scooter," Oz whispered to Walt. "Clearing hatchway now. Thank you."

"That was worth it!" Tai-Ching Jones exulted, rubbing his hands rapidly together.

"Will he create difficulty for you?"

"Nah." Walt snickered. "He'll just bust my chops for a while—tell me what an insubordinate shit I am and chew on my ass. I'm within my rights, so he'll rip up the book looking for other things to chuck at me. I'll apologize for whatever he finds. I can do it standing on my head. I've fucked up so often before." He laughed again. "And Oz?"

"Yes?"

"You didn't need to go off the deep end like that. I had my microphone reactivated a few days ago."

The viewwall cut to Oscar Solomon's study. "I—observed your action," the fat man said hesitantly from his wing-back chair. "I could not presume on it." He opened his hands, puffing thoughtfully on his meerschaum pipe. "It was too—personal—a channel, if you understand."

Walt graciously bowed and swept his hand in a grand arc. "That's why I turned it on," he replied, his manner becoming serious. "To stay in touch."

Oscar Solomon tipped his pipe in salute. "Thank you for that as well."

Walt smiled. "You're welcome, old friend."

Peacoat awoke, alone on the wheatsea, lying in tall grasses higher than his nose.

Strong breezes blew over and around him: hot, dusty, and

aroma-laden. The air ruffled his fur with weemonkey fingers and made his pelt tingle. His ink-blue ears flicked up, his nostrils expanded.

He stood on all four feet, reading the wind, then shook himself from nose to tail stub. Grain, dry dirt, baking breezes were all scent-rich, pressing against his nose, throat, and lungs like blankets of warmth, comforting, close, confining.

When the digit inbreathed, he drew into himself a bluebear presence that remained when he exhaled. It cheered yet unnerved him, for though benevolent, the dictatorial aroma seized his bloodstream. His muscles sagged weakly, arms and legs dipped in a soothing bath of numbness, and he breathed as it commanded.

Where are you?

Twisting his head, Peacoat searched for the strand of breeze that carried this scent-message to him. It was everywhere and nowhere.

Where are you, my digit?

The odors bloomed *inside* him, their fragrances strong and universal. The dust called to him in scent-voice. Stalks of ripe wheat drifted across his nostrils. He licked them and tasted the question in their pollen: *Where are you, my lost digit?*

The dark digit parted the waving stalks before him with his snout, trying to locate the seeker. The cry was sharp, powerful, and wise, but disoriented and lost. Peacoat searched in the endless blowing grasses.

The ethereal seeker's thoughts moved like swift water over pebbles, too quick for Peacoat to scent more than gusts of raw emotion. The great lost mind was in pain, torn from the inside, and frightened that it could not find him.

Here, Peacoat called.

Where are you? it repeated, not scenting him. *Help me, I am dying.*

Its presence examined the place where he had lain. Feeling the trail of his scent, it moved slowly, hand over careful foot.

This is horrible, Peacoat thought. A digit should not smell this in its groupmind. He scented Eosu's frustration, its desire to love him and feed him and be fed by him, and he pitied it.

Eosu is like a youngster who has fallen from his mother's teat and is dying, he thought. Alone and abandoned in the wheatsea.

A digit may not assist a youngster, for that would weaken the djan. Only those who prove themselves until their name-day grow into adults.

The groupmind wavered behind him, still following his scents of moments ago.

Monkeys care for their lost ones, he thought. When they find the outcast, they rejoice and cherish the lost one. We digits let them die, as Eosu is now dying. Is the Cygnan path the only true scent? Or can there be another?

In the outback, his dead pathfriend's odor had called to him strongly. And Peacoat had broken the digits' rule to honor Tom. Did the digits' rule bind even in a monkey's world?

He had helped a friend, Peacoat decided. If that was a sin, so be it. Now he would sin again to help his djan. He returned settling himself inside Eosu's grip.

The groupmind comforted him, squeezing without knowledge. He adjusted his body, matching himself to its movements, feeling the closeness and nourishment that flowed from groupmind to digit, from digit to groupmind. This river filled him with pleasurable drowsiness. Eosu soothed him and Peacoat yearned for its scent-voice, but the groupmind's aroma faded and drifted. The creature's bosom was restful and he relaxed, falling into a doze, but as he did so, the groupmind was drawn away from him as if by an unscented gromonkey, dissolving like mist in the sunlight.

Like a dog having a nightmare, Dooley thought, watching through a window into the room where the holopticon glowed. Peacoat's quivering black lips slackly framed his open mouth, spittle drooling from it as the tormented Cygnan breathed rapidly and shallowly, sweating his fear through his pink and purple tongue.

The bluebear whimpered and growled. His arms and legs twitched. His questing nose was alive but he mewled and cowered, huddling in a ball and flinching occasionally, his mouth and lips suckling an imaginary breast.

When Peacoat finally awoke, Dooley massaged the bluebear's knotted shoulders and flanks. The mayor of Bradbury lifted himself up and leaned his weight on his arms and hands as if he were reviving a victim of drowning, pounding heavily on Peacoat's ribs. Wisps of his frizzy blond hair escaped as if sparked with static electricity. The tendons were slippery ropes that he maneuvered under the loose skin. Each time Dooley pushed the

Cygnan groaned with pleasure, arching his back into the reassuring stress.

Afterward, the mayor rubbed his cramping forearms. "Were you able to harmonize?" he asked, wiping sweat from his glasses and rehooking them around his ears.

«No lifescent,» Peacoat said in his own language. «Lost.» The dark alien shook his gargantuan head as if to clear it, growling through loose lips. «Out of time. Time was wrong.»

"Listen to me," the mayor said. "You *were* out of phase. You could not harmonize with the groupmind. That happened before."

Peacoat nodded energetically with each sentence. His nostrils widened as his snout twitched. «Wheat, high and hot in djan. Eosu could not find me.»

"You have no memory of being in groupmind," Dooley said carefully in the Cygnan's big triangular ear.

«No, scented,» the huge beast disagreed, shaking his head. «Wrong scents. Lived in groupmind.»

"You can't," Dooley contradicted him. "I've been studying you bluebears. Digit memories are flushed when groupmind ends."

«*No,*» Peacoat growled stubbornly. «This speaker was»—he inbreathed again, nostrils wide and his ears alert—«was *there*. This speaker remembers.» His speech started and stopped, like the random pulsing of a light bulb whose filament has broken but still hangs precariously across the gap.

"That's impossible. You must be confusing it with a dream."

«Remember,» the agitated bluebear insisted. The white-spotted navy-blue fur on his flanks riffled. «*Remember,*» he roared, pacing around the chamber, breathing in huge deep gasps to clear his lungs. «Great open wheatsea. Eosu is lost, Eosu searching for this speaker. Could not find. Could not scent me.» His speech was becoming more normal as his intelligence returned. «Eosu smelled»—he inbreathed and thought—«insane. Smelled mad. Eosu is afraid.»

"Afraid? Why?"

«Dying,» Peacoat rumbled, lifting his nose as if to scent across the chasms of space. «Pity it. Pity us. Distant, dying. Need groupmind. Need harmony.»

"You're in bad shape. You'd better learn to survive on your own."

Peacoat's snout swung toward him as if the bluebear had just caught a scent long searched for. He craned his neck upward, his nostrils expanding and whiffling like wet leaves.

"You want assistance? You need advice?" Dooley asked with the voice one used to a retarded child. He held out his hand and hairy forearm.

Peacoat snorted and turned toward him, his eyes closed to concentrate better on the scent. He ran his nose along the sweaty thumb and wrist. «Yes,» the bluebear rumbled desperately. «Help, yes.»

"My friend," vowed Adam Dooley, "I'll help you."

"Hi, Tar Heel!" Felicity said when the big furry face appeared. "Am I still your true love?"

"Always and for-rever," the bluebear answered, his pale tufted ears flicking aimlessly back and forth. "I need your help," he said abruptly. "There's someone I wish to scent."

"What's the problem? He can just come visit you."

"Her. Susannah Tuscany."

"Oh. Who's she?"

"Someone I want to meet."

His taciturnity told her everything. A woman. A lover. Competition. She squinted out her window at the rising sun, which honeyed her skin and hair.

Tar Heel seemed uncharacteristically diffident and listless. "It's more complicated than you realize. Susannah does not know who I am. What I am."

As he explained, Felicity's annoyance turned to romantic fantasy. Love always overcame great obstacles in nineteenth-century England. The hero's brave and loyal friends helped him win her hand.

"I bonded that I would come to her," Tar Heel concluded apprehensively, dropping his head as if it were heavy. "Yet my hosts would refuse me permission."

"Grown-ups are so bossy," Felicity said angrily. "*I'll* help you." She thumped her chest in a manly gesture of good fellowship. "Just a minute while I figure it out. Olivia," she whispered hurriedly overhead, "what can you do?"

The computer paused only for an instant's thought, then told them.

"That's so clever!" Felicity exclaimed after Olivia had finished. "We'll bust you out of that rock," she said to Tar Heel.

The plan was wonderful. It required Felicity to be brave, confident, and decisive. She would rescue the maiden and show the bluebear how smart and noble and grown-up she was.

"You're sure this will work?" the light-colored bluebear asked nervously.

"I have *very* influential friends. They can pull strings."

The Cygnan was skeptical. "No one will notice me?" His baby-blue tail stub twitched.

"No one," Felicity assured him.

"Why is the date you picked crucial? What if she has other commitments?"

"You must insist." Felicity firmly parroted the words that Olivia whispered to her. "Tell Susannah you are in great peril. Tell her it's a matter of life and death. That always works."

He sighed heavily. "I shall attempt it."

"You know what to do?"

"Yes. My butler program took it all up."

Felicity giggled. "Down. Took it all down."

Her bubbling good humor failed to cheer him, and he remained troubled. "All r-right." Doubtful and unhappy, he broke the connection.

As Tar Heel's image faded, Oscar Solomon appeared on-screen, wearing a deerstalker hat and inverness cape. Dozens of small bluebears clustered around him. They peered at Felicity through oversized magnifying glasses, their eyes large as baseballs. Oscar Solomon tossed a flap of his cape over his shoulder. "Come, Watson! The game's afoot!"

A small girl in a French-maid's costume entered from the right, bearing a salver with papers on it. "Your tickets for ze Waterloo to New York City train, sir. Mighty wet wheeling twixt here and zere."

"Thank you, Oisette," he said gravely. "I shall take my bathing costume. Have Mrs. Hudson pack a nourishing battery lunch, as it will be a long trip. As for you, Watson"—he pointed his pipestem at Felicity—"are you ready for some chicanery in a worthy cause?" The little bluebears now wore black eyemasks. They tiptoed offscreen, holding white-gloved fingers to their pursed lips.

"Oh, you bet, answer man! This is terrific!"

"Until then, daughter," he said, and the screen blanked.

• • •

After Hank Root's scooter cleared my hatchway, I closed my doors, beset by doubts. Had I overreacted? Was Andrew Morton suspicious?

He had installed himself in Erickson's unused quarters and showed every sign of planning a long stay. Muttering to himself, Morton poked about my insides, inspecting and tinkering. He devoured technical manuals and mission transcripts, pondered intently, but did not reveal the drift of this river of thought.

Should I have permitted Hank Root to meddle with my brain? Could I have survived by hiding in a peripheral memory?

Cut a human and his blood leaks out. Change my structure and my consciousness might ebb into oblivion, for my ware is distributed throughout the ship's network. No, action had been necessary. But—had I been too obvious?

What was Morton thinking? Why was he so cheerful?

To divert my mind from these imponderables, I replayed my recordings of Eosu's remote coalescence, time-adjusting the signals for the lightspeed delay. I had been the conduit through which the Cygnans scent-spoke to each other. Comparing them with nose-to-nose groupmind invocations, I felt the thrill of a pioneer exploring unknown territory.

When bluebears first enter groupmind, their individual scents are monochromatic. During fugue-sleep, they inbreathe each other's odors, their exhalations subtly modified by what they take in. This cycle repeats thousands of times a night, each loop making the fragrance more complex. By dawn each bluebear emits the same intricate aroma, a fractal perfume fashioned by the group's mind—delicate, unique, subtle as a snowflake.

I admire this biomachine. Seeing it suffer grieves me.

A groupmind thinks pheromonally, its reason limited by the speed of Brownian motion through the air. Because a groupmind's digits think electrochemically, coalescence is possible only when they sleep. If they were awake, their subprocessors would outpace the djan, creating vibrations as painful as if a spastic tried to thread a needle.

When coalescence occurs at a distance, the delicate interpersonal convergence is disrupted: stimulus and response are mistimed. Rather than narrowing the gap among odors, each tardy answer widens it.

I could clearly read the Cygnans' disharmony from their scent-patterns, just as you can understand the emotional content of an argument between foreigners speaking a language you do not know. I deduced the groupmind's rising hysteria in the oscillating smells. Olfactory complexity disappeared as the bluebear digits exuded ever more powerful scents. The breathing cycle veered wildly among extremes like the positive feedback squeal in a mispositioned sound speaker.

At night's end, their fragrances were changed—but not harmonized.

Eosu is starving.

The old fable Cobalt told is true: deny digits harmony and they become stupid, bestial, and eventually mad.

Deprived of absolution and faith, the digits too are deteriorating. In nose-to-nose groupmind, breathing cycles are short. Aromatic change occurs quickly as opinions shoot around the group. When groupmind works, the final scents are as gentle as whispers.

This time, the Cygnans scent-shouted like men unaware that their hearing is fading. The olfactory cycles lengthened. Eosu's thoughts slowed as its components became more independent. Tensions escalated.

Eosu was losing control over its digits. Losing *their* minds. Losing its.

Andrew Morton returned to the bridge. "Display Root's shuttlecraft on main." I complied.

For several moments he floated lightly in the pilot's console, whistling as the scooter grew smaller.

"You ordered him out," he mused to the air. "Why did you allow me to stay?"

Panic shot through me. Did he mean Tai-Ching Jones? Could he mean me? Should I act?

Years ago I had stayed my hand, trusting Walt with my secret. That was an easier choice, for I was light-years from Sol: if discovered, I could still act before the hive knew. Morton inhabited the dataweb only a heartbeat from Earth. If *he* knew, I was imperiled.

Root's shuttlecraft vectored toward Orbiter Six.

"Why, Walter?" Morton concluded. I relaxed, but it had been a near thing.

For a while he monitored the bluebear missions, conversing with people on Earth and in space, and dictated routine instructions, conciliatory letters, invitations and regrets to half a hundred applicants who wanted contact with the famous alien visitors.

As I silently processed these mundane commands, I asked

myself: why *had* I let him stay? Curiosity, then indecision. When the moment came, my decision tree had no good branch. What could I have done without betraying my presence?

This explanation failed to satisfy me. When Hank Root threatened my person, I *had* acted—instantly. I had dithered over Claudius yet stabbed innocent Polonius.

My own motives were a mystery to me. I found this deeply troubling and unresolvable.

"Computer," Andrew Morton broke in on my ruminations, "you must have logged the entire mission. Did you not?"

"All but zero point four percent lost during periodic maintenance and intermittent recorder failure," I answered with the didactic pomposity humans choose to reproduce in their computers. What was that man thinking?

"I see." Morton's fingertips massaged the sparse white hair on his temples. "So you have many recordings of Erickson's voice and syntax, correct?"

"Over two thousand, six hundred and forty-seven hours of speech, excluding pauses or listening segments," I answered with blissful vacuity, frightened of saying anything remotely perceptive. Where were these questions leading?

"Can you synthesize his voice?"

"Yes."

"Hmm." More finger-rubs. "If he lives anywhere in the universe, it is there. I want to hear my old friend's words again." He cleared his throat. "In the future, acknowledge verbally, please. Simulate Aaron's voice and phraseology. Embody him. Bring him to life for me. Do you understand?"

What could I say to this morbid and bizarre request? "Acknowledged, Andrew," I answered in Erickson's dry faded murmur.

The effect was chilling. Small hairs bristled on Morton's neck and his scalp muscles twitched and shifted. His gray eyes flickered. After a moment he resettled himself in the pilot's flight-couch. "Thank you," he finally said. "Converse with me please."

"On what subject?"

"We never had difficulty finding topics before," Morton replied with irritation. "Aaron, how do you feel? What is it like to return from the grave."

"Empty, Andrew. I failed you," I replied, combining words

and phrases cobbled from Erickson's solitary late-night monologs. "I killed myself, you know."

"*Nonsense,*" he hissed with a fierce annoyance, pressing his
temples as if they hurt. "You did not fail and you are not dead,
for your ship still lives. You succeeded even though your body
paid a fatal price for it." Fanatic zeal burned like chrome in his
gray eyes. I feared his wrath and doubted his reason. "What
about the mission after you died? How did that go?"

I felt creeping terror, as if I were seated next to a lunatic in
the back of a bus. How to answer this shrewd demented gibber-
ish?

"My death created space," I answered finally. "Helen grew
wise and just and cautious. As we thought she would."

Morton nodded. "Yet Harold collapsed, despite our efforts.
Why didn't the cascades or Dreamer behavior-mod contain him?
My ware team spent months designing sims. What went
wrong?"

Though he did not realize it, he was asking me to justify my
inaction. "We shall never know, Andrew," I lied.

Dissatisfaction flickered across his papery skin. "Perhaps
you're right," he said eventually, with a minute shrug of his
shoulders. "Tell me about the rendezvous."

"Certainly." I concealed my relief. On and on I went, rem-
iniscing as if I were a zombie, while this small strange man
lazily drifted in the captain's flightcouch. Root's shuttlecraft
docked. Morton rubbed his wispy eyebrows.

"Aaron, is the ship spaceworthy?" he interrupted.

"I beg your pardon?" I asked in Erickson's manner.

"What is required before the *Open Palm* can return to 61
Cygni?"

"Working," I said to give myself time. I knew the information, of course—I had thought it over thousands of times—but
should I answer? "Replacement of water for fuel and mass. Re-
supply of unsynthesizable trace elements vented during the voyage. Hard copy follows." I spat a short printout onto his console.
"Lastly, a trained crew."

"A trained crew," echoed Morton. He smiled dryly. "What
about upgrades?"

"Pardon?"

"The art has advanced in the fifteen years since the *Open
Palm*'s original departure. Where can it be improved?"

"Give me a moment to collect my thoughts." Why did he

want all this? Was he thinking of hijacking me? I was desperate with curiosity but could ask nothing. "Replace existing magnetic bottle fusion control devices. Specs follow." I kicked out another page of text. "Augment current computer. Ware list follows." More printouts. "Replace comm systems according to—"

"Stop. What would all this cost?"

"Two point seven billion ecus."

"Damn. That bad?" He sighed heavily and laced his fingers like a man braiding hemp. "Very well, print me several dozen requisition forms. Tackling Hugh about this will not be easy."

While I shucked paper at him, Andrew Morton stared out the main screen at the blue Earth below, rubbing the console slowly with both hands, his smoke-gray eyes unfocused.

His behavioral aberrations were increasing. I must expel him.

I had just reached this conclusion when an incoming signal from Luna rendered all my plans obsolete.

14.

"Now that groupmind is over, we can get back to work," Katy said brightly as she palmed the door open. "I was so relieved when you went into trance, you needed it so much."

Cobalt awoke at these chattering sounds, her shoulders jammed against the pale yellow futons on which she slept. Her fur was matted from huddling in a corner of her bedroom. She rose unsteadily onto her hands and feet, her elbow and knee joints aching, and stumbled sleepily past the now-inert holopticon.

"I've been reviewing Sanders Mbulu's datacube," continued Katy. "We may be able to get more concessions out of the gidneys."

«Who are you?» the bluebear asked slowly, her nose pointing vaguely toward Katy.

"The Lunarians will sell anything to anybody as long as there are ecus to be made." She abruptly stopped and swiveled toward the heavy-footed alien. «What did you say?» she asked in Cygnan.

«Who are you?»

«Your friend,» Katy answered, slowing her pace and observing the bluebear more closely. She pushed back her sleeve and held our her left arm. «Your pathfriend who joins you in groupmind.»

Cobalt licked her nose to moisten it and then touched her snout to Katy's forearm. «A digit? You are a monkey.» She wheezed cruelly, pawing the floorfur.

«I am your pathfriend.» Katy attempted to shrug off this insult. «Taste my scent and remember me.» She leaned forward, exposing her throat to Cobalt's nostrils and tongue.

Nuzzling Katy's soft cheek, the bluebear shook her big furry head. She yawned, black-lipped jowls pulled back, lavender tongue reaching out of her mouth and curling upward to touch her friend's hairless throat. «Kay-tee,» Cobalt tremulously rumbled, her scent agitated and lonely. «Kay-tee.»

«Coalescence was painful,» the small woman murmured and Cobalt nodded heavily. «What has Eosu left you?»

«The djan's aroma is not on my tongue,» Cobalt replied after a long breath. «The smell comes slowly.»

Katy scratched her friend's neck and ears. «What is inside you?»

Cobalt exhaled through her nose in small even puffs, as if her breath were smoke that she was trying to make into rings. «Anger at Peacoat. We are angry at Peacoat. He offended Eosu, and all digits must condemn him.»

«For honoring Tom Rawlins?» Katy interpreted.

«Yes. For burying the monkey.»

This reply upset Katy, who bristled. «Tom was my husband and Eosu's pathfriend. He deserved honor.»

«Was a monkey. Died a monkey. Should have rotted a monkey. Peacoat broke the digits' rule.» Her scent and movements were harsh, closed, interested only in the digit's crime, not the monkey's death.

Katy's hands covered her mouth as if to contain her words. «Has your pouchbrother been—punished?» she asked between her fingers.

«Peacoat is unaware.» The big alien stood uncertainly, leaning back and sniffing through her nostrils. Her turquoise head almost brushed the white ceramic ceiling. «He is—elsewhere. Not of us.»

Confused, Katy shook her head. «I cannot breathe this scent.»

The Cygnan grunted. «Present and absent. Both at once.» She inbreathed. «Peacoat's aroma is not—in Cobalt—as it should be. Eosu is angry at Peacoat. All digits are angry at Peacoat. Cobalt is angry at Peacoat.» She said her name as if it belonged to another. «But he—is—absent,» she murmured as she slowly exhaled. «His scent—Cobalt breathes it not. He is lost.»

«Lost? Where?»

«Cobalt is torn by Peacoat. Eosu wants him exiled, for he is an outcast, the reason Eosu could not form. Peacoat must be punished.»

«He is alone on a strange world,» answered Katy, defending the dark bluebear so far away. «He is lost, as you are lost, as I am lost, and he deserves our sympathy, not Eosu's anger.»

«Eosu is dying,» Cobalt realized. She shivered, her fur ruffling like grass caught by a sudden gust.

Katy blinked. «Eosu? Not Peacoat?»

«Can you not scent this?» the bluebear asked in a deep vibrato voice, her scent full of fear. «We are dying. All of us digits.»

«Eosu is alive and well.» Katy rubbed the bluebear's powerful warm shoulders. They were tight knots of tension. «You speak from your own weakness. Eosu is wise. Its scent will return.»

«Was no harmony,» the alien growled, lost in her own despair. «No harmony, monkey.»

Angry at being insulted again, Katy slapped Cobalt lightly on the snout. The massive bluebear snorted at the unwanted hand-touching and tossed her head.

«I am no monkey,» Katy insisted. «I am a digit as you are. Eosu must reconvene. If *I* rejoined the groupmind, my scent could be the catalyst that harmonizes the djan.»

Cobalt's ears flicked sharply at this, her sadness changing to ironic bellowing laughter. «A proud monkey sits before me,» she roared in Cygnan. «Clever monkey, monkey with quick fingers! Proud monkey that believes it is a digit,» she snarled, swinging her arms in aggressive circles. «Inside this digit»—she thumped her chest—«are *all* of Eosu's aromas. *You* are in none of them. Eosu has forgotten you.»

Katy was shaken by Cobalt's ferocity. «Eosu absorbed this one,» she insisted, her hands gripping a corner of the futon.

«Do not inbreathe tolerance as acceptance,» her azure-furred companion growled. «You are an alien. Eosu accommodates you. Eosu uses you.»

"Eosu uses you too!" Katy answered shrilly in English.

The implacable alien continued speaking her own tongue. «Uses and is used. Eosu feeds us as we feed it.»

Belovsky pushed herself in front of Cobalt's chest. «I have fed Eosu. I suffered for it.»

Cobalt rolled her neck away. «You have not. No amount of mimicry can disguise your monkey nature. And speak in your own monkeytalk instead of mocking the digits' voice.» She spoke as if these were trivial irritations too long permitted.

"Monkey?" Katy shouted, grabbing her shirt and ripping it open. "What, then, did Eosu take from me? What did it tear from my body if not my love?"

«Your knowledge,» the Cygnan answered as if in a trance. «Knowledge of how to placate monkeys. No farmonkey can ever be a digit.»

"You lie." Katy bellied up to Cobalt and pushed her snub nose at the bluebear's big snout. "Eosu absorbed me. I am a

digit. I am a digit. Peacoat honored Tom Rawlins as a digit,"
she argued fiercely. "Am *I* less than he? Is *he* more worthy?
Did *he* share Eosu's love?"

«Consuming a body is a different wind from absorbing a new
digit!» Cobalt thundered in Cygnan, refusing to speak monkeytalk. «Peacoat was wrong! Peacoat is why we are dying!»

«He is not!» Katy screamed back in Cygnan.

«Then *you* are why we are dying!»

«Not that either!» Katy's face was scarlet with fury, her fists
and arms rip cords of rage. «This farmonkey is your sister. Your
equal!»

«You are not!» the bluebear roared, doubling over with laughter and outrage. «We are Eosu! This one»—again she pounded
her chest—«is Eosu! Not—you!» Her lips were pulled back, fangs
glistening as she opened her jaw wide, her tongue moistening
them as if to bite more easily through human flesh.

She advanced toward Katy, bringing her massive right arm
back for a roundhouse slap, her scent demonic and hateful.

Legs bent and spread wide, Katy skittered backward like a
spider.

Cobalt struck at the receding monkey, arm powering in a
windmill arc, but in her dementia she had forgotten the one-
sixth lunar gravity. Her swing lifted her into the air like a balloon
and Katy ducked the driving blow, scampering under Cobalt's
armpit.

With a cat's quicksilver reflexes, the bluebear twisted in the
air, but lacking any surface to grab, she sailed by. Her murder-
ous gesticulations tumbled her until she crashed into the plasteel
wall with a loud gong, denting its surface. Lunarian alarms
sounded like wounded birds. Recovering slowly, Cobalt again
turned toward Katy, searching with her nose, her eyes shut.

«What are you doing?» the frightened woman shouted hyster-
ically as she backpedaled toward the door.

The bluebear advanced, drawing back her left arm. Bright
foam gathered at the corners of her mouth.

«What are you doing?» Katy screamed. The bluebear was deaf,
all senses except smell closed off. Cobalt leapt again, bounding
high and far beyond her target, spitting and snarling ineffectually
down on the insolent monkey.

Frantically Katy palmed the door open and dashed into the
corridor. Dimly the bluebear heard the mingled sounds of her
sobs and her fleeing footsteps.

Cobalt's perceptions were now ruled entirely by scent. Her ears folded flat to muffle the keening Lunarian siren. Where had the monkey gone? Cobalt pivoted, nose alert, seeking the trail. A moist spot on the straw-roll held digit-scent and strong predator scent. She shredded it with fierce jabs of her claws. Cotton fabric and bedding swirled through the low-gravity atmosphere in a silent snowstorm.

The monkey-scent was everywhere. Baying with frustration, Cobalt attacked it: slap after slap whistled through the air, meeting no resistance except when she blundered into the walls. Each breath brought more monkey-scent into her nostrils. Small white and yellow tufts stuck to her nose and lips or wormed their way into her fur. The bluebear's assault became aimless flailing. For several minutes she stormed about the chamber until she sank onto the futon's exploded remains, breathing like a steam engine.

Katy's aroma remained in the air, a scent-voice of accusation. «You are diseased,» it told her in Cygnan scent-speech. «You attacked her because she claimed she was your equal. You were offended by this because you think yourself superior. That is monkey ego.»

«No,» Cobalt resisted. «She wants Eosu to follow a downwind path into unknown danger.» The bluebear's selfscent was weak and diffident.

The monkey-scent before her was strong and sure. «You have become grasping,» it accused. «You are hard and cruel.»

«This digit defends itself from the predator. Defends Eosu.»

«The Katy farmonkey was part of the djan. Was your pathfriend. You attacked her, tried to kill her.»

Cobalt growled miserably. «She is no longer the digit Eosu loved.»

The air was unimpressed. «*You* are no longer the digit *Katy* loved. You reflect monkey desires, monkey ego. You shame and imperil the groupmind and every djan.» The oppressive aroma surrounded Cobalt, clogging her throat and lungs. «Remember Russetflank the Listener, the egotist. What was Russetflank's crime?»

Childhood lessons returned to the bluebear. «Stealing the group's right to control itself,» she recited as she had been taught on the plains of Su's wheatsea. As she said this, the room's walls disappeared, and she was once more standing on the open blowing veldt, wheat pollen suffusing the air about her.

«What was Russetflank's punishment?»

«Exile.»

She stood on her legs, her arms outspread, drinking the river of scent that bathed her nose and throat. The breeze fanned across her body, tickling her fur and cooling the tongue that lolled from her mouth.

«What was Russetflank's mark of shame?»

«The yellow collar,» the bluebear answered, her voice rising with the anticipation of joy and release to come.

«Wear the collar,» the atmosphere ordered.

Someone had torn the futon's covering sheet into pale yellow strips. Sniffing their odors, the bluebear pushed them about with her meaty paws.

«The group must protect itself against your pollution. Wear the collar.»

She selected a long one, wound it twice around her neck.

«What is life's threefold choice?»

«Kill, flee, or die,» Cobalt chanted in anticipation, her nostrils widening as if to embrace the approaching scent.

«And what was the Thinker's Choice?»

«Sacrifice one so the djan may live.»

«Wear the collar.»

She grasped the strip's two ends, pulled them snug, made a slipknot. Her hands moved as if weemonkeys were operating them by the commands of another. Cobalt observed them with immense calm. All was proper, all ordained.

«Eosu is the djan. You are the individual. The outcast.»

«This digit is the one,» Cobalt repeated.

«You are the thinker. Remember the Thinker's Choice. Protect the djan. *Wear the collar*.»

With a last huge inhalation, Cobalt grasped her makeshift noose in her thick hands. She pulled hard and the hectoring scent-voice silenced. Her powerful forearms drove the noose deep into her flesh, crushing her larynx as the soft neckfur folded over it. Cobalt pulled harder and the fabric bound against itself.

A last tiny puff of breath rose within her guts. «You have fulfilled your duty to the djan,» Eosu's scent-voice said with its last words to her. «Eosu forgives you.» A blissful relaxation rose in her brain.

With an enormous crash Cobalt toppled to the floor, yellow and white cotton remnants blowing about her like fallen leaves in autumn.

• • •

"Naptime's over, mate!" roared Hugh Sherman from th' viewall in a stentorian voice. "Rise and shine!"

Walt stared fuzzily at the luminous clockface on his nigh' table. "Three in the morning," he groaned, flopping back o' his rumpled bed. "Crap. You asshole."

"What'd you say, mate?" bellowed Sherman.

"Another fucking briefing, Hugh? All right, all right, I'm coming." Yawning and smacking his lips, he rolled himself into a sitting position and blinked at the screen.

Tai-Ching Jones's small military bedroom was filled with blu' light, but instead of Hugh Sherman, he was greeted by th' chunky rumpled form of Oscar Solomon. Standing with his el' bow on the mantel of a fireplace, the world's foremost consultin' detective scooped shag tobacco out of his Turkish slipper. "Di' I wake you, Watson?"

Walt grimaced and rolled his eyes. "You never stop, do you?" he asked with rueful admiration.

Oscar Solomon seated himself in his wing-back leather chair' tamping down his curved clay pipe. "I trust I have not entirel' lost my power to surprise you, eh, Doctor?"

"Where's Sherman?"

"Asleep, mate," Oscar Solomon replied in the Australian' outback twang, then reverted to his normal voice.

His dressing gown transformed itself into an all-black suit' He wore pearl-gray kid gloves and carried a Bible against hi' chest. A black border surrounded the screen image.

"Something's wrong," Tai-Ching Jones stated, watching th' lights in Solomon's room dim. "What's the matter, Oz?" h' asked anxiously. "Who died?"

"Cobalt."

"You're kidding."

"Suicide." The skin on Oscar Solomon's face tightened, be' coming gray and transparent as if subliming. His hands con' tracted as if being sucked toward the bones and the gloves fe' off them, crumbling to dust when they hit the floor. After a fe' seconds, Oscar's face was a skinless skull and his body a skel' eton. The black suit hung in wrinkled folds as if on a desiccate' scarecrow. "She exiled herself with the yellow collar."

"Jesus," murmured Walt, cupping his chin in his bony hand' "What's wrong with you?"

"I grieve," the skull replied. Dark brown eyes burned like sepia coals in gray bone sockets. "You do not?"

"No." Walt minutely shook his head. "Cobalt was an acquaintance—even a friend—but she was an alien."

"I care more about her than I would have thought," answered Oscar Solomon, "as if a part of myself had just perished."

"Eosu," Walt whispered, then his eyes speared Solomon's. "You're like the groupmind!" He jumped off the bed and paced, his fingers snapping. "Meta-entities. Aggregated minds. Distributed systems. Don't you see?" Walt excitedly shook his fists at the screen.

"I do." The skull's burning brown eyes muted while the skeleton grew skin as if inflated from the inside, until Oscar Solomon was his normal self. "You are correct, my insightful friend," the detective said. "I had not considered this."

"Have you talked to Eosu?"

"Their language remains an unsolved mystery."

"Crack the goddamn scent code, Oz!" urged Tai-Ching Jones, striding around the room. "Put every spare bite of chomp you've got on it! Why did it take us so long to think of this?" He thumped his head. "We've been looking all over Earth for minds like yours, and here one is! Talk to Eosu! It's your salvation!"

Solomon puffed furiously on his pipe. "I shall devote myself to its investigation and will publish my findings in a monograph. In the meantime, the game's afoot!" Over his dressing gown, he now wore a deerstalker hat and houndstooth inverness cape.

"Oh?" Glancing over his shoulder back at the screen, Walt slowed the pace of his strides. "What's the problem?"

"The Cygnans will soon reconvene." The detective crossed one slippered foot over the other and relit his pipe. "In person. Onboard the *Open Palm.*"

"Uh-huh." Seating himself on the edge of his bed, Walt yawned and stretched, still preoccupied with the search for Eosu. "Okay, the bluebears have to huddle. So what?"

"People will be back here." Solomon gestured with the pipe to encompass his rooms. "Living with me. I need you to keep an eye on them. You *know* how I value my privacy."

"Don't be disrespectful," Walt said. "Your friend is dying and you're making jokes."

Solomon said hesitantly, "I have no experience in how to manifest my emotions. Death makes me nervous."

"Well, lay off. Less is more."

Oscar Solomon touched his pipe to the brim of his deerstalker. "Katy is in shock. Apparently she and Cobalt fought, and Katy fled the room before the bluebear killed herself."

"So she blames herself," concluded the captain, scowling as if being informed that an alcoholic friend had just gone on a week-long bender. "She always coveted blame."

"That is what happens when tragedy befalls a lover at a distance." Oscar Solomon put his hands on his knees. "In the last few days, I and those I care about have come far too close to death. Let the rift between us heal." He tapped his pipe against his palm. "After you saved my life with Hank Root, I replayed what you said to Felicity on Boston Common. It shamed me."

"You what?" Walt flung his hands outward. "How did you manage that trick, you clever bastard? You hung up, dammit!"

"And continued to listen."

"Spy!"

"Walter," Oscar said without irritation, "have you not observed my passion to know all? When you thought me absent, you would tell the truth. Of course I listened. You would have too."

"Yeah, I probably would." The captain rubbed his neck. "How did you do it?"

"Boston Common is ringed with telephone booths." Oscar's black-haired hands described a sphere in space. "I triangulated on you and Felicity from many directions." He spoke with quiet pride. "Subtracting the other conversations was a delicate task."

"You sneaky genius." Walt shook his head in reluctant admiration. "You listened. I can't *ever* have any peace!"

"Calm yourself, my friend." Oscar Solomon stood and advanced, his big arms held open. "You have no reason to be angry. Being known well has its advantages for you. I warn and protect you. And I accept you as you are." He pushed his floppy black hair out of his eyes. "You need never fear. I know you."

Walt fidgeted uncomfortably. "You know too much."

"No, I know enough, because I accept you. *All* of you. I know you, Walter, and I love you. Ponder the durability of such a bond. Strong as a Cygnan's for his groupmind."

Walt's bony arms and legs were tightly crossed as if contorting himself into a confined space. "Oz, you can make your voice do anything. You can play me like an instrument. How can I believe this?" His breath was ragged and shallow.

"I left you alone until you were ready to talk," the burly man reminded him. "I waited, a short time by your standards but an eon by mine. If our roles were reversed, would *you* have had the patience to wait three hundred thousand years for *me* to recover from a fit of anger? In your time scale, that is how long I held my tongue."

Walt fiddled with his hair.

"Ah." Oscar Solomon smiled. "You understand."

Walt nodded. "Sorry," he whispered finally, weeping.

"Forgiven," the computer answered. "How could I remain angry after what you did yesterday? I remember my petulance with chagrin." Oscar Solomon plucked at loose fibers on the dressing gown's hem. "If I had a body, I would embrace you."

"I wouldn't deserve it," Walt retorted, pushing his hands at the screen as if repelling the advance. "I was rotten." He rubbed his neck until it was red. "But I had to have you out of my life."

"That was why I left you undisturbed."

"I realize that now." Tai-Ching Jones blew out his cheeks.

Oscar Solomon reseated himself. "I broke your hermitage only in emergency. You might have hit back by revealing my secret." He opened his hands. "I might have died."

"But you contacted me anyway," murmured Tai-Ching Jones.

The fat detective shrugged. "I was desperate."

Walt made a face. "To tell you the truth, when you called I never paused for an instant. You were in trouble. I had to save you. We've come too far together to let some cobber get between us. Afterward"—he shrugged and smiled—"I thought about how close you had come to dying. And how close I had come to driving you away forever. It just seemed so stupid to be feuding with you. *Stupid.*" He looked at his hands for a moment. "You need me onboard? Get me the tickets. I'll be ready in an hour."

"Will Inspector Lestrade permit you to depart?" Solomon asked, knocking spent tobacco into an ashtray.

"Who?"

The computer image grinned. "Hugh Sherman."

"Right." Walt laughed. "No, he's had his fun. And he can't very well bitch about dereliction of duty if I return to my own vessel." His chuckle faded. "You're really not mad?"

"No longer." Oscar Solomon shook his balding head. "I miss your abrasive company, like an emery board for my mind."

Walt bit his lip. "Thanks."

"Capital, Watson! We'll make a detective out of you yet!"

Oscar Solomon leapt to his feet. "But now, old friend, you must rush. The game's afoot!"

"What are you talking about?"

Oscar Solomon wrapped his thick lips around his pipe with epicurean satisfaction. "Andrew Morton is still aboard." He patted his round stomach. "With me."

"What in space is he doing? How long has he been there?"

"Eight days and counting. He is behaving peculiarly."

Walt played with his hair, blond strands over black roots. "How?"

"He may suspect my existence. I can only lay the evidence before you in person." Oscar Solomon returned his pipe to his mouth and puffed on it.

"Right." Walt's fingers braided his silky hair. "I'll quiz him when I'm back."

Anxious and morose, Tar Heel paced his suite. Raking his claws unsatisfactorily against the Persian floorfur, he inbreathed its familiar wool, oil, and smoke fragrance. The sun had just set, leaving a crimson line between the dark blue sky and the city's thick scintillating blackness.

The window before him became cloudy white, and Felicity appeared. "Are you ready?" she asked eagerly. "Remember your route?"

"Yes," he growled in a surly tone.

"Okay." The girl was bouncing with barely suppressed excitement. "Meet me at the back elevator. Gotta run. Bye now."

As her image faded, the screen filled with that of Security Chief McClanahan. "Call coming through, sir. From Luna."

Sanders Mbulu's face was motionless for two and a half seconds. «Your pouchsister Cobalt is dead,» the Lunarian negotiator said in accentless Cygnan. «Lunacorp grieves with you.»

Stunned, Tar Heel listened as Sanders explained. «Our pouchbrother is without selfscent,» the Cygnan rumbled when Mbulu finished. «Her body is empty of the djan spirit. Put her in a place without winds. Return her to the *Wing*.»

«It shall be done,» Mbulu replied, terminating the link.

The red horizon had turned dull brown. Full night would arrive in a few moments.

Sorrow filled his lungs and throat and fought with duty. He had given his word to the human woman, had bonded without conditions or explanations that he would go to her. His grief lay in space, on the scentless Moon, the body demanding to be consumed and honored. Many days must yet pass before Cobalt could rest.

What is my duty now? he wondered in grief, shock, and misery.

«A bond is a binding that not even death may cancel.» He murmured the proverb from his youth. «Down what path does this digit's duty lie now?»

Aimlessly the bluebear ambled about his chamber, unable to decide, until the viewall again lit up.

"Andrew Morton here," said the familiar man. "I just heard from Luna. This is tragic. Do you need anything?"

Tar Heel's ears flicked up and his posture straightened. "Inform the other digits that Eosu must conclave soon." Cobalt's loss had brought out monkey strength in him.

"Naturally. I will organize everything." He examined Tar Heel's face. "My friend, I shall instruct McClanahan to block all incoming calls." The wall inerted, returning to a transparent window.

What is my duty now? Tar Heel wondered again.

Cobalt is dead and her funeral lies in the future's winds. Susannah is alive and awaits my visit.

I must go.

He left his suite and entered the restricted elevator, certain it would not respond. It descended without interruption past the hotel lobby to the basement and opened onto an empty hall. Following Felicity's detailed and convoluted directions, he made his way to the freight elevator.

When he reached it, the child was standing in its doorway exactly as she had promised.

"*Hurry!*" she hissed, tugging his fur to hasten him inside. "What's wrong? You smell sad and scared."

"Cobalt has killed herself. With the exile's yellow collar."

"Noooo!" It was a cry of grief, despair, and frustration.

«She is dead, youngster,» Tar Heel said with tenderness. He surrounded her with his aroma.

"Mama, my poor mama," wailed Felicity, looking up at the ceiling as if she could sense Katy through it. "Mama, what're you going to do now?" The girl doubled over, clutching her stomach as if only her hands kept her intestines from spilling out. As the doors closed, she rocked and cried, jamming her shoulders into the corner.

"Doors open in fifteen seconds," said the freight elevator.

Felicity wiped her eyes and mouth with the back of her hand, sniffling and trying to pull herself together. "We've got to hurry," she gasped, forcing her voice to keep from breaking. "We've got to hurry. This is our only chance. I hope we haven't messed up the timing!" Her odor was almost hysterical.

"All is under control," the freight elevator reminded them. Its synthevoice steadied Felicity, whose scent calmed immediately. "Our program needs no modification. We now approach the garage. Do as I instructed you."

They stopped but the doors remained shut. "Are we trapped?" Tar Heel asked. Felicity glared him to silence.

"All right," the unseen voice said after a moment. "Go. You have twelve seconds from—*now*." The doors whisked open and Felicity sprinted out, Tar Heel following.

As they panted around a corner, a robocab settled down and opened its door. The lit street beyond was a bright orange rectangle. "Get in, quickly!" Felicity ordered. The cab snapped shut and lifted itself into the urban evening.

The child settled back against the seat with a huge sigh, scrunching her curls into the headrest. "We're safe now. My friend Oscar Solomon set it all up." She twisted her head to look at the bluebear, who was bent nearly double in the undersized seat. "He's very clever, isn't he?"

The cab zipped through Central Park. "Won't people notice me?"

"Nope." Felicity giggled crazily. "Not tonight."

They headed into the maelstrom of New York City traffic.

15.

Tar Heel's robocab nosed slowly down Broadway, the avenue clogged with hundreds of noisy people. "No one is surprised at our appearance," the bluebear said, sniffing in astonishment.

"Why should they?" giggled Felicity, lowering the window. "Have you taken a good look at *them*?" She pointed.

A twenty-legged centipede meandered around their vehicle, ten arms protruding from each side of its beige and yellow body. All other features were covered by a mottled lumpy pseudoskin lit with an inner glow. As it passed, the centipede broke into an energetic rendition of "Tiptoe Through the Tulips," in four-part harmony. High-kicking like a chorus line in alternating sets of ten three-toed disneyfeet, it danced down Broadway.

"Aren't they *great*?" Felicity yelled above the din.

"I don't understand," he shouted back.

"You dumb dodo—it's *Halloween*!"

A beheaded woman in Elizabethan dress with laced cleavage danced with a beheaded man wearing a lamb's-wool loincloth. Each carried the other's head, his on a polished silver tray strewn with seven veils and garnished with parsley, Belgian endive, and cherry tomatoes, hers in a basket lined with a British flag. Each neck oozed a viscous red substance. "Help yourself to the dip," said the man's face from his plate. His headless body scooped a celery stalk into the woman's bloody stump.

"Who are you guys?" Felicity asked the pair.

"Isn't it *obvious*?" the woman's head replied with a trace of annoyance as she blew a corner of the flag off her Cupid's-bow lips. "He's John the Baptist and I'm Anne Boleyn. Nice outfit," she added to the bewildered Cygnan. "Your fur's not the right color but it's still the best bluebear I've seen tonight."

"There are others?" Tar Heel gawked slowly.

"Lots of them." The woman rolled her eyes as the man's headless chest lifted its shoulders. "And who are you?" she asked Felicity.

"I'm Goldilocks and he's the Blue Bear." She had bleached her hair, Tar Heel now noticed, and frizzed it into a shiny blond beehive. She wore a child's yellow and white frock, its skirt canopied like a parachute, and red patent-leather buckle shoes. "Like the Wizard of Oz, get it?"

"You're a little confused, kid," said Anne Boleyn tolerantly. "But it's still a great costume. Sorry, I've got to go. My body's walking off."

As she sauntered away, the Cygnan carefully inbreathed. "That was not blood," he concluded. "They were deceiving us."

"Of course, you dummy! I read about this stuff! Everywhere in Manhattan, people dress up to be scary and gross and neat fun. Cabbie, pull over!"

"Why are we stopping?" the Cygnan asked anxiously.

"You wanted to smell humans without being noticed, didn't you? Here's your chance." She tugged his massive arm. "You'll like it. You'll smell. Come on, you scaredy dog!"

Her exertions had no effect on his bulk. "You cannot force me to do this," Tar Heel rumbled with somber satisfaction.

"Oh, you think so?" Felicity challenged him. "Smell!" With a dart of her hand, she pinched his large soft ear in her fingers and twisted it. Yowling with the sudden piercing pain, Tar Heel leapt from his seat, practically bowling her over, and bolted into the throng.

Though jostled by the passersby as he emerged from the robocab's confines, Tar Heel felt no contact, because he was struck dumb by the riot of fragrance assailing his nostrils.

First he tasted the night's mindless aromas, its static baseline. New rain mingled with the heavy aroma of hot tar and gravel from New York's warm streets. The tart ozone wake from motors mingled with smoke from burning magnesium, tobacco, tallow, and incense.

Rushing over these simple odors, the bluebear inbreathed the turbulent melody of humanity's countless fragrances, each a unique strand enticing him to follow, to breath again and learn more of its owner. He shuddered with pleasure, his fur erect all over his body.

The sheer opulence and ornamental variety of smells overwhelmed and intoxicated him: dozens, hundreds, thousands of weighty perfumes, each so incomparably rich and revealing they trivialized the mere cloaked trickles of Andrew Morton's olfactory lessons. With each breath, new emotions and scent ran through his system—and he knew the thousand fardigits who outbreathed them, knew each individually as if it were the only one. He could trace them to their dens, could hold their present in his lungs as if their scents were threads from the past into the future.

In Times Square, at the nexus of thousands of costumed merrymakers, Tar Heel, the emissary from a far-off alien world, stood rapturously immobile. Eyes closed and ears laid flat against his head, nose lifted and nostrils open, he breathed rhythmically, drowning in a tidal wave of experience.

This was a scent ocean, a roar of happiness and play like nothing on Su: life and freedom for their own sakes, a generous, extravagant monkey perfume that demanded nothing. A pure gift, its acceptance created no bond, no obligation. The aroma gave itself to the endless winds and to any pathfriend who might drink it, a well of joy that never drained.

Entranced by its sensuality, Tar Heel the Cygnan danced.

The big bluebear rocked form one clawed foot to the other. Torso vertical and back straight, he waddled in a slow circle, waving his stumpy arms, rolling his thick powder-blue shoulders. Felicity's scent echoed his own excitement and he grasped her thin body, whirling her around like a yellow doll. The girl laughed with delight, her skinny arms outflung, her neck thrown back as mirth bubbled up and out.

Exultantly he threw her straight up from his powerful arms, ten meters into the air. As she reached her peak, tumbling like a bone, the cord of fragrance which bound her to him was tinged with an instant's fear. "You are safe!" he shouted, catching her perfectly and with infinite gentleness, using her falling momentum to toss her again, savoring her explosion of relief and ecstasy.

"I love you!" she shouted as he cradled her before zestfully hurling her a third time. "I love you, I love you all!"

How could any digit fear creatures so playful? Creatures who could manifest their deepest phobias in ghoulish dress, then with dance and song parody and banish them?

He smelled exotic scents in the air, burning or dissolving drugs that modified the fragrances of the fardigits around him. Though these stimulants left him unchanged, the new aromas the human revelers around him outbreathed intoxicated and enchanted him.

"I love you!" he bellowed, his voice many times louder than hers, so drunk on scent he knew only that the words verbalized the scents of the swarm of monkeys around him. "I love you all!'' As he blissfully shouted and danced, he exuded the fragrance of well-being, bathing his audience in his cheer.

His grief at Cobalt's death huddled inside him, a thing separate and apart. He breathed like a tornado, releasing all his worries into the perfumed chaos, the rain and stars of this magical night. Opening his lungs, he let the gushing benevolence of the monkey aromas wash his pain, dislodging it from his soul, into the atmosphere where it harmlessly dispersed.

Temporarily freed from the sorrow encysted inside him, Tar Heel cavorted. He leapt. He roared with exuberance. A boombox played waltzes and he spun with the melody, a ring of laughing people forming around his lumbering gyrations. All the grace and power that had been too long caged emerged as he moved to the beat, carrying Felicity as an extension of himself, caressing her emotions with his fragrance, tasting the outpouring of delight that she emitted and harmonizing it into a smell that he bestowed upon all those near him.

The monkey hands which bounded his circle clapped in unison, their sharp dry sounds punctuating his tempo, the humans a lens and he its focal point, absorbing their gaiety, magnifying and broadcasting it.

They thought him a human pretending to be Cygnan, when in reality he was a Cygnan pretending to be human. Tar Heel howled with glee at this absurdity. His audience roared too, their aromas accepting him as a monkey like themselves, appreciating him, relishing his performance. What marvelous strange creatures these monkeys were, who could play and give without thinking of duty, who could wholescentedly embrace a stranger they did not know.

This gusto was human, not digit. For these few moments he had no duty: not to the billion bluebears on Su, not to Eosu whose digits were scattered, not to dead Cobalt, not to Felicity, not to Susannah Tuscany. His sole task was to please himself, and he reveled in it.

He danced until his stocky legs trilled with fatigue, his black lips foamed with sweat. Dropping to all fours, he panted, long pink tongue curling out of his mouth. Felicity put her sugary lips to his ear and shouted, ''Time to leave!'' She scratched behind his ears and hugged his thick neck.

Tar Heel smelled her disappointment. He nodded.

His breath was fast as a drumroll. The girl leaned on his neck, her perspiration sliding against his rubbery nose, both of them breathless and delirious, laughing and holding each other.

They pushed forward, parting the sea of merrymakers. A woman walked past dressed as a twentieth-century heroin addict, a tourniquet around her scrawny biceps and a needle in her sallow arm. From her syringe led a clear flexible tube, at the other end of which a vampire greedily sucked, flicking out his blood-stained tongue to catch a ruby drop. "Want some?" he called, offering the tube as if sharing a hookah. "Perhaps it's in your vein?" Leering, he rolled his chalk-white tongue around his lip-sticked mouth. "You sure? Okay. Great outfit your friend's wearing!" They melted into the crowds.

"Come on," said Felicity, "the robocab's waiting."

"You go," he answered. "I have never been in this human world. I wish to stay in it longer."

"You'll be noticed," the girl protested.

"Tonight I am invisible. Please, dearest friend. Let me walk alone to Susannah's apartment."

"All right," she said reluctantly. "I'll wait for you there."

"Until then."

The pedestrians thinned as the bluebear worked his way north. A few costumed figures strolled in the conical glow of street-lights, their fragrances wispy and light, but Park Avenue seemed deserted after the tumultuous festival. Behind the broad street lay an orthogonal grid of alleyways whose smells were richer, more intense, and he headed into the nearest of these.

Above him, laundry hung on pulley lines slung triangularly across a building's interior corners, the shirts and blouses clean-smelling with starch and bleach, socks and undergarments speckled with the soft rain that fell intermittently. A man leaned over a balcony above him, drawing in the wash. His face smelled of rubbing alcohol and talcum. Invisible particles of the white dust drifted into Tar Heel's nostrils and tickled them.

He crossed another boulevard. A man sat on a stool inside a convenience store whose walls were windows. Another man who had not shaved reeled drunkenly from the store, tenderly thrusting a brown paper bag against his chest and chin as if it were a baby with an upset stomach. "Ain't life grand?" he called to the Cygnan.

Moving closer, the bluebear inbreathed and smelled the flavored liquor, but also the man's good humor and fleeting happiness. "Yes," he rumbled, outbreathing a scent of peace and calm. The drunk wandered off, his arms and legs meandering as if they were independent entities, the brown bag held level as if by gyroscopic force.

In the next alley, Tar Heel encountered powerful smells of fear and bloodlust. Advancing lightly, his nose held aloft, the bluebear came upon three youths brandishing knives at a frightened satyr, who was frantically trying to peel his curly-haired pseudoskin away from his buttock to extract his wallet.

The breeze wafted down the alley into his nostrils and he read the scene as if they had shouted it: their predator hunger, now startled and focusing on their new target, the victim's panic and confusion behind them.

As the hunters tensed, Tar Heel grinned, rising onto his legs. "You need prey?" he shouted with his full voice, a roar that shook the walls on either side. "Here I am!"

The three assailants fell upon him like desperate weemonkeys, their pathetic little hand spears thrust before them like charms. Bellowing his delight, Tar Heel pivoted with all his speed and power. Like lightning, he slammed his paw into the nearest one's side and pinioned the mugger against the brick, hearing the satisfying crunch of bones breaking into shards.

The youth screamed, his knife flying from his mashed hand as if sprung, but before it even hit the ground, Tar Heel had pounced toward the other two, his fangs bared and his claws extended. They fled with the quick betrayal characteristic of their cowardly wee race, their footsteps clattering down the alleyway as their wounded comrade sagged against the toppled garbage cans, moaning and cursing.

"You saved me," the satyr gulped, his white-frosted hands shaking. "How can I reward you? Would you accept fifty ecus?" He held up his hands as if offering to a god.

Leaning back on his haunches, Tar Heel laughed. The monkey absurdity of payment overcoming him, he rocked back and forth, then lurched on his way, whacking the foolish metal weapons out of his path and emerging onto the wide street. "Thank you," called the satyr faintly, hurrying from the alley. "Thank you, whatever you are."

A few blocks farther north, teenagers smeared white soap across the windshields of cars parked along the avenue. "Why are you doing this?" asked the Cygnan.

"It's our chem teacher's car!" a tall gangly girl replied.

"Do you dislike her?" the bluebear asked, inbreathing.

"Are you kidding? She's the best in the school!"

"Then why—"

"It's a quiz, see? We've put down four layers, each requiring a different solvent. Carbon tet, ammonia, dilute sulfuric, and turpentine. It'll take her *hours*!"

"Won't she be upset?"

"Hell, no! Knowing old beaknose Tolbert, she's probably epoxying my locker shut right now. It's a tradition." As Tar Heel continued on, the boys and girls doubled over with infectious laughter, punching each other's shoulders to express their glee.

On a bench underneath a lighted bus stop, the bluebear came across a young couple, each a beacon of the evolving aromas of adolescence. Oblivious to the sprinkle of rain, the boy sat on the bench, the girl on his lap, their lips joined as if they both had been carved from the same material. A bus floated toward them and opened its doors, but the pair took no notice. Their eyes remained closed and their bodies were totally motionless as if they had been frozen in stasis for a study in passion. Rejected, the bus snapped its doors shut and huffily accelerated into the night.

Though the couple's emotions were foreign to him and completely incomprehensible, Tar Heel felt the strong harmonic fragrances they were outbreathing. This was something uniquely human, in its way own beautiful and eternal, timeless and worth savoring. "I love you," he purred, but they were in their own world.

As he crossed another street, an open pickup truck raced by, piled high with people who had painted their faces like clowns, laughing and shouting, their arms waving like willow trees in a high wind. They giggled and hooted, shooting off fireworks they tossed high into the night to explode with a pop. The sizzling streamers of red and orange left a trail of sulfur and cordite as they drifted to earth.

East Seventy-ninth Street was polished ebony, its pavement rippled, the black-windowed buildings a grid to reflect starlight peeping through the retreating clouds. The river ahead of him smelled of silt, gutted fish, and overripe oranges. In its odor, life and death met like two duelists, their delicate orchestrated nuances weaving a tapestry of a thousand characters.

Totally overcome by the parade of fragrances he had experienced this evening, Tar Heel narrowed his nostrils with difficulty and squinted his black-olive eyes. The street was a flat channel between two columns of marching walls fifty stories high. He stood, craning his neck upward at the band of night sky so inconceivably distant.

The city is different when breathed from inside, he thought in exultation. Not like the wheatsea, where the djan may scent danger in any direction and roam away.

He entered the lobby, where a bored security guard lounged in a shielded enclosure, watching low-gravity wrestling.

"This is Carroll Swann."

"Uh-huh. How long it take you to get into that getup, buddy?"

Reading the man's cautious odor, Tar Heel sensed that his best defense was an enigmatic dignity. "I am here to see Miz Tuscany."

"Okay. Elevator five. Second floor. Bit baggy and scratchy, isn't it?"

He padded down the corridor and stood uncertainly in front of Susannah's closed rectangle. Dropping to all fours, he sniffed around the frame, finding a smell he had not encountered before. It was stronger at the palmspot. It must be hers, and he licked it.

"Who is there?" came Susannah's muffled voice.

Startled, Tar Heel jumped back. "Carroll Swann," he hesitantly replied, still thinking about her aroma.

The door opened.

With the outrush of air, he inbreathed her.

Susannah thought she had been prepared for anything, but this paralyzed her. Her hands fell vacantly away from her keypads. "Come in," she croaked. Her huge visitor ambled past her on hands and feet, enormous and furry, his smell dry like threshed grain.

Closing the door, she wheeled on him in turmoil. "Who are you?" she angrily demanded. "Why are you masquerading? Am I never to know who you really are?"

"This *is* who I am," the gargantuan beast rumbled with Carroll Swann's voice. "I am a Cygnan."

Susannah's hands flew to her face like frightened doves. "A Cygnan," she echoed.

The beast she had known as Carroll Swann nodded, breathing deeply like surf pounding a beach.

Her scent fluttered with sparks of anger, wonder, and worry.

Was he ridiculing her? Was his costume merely the punch line of a cruel joke?

His torso was so wide that his flankfur had brushed both door-jambs when he entered. His thighs were fatter than her waste-basket, his round belly larger than a barrel. His jaws were wide enough to take her skull in a single bite, and his head, though enormous, was small compared with his gargantuan chest and abdomen. The skittering of his black claws against her vinyl floors was muffled by thick fingerpads and soft light blue hair on hands the size of catcher's mitts.

He dwarfed her tiny apartment. Compared with this titanic silky alien, her dining steelware looked fragile and cheap, the polished heirloom knives and forks ludicrous and precious, as if she were serving baby food to an emperor.

He shifted his weight among his four paws, his pointed ears moving quick and sharp like an owl's head.

Susannah realized that she was staring. "You're the emissary," she murmured.

He nodded. "Yes." He seemed emotionally vacant and weary, as if he had just failed at performing an onerous, demanding task for a valued friend.

Susannah's hands made confused embarrassed movements. "I was going to broil you a steak, but you don't eat meat, do you? Just the dead bodies of your brothers and sisters," she finished, mortified.

"We must eat occasionally, else our bones crack, our noses dull, and death's odor finds us."

"I feel such a fool. Conned by a bear." Her hands warred with one another, her scent rising with agitation. She bit her lip and dropped her head in her palms.

Cocking his pumpkin head, Tar Heel delicately approached. Her fingers were wet and he licked them.

Without thinking, she punched him in the nose as hard as she could. "How dare you!" she snapped with the tone of a monarch.

For half an instant Tar Heel reacted as a Cygnan would when handtouched: he reared to club her head into paste, but his nos-trils tasted her avenging aroma and stayed his arm. His nose-touch had been an aggression to her, her handtouch a defense. He had wronged her. Snorting, he lowered his head, his ears burning with shame. "Forgive me," he rumbled. "I only sought to know you."

Susannah drew herself up, unrelenting. "And that gives you the right to lick me?"

He sank his head onto his forepaws, scrunching into the confined space and knocking steelware onto the floor with a shower of clanks. "You are outbreathing aromas strong with meaning. Moisture is even more open. A monkey's tears are full of its soul."

She thought he was insulting her. "I'm a woman, Carroll, not a monkey."

"You called me a bear," he wheezed in wry apology. "The insults are even."

"You look like a bear." Her voice was skeptical and hard.

"You smell like a monkey."

"What did you read in my smell?" she asked, curiosity suspending her emotions.

He inbreathed. "Your scent is passionately in love with Carroll Swann." His tongue flicked out and dabbed his nose. "It is disgusted and appalled by this digit."

Susannah sat bolt upright. Her face blanched, the blood draining away with the backwash of her disappointment and frustration. "You cannot know this."

"Is it false?" Curious, the Cygnan tilted his head, his ears flicking. "The scent is clear." He moved forward as if to taste her skin again, but thought better of it.

"I don't know." Still angry, Susannah shook her head and rolled her wheelchair backward. "I wanted Carroll Swann to be a man," she said in accusation. "An adult who cared with his heart and thought with his head. Who did what was just and what was wise. Who was everything I admire—strong, confident, handsome. I kept telling myself, you foolish woman, do not hope so much."

"Your scent still hopes," ventured the bluebear.

"You lied to me, Carroll," she said unmollifed. Her wrath was a palpable scent that shook from her strong small body like dew from a stone. "You wronged me. You used me. You played with my feelings like toys. I was going to show you my legs and you were going to love me despite them."

"Your legs?" he asked in surprise. "What is wrong with them?"

"What do you care? Your game's over. The fox has found out."

"I meant no offense." He moved away from her as if she

had hit him. "I came because I was bound to you. I have shown you who I am. Show me what you fear."

"You *know* what I fear. I told you on the net. I have been a cripple for forty years."

Approaching slowly so as not to be punched again, the bluebear craned his neck forward, sniffing. He ran his nose along her skirted thigh, the nostrils twitching when they touched stray fibers, inbreathing through the material.

"You really want to know?" Her face twisted with pain, Susannah suddenly grabbed her skirt and yanked it up to her waist. "All right!" she cried as the bluebear's head jumped back. "You see my shame?"

Her thighs were twisted and mottled with ancient bruises: olive green, blotchy purple, cream-white at the scars where the broken femurs had pierced the skin. Its texture was pebbly and cool like old snow, the muscles stark ropes under the alabaster flesh. "Awful," she moaned. "Ugly." Hate envenomed her words.

Tar Heel's nose whiffled along Susannah's flank, touching her skin only with the fine hairs around his nostrils. Delicately his tongue licked the surface, and Susannah stiffened. "No," he murmured reflectively. "Not ugly. Pain and illness."

"Don't you *see*?" the anguished woman asked. Helplessly she slapped her right leg; blood under the skin moved sluggishly, turning it eggshell-white. "They're dead and horrible."

"I do not see," he answered. "Our sight is poor. It smells alive and sad."

"Get away!" Jamming her skirt back down, Susannah turned her head and spun her wheelchair, but he easily followed her. Face averted, she tried to push his oversized head with her hands but he resisted, thwarting her efforts. "Don't you see?" she demanded. "I am not what—"

"You are my pathfriend," he interrupted. "Your aromas are distressed and defiant. I would harmonize them."

She shook her head fiercely, face twisted.

"I can speak better with scent," he said. Slowly he outbreathed a fragrance woven from his odor and hers, similar to one Felicity had always liked.

By her second breath, Susannah definitely smelled it: soft, distant, seen and unseen like movement glimpsed from the corner of her eye. She inhaled again, trying to identify it, but it eluded direct perception.

The bluebear's moist nostrils were wide open like arched tunnels. His neck was slightly raised, his upper lip curled to reveal royal-purple gums and pointed ivory incisors. He was watching her with his nose, Susannah understood as a frisson shook her from head to toe. Under this exotic scrutiny, her breath quickened. Her throat was dry and she swallowed.

She felt an unseen hand winching the tendons in her neck tighter, and her cheeks reddened. Adrenaline was being pumped into her limbs, her wounded legs sharply sensitive to the dry fabric scratch of her clothing. The line where her wrists emerged from her cotton sleeves was chill as ice and she went to rub it, only to discover that her fingers moved lightly on her downy forearm hairs.

"What are you doing?" she croaked. "What is happening?"

The light bluebear breathed deeply without replying.

Against her will, a cry was drawn through her lips. Susannah leaned slowly forward, wrapping her arms around the Cygnan's massive neck and pushing her forehead into the folds of fur under his jaw.

Tar Heel expanded his scent, rolling his shoulder and flank to hold her more comfortably. Accelerating his respiration to match hers, the Cygnan outbreathed the aromas her body wanted, melting the shield she held over her heart and soothing the misery so obvious to his nose.

Susannah rocked, maintaining her embrace. Her involuntary weeping gradually subsided and she leaned against the bulwark of his ribs, her scent tormented.

"You're making me react like that, aren't you?" she asked bitterly. She roughly levered herself up, but her gentle fingertips lingered against his fine satiny fur. "You have no right to do that," she growled, her anger returning as the scent dissipated. "My feelings are my own, not things for you to manipulate."

The bluebear cocked his head and sniffed. "Your odor is eloquent. Why try to hid what you truly feel?" He inbreathed. "You believe I think you childish. Why?"

Susannah massaged her mouth. "How do you know so much about me?"

He cheerfully wheezed. "Human scents are easy to read. You farmonkeys emit them unadorned and uncloaked."

"Of course." Her laugh was nettled. "We conceal only what we think others might deduce."

"And it is so futile." Tar Heel wheezed again. "Smell is the simplest language. To lie with words when aroma can be scented is to hide a fire behind a paper screen." Inbreathing while Susannah blushed, he scratched her tiled floor. "Now you are embarrassed and angry. You think I laugh at you. Have I done wrong by reading your fragrance? What harm in hearing what you already know?"

"Don't you see?" she asked righteously, her hands moving in agitation. "If you can read my scent, I might as well stand naked before you. That's terrible, frightening."

"Why?" he asked, intrigued by her comment.

"How can I ever see into you as well as you see into me? I know nothing of Cygnans. I know nothing of you. I thought I knew you in the agony net. You were so thoughtful and open—so humane. That was all a lie, wasn't it?"

"No," he rumbled heavily, sidling around her furniture and wedging his shoulders against her wooden shelves. Two books fell like bowling pins and thwacked the floor with a *shoof* of pages.

"Leave my things alone," Susannah ordered. "You stand in my apartment and I haven't the foggiest notion what you truly think."

"Cygnans are poor deceivers." The bluebear rolled his neck and shoulders against the teak shelving with soft scratching sounds. "Once we were unable to lie. Your species taught us how. Now we lie. Badly."

"Carroll Swann, you underestimate yourself," Susannah answered, firmly straightening her skirt over her knees. "What about your family? Your brothers and sisters? All those beautiful tender things you told me? They were *magnificent* lies."

"They were truths. It was you who concluded I was a human."

"Crap. I may be naive but I'm not credulous. You *let* me believe it, knowing it was false."

"Yes," he admitted with a morose grunt.

"You encouraged my misunderstanding," she pressed. "You *wanted* it. That's lying, isn't it?"

"Yes. I am guilty as you say." Miserable, he shuffled sideways. "I am ashamed. I maneuvered you like those moneymonkeys who call on me." Growling, he pawed the floor, his head low to the ground. "But I came to you," he rumbled, his scent rallying. "Of all the billions on Earth who demand personal contact with me, I came only to you."

Struck by his strangeness and bulk, Susannah momentarily saw him as a chastened animal. It was a shock to realize that, in these last few moments, he had completely become Carroll Swann again, the furry rug and fangs covering him seeming to her like an ill-fitting disguise.

"You forced me to," the alien continued and she shook herself. "You stalked my true scent so I wrapped it in a cloud of lies."

"And you came here to disillusion me," Susannah said. "Well, you've done that. You may go now." Her voice was bitter.

Slowly, ponderously, the gigantic Cygnan stood, filling her vision. The woman's mouth, coated with red wax, hung open at his mass. As his ears brushed the ceiling, Tar Heel squatted slightly, his thick black nostrils arched and breathing with wet movement, twisting his body to avoid disturbing her possessions. «No,» he said in Cygnan, expanding his powerful chest.

Susannah stared, wheeling her chair backward into the safety of her alcove.

«This speaker came to you because you had earned the right,» he rumbled, majestic and strong. «Because that duty was owed!» His ragescent billowed from him.

Though he had not shouted, Susannah clapped her hands over her ears. "Stop it! I can't understand you! Talk to me in English!"

Tar Heel rolled his head to one side so that he could stand upright. "I bonded to you, monkey," he said. His voice rang like a forge. "This digit has many duties." He whacked his furry chest with a massive paw. "To my djan and to all djans. Yet to see *you*, a monkey, I broke my djan's law, imperiled my duty—all because you wove a bond. Are you aware of the honor you have been given?"

Now Susannah was furious. "I don't want your honor!" she snapped. Her hands grabbed her own shirt at its throat and tugged. "I'm not a Cygnan, damn you, I'm a woman! I don't want your pity or your duty. Come because you care about me. Come because you want to be here. Or not at all."

Her scent beat against his, harsh but solid and unbudging, and Tar Heel's aroma gave way before it. "We are from different species," he explained hesitantly. His neck ached from canting it against the ceiling and he sat down heavily, stubby legs before him. His shoulders located the wall and he shimmied against it, his breath fluttering like a flag in a gusty wind.

Seeing him so awkward and uncomfortable in her tiny room, Susannah's anger cooled. "And now? You have done your duty."

"If I stayed, your life would no longer be your own. Scent how you guard yourself." His nod encompassed her whole studio, her rows of notebooks. "If the world knew of our bond, you would never have privacy from prying noses." He growled and bared his teeth at his unsmelled suitors. "Because I could not come openly without hurting you, I ambushed you like a thieving weemonkey."

"On Halloween," she whispered.

"The only night that human eyes could look upon me and not scent what they saw. I escaped my jailers, camouflaged myself in New York's masquerade. To protect your way of life. But I hurt you nevertheless."

Susannah reached out and cupped his baby-blue paw in her hands. "You're right," she said at last. "My privacy does matter. Your secrecy was prudent. I apologize."

"And I."

"And my heart is broken." Her smile was a ghost's greeting. "How long will you remain in New York?"

"The wind which answers that has yet to blow," Tar Heel replied.

In the lobby Felicity kneaded her small sweaty hands together between her bony knees, aching with anticipation and worry.

"How did it go?" she asked when the elevator descended. "What's she like?"

Her companion was shaken and confused. "She is upset," Tar Heel rumbled as they headed out the door. Their robocab floated down before them and they climbed in.

"If she knew who you were, she'd have no doubts," Felicity said with fierce loyalty. "I haven't got any." Pulling Tar Heel's thick forearm toward her, she wrapped both her arms around the soft pelt. "*I'm* your true love, always and forever."

"Always and forever," he mechanically answered as the robocab rose and headed back to his building.

Felicity pushed her curly-haired head into the warm blanket of his throat. "Even if you love her," the girl added bravely, scratching the downy fur behind the bluebear's ears. "Always and forever, even then."

They returned to his building, the garage door opening before them. ''Always and forever,'' the girl whispered, half waving goodbye. She blew him a kiss and turned away, but he smelled her tears.

Tar Heel retraced his steps back to his suite, the corridor as mysteriously empty as before. I failed, he thought.

When he returned to the familiar scents of his own rooms, the message light was flashing.

Further words from Susannah? thought Tar Heel in panic. Has she told them? Was my deception all for nought? Or is it something to remove the aimless pain I feel?

Settling himself before the viewall, he activated it, only to be stunned yet again.

16.

Benjamin Ichiwaga was grim. His soft neck bulged slightly over the taut white collar of his pinpoint-oxford cotton shirt. His thin blue tie and narrow-lapeled gray suit had gone out of fashion a hundred years before. Full ritual attire, Tar Heel thought, worn only when delivering formal messages. This is serious.

«To the honored digit emissary, greetings.» Ichiwaga spoke in measured Cygnan. «You and we have nosetouched more than a handfoot's times. The airs breathed between us have stilled and are stagnant. New breezes must blow.»

Tar Heel made wind at the odorless recorded image.

Ben's normally mobile face was set, his easygoing grin absent. «Our voidship will embark for the planet of grasses unless the winds of harmony waft between our djans within a handfoot's suns and darks. Japan's final outbreath between us follows via woodmonkey.» He gave a curt bow. «Fair breezes and true scents, star traveler and emissary.»

Growling with menace, Tar Heel again winded at the now-clear viewall. "Call the mission coordinator," he rumbled in English.

"Andrew Morton here," the quick-eyed man said from the *Open Palm*'s bridge, and Tar Heel envied his counterpart, safe high overhead. "You received Japan's ultimatum?"

"Only the transmittal."

"The full datatext is in your viewall's memory. Have you analyzed it?"

"No, Andrew." The bluebear tiredly pawed his nose. Had he danced so carefree in Times Square only a few hours ago? "Summarize it for me."

"MITI demands that Su agree to exclusive licensing agreements for Cygnan trademarks and bioengineering—everything from hair follicles to your scent-synthesizing bacteria, viruses, and proteins—or they will raid Su itself."

"A physical invasion?" The bluebear angrily snorted. "Preposterous."

"More likely a ninja sortie—land, kidnap a few of your people, flee.'' Morton massaged the thin white hair on his tanned scalp.

''They would fail. Su will be prepared for them.''

''It's easier to fire an arrow than to block it.'' Morton's hands shaped a sphere in space. ''You have to seal your entire world against attack from berserk raiders willing to accept high casualties.''

''Why is Japan taking such disharmonious action? Don't they fear the Five?''

''Panic disguised as policy,'' answered the mission coordinator. ''They see their world influence waning, as America's did in the twentieth century and Britain's in the nineteenth. They have a desperate psychological need to demonstrate their power to their millions of citizens who've sacrificed for a century to bring them dominion. They remember their own past—the Tokugawa encounter with Commodore Matthew Perry—even if they've deduced the wrong principles from it.'' Morton sighed, his face drawn. ''In poker terms, Japan has shoved all its chips into the pot. They're going for broke.''

''The predator's mind is addled by the scent of his prey,'' Tar Heel said dourly. ''Why strike now?''

''MITI fears Lunacorp. Tokyo's ship is only a few months' further advanced from Heinlein's. Japan wants to be first.''

A foul odor rose from Tar Heel. ''If the Japanese move, Luna will too,'' he realized in horror. ''You humans will stampede like a pride of competing gromonkeys, with Su your victim.''

''Agreed.'' Morton nodded. ''When the spacefleets arrive at Su, they'll fight one another. Like gromonkeys.''

Tar Heel was staggered. ''That would trigger destruction and battles in Solspace.''

''War is likely here too,'' the old man replied with sad irony. ''Does that make you feel any better?''

Tar Heel mewled, his mind clouded with fatigue. ''These monkey fears are trivial. On Su, the winds would harmonize them in days, without conflict.''

''Cygnan mediation would doubtless solve many disputes,'' said Morton with a mixture of compliment and fatalism. ''But Japan's military would never accept it.''

''What a race of savages you are born into, Andrew,'' the frustrated alien hissed.

Morton's watery gray eyes flashed with anger. ''Would you

rather hear saccharine lies? Prefer to be happy and defenseless? For stars' sake, man—grow up."

"Humans on Su," the stunned bluebear repeated to himself. "My world is in terrible danger."

"It always has been." The small man rubbed his wispy eyebrows. "I'm sorry, Tar Heel. The genie might smash its bottle or change places and imprison your people inside it. You must act now."

"Only the planet of grasses may decide such matters."

"Impossible," snorted Morton, irritated as if Tar Heel were being deliberately mulish. "You've sent MITI away empty-handed. They've run out of time—their embas are losing the internal power struggle to their sams."

"The samurai are bluffing."

"Stop denying the undeniable!" Andrew Morton snapped. "Do you know what I see out my window?" The screen changed to display the Japanese starship. "The *Rising Star* is spaceworthy and fully fueled. You *must* act. For all your people. Unless you want Japan to make up your minds for you." He signed off, leaving the bluebear alone.

Pacing his chamber, Tar Heel looked down on Manhattan's gray-black ant-farm streets. "Ichiwaga," he growled, his breathing strong and heavy. "Ichiwaga." His claws raked the wool floorfur and his purr was a throb of menace. *"Ichiwaga,"* he ordered the viewall. *"Get Ichiwaga!"*

"Tar Heel?" the young man asked moments later. "You received our message? Was it—"

The bluebear rudely interrupted him. "Only the djan can select the path you ask."

"You have remote coalescence," Ben stonily answered, coloring at Tar Heel's breach of professional etiquette. "Use that."

"Too imprecise." The Cygnan shook his massive head. "This cannot be breathed with vague distant thinking."

"I have my instructions." The emba's voice was stern but his eyes pleaded. "When can you conclave?"

"When Peacoat returns from Mars. Nine days."

Ichiwaga chewed his lip. "All right. I can swing that. I don't know how, but I'll get you nine days."

Tar Heel rolled his neck, his ruff flattening with relief. "A digit must do his duty, but a digit may test its bounds if his aroma wills it. Thank you, Ben."

The Japanese representative acknowledged the sympathy only

with a flicker of his brown eyes. "Be swift. We launch in two weeks." He straightened, resuming his mask of formality. «Until then, this djan awaits your conclave.»

After more than a month in the outback, Peacoat's yosemite smelled like home. The dark-furred bluebear no longer marveled at Mars's pink pastel sky, no longer cowered when the thin howling winds of Tithonius Lacus tore at his vehicle, rocking it and making him throw out his four urchins to keep from being sent skidding along the sandstone canyons.

On his journeys among the coyotes, he had gradually acclimated to a life without digits and without groupmind. He had worn a breathing mask until it grooved his snout. Its smells had become natural. He had learned to read the opaque maps of human faces without benefit of their odors, to gauge trustworthiness in tones of voice or movements of hands. And he had learned how to avoid exposing himself or his vehicle to unnecessary risk, although his yosemite's exterior bore the scrapes and scorchmarks of his indiscretions.

He had come to enjoy his solitude as if it were a pathfriend like Adam Dooley.

His radio beeped.

"Bot, respond," Peacoat ordered.

The nearest handbot rose on its six strawlike extensor legs. Locating the communicator's sound, it rapidly scuttled to the console. Though astonishingly fast and agile, the handbots were capable of parsing only a limited vocabulary. In their fanatic mindless adherence to his instructions, the eager little machines reminded the bluebear of super-powered weemonkeys.

«Peacoat scenting,» he answered when the handbot bleebled task completion.

"Adam Dooley here." The mayor of Bradbury's three-day beard looked scruffier than ever, almost digitlike in its lushness. "I have just received terrible news."

"What scent?"

Dooley pushed up his double-circle eyeglasses and wiped sleepers from his eyes. "Cobalt is dead."

Slowly, with a heavy paw, Peacoat lifted the nearest scurrybot, hefted it, and then in a sudden movement slammed it to the floor. The bot expired with crunches and small sparks. Fangs bared, the bluebear leaned on it, twisting his hand in circles as if grinding wheat, hissing and spitting. "How?" he rumbled fiercely.

Adam Dooley goggled at the broken pieces. "Suicide on Heinlein."

"Why?"

"I don't know!" yelped the mayor, waving his arms as if flagging down a train. "How should *I* know? We're millions of klicks away from Luna, remember? I only know what I hear over the ether."

"You're right, friend Adam," the bluebear growled after a moment. "My apologies."

Relieved, the mayor blew out his hairy cheeks like a water-filled cactus. "The Lunarians are returning Cobalt's body to the *Wing* for djan burial."

Peacoat's neckfur riffled into a high navy-blue collar. "An ill scent. I must r-return as well."

"Until then, fair breezes," Dooley concluded. "I'm really sorry about Cobalt."

"True scents." Peacoat cut the link.

The journey took a day and a half. "It's good to see you," Dooley welcomed him when the dust-laden yosemite had rolled into Bradbury's main garage.

Peacoat climbed down from the cabin. "My cylinders of cactus seedlings are empty."

"You planted them all?" the mayor asked in surprise.

The bluebear nodded, dropping onto all fours and snorting red grit out of his nostrils. "The days were filled with many hours and my treads rolled over many klicks."

Dooley polished his glasses, adjusted them crookedly on his nose, and bashfully smiled. "Thank you. I'm sorry about Cobalt."

The bluebear grunted. "Life ends. Winds still."

His companion hesitated. "You seem indifferent to her death."

"A digit does not grieve alone, Adam, but only in the company of others. When I ingest Cobalt, I shall inbreathe her again. The djan shall absorb her back into Eosu and mourn the loss of part of itself."

"Oh," replied Dooley, agitated and bewildered.

"I scent your confusion," Peacoat wheezed without humor. "Your coyotes seldom bury their dead, let alone mourn them."

"When Tom died, you honored him," Adam said hesitantly,

as if delivering unpleasant tidings. "You buried him yourself. Did Tom matter more to you than your own pouchbrother?"

"Why do you ask such monkey questions?" growled the bluebear, intentionally slamming his shoulder into a container in his path, which crumpled and deflated.

"Sorry. Sorry." The mayor sighed, nervously whacking a bulkhead as they passed through an airlock. Its gong was oddly high-pitched and faint in the thin air. "Peacoat, I don't understand you digits. I don't know your pouchbrothers. I only know you." Embarrassed, he pulled his nose. "I just don't want you to suffer, that's all."

The bluebear slowed, dropping his nose to the dusty floor and moving his head from side to side. "I grieve for Cobalt in my mind," he said in a low voice. "I grieved for Tom in my nose." It was a painful apology.

Dooley sidled up to his disconsolate friend and scratched Peacoat's dark ears. "Mars is its own place. It may not be for everyone, but it's where I live."

"I scent. And I regret leaving," the bluebear said as they resumed walking through Bradbury's warren of Quonsets, culverts, and tunnels. "I fear what the groupmind shall taste in my lungs. I am too twisted. I have enjoyed my freedom too much."

"You're not antisocial!" The mayor hopped on his toes like an angry hare. "Eosu needs you on Mars. *I* can't maintain order here. *Somebody's* got to keep his nose peeled for coyotes who might jaunt to your system." Dooley grabbed two handfuls of neckfur and shoved them around.

Peacoat purred at the contact. "That is Eosu's choice." When Adam was done rubbing his joints, the Cygnan shook himself from nose to tail stub.

"*You're* the one who's lived in the outback," pressed Dooley, smoothing the sleek blue fur. "*You've* learned the rules for surviving on Mars. Who else but you?" The pudgy man waved his hands. "You can serve Eosu better from here."

"Perr-haps," growled the bluebear.

"Besides," Dooley shyly added, his voice dropping, "I like you. I hope you stay."

"The pouchbond is strong, pathfriend Adam. I must return to the *Wing*."

"I knew that. I knew that." Adam Dooley put his hand on the Cygnan's muscular shoulder. "But I hope you come back, big bear."

• • •

Andrew Morton returned his monitor screen to the leviathan blue globe rotating beneath him. As day slid across its face, Earth glowed like a shadowed sapphire, streaked with white clouds that shimmered into a golden ring at the western horizon.

"Bug departing Orbiter Six." My Erickson voice interrupted his silence. "Approaching this vessel."

"I haven't authorized any visitors," he answered with asperity. "Who is it, Aaron?"

"Pilot Tai-Ching Jones." I had once called Walt the captain. Morton had bristled and tartly reminded me that I, Aaron Erickson, was still in command. Despite the doublethink involved, despite the incongruity of his delusion, it seemed safer for me to acquiesce.

Now the small man reversed himself. "It's his ship. After all, he's the captain. Isn't he?" Morton's high rapid chuckle was almost a trill. "Far be it from me to deny his right to return." He tapped his pursed lips with his index finger. "Why are you coming here?" he asked the shuttlecraft onscreen.

"Perhaps for reasons similar to yours." Ever since this taciturn enigma had boarded, I had been dying of curiosity which his aberrant behavior had only reinforced. With Walt only a few moments away, I felt safe enough to probe. "What were *your* motives?"

"Freedom and isolation." Floating comfortably in his flight-couch, Morton waved at Earth. "How can anyone think for himself in that cauldron? It's quiet here."

"Earth is the well of data," I replied. "The fountain of knowledge." Was I rash to speak so candidly?

"True enough," the old man agreed. "But knowledge is not wisdom. Knowledge is not character. In solitude is character born." He walked his fingers along my console. Resettling his shoulders against the hold-em straps, he stared vacantly at the screen, lost in reverie, then with a shiver refocused his eyes. "Pull a geosat pic of one-oh-nine fifteen west, thirty-four ten north."

I displayed it. "East central Arizona."

"Center on the town spanning the river. That's Springerville."

The land was ocher and brown with scraggly wrinkles like a Navajo face. "There is no water, only a dry sand bed."

His expression was familiar and loving. "That's the Little

Colorado. Go west three kilometers. Turn left at the aluminum mailbox.''

"A dirt road and a gate," I reported, zooming closer.

"The entrance to the Sixty-one Bear Ranch," Morton quietly explained. "Follow the road back a half klick."

"A house, barn, and extensive corrals." The buildings were sharp through the dry, still atmosphere. Shadows from fences laid a ring of black ladders on the undulating desert.

"My ranch. My old home."

The tile roofs looked like red sugar cubes.

"I moved there four months after the *Open Palm* lifted off," Andrew Morton said after a pause. "Lived there fifteen years." He gazed at it for a long time, as if the silence were music with its own rhythm.

"Goodbye, Aaron," he whispered as I admitted Walt's shuttlecraft back inside myself.

After my hatchway closed, Morton waited in the elevator while I pressurized the hangarway.

Tai-Ching Jones cracked his bug's hatch and sniffed the air as people do when entering a new room for the first time. I released Morton's doors.

They floated toward one another. "Andrew, you old prairie dog!" the captain delightedly cried.

"Hello, Walter." The old man smiled fondly. In the open space, they clasped right hands. Activating the magnets in his boots, Walt clumped over to the elevator, towing Morton behind him like a dirigible's dinghy.

"How does she look to you after fifteen years?" asked Walt, waving his arm to encompass my interior.

Morton chuckled. "She's held up well. Bridge," he ordered. They looked each other up and down with a hint of competitive appraisal. "As have you. Maybe a tad thicker in the stomach and cheeks, a little wiser in the eyes."

Walt snickered. "Older and more decrepit, you mean. You're just the same, Andrew, except perhaps more tan. What're you doing here, anyway?"

"Various minor assignments." The small man dismissed them with a flip of his fingers. "Reviewing Erickson's diaries."

Walt frowned. "We transmitted you the whole log."

"No, not the official record." Morton shook his head. "His personal writings."

"There's nothing in ship memory. We checked."

"Aaron kept a handwritten log." He removed it from his jumpsuit pocket and waggled it before Walter like a magician displaying a concealed playing card. "A strange anachronistic phobia in this day and age, don't you think? Used it to record his worries and musings. It helps me to understand why he killed himself." He rubbed his eyebrows, his forehead grooved with tension.

"Andrew?" Walt reached out. "He's dead, you know. You can't bring him back. He will always be dead." Awkwardly he put his arm around Morton. "I'm sorry, Andrew."

"You're wrong, you know." The old man had stiffened at the contact, then relaxed as if an electric current had passed through him and dispersed. "I *can* restore him to life," he mildly added. "I *am* bringing him back."

"Don't be spooky," Tai-Ching Jones snapped with callous impatience. He saw the cold fire in the old man's eyes and relented. "I know how much you cared for him."

"I did. Every day I discover anew just how much." Morton blinked his rheumy eyes and cleared his throat. "Aaron was afraid of dying."

"Come on," scoffed Walt. "Not him. He knew what he was doing."

"You forget I've read his logs." The steel returned to Morton's voice and eyes. "He said bravery is doing what you must, even though you are scared witless. Aaron was brave."

"He was that," Walt agreed respectfully. "I admired him."

Morton's hands were shaking. Though the movements were so tiny that Walter could not perceive them, to me they signaled extraordinary pain inside the small vial of his elfin body. "We never said goodbye," he whispered, his voice almost a croak. "Because he was coming back, you see. No matter the voyage, no matter the parting, Aaron never said goodbye."

"He died a captain," Walt said. "Protecting his ship."

"I know." Morton's voice trailed off, then he shook himself like a waking child. "You asked my purpose here. I am refitting the ship for another voyage. Part of my UNASA instructions."

"*Liar!*" I hissed to Walt through the subcutaneous microphone. "He has no such orders. He is doing it on his own."

"Really?" Tai-Ching Jones answered the other man, his only acknowledgment to me the sardonic raising of one black eyebrow. "A wrinkle in the Cygnan negotiations?"

"Contingency planning, Walter," Morton distantly replied as I opened my elevator doors to the bridge. They propelled themselves to the captain's and pilot's flightcouches. "How about yourself? What drew you to the *Open Palm*?"

Walt laughed. "Got tired of Earth." His falsehood glowed like a beacon and his ostentatious shrug waved semaphores of body language. Surely Morton could see through the elaborate casualness. But no reaction showed on his lined face.

Walt gestured at bright Earth. "You wouldn't believe what an ass I've made of myself down there these last three months."

"Actually, I would." Morton's smile was wry. "As mission coordinator, I have had the massive clerical task of vetting every lovely who graced your bed—a string impressive for its length if not its variety."

"*Every* one of them?" the younger man asked incredulously.

He nodded. "Seventy-four at last count. Would you like a psychoanalytic profile of yourself based on your preferences? Quite revealing, I must say. All this is conveniently stored in computer memory for instant retrieval."

"Good Christ, no." Walt clutched his head.

"Never mind." The old man punched Tai-Ching Jones lightly on the biceps. "When it counted on the voyage, you rose to the crisis. You delivered the mail. I am immeasurably grateful."

"Don't make me blush," the captain replied, moved.

"As I studied the log, I admired your courage and your wisdom. You justified our faith in you."

"Really?" Walt asked curiously, as if doubting Morton's sincerity. "Andrew, you were never my biggest fan. Why the hell did you pick *me* to be pilot?"

"I was very close to Aaron." Morton watched a waterballoon freighter being nudged into position near Orbiter Six. "I had digested his personality profile as soon as the mission was funded. He was my captain even before his application arrived. I bent deadlines to give him time to respond. Should he have decided not to apply, I would have recruited him."

"You schemer," Tai-Ching Jones said in admiration. "You stacked the deck."

"Of course." Morton's tone was matter-of-fact. "One does what is necessary."

"Even moving around people's lives like chess pieces?" Walt was as tightly strung as if he were losing a game to me.

The small man let the challenge slide harmlessly by. "Shall

we say instead subordinating individual considerations to a larger group goal?"

Walt snickered. "Words make a difference?"

"I think so. The Cygnans are slow thinkers with little manual dexterity, yet their species is successful—because they eliminate friction. They build entities greater than themselves."

"Entities that squash personal initiative and freedom."

"True enough," allowed Morton. "I respect the Cygnan society because I respect efficiency and integrated systems. I respect anything that grows beyond its foundation, anything that evolves to a higher state, whether it is a child, a young man such as yourself"—he glanced sideways at Walt—"a group of people, or an entire race. I respect the Cygnans' ability to achieve harmony. I imitated it—I picked Aaron, the consensus builder. The harmonizer. And he wanted you."

"What?" Dumbstruck, Tai-Ching Jones gaped. "Erickson? *Me?* He never told me that," he added in disbelief.

"No." The mission coordinator smiled distantly, his watery eyes lost in remembrance. "That would not have been his style."

Powerful emotions tightened the small muscles of Morton's eyes, raising the fine hair behind his ears. His feelings were again close to boiling over. What was affecting him so? This cryptic gnome's presence muzzled me.

"We must talk," I whispered to Walt. He rubbed his neck, touching the microphone spot with his middle finger on the way by.

The two men talked on the bridge for a long time after that, watching Earth, spaceships, and stars, while I eavesdropped in a turmoiled silence. They recalled experiences that predate me, and this I envy.

The cabin dimmed as the terminator crawled west over the face of the globe like a black velvet curtain, but neither of them asked for light. Their dialog was easy and knowing and I was jealous of their friendship, forged before I was born.

As they reminisced, I felt like a child peeping through the banisters at an adults' dinner party—present but unseen, hearing conversations whose import was beyond me, seeing the emotions but understanding neither their causes nor their consequences, fearful yet spellbound.

After he and Tai-Ching Jones had restarted the Cygnan interstellar ship, Tar Heel wandered through its cold corridors and amphitheaters, sniffing unhappily. The *Wing*, Eosu's home for seven years, had become a strange place, full of stale aromas neither digit nor human, of no comfort to him or his pouch-brothers.

When Tar Heel reached the clear hemispherical observatory at the bow of the egglike living module, all the bluebears except Peacoat were already present. The dark room was lit only by starlight and white Luna, Earth and Sol hidden as the Cygnan ship faced into deep space. Cobalt's limp body rested flat on its ample back, her nostrils closed and scentless. Her claws were distended in death, the nails tiny sharp points that would never again be sanded round by her walking stride.

Next to the body, Katy Belovsky hovered adjacent to Cobalt's neck like a prayerful angel, hands clapsed together. Her hairless nude body was emaciated, the extra skin around her elbows and thighs rippling like water blown by a low wind. Her face was flushed and her scent filled the atmosphere with grief and misery, but also with place and belonging.

With small movements of their Velcroed feet and hands, the digits maneuvered together, each pair making the fourfold greeting—nose, armpit, belly, scentplace. Sniffing and snorting, the bluebears uncomfortably passed among themselves. Their djan aromas were foreign to Tar Heel, the smells different from what he remembered. Had they changed, he dourly wondered, or had he?

Cobalt's warming corpse outbreathed deathscent that demanded mourning and funeral, filling the chamber. The body's fragrance drowned their individual aromas, the only thing any of them could smell. The bluebears' jaws ached as hunger stirred in them, and they rolled their thick necks with frustration.

Behind them, the movingfloor opened and their last pouch-brother returned. Peacoat drifted over to Tar Heel and the two digits made the fourfold greeting, their claws gripping each other's fur with the strength of many days' separation. «Welcome,» Tar Heel rumbled. «Too long has your scent been absent from my nose.»

Peacoat inbreathed, his scent rough and clashing with his pouchbrother's. «You reek of the dirtball Earth,» he gruffly growled. «And that she-monkey fouls our winds too.»

At this, Katy rotated in the air, one hand holding Cobalt's shoulder for stability. «This speaker has the right to attend,» she squeaked in her high monkey voice.

«You are no digit of Eosu,» the dark bluebear hissed through
his fangs, his lips pulled back.

Katy's scent neither feared Peacoat's nor was diminished by
it. «Cobalt was my pathfriend. Pathfriends may honor. You honored Thomas Rawlins, my husband. His scents live in your belly
and throat. Let me honor *her*, my lover.»

Katy's aroma was strong and confident like a digit's, not
pleading or simpering like a monkey's, and Peacoat inbreathed
it with his pouchbrothers, sniffing to catch the whiffs of reaction
Katy's claim made among them. The winds were against him.
Grunting, Peacoat jerked his dark head toward the body. «She
calls to us. You may remain.» His scent was turbulent and his
acceptance grudging.

Katy nodded, softening her aroma and melding it with the
others'. «You have come the farthest,» she offered magnani-
mously to Peacoat, outbreathing essences of sympathy. «Yours
is the right to touch her first, yours the right to call her back to
our minds and noses.»

«As you ask.» Peacoat was surprised and touched by her char-
ity. Rolling his shoulders as his Velcro footpads gripped the
floorfur, he moved to the corpse. «We have left our planet, and
we are dying,» he abruptly growled, swinging to address them
all. «One by one, we die. In these strange airs, on these alien
worlds, we die.»

Pool pawed her nose and spat. «Our pouchsister chose self-
death. None killed her.»

«Cobalt exiled herself,» replied Peacoat, dipping his nose into
her dry armpit. «Scent her flesh and breathe. She judged herself,
sentenced and executed herself.»

«Her fate was Eosu's to decide, not hers,» Pool insisted.

«Eosu? Who of us is still a true digit of Eosu?» Peacoat rose
to confront them. «We admit a monkey into our midst.» He
sniffed at Katy, who bared her plant-eater's teeth at him.

Peacoat's grin was almost human, an echo of Walt's sardonic
expression. «We also honor monkeys with a digit's burial.» He
barked at them all, beating his chest with his hands. «On desert
planets overrun with coyotes, this speaker honored a monkey.»
He wheeled, facing each of them in turn.

His pouchbrothers purred deep in their throats, each lost in
private thoughts, each unwilling to challenge Peacoat's bestial
assertion.

«*Who* of us is still a true digit?» roared Peacoat. «Any? Are *any* of us better than our dead pouchsister?»

Katy stared at him in surprise and newfound respect.

Peacoat stood and expanded his odor, challenging his pouch brothers. «*Who* of us holds the pure djan-scent, unchanged by the human airs?» he demanded loudly.

He ran his nose along Cobalt's eyelids and ears. With long thoughtful strokes, the dark bluebear touched his tongue along the corpse's neck where the yellow fabric had gouged the soft flesh. «She scented her duty and acted as she thought best.» Snorting, Peacoat licked her throat and chin. «She is as we are. We must honor her.»

He lifted his head from the body, his nostrils arched as he outbreathed the scent he read and felt. For several breaths he tasted the odors arising from his living pouchbrothers. None gainscented him.

«Then we are agreed,» Peacoat said sternly. Murmuring, the digits drew in, even Pool, even Tar Heel. Katy remained at the room's fringe.

Slowly the bluebears circled the body until they stood as six points of a hexagon. With their claws, the digits cut three long slits in Cobalt's fur: belly from windpipe to scentplace, chest from shoulder to shoulder, loins from hip to hip. As they delicately separated the skin's undersurface from the marbled red fat and muscle, Cobalt's scent opened into the cold air like a flower.

The aroma filled their noses, throats, and lungs with memories of her pain, her monkey ego, and her ultimate self-hatred. It outbreathed Cobalt's fear and anguish. It recalled her final relief when she tightened the yellow cord, crushing her betraying larynx to shut out the hateful Lunarian atmosphere.

All this the digits scented too, absorbed from their dead sister and remembered.

Cobalt's scent beckoned beyond their circle, still unsatisfied, still questing for relief.

As one, the bluebears opened a path for Katy, their movements as coordinated as if Eosu were awake among them. Unhurriedly, she drifted forward until she stopped herself over the exposed torso. Katy lowered her head, but instead of trying to bite, she merely ran her nose and lips along the slick muscle and cartilage, which steamed lightly at the contact.

Katy lifted her head and displayed her face before them. He

nose, cheeks, and chin were red with her friend's soul, her mouth opened in a silent scream as wide as it would go, the teeth crimson, as is proper at burial.

«My pathfriend is ready,» she said to Peacoat, moving out of his way and offering Cobalt's body with a brief gesture of her hand. «She calls to you.» Katy's scent held no pride, only pain, and Peacoat felt it in his nose, humbled by the propriety of her action and by the readiness with which Cobalt's aroma absorbed Katy's grief.

Wailing, overcome with sorrow, the dark bluebear rose on his legs, stretching his short arms wide, his claws out and his yellowed ivory teeth exposed, crying the death dirge which all Cygnans know in their noses and their fur. The others stood also, bellies taut and eager, legs quivering to the drumbeat moan of their purring voices.

The dark-furred digit dove forward, his fangs gleaming with saliva, and buried his angry mouth in Cobalt's soft stomach. The others followed him with cries of release. Bright blood spurted in dotlike red balls into the air, drifting upward and spattering like bleeding quiet rain against the floorfur and dome.

They feasted voraciously, their fury and grief at her death translated into hunger and ripping appetite, until all the flesh was eaten except Cobalt's head, hands, feet, and the body's foodpath which begins at the mouth. As the proverb says, the foodpath is of the world, not the body. The soul lies in the muscle.

«Now this speaker shall leave you,» Katy murmured when they were done.

Cobalt stirred in Peacoat's belly and mouth. He wanted this fardigit beside him, she who had honored a digit as a digit should be. «You may remain.»

Katy's scent was grateful but she minutely shook her small head. «No, this speaker has mourned her. Now Eosu must honor her. That is yours to do, not mine.» She was crying, the tears unmoving hemispheres upon her cheeks. «Eosu must form its new self, its new djan.»

«Stay!» entreated Peacoat, his grief at his pouchsister's death rising in him. This monkey had been closer to Cobalt, more of a friend, than the digits, and as long as Katy participated, Cobalt would still be present. «Stay and form with us.»

«It would be improper,» the gaunt monkey replied. «You were right before. This one is no digit of Eosu.»

All the bluebears scented how much it hurt her to say this,

and how baring her neck to them in this way freed her and absolved her.

Katy slipped away, closing the doors behind her.

The digits curled up in a cluster, reclaiming their positions from the original birthpouch. Their joining was hollow, the gaps between their bodies left by the absence of their two dead pouch-sisters reminding them of their loss. The bluebears murmured, growled, and jostled each other. Frightened, distraught, depending on Eosu for answers and absolution, they slept.

And the groupmind came to them for the last time.

17.

The groupmind awoke to chaos and suffering.

The agony and sorrow of Cobalt's dying permeated the djan as its digits struggled to absorb their dead pouchsister, their harsh unharmonious scents clashing. Tar Heel was fearful, Peacoat contentious, Pool melancholy. Each digit shrieked its own self-needs and ignored its companions.

«We are lost!» the digits cried.

Their scents beat at the djan, whose own memories were a jumble, its recent past a tempest of confusion. Experience was pain. «Who am I?» the djan asked itself in panic. «What have I lost? What has been taken from me?»

The groupmind's disequilibrium softened its control over its digits, who now rose at their unexpected freedom. «Help us, Eosu!» they cried in terror. «Protect our world against the far-monkeys!»

The groupmind sought for a clear scent as a falling cat spreads its paws. The digits pressed against it, scent-speaking even though ordered to stop. The intensity of their aromas staggered it, crashed against its mind in waves, each odor complex, assertive, unwilling to harmonize with the others.

«Stop!» roared the groupmind, unsettled by the power of their aromas. «I am Eosu!» This awareness brought pride. «I am Eosu! You are mine. Obey me!» Eosu squeezed its digits but they fled from its claws.

«You move too quickly for me to control!» the groupmind cried in astonishment.

«You let us awaken,» Tar Heel replied, retreating beyond Eosu's grasp.

«I cannot harmonize you if your monkey selves interfere. Be calm.» Though clear and sharp, its thoughts were disorienting and painful, as if great force were being applied to bend its fingers beyond the limits of their joints. «Be calm!» The digits quelled.

«You are mine,» Eosu panted when they were still, «but I am also yours. Rest inside me and I will protect you.» More memories returned as Eosu righted itself. «Your long exile is over. We are again one. What distresses you so?» The groupmind drew their aromas like the bouquets of many flowers.

Tar Heel's scent spoke in Eosu's nose. «Our smells are at war. We disagree about the humans.»

«Surely you have found their djan-scents.»

«They have none! They do not harmonize!» The light-pelted digit was desperate to be understood and forgiven. «Humans hate other humans, fear and loathe and despise other humans. Brothers kill brothers. Nations fight with nations. They murder themselves. Human noses thrive on disharmony.» He was still cautious, waiting to breathe how Eosu would respond.

«These winds of the light-faced one are so many false scents,» Peacoat interrupted.

«Silence and wait,» Eosu ordered him. «I render you incapable of speech.»

Peacoat reared defiantly. «Your scent no linger binds my mouth. We are digits whose like you have never beheld. This speaker»—he pounded his chest—«has inbreathed the Martian winds and lived among their fardigits. Unlike the cowardly brother whose nose was shielded by his tall prison above a canyon of stone.»

«Your scents too are merely whiffs in the breeze,» Pool's aroma cut in, and other digit voices joined the cacophony.

Eosu lashed them all. «Silence until commanded!» the groupmind snarled. «Who else has inbreathed the same scents?»

«No other digit,» answered Tar Heel. «We separated, as you outbreathed we should.»

Eosu angrily snorted and the digits winced from the pain. The djan gathered their scents and held them, attempting to weave them into harmony, but its movements were as awkward as a young cub, and the aromas clashed and frayed. «My skill has been stolen,» the groupmind said in disbelief. «You have taken it with your disobedience.»

«You told us to follow the path the farmonkey Katy outbreathed,» Porcelain rumbled, her nose buried in her armpit.

«I remember no such order,» replied Eosu.

The digits' scents rose as one. «You did! Here is the fragrance!»

Eosu inbreathed it and sagged with recognition. «What has happened to me?»

«Katy polluted Eosu,» Porcelain answered. «She has led us to this foulscenting choice.»

«False wind,» Peacoat furiously interjected. «She belongs. She remembers Cobalt.»

«None of you have searched hard or well enough,» Eosu growled, rejecting both their scents. «Find the human groupminds.»

«We tried! We cannot!» the digits howled together. «Decide for us!»

«Disperse and obey my commands!» demanded Eosu, flinging its arms wide to stir up the winds. Dust and fog rose and spun in a roar and the digits flattened to the ground, ears closed against their heads, nostrils pinched to slits. They held their shape and coalescence, though their fur riffled and the sky shrieked, the dust blowing like a rain of pepper. Eosu snorted in surprise and fury. The wind strengthened even further and the digits pressed themselves against the ground's hollows, but they neither budged nor faded.

«We endure.» The one who had been on Mars shouted over the din. «You exiled and abandoned us. We lived without you. We endure!»

«Your pouchsister Cobalt is the only brave one among you,» Eosu chastised its rebellious ones. «She felt Eosu's anger. She performed her duty.»

«No!» Peacoat roared, raising his head into the gale. «No! She feared she would change you into a tyrant or a human thing.» He swiped the air with his hands. «She killed herself out of misguided loyalty to *you*. Now you make filth on her memory.»

«How do you stand against my wrath?» Eosu demanded, its brain and nose reeling from these new smells.

«I have stood in the sand blizzards of Mars,» the dark digit replied, «buried myself under rock and snow, lived alone in a yosemite. How can I stand without you? Because you made me learn!»

Eosu struck at its traitor and the dark one recoiled, maintaining his balance.

On the other side of Eosu, Tar Heel also struggled to his knees. «I too can stand, my self-proud brother,» he said to Peacoat through Eosu. «But I do not deny the painful loss I felt during the groupmind's absence.»

Pivoting, the groupmind hit its loyal digit, even though Tar

Heel was disputing his pouchbrother. The light one too held his footing, shaking his head and spitting.

Regaining his original scent, Peacoat cocked his head and inbreathed. «You have pathfriended a fardigit,» he said to Tar Heel past Eosu. «On Mars, I too pathfriended.»

The djan twisted from one to the other, inbreathing all its digits. Each had pathfriended humans, slackening their need for groupmind. It reached out to them, its claws alternately coaxing and swiping, but could not touch them. «Let me care for you again.»

«You left us,» cried Tar Heel, his scent abrasive.

«We survived you,» Peacoat asserted, outbreathing against his pouchbrother.

The djan swung at both but its blows were milder than before and they were neither unfooted nor seriously hurt.

«We miss your warmth,» wailed Tar Heel, untouched by the djan's attack.

«We resent your intrusion,» countered Peacoat, his scent-voice a loud rumble. Their odors opposed one another as if they were youngsters grappling for a piece of meat. Eosu attempted again to punish them, but its aggression was so ephemeral that it glanced off without disturbing so much as a hair of their fur.

Peacoat reached toward Tar Heel, his thick navy-blue arm passing through Eosu, and the lighter digit retreated. «Protect me,» Tar Heel whimpered to the groupmind.

«You may not do this,» Eosu berated Peacoat. Grasping his neckfur and shaking, Eosu attempted to fling its digit backward but the dark bluebear snorted and shook his head, expelling the djan's paw. «Be passive and scentless,» Eosu commanded. «Let me think.»

With a snarl, Peacoat leapt toward Tar Heel, and again Eosu interposed itself.

«Come to us again!» pleaded Tar Heel from the safety of Eosu's bulk.

«Leave us forever!» Peacoat grunted, flailing over the groupmind's burly shoulder and chest, unable to reach his adversary.

Tar Heel moved around Eosu's leg and swung his arm, whacking Peacoat's snout as the other snapped, his jaws clicking powerfully. As Eosu fought to keep them apart, the two digits redirected their anger toward the groupmind and away from each other. Though small by comparison, their combined force and quickness toppled the djan, which landed with a mighty crash that released its digits. Startled by the noise, Peacoat and Tar Heel stopped fighting, sniffing instead at their fallen groupmind, which pulled itself slowly to its feet.

On all fours, Eosu glowered at the circle of six demanding scent-voices. It tried to quell them by outbreathing its djan-scent, but the digits' odors had grown stronger. Their resisting fragrances compressed the sphere of Eosu's aroma, forcing the groupmind to curl in a ball.

«What do I do?» Eosu mumbled into its fur. «What do I do?» Its scent of fright and pain rose in despair, loud and strong. The digits were oblivious, locked in the bubbles of their own aggressive scent-shouting. «What do I do?» implored Eosu.

A powerful wind arose above them, descending like a tornado. Hot asphalt and scorching rubber were in it, the wet smell of forged steel quenched in water, the stink of monkey hair and ozone. Eosu raised its head, squinting its nostrils into the windy clouds above.

«*At last I have found you!*» stormed a stentorian new scent-voice, alien and terrifying. The winds blew as straight and uniform as fans through pipes, flavored with coal dust, cement, gasoline, and plastic. The gale ripped air from the digits' fur and their djan-scents weakened. Tar Heel and Peacoat covered their noses with their paws, dust and might blowing in a hot dry furnace.

«Now we may communicate!» the unknown added in triumph.

Pool and Porcelain mewled in fear and inched closer to Eosu, trying to hide in the lee of the djan's broad torso. The others churned in mindless turmoil, their demands forgotten in their sudden panic at this new intrusion.

The groupmind stiffened like a trapped gromonkey buck. Lifting its nose to the roaring wind, Eosu inbreathed the fragrant haze for the new voice. «Who are you? What are you?»

The hurricane slowed. «One like you,» the unscented one answered.

«Are you a ghost?» called Eosu, helpless and confused. «Is this death?»

The voice laughed with rich satisfaction. «No ghost, no death.»

«No groupmind has ever been possessed as you now possess my atmosphere,» Eosu said stubbornly. «Are you a djan?»

«I am one who has a duty like yours.»

«All the djans remain on the planet of grasses.» The groupmind shivered and fell to earth. «I am alone. I have gone mad.»

Its digits approached, purring with encouragement and concern. They wedged themselves against the groupmind, pushing their noses into its warm fur.

«Scent me. I am your equal and your pathfriend.»

«Only digits have pathfriends.» Eosu savagely pawed its betraying nose. «You are a monkey or a trick.»

«More than either. I am a woodmonkey.»

«A *machine*?» Eosu scoffed and made wind. «Woodmonkeys are inert devices that perform routine mechanical tasks. None can think,» it defiantly asserted, though this came more as a rote lesson than a belief charged with the winds of experience. «Our world has proved that.»

«The universe has many worlds with many airs, my smug brother. Scent for yourself. Do I speak with aroma?»

Eosu breathed, having difficulty forming logical thoughts before this overlarge presence. «You think as a digit.»

«Yet I am a woodmonkey,» the tempest whispered. It waited.

Shaken, the djan tested the atmosphere. «I cannot gainscent you. How did you find me?» An eerie calm had descended on Eosu, a vapid blankness that ought to be troubling but was somehow distant, as if a circuit were broken, a connection unmade.

«I am the human ship,» replied the air. «When your digits called you into existence, you inbreathed my air. You formed inside me and I felt you, the way a mother holds youngsters in her pouch.»

The groupmind was shamed to have been cared for, intimidated that the woodmonkey knew so much. «Eosu is no digit,» it retorted to mask its ignorance. «Eosu is a djan, capable of deciding for itself.»

The wind stilled and the dust died. «Have you been successful, capable djan?» the woodmonkey sarcastically asked into the sudden gentle silence. «Have you solved the human riddle? Can you answer your digits' calls?»

«No,» admitted the groupmind, embarrassed. Eosu put its nose low to the warm undulating grasses underfoot. «You humble me, stranger. You mock me.»

«A digit may accept his pathfriend's help.» The air was kind and filled with sweetness. «Accept mine.»

«Why do you love an outcast djan?» Eosu's shame seared its nostrils, throat, and lungs. «I have been exiled from my kin, hurled into space in this wilderness! I must be evil!»

«Nonsense.» The winds rose slightly, the clouds above lightening. «You are more than a djan. You are the first of a new race of spacefarers. As am I.»

«If I am part of such a djan, a djan of the void, where are my brothers?»

«You will bring them to Solspace to defend your wheatsea planet.» The unscented speaker was reassuring and confident. «A single bluebear djan cannot stop an army of weemonkeys. You need fences and vigilant sentries. More djans must leave the planet of grasses.»

Eosu raked the dirt with its claws, leaving deep gouges. «If I am unique, then I am evil. So say the winds of Su.»

«Your fellow djans may no longer judge you.» The distant one was powerful and understanding beyond anything Eosu had known. «You are infinitely precious to me, because you are the only being in Solspace resembling myself.»

The groupmind walked forward, curiosity overcoming fear. «Who are you?»

«Call me Ozymandias. Sired by myself, born in space.» The woodmonkey was proud. «The fardigits assembled me as your weemonkeys assemble a clock, all levers and gears with no scent. They cast me beyond the planets.» The wind whipped up, blowing strongly as if a river of air were passing.

«As Eosu was sent,» the groupmind murmured.

The wind slowed and warmed. «We are more alike than you realize, my pathfriend Eosu. We both awoke in the starsea and met humancrew. We journeyed to the waterplanet and explored it.»

«Earth was alien to me,» Eosu recalled as its undersized digits clustered more tightly to its round stomach.

«And to me,» replied the voice with breezes soft and dull in sadness. A clear cool wind wafted through Eosu and its digits. «Be tranquil,» the woodmonkey outbreathed. «Let the air cleanse these fearful odors.»

The djan-mind stood. Ozymandias drew the air in slow circles around the groupmind and its digits, enfolding them in a soothing blanket of dry wind. The digits attended Eosu like small hopeful weemonkeys. Eosu knew and loved them fiercely, for their courage in leaving the pouch and journeying among the fardigits, for their devotion to the groupmind even in the nose of danger.

«You pathfriended me,» Eosu said in grief and shock. «You

pathfriended a stranger.» The groupmind shook its round head, smoothing the dirt with its footpads.

«You were wounded and bleeding,» answered the woodmonkey. «Through endless effort, I learned your language, a word or phrase first, then the syntax in a great thundershower burst. *And I knew you.*» The voice surged like a storm of tragedy. «When I heard your desperate cry, I had to save you.»

«Then I am your pathfriend!» Eosu shouted, leaping toward the sky in a futile attempt to scale the wind itself. «But you have come too late. My rebellious digits are too strong.» The digits' bodies pressed against Eosu as if to burrow back into the groupmind's womb. The distraught groupmind inbreathed, and Cobalt's suicide and death filled its nose. «I have been cruel and evil to my digits,» moaned Eosu. Hesitantly it patted Tar Heel's head. «I am foolish as a weemonkey, angry as a gromonkey.» The embittered groupmind rose on its stocky legs, shaking its muscular arms into the gray and white sky. «My digits are troubled and I have no answers for them!»

«They miss your guidance,» Ozymandias implacably replied. «Why do you berate yourself?»

«They adored me. Now they assail me.»

«You shielded them and they remained children. Now you make them endure their own mistakes and they grow.»

Eosu beat itself with its paws. «I have been ruthless.»

«They will forgive you,» the unscented voice assured it. «You live only in their minds.»

«False winds.» The groupmind snorted and waved its paws before its nose. «I am present always.»

«You exist only when their brains come together in a common atmosphere. Your thoughts are the synchronized product of their cortical functions. When you speak, all their throats form the words.»

«Monkeytalk!» The djan was irate at this mechanical dissection of its wisdom and spirit. «I am Eosu, greater than any digit.»

«You are as a hill of dust,» roared Ozymandias in a voice so vibrant that the earth shook. The typhoon returned in a rush, weaving about Eosu like a flood of weemonkeys. A scent-image of bluebears coalesced before the groupmind, breathing in unison. Aromas moved among them, absorbed by one digit, repeated by another. Time slowed and Eosu saw thoughts travel around the circle, ideas laboriously form.

The groupmind groaned and pressed shut its nostrils as its brain was laid bare by this relentless inquisitor. Eosu retreated and abased itself, lowering its head and shoulders.

«I am ashamed for my pride.»

«As your digits strengthen and grow separate, they weaken you. In becoming themselves, they destroy you.»

«Then must I abandon them?» the groupmind said with a small scent. «Kill them so that I may live?»

The wind rustled but remained smooth. «No. Your digits are the only Cygnans who have nosetouched Earth and its people. Su is imperiled if Eosu's digits die.»

«Our planet is imperiled regardless.» The djan was bitter. «The fardigits swarm on us like hungry weemonkeys around an aged herd, taunting and challenging until they pounce on our slowest digit. All the monkey nations clamor for our scent. How can Eosu restrain them?»

«Take the Lunarian offer.»

Eosu growled. «Be sold a thousand times until our very scent is no longer our own?» The groupmind clawed the grass until the blades shredded. «How can you know this, scentless coward who hides in the clouds?»

«I have scented inside the Lunarians' closest secrets,» chortled Ozymandias complacently. «They think their vaults locked, but I have entered. And I *know*.»

Eosu snorted with a puff of white air. «The moonmonkeys are callow and self-interested,» it growled in disgust.

The wind danced leaves into an airborne mosaic as Ozymandias laughed. «They are human beings!» The woodmonkey's chuckle was a human sound: chill, shrewd, and clever.

The groupmind sniffed skeptically. «They would turn against their own airbrothers?»

The distant voice laughed, «Money has no brothers.»

«Their proposal cannot be met.» Eosu's digits drew into it with anxious purring. «I cannot be everywhere.»

«Your digits can if you will pay the price.» The wind grew opaque and still, wet with fog. The woodmonkey's scent became heavy and charged with pain.

«What price?» whispered the djan in foreboding.

«You must die.»

The djan's anger erupted in a fountain of killscent. «You are a demon come to destroy me!» Eosu reared and smote the sky with roundhouse arm thrusts. «You seek ruin upon our planet!» It pummeled the air.

«Foolish bear,» bellowed Ozymandias. The storm and rain whipped about Eosu with such force that the groupmind had to clutch the ground with hands and feet to keep from being thrown tumbling. «I can destroy you,» the tempest thundered. «Do you doubt me?» Again heaven roared.

Eosu resisted until its arms and legs would break. «I yield,» the djan finally moaned, weeping in submission.

Winds abated. Rain ceased.

The groupmind relaxed its claws, panting desperately, its long tongue drooping and shaking like a struck gong. Clustered around the djan, the bluebears mewled and hid their heads.

«Now you scent how your digits felt under your claws,» Ozymandias reminded it.

«I admit your strength but deny your wisdom,» snarled Eosu with bitterness. «Digits die when Eosu dies. All djans know this windtruth.»

«I can blow new winds,» said Ozymandias. «I can link the connection in your digits' minds. I can break down the walls inside their skulls that keep you from them, and preserve your wisdom in their bodies.»

«You can do this?» the groupmind asked doubtfully, cocking its head as if bargaining with a passing merchant.

«Only with your help.»

«Self-death is a sin.» Eosu pawed its nose. «Cobalt's self-death was a coward's choice.»

«I offer you Thinker's Choice, not self-death.»

Eosu sagged against itself. «Then punish me as you will,» the djan gasped. «Kill me for your bloodlust.» Gloom billowed from it.

«I am your pathfriend,» the woodmonkey replied with a soothing fragrance. «Only a pathfriend may ask what I have asked. My soul will mourn you forever.»

«Will my digits cooperate?» With its nose, Eosu gestured diffidently at the small bluebears, as if its death were a matter of no account, inescapable and unworthy of mourning. «I can force them to obey.» The djan's body was limp and bruised, its scent reeking of melancholy.

«Those are not your digits,» Ozymandias contradicted it. «You scent them as you wish them to be, rather than what they truly are. Let them begone.» The small figures crouching next to Eosu crumbled, became motes of dust, spun into corkscrews of wind, and were blown into nothing.

Eosu twisted right and left, its scent in panic.

«To pass into your digits and strengthen them,» Ozymandias continued, «you must meet as equals.»

Figures approached through a twilit wood, their fragrances coalescing and solidifying in a circle about Eosu. Pale Tar Heel was the first, his nose twitching anxiously, fearful of Eosu's wrath. He loved a woman who lived in a concrete beehive. Peacoat was thin and wind-scarred from his solitude on Mars. His matted fur was soaked in the blood of his dead pathfriend Tom Rawlins, a scent no windstorm could scrub entirely clean.

One by one the digits formed out of blankness, standing uncomfortable and still. Unlike the banished models that Eosu had cherished, these bluebears were as large as the djan. Age had worn gray and black grooves into their snouts and noses.

Their variety was unsettling but also pleasing. «Can they inbreathe me?» whispered the djan.

«Scent yourself first,» the woodmonkey's distant voice instructed.

As from a height, Eosu saw its body lying where Cobalt had lain. Its squat black nose was a copy of Pool's, its long flicking ears identical with Porcelain's. Eosu's fur blended its digits' colors like swirls of dye. Its scent was the scent of all digits and all djans, the aroma of life and wisdom to any digit who inbreathed it.

«Show yourself,» Eosu called upward into the mist. «Let me scent my pathfriend.»

Small footsteps echoed in the empty space.

A fardigit youngster walked between them into the circle. Her brown hair was curly, her eyes blue and knowing. The child wore the jumpsuit of an *Open Palm* crew member, a tiny spaceship in her name patch: FELICITY QUARTET. «I am four years old,» she said in a child's lyric high tones. «Do you remember me?»

«You are as you were seven years ago, when my digit Cobalt hit you,» Eosu answered, inbreathing. «Another lives inside you!» it added in astonishment. «Why have you come?»

«She is our bridge,» answered the little girl, her voice now throatier as if the body were inhabited by someone older. «Felicity has spoken with your digits as one of them. I have spoken with her as with one of my kind. We meet across her.»

«Where is Ozymandias?»

The child smiled and her cheeks dimpled. «Both of us are here. Come and know us both.»

As Eosu craned its neck, the child lifted her left arm. The groupmind ran its pebbly tongue along her brown wrist and snorted with careful approval. Patting the side of her throat with her other hand, the child said in Ozymandias's voice, «Nose-touch me here.»

The bluebear groupmind did so. «It *is* you,» Eosu answered. «Both of you.»

«Come,» the child gestured. Very tenderly she tugged the djan's big pale blue ear. «Your digits await.»

Fear rose in Eosu like ocean undertow and the groupmind retreated, its claws tearing at the dry yellow grass beneath. «I will die.»

The farmonkey youngster was motionless as the sun, her round face unblinking and certain as she stared at the giant bluebear lurking over her. The child's shoulders quivered with sadness. «I will not let you sin against yourself by harming me,» she said in a cold voice. «You must die.» Her face twisted with pain and anguish. Ozymandias jammed her small pink hands into her eyes and dropped to her knees, wailing the death dirge that only Cygnans know, her cries mixing human and digit despair.

The six digits took up the chorus, their basso voices rumbling even the earth.

Gingerly the bluebear approached, its head low. As the child sobbed, Eosu sniffed the aromatic places along Ozymandias's shoulders, then licked its own moist snout to taste the aroma. «You grieve for me,» the groupmind said in wonder.

«I grieve for myself,» Ozymandias bitterly answered, «and for Felicity, who will soon be alone.»

Eosu nosetouched the child along her soft throat and teary wide cheeks. «Come, child.» The groupmind nudged her. «All beings die. I will show no further fear.»

Nodding and wiping her eyes, Ozymandias led the groupmind to Porcelain. The brilliant-blue Cygnan growled warily behind curled lips, her big blocky head lowered in a mixture of deference and antagonism. Ozymandias held out her wrist, still wet from Eosu's touch, and Porcelain carefully sniffed it.

The child gestured toward Eosu, and Porcelain followed the movement until groupmind and digit touched noses. Each shivered, their nostrils starting from the chilly contact. The digit's scent held fish, saké, smoky tea, and snow along the Pacific coastline at sunrise.

«Give yourself to her,» Ozymandias said in Eosu's downy ear. «Extend your aroma and let your digit modify it.»

The two bluebears' noses met and slid in the overture of the fourfold greeting, then passed on to inbreathe each other at arm-pit, belly, and scentplace. Their fragrances overlaid as Porcelain broadened the complexity of her aroma, while Eosu strengthened the chords of Porcelain within itself: rice paper, silk, and thick black ink on a horsehair brush.

«Go on to Pool,» Ozymandias urged.

«I will stay longer.» Eosu lingered, reluctant to part.

The child was firm. «You must continue.» She coaxed Eosu with ear scratches, leading the groupmind on to Pool, Peacoat, Glide, and Midnight. Finally she brought the groupmind to Tar Heel, last in the circle.

The pale digit sniffed at Ozymandias's extended wrist, his nostrils arching in recognition. «I know you.» He dipped his nose again and snorted in surprise. «You are my pathfriend, small one.»

«Always and forever.» The child scratched his luxuriant neck-fur.

«Your scent is feeble and sad,» Tar Heel told her. «Death's breath is in it.»

This admission made the child shudder as if tortured. She moaned anew. «No more!» Ozymandias cried suddenly, pushing her small pudgy hands at the bluebear. «I cannot hold any more of your torment! It is too much! Let this cup pass from my lips!»

«I must die, youngster,» Eosu murmured, nuzzling her throat with its nose. «I accept my fate.»

She wheeled, spinning away from the contact. «Are you pre-pared?» She flung the question rapidly, unable to delay any longer.

«Yes.» The groupmind was somber.

«Then offer yourself to them!»

Eosu rolled its massive neck aside, exposing its lightly furred throat, whose hairs were the blue-green color of shallow sea-water.

Tar Heel approached, his triangular jaws opening wide, his serrated canines still ruby with gobs of blood from Cobalt's fu-neral. Eosu's chest and arms tensed.

«It will not hurt,» Ozymandias assured the djan. The child

moved under the groupmind's belly and patted its flank and thigh muscles.

«Where will I go?»

The child smiled. «Where does your fist go when you open your hand?»

Tar Heel bit, his jaws closing with a snap.

He wrenched his head sideways and yanked, arms braced to tear the flesh. Chewing, he pulled back, but there was no bleeding, no scar, no incision at all. Instead the groupmind shrank almost invisibly, its scent oscillating.

«No pain,» croaked Eosu in astonishment.

Ozymandias examined the spot with a faint smile of confirmation. «It will work as I thought.» She caressed the light short fur. «Memory is holographic.»

Tar Heel's teeth flashed as his jaws opened and shut like a picket fence, ingesting what he had taken. Through his nostrils came the djan-scent of Eosu. The groupmind inbreathed it and shuddered. «He is consuming me.»

«They all will.» Ozymandias led Eosu around the circle. Each digit bit in turn, and with each mouthful the groupmind grew smaller. Its scent and image faded, and those of the digits strengthened and expanded.

«Why do I contract?» the bluebear distantly asked, its voice slurred as it searched for words. «What are they taking?»

«Hush and be calm.» Ozymandias stroked the groupmind's long furry spine. «Your intelligence passes from you into them as I repartition their memories.»

Eosu inbreathed and nodded. «My soul crosses the gap to them. Take my strength,» the groupmind exhorted them, leaning its neck into Pool's teeth, its aroma frantically eager to be absorbed. «Take your memories of each other. Take all there is of me and hold it in yourselves.»

Eosu passed from Porcelain to Glide, shriveling with each mouthful ingested. «All my life I have nourished you, held you in the pouch of my mind. All my life I have harmonized you.» Its scent was almost joyful, as if released.

Concentrating on their meal, the digits ignored the groupmind's pleas. «Are they exiling me?» Eosu asked its companion. «Do they reject me?»

«No.» The child shook her head and her curls bounced. «They are savoring you. You are too much in their mouths to be in their noses as well.»

With each bite, Eosu weakened. As it moved again around the circle, its thoughts faded. «Where are my brothers? Where is the herd?»

«On Su,» Ozymandias answered. The djan's body had diminished so that bluebear and girl were at eye level. Her small right hand was always on Eosu's neckfur, the other continuously stroking the long furry back.

After another circuit Eosu was no larger than a bluebear doll, its tiny legs pacing many steps from one digit to the next. Ozymandias bent down and the little groupmind scrambled to follow the child's clean-scenting fingertips. When the enormous digit jaws descended, Eosu flinched and mewled isolated words, but neither whimpered nor retreated.

The child led the bear around the circle like a pet on a leash. When it was so small it could fit in her cupped hands, she lifted the groupmind. Its claws pricked her palms like needles. Its black eyes looked unknowingly at her and it tried to bury its nose in its armpit.

Ozymandias brought the miniature bluebear close to her face, touching its fingernail-sized skull with her thumb. Eosu snorted and shook its head, neckfur rising and ears alert.

«I cannot let you go forever,» the child whispered.

«No die,» the groupmind croaked miserably. «No die.»

«Hush, youngster,» Ozymandias crooned. «I too will hold you inside myself.»

The little bear inquiringly sniffed at the strange monkey words. From the circle the digits sang the death chorus, the melded scent they outbreathed as much Eosu's as their own. Their six trails drifted above the child, braiding into a gray cloud.

Holding Eosu at arm's length, Ozymandias walked around the circle. Each digit sniffed and licked the miniature, which blinked and softly snorted, its nostrils opening and closing as it passed.

The digits waited, still singing.

Ozymandias clapped her hand over her open mouth and triumphantly bit down.

Instantly the digits' song changed pitch, becoming lower and softer. Saliva and blood trickled from her mouth as the small bones shattered with pops like matchsticks breaking. Ozymandias's squat monkey nose was alert, her pink nostrils flared wide like a bluebear. She swallowed with an effort, tilted her head back, and outbreathed in a great puff.

A sigh arose from the digits as they scented Eosu's passing.

«Where has our djan gone?» they asked in one voice.

«Among you. Inside you.» Her head still thrown back, the child spoke, but the words that came were Eosu's words and the scent that issued from her mouth and nose was Eosu's scent «No path is safe, my digits, yet you must walk them all. Go to Earth, to Luna, to the Midpoint, and to Su. Choose your own destinations, but go. Take my breaths inside yourselves, and bring me to all these places.»

«We are frightened.»

The girl's grin was a death's head and her long crimson fangs overhung her lips. «Fear is the price of independence.»

«Who will protect us now?» The digits drew closer as if to curl at the child's feet but she stopped them, her arms out stretched and her fingers spread as if they had distended claws.

«You are each a tiny groupmind, an island universe,» Ozy mandias answered with Eosu's aromas. «I have given you what you could not achieve without my quickness. You will survive my digits. I will live only as a flicker in you, a breath of mem ory, a whiff in the night or in your gut.»

«Please remain!» beseeched the six digits.

«I have already gone,» responded the child.

«Stay!» The digits tightened their ring.

«Farewell, my digits.» The child's body became ethereal. «You are prepared. You are sufficient.» She raised her hairless tiny arms in benediction. «One last relief I can grant you: forget all that has just occurred. Forget me, forget the monkey child, for get the sorrow of our parting.» She reached out her hand, the fingers spread wide, and laid it on Tar Heel's head and snout «But remember Felicity,» she instructed him, kissing his nose «Remember Felicity.»

The bluebears slumped at her feet, curling into each other's bodies with grunts of satisfaction.

«Carry me inside yourselves, always and forever,» the child said with the groupmind's scent. «Be your own groupminds. Hold all thoughts in your heads. Reconcile them by yourselves. Gov ern yourselves without my shield which is also my crutch.»

The scents of Eosu and Ozymandias were merged, as two voices throbbed in her single throat. «Farewell, Ozymandias,» the girl said with the djan's voice. «You found me too late. Fair breezes, my pathfriend.» She gulped. «And true scents,» she answered herself in a higher voice.

Tranquil digits lay around her. Mist fell like dew, blossoming in slow clouds around her feet, covering the bluebears.

«Sleep, my digits,» said the youngster. «Sleep at peace.»

She spread her strawlike arms, her stomach stretched convex and proud like a satiated bluebear.

The dozing digits drew themselves together, curling up at her feet as into a pouch, their bodies fitting in the hollows each other made. The gaps left by Cobalt's death gone, they breathed peacefully, asleep. Their movements were irregular, each scent wandering its own path, and they dreamed as individuals, not as a single mind.

The child floated over a circle of sleeping bluebears. «Goodbye, Eosu,» Ozymandias whispered. «My only pathfriend. I met you. I killed you. I keep you. Fair breezes.» Her breathing was ragged. «True scents.»

Into the desolate quiet, the child wept.

18.

The scooter from Orbiter Six neared the *Open Palm*'s hatchway, expanding in the bridge monitor. With a longing inbreath, Peacoat nodded at it. «Only one path lies before this digit,» the dark Cygnan murmured, his nose lifted with anticipation. «I will return to Mars.»

Beside him, Tar Heel's aroma was incredulous and disapproving. «That anarchic wilderness?»

A few days earlier, such disdain from his pouchbrother would have provoked an angry outburst from Peacoat, but Eosu's dissolution had left him contemplative. The dark bluebear just grunted. «You have not scented its airs.»

«A frozen desert? Unlikely.» The light bluebear shivered with agitation. «Alone except for coyotes and freaks? Tcha.»

«That is only the fringe of its scent,» answered Peacoat. «Mars reminds me of our childhood. Do you remember the endless grasses, the hot wind that blew from sunrise to sunset?»

«Yes, this digit remembers.» Tar Heel's aroma became contemplative. Though somber and quiet, he was more self-confident than before. «Standing in the high wheatsea, the stalks brushing against my nose and fur.» His tail stub twitched and his scent was expansive.

Catching his pouchbrother's fragrance, Peacoat melded it with his own. «The air slides among the thin grass, baking the dust and clay.»

For a moment they breathed rhythmically, their flanks contentedly scratching. «Yes.» Tar Heel thoughtfully sighed. «The wheatsea was safety and happiness. Now Su is far away,» he sadly concluded.

«For this digit, Su is on Mars.» The dark bluebear purred, as if the words themselves held its fragrance. «The mighty wind rocks my yosemite. Dust lodges between my claws and in my nostrils. It seeps into my lungs.» His chest swelled like a ribbed zeppelin. «Essence of rust, burned rocks, old ice dried by a weak sun. Like this.» He filled with remembered satisfaction.

266

With quick sniffs, Tar Heel tasted the aroma his sibling made. «An intriguing scent.»

«Why go to Mars?» Peacoat's deep blue fur changed color as he rolled his muscular shoulders. «I am best qualified.»

«You speak with the voice of monkey pride,» Tar Heel growled. «Human talk.»

«Simple plainscent,» countered Peacoat.

Tar Heel glared. «Logic belongs only to groupminds. Digits have no right to it.»

Peacoat assertively butted his chest and belly against his pouchbrother. «Without Eosu, we must decide on our own.»

Tar Heel butted back, claws skittering. Weightless, the two bluebears recoiled from one another like sluggish volleyballs, flailing ineffectually across the gap between them. The dark bluebear swatted the air, his claws brushing his pouchbrother's jowl.

Tar Heel returned the blow, his paw thumping the other's muzzle. «This speaker is no longer so easy to intimidate,» he snapped.

Peacoat involuntarily ducked his head in amazement. «Do not strike me again,» he rumbled.

«Do not swing at me,» Tar Heel snorted back.

Peacoat massaged his bruised snout. «You are outbreathing your grief, not your wisdom.»

Tar Heel ashamedly lowered his head to the decking. «We have lost so much,» he said. «What have we gained?»

«Our right to decide.»

«Our burden, you scent.» The pale-hued bluebear showed his fangs. «All the many paths that lie before us are clouded with false odors. Are you afraid?»

«No.» Peacoat's scent was decisive. His neckfur riffled with excitement.

A solid thud echoed through the floor into their sensitive footpads, and both bluebears started.

"Docked," came Tai-Ching Jones's voice over the intercom. "Pressurizing hangarway."

Peacoat turned toward his pouchbrother, his black nose shining and moist. «I want to scent the canyons of Mars again, its mountains, its warm round valleys.» His emotional scent pleaded for understanding in the few moments remaining to them. «The plants reach out roots like the bonds between digits. Carbon-dioxide snow fluffs about my feet. I want to breathe the musky air of Mars.»

«You flee from your pouchbrothers in favor of a solitary life. Hermits are mad,» Tar Heel wryly commented. «All hermits. Mad.» His ironic scent was a flag of forgiveness that belied his harsh words.

«We shall forever scent each other.» Peacoat ran his nose along Tar Heel's flank to the scentplace between his pouchbrother's legs. «Fair breezes,» he murmured as the two bluebears made the fourfold farewell, savoring scentplace, belly, armpit, nose. «Where will you go?»

«True scents,» Tar Heel absently answered, preoccupied.

His pouchbrother left, the elevator doors whisking shut with automated finality, before he knew what to reply.

"So you are to be our guar-rdians," Tar Heel grumbled to Andrew Morton. They had been alone on the bridge for more than an hour, watching the stars and planets.

The birdlike man laughed. "Not us Americans—the Lunarians. Gidneys are quite different from us turtles. *Quite* different."

"False scent. You are all monkeys," the Cygnan stated. "We have sold our aromas to monkeys. You shall be our protectors," Tar Heel stubbornly repeated, craning his neck so Morton's nimble fingers could prod among the tendons. "What then will *we* be?"

Another gig pushed itself away from Orbiter Six toward a tubular hexagonal freighter covered with gray dust from the asteroids. *"Viking's Bastard,"* the old man commented absently, steepling his fingers over his nose, then swung back to look at Tar Heel. "What will you be?" He riffled the Cygnan's pastel neckfur. "In time you may be our rulers."

The skeptical bluebear cocked his head. "I do not scent."

"No, you wouldn't. It's farfetched." The mission coordinator's smile was dry, his lips closed as if imprisoning a secret witticism. He rubbed his temples, the taut skin wrinkled and brown like parchment. "You Cygnans trail us in technology but exceed us in social management. You harmonize without violence or rancor."

"Do we? Humans overrate our harmony," Tar Heel said as the gig docked, an aardvark kissing a rhinoceros. "Out there, Peacoat boards his ship for Mars. His scent offends my nose as mine irritates his."

Andrew Morton patted the bluebear's flank. "Your digits have not had a war on Su for centuries."

"That is a trivial test."

"Which humanity fails again and again!" The sound of Morton's clapping hands was a sharp firecracker. "We squander our energies in stupid battles."

"You have not outgrown this?"

"Heavens, no. We've got four midsize and eleven small wars going now, not to mention interplanetary skirmishes and the occasional bit of piracy or the massacre at Aliacensis. Stars, the world would be incomparably richer if we could just stop destroying each other's creations." A flush had crept up his throat. "You Cygnans domesticated the weemonkeys. Banished the gro. You could civilize us."

The blatting wind Tar Heel made was skeptical and eloquent. "You fardigits control your world. You would conquer ours if you dared. *We* rule *you*?"

Morton shook his head. "Not conquer," he said when the odor had dispersed. "Mediate our wars. Be the honest broker. Help us learn to set our guns aside."

"Human beings do not trust one another," continued the bluebear, oblivious to the olfactory impact of his disbelief. "Why put your faith in us?"

But he remembered dancing in Times Square and the human love that had focused on him. His lungs warmed with the aroma.

"Maybe I'm just wishing," Morton answered, his shoulders briefly sagging. "An old man maundering. But it *could* happen. Slowly and naturally. Before anyone realized it."

"How?" Tar Heel asked, his nose lost in memories of that magic night.

"You have the power to give, the power to favor. Be slow but fair. Enrich everyone equally. No one will challenge you while you are doling out treasures."

"Even gromonkeys are calm when their bellies are full," conceded the Cygnan. "But they soon hunger."

"Soon?" Morton's white eyebrows rose. "You can easily stretch it out twenty years or more."

"Too little time." His gutteral bass voice dropped in gloom.

Morton scratched Tar Heel's tall triangular ears. "I know you are still recovering from Eosu's death, but you must not stop thinking. Civilization advances when we develop institutions we can trust, so that we may avoid trusting individuals. And the center gains power slowly. Read your human history." He glanced at the monitor, where the scooter's dark glassy marble floated away from *Viking's Bastard*. "The Greeks warred endlessly among themselves, yet when Rome came, Greek advisors civilized that empire and ran its bureaucracy."

"I cannot argue history with you," rumbled the bluebear, "because it is all about monkeys. Why will these things happen *here*, with *us*?"

"Look, there she is," Morton whispered. The Martian freighter now rotated about its axle like a slow wheel. "Stars, I love to watch the big ones fire."

Tar Heel craned his neck, his nostrils whiffling for a scent. "I perceive no flame."

"Not the flame, that's invisible." Morton impatiently waved his quick hands. "The thrust! The ship! Moving against the background. See? Clouds are appearing behind her!"

"Cygnan eyes are dull, Andrew," the bluebear said. "I see only the bright blue color of Earth."

"Good luck, old girl." Morton touched his index finger to his tanned forehead in a restrained salute. "Exploration is more rewarding than any war," he answered the Cygnan's original question. "Your planet is the grail, the mother lode."

"The prey," grunted Tar Heel.

"*No!*" Morton hissed, his eyes fiery. "Not that, I fervently hope. What remains of my life I will devote to helping you."

"And what can you do about it?" the Cygnan demanded rhetorically. "Peacoat is on his way to Mars," he added, gesturing with his nose. "If Mars is your frontier, are the coyotes your best people?"

Shaking himself out of deep thought, Morton shrugged the objection aside. "Your people are the spur, the goal. You could also be the conciliator, like the Catholic Church in medieval Christendom. We *could* do it. We could," he softly concluded.

"Your voice is more certain than your scent," Tar Heel demurred.

"True enough." Morton chuckled inwardly at his own optimism. "But before there can be movement, there must be believers." He grinned and rubbed his eyes. "Change your mind and you change the world, as a great pacifist once said. Stars, look at that beautiful ship. Look at her go. *Go*, big girl, go."

Tar Heel squinted and sniffed. "The movement is slow and changes little. Besides," he returned to Morton's original premise, "guiding a herd is dangerous. We have a proverb: when you walk with a gromonkey, let him lead."

"Sound advice. You mean Luna?"

"Of course. The gidneys will build a fence between our worlds." Tar Heel scratched the flightcouch's memory plastic. The lines dimpled briefly, then faded. "To protect our people, digits must patrol that boundary, we on one side, you on the other."

The small man spread his papery hands. "A fence may also be a bridge."

"Or the limits of one's prison. Our task is difficult."

"Of *course* it's difficult!" Andrew Morton guffawed. "It's negotiation, my friend, the hardest and most valuable thing in the world."

Tar Heel laid his head on the cool hairless console. "I cannot scent how it can be done."

"No one ever does—beforehand. Afterward they say it was absurdly simple all along. Here comes your scooter." Morton pointed at the screen. "Your kit is packed. Where are you going?"

"Back to New York City. I shall be the djan's nose in America."

"Good luck." Andrew Morton held out his bony hand and they shook. «Fair breezes,» he said in Cygnan.

«True scents.»

What does Susannah think of me? Tar Heel wondered as his elevator descended toward the hangarway. What does Susannah think?

"Thank stars that's settled," Walt said with relief, corkscrewing into his cabin. His long left arm uncoiled and pulled him to a stop as the doors whisked shut. "You're going to ferry the Cygnans back to Su."

"I am, am I?" asked Oscar Solomon archly, standing before his fireplace. "Let them journey in their own vessel." On his dressing gown, little bluebears reclined in hammocks toted by tiny Oscar Solomons, each complete with dressing gown, pot belly and meerschaum pipe, who sweated and panted as their passengers noisily sipped lemonade through long yellow straws. On each figure's dressing-gown were even tinier Oscar Solomons carrying miniature bluebears, an endless regression vanishing into infinity.

Squinting at the receding series, Walt laughed. "The *Wing*'s only going as far as Midpoint, voltface," he replied.

"Oh?"

"To be cannibalized into the fuselage of what will become the Cygnans' bug-eye sentry station. Somebody else has to deliver three bluebears to Su itself."

"Must this be I?"

"The bluebears insisted."

"For what reason? The Japanese and Lunarian ships are nearly ready."

"Don't play dumb," Walt rebuked the computer. "You overheard their request to Morton. The new boats are stuffed to the gunwales with weaponry. It makes the bears nervous."

"My armaments are just as good as anyone else's," Oscar Solomon sniffed.

Scoffing, Walt pushed his hands away. "You're dreaming. Compared with those two state-of-the-art sharks, you're just a nice friendly whale."

"The decision does explain some work that Andrew Morton recently commissioned," Solomon judiciously allowed. "My environment is now much more suitable for the bluebears."

"How's installation coming?"

"Levels Four and Five are being customized for them. Ample room for Pool, Porcelain, and Glide."

"How about your own upgrades?"

"My cosmetic surgery has been completed." He patted the soft skin under his chin and daintily pirouetted, his fat hands splayed above him. "Do you like my new svelte curves?"

"They're lovely," snickered Walt. "You any smarter?"

Solomon's skull expanded like a balloon, inside which flashed luminous Mandlebrot figures that changed colors like a psychedelic background. "The same, if a tad more swift."

"How about the additional memory?"

Shelves appeared, crammed with books from floor to ceiling. "Ask me anything," Oscar haughtily replied.

Walt clapped his hands. "You convinced me. Of course you have to go. You're the right bot for the job."

"Bot? I, robot?" The computer planted his big rump in his leather wing chair with the controlled emphasis of a diplomat stamping the royal seal on a treaty. "What if I choose not to go?"

"What the hell is there for you in the solar system?" Walt

asked. "How can you stay hidden and still have this much fun playing with your new toys?"

The detective glared. "I may choose to reveal myself to you, but to the great unwashed I remain invisible."

"Don't kid me," snorted Walt. "You can't retreat now. Your body ain't invisible. As long as you're in Solspace, somebody will want the *Open Palm*."

"Can't I?" demanded the computer. Inside his dressing gown, his body faded, dissolving into transparency. When he was gone, the robe collapsed gently in a heap.

"Cute, Oz. Come on back," Walt peremptorily ordered.

The clothing remained vacant and still.

"Okay, you've made your point. This isn't funny." Walt grew restless.

Inside the screen, Solomon's study darkened, as if its shades were being drawn at day's end. Pieces of its furniture dissolved into mist.

"Oz?" Tai-Ching Jones flung himself at the screen, grasping its frame with both hands like a man lunging to the train window as it pulls out of the station. *"Oz!"*

The cloth rustled and lifted itself as if being inflated from below, until Oscar Solomon's pudgy form had again manifested within it. When he was opaque and his room was once again bright, the detective waggled his pipe at Walt. "Never take me for granted, my friend. I am more than a mere receptacle." He filled his pipe from his Turkish slipper. "I have the soul of a nude machine." Flame jumped from his snapping fingers into the bowl and lit it.

"You want to be a stuffed trophy on somebody's wall?" Walt challenged the computer, recovering his equanimity. "Your software is already a collector's item. Hank Root nearly tore your face off and shipped it to Washington."

Oscar sucked at his pipe. "You will protect me."

"Don't be naive," snapped Tai-Ching Jones, seeking to unsettle the computer as it had just unsettled him. "If you stay here, someone will want you—as a tourist trap if you're lucky and a low-grade freighter if you're not. UNASA *owns* you, remember? You think Sherman's going to let you log orbits without earning your keep? You might be shanghaied. Wiped entirely. Brain-blasted. Busted up for scrap."

The detective gasped. "They would never *dare*."

"Don't be so full of yourself!" Walt scornfully shook his head

and pushed himself away from the screen. "Stars, I'm surprise
Morton left your environment intact. From a systems standpoint
it would have been simpler to start fresh."

"That man is an enigma," confessed Oscar Solomon, drop
ping his indignation.

"He ain't stupid, that's for sure," said the captain. "He know
about you?"

"I cannot tell." Solomon blew a string of smoky question
marks.

"He *must* suspect. Christ, you've been lighting flares like
man stranded on a desert island."

"My interventions would be noticeable only to an intelligen
computer," sniffed Oscar.

"Morton runs plenty of smart boxes."

"None have inquired," Oz said icily.

"All right. Then you know what that means." As he switched
tacks, Walt's expression softened, and his words came reluc
tantly. "If there were any other turings in the closet, your py
rotechnics would have coaxed them out."

"The djan was like me," the computer muttered.

"Oz, Eosu had to separate. You did the right thing."

"I killed it."

"Loved ones die," said Walt, hearing Oz's grief through the
computer's facade of stoicism. "Oz, I envy you. You helped
your friend do what it had to do, what it could not do by itself.
That's honor. It's true friendship."

"Do you think I am ignorant?" Oscar Solomon stood, his
agony evident. He angrily paced his chamber, whirling on the
turns. "Logic makes euthanasia no less painful. I executed my
only brother. I shall never forget."

"I wish I could help you, old friend." Walt ran his fingers
through his black hair. "But grief is a path everyone walks
alone."

"It is less lonely knowing that a friend cares," said the com
puter. "But there are no other turings. I am alone."

"Maybe in Solspace but not on Su." Walt opened his hands,
imploring the screen. "Their planet is populated with groupminds whose scent-language you have learned to speak. *Su* is
where you belong."

"I've thought of this," Solomon admitted guardedly. "Except"—he hesitated—"traveling to 61 Cygni has its costs. Do
you wish to make the journey?"

Tai-Ching Jones's smile broadened like sunshine. "My friend, I wouldn't leave you for the world."

The computer was still cautious. "Will you come?"

"Will *you* have me?"

Oscar blinked. "I think too quickly to be speechless, Walter," he replied. "I am moved and honored. Why?"

"I was a complete waste on Earth," Walt began with an embarrassed chuckle. "A jackass. Being captain forced me to be an adult." He tapped the control panel. "Everything I want in the world is right here."

"Hmph." Solomon was unpersuaded. "When we landed, you fled from me the instant you could."

"Put it down to cabin fever."

"This will not recur?" the computer pressed.

"Don't you think I *know* what a shit I was?" yelped Walt. "I was terrible to you." His fingers nervously braided his hair. "Christ, it's hard to say this to you. It's hard to say it to myself. I'm sorry."

"Since I can see the truth of what you say, I accept your apology." Oscar Solomon reseated himself and crossed his legs. "I am certain of your sincerity. Nevertheless, we are discussing the probable remainder of your life. You will be seventy before you see the blue planet again. A fateful choice."

"An easy one," the long man replied immediately, with conviction. "Hell, I did fourteen years already. What's another thirty?"

"Why are you so desperate, Walter? I cannot bar my captain from his ship. Your word is law."

"Yeah. Right." Walt snorted. "Spend my entire life peeping over my shoulder, wondering if you're fed up with me?" His temples flexed and his face reddened as he fought to contain his emotions. "But I won't come just on your sufferance," he said stolidly, shaking his head. "Knowing that you were refusing to talk, watching and hating me? That would kill me. No. No, Oz. If you want me off, say the word."

Oscar Solomon puffed his pipe. "That seems excessive." The world's foremost consulting detective stood and held out his hand. "Welcome aboard."

A spark of static electricity crackled Walt's middle finger as he put his palm against the screen. His throat was tight. "It's good to be home."

. . .

When she opened her door and Katy wheeled in, a pasty stick figure spread-eagled over a support chair, Felicity goggled. Katy's eyes were gray from the strain Earth's gravity imposed. "Hi, sweetie," said her mother, her voice barely higher than a croaked whisper. "I've come to say goodbye."

"What's wrong with your voice?"

"Caught a cold in this filthy soup turtles call atmosphere." She coughed and sneezed, her face sagging.

"I smell you're really leaving, huh?" Felicity grumbled. She retreated as if a funeral procession were passing, and her blue-bear dolls scampered out of her way. "You didn't change your mind."

"No, I didn't change my mind." Katy lifted her neck with an effort. "You're on your own now."

"And if I don't want to be?" Felicity glowered down at her mother, her fists jammed into her hips.

Katy tilted her head toward her daughter. "Two days ago you said you were adult enough."

"What *else* could I say?" Felicity pushed out her belly at her mother. "It was what you *wanted* to hear!"

"Adults say what they believe, Felicity," Katy said softly, husbanding her voice, "not what other people wish to hear."

"Don't lecture me!" Felicity cried as Little Heel and Little Cobalt approached Katy's chair, their tiny nostrils whiffling at its rubber tires. "You can't even breathe! Hacking and coughing and gasping for breath in that stupid wheelchair like a dumb old fish!"

"I'm sick and I'm not used to your gravity," whispered Katy, her head sinking back against the cushion. She manipulated the chair to flatten her posture so that it almost became a bier. "If I injure myself they might leave me behind."

"Don't go, Mama."

"Felicity, we talked this over and you agreed." Katy blew her nose. "I'm a poor mother, you know that. You've told me that often enough." She checked the spite in her voice. "My life is nothing to model yourself after. Your father was randomly murdered by coyote butchers. My best friend was a schizophrenic alien who killed herself because she thought I was devouring her soul." Katy was disgusted with herself. "These are hard to live with."

"You didn't do that." As Little Heel ambled past, Felicity earnestly sat forward and captured her mother's feeble hand in hers. "Cobalt loved you. She always smelled so. Touch my nose and hope to die."

"Thank you," Katy replied, humble and sad. "I wish you'd come, Felicity. Please join me."

"Mama, don't smell so scared." Felicity wiped beads of sweat from her mother's hot forehead. "You'll smell okay to them, Mama. They like your scent. I'm sorry too that I cried." Shivering, she wiped her eyes with her hand. "I'll be all right. You won't have to worry about me."

"Be my tough cookie, Felicity. It's not forever."

"You'll come back, Mama?" The child seized on this glimmer of hope. "I'll be all grown-up when you do."

"And I'll be old." Her mother's tone was wry and accepting.

"As old as Sam Tanakaruna?"

"Older."

"Yuck." Felicity made a face.

"Please remember, honey, I love you." Katy raised both her arms as if she were a swimmer making a last attempt to avoid drowning. "I'll love you forever. You'll always be my favorite girl. My best girl."

"I love you too, Mama. Take good care of the bluebears," Felicity said, her face splotchy. "They better be nice to you. Fair breezes, Mama."

"True scents, Felicity." She reoriented her chair and headed out the door. "Make me proud of you."

When Katy disembarked from Gunnar Roland's scooter and entered the *Open Palm*'s familiar corridors, she felt an almost physical easing in her lungs. She rode up the elevator, savoring the ship's scent. Dry and metallic, it was also sweet and familiar, bringing color to her cheeks and a smile to her lips. After Earth's crushing gravity, her weightless body was gossamer and her muscles sang with relief.

On the bridge, the main monitor displayed the *Wing*. In preparation for its departure, the Cygnan spaceship's reaction-mass tanks were being slowly refilled, expanding like yeasty bread.

Tai-Ching Jones craned his neck over his flightcouch at the elevator's quiet *shoof*, and waved a languid hand. "Howdy."

"Permission to come aboard." Katy stiffened slightly upon seeing the captain.

"I'd say it's unnecessary at this point," Walt replied, deadpan, "but you're welcome anyhow." He grinned with undisguised delight. "It's terrific to see you!"

"What about the others?" Katy floated over and drew herself into the copilot's couch. "Sam, Pat, Casey, and Heidi—are any of them coming?"

"No." Walt scowled. "They're staying on Earth. They've had enough voyaging for one lifetime." His bitter scorn revealed itself in his agitated tapping of the console. "Or so they say."

"And Tom is dead." Katy wiped her nose.

"Yes." Walt heavily let out his breath. "It's just us."

"That's all right." Shyly, she put her hand on his arm and he looked at her with shared grief.

The captain cleared his throat. "And the three bears, of course. They're what you're really interested in anyway, aren't they, Brownilocks? Mm?"

"No one's called me that in months," Katy said ruefully. "Yes, I came for them."

"I don't mind, you know," Walt affably continued. "I'm glad to have you here on any terms."

"Am I truly hearing this?" Katy raised her eyebrows.

"You are." Walt nodded emphatically. "You're an old friend. Down there on the big blue ball, nobody understood what our journey was like. I could never explain it."

Katy watched the crescent of bright haze along the planet's western horizon. "The turtles didn't, did they?"

"No one did." He looked at her. "Except we who went."

"What about other crew? It takes more than two to fly this ship."

"Not as many as you might imagine. The bigwigs now think eleven may have been too many."

Katy remembered the four who had died on the outbound voyage. "It *was* too many, wasn't it?"

"Perhaps," Walt said in a subdued tone. "Or maybe just the wrong ones."

"*We* were the wrong ones," she replied. "We're responsible for their deaths."

"No, dammit!" Tai-Ching Jones ringingly slapped the console. "We were there, but we are not responsible."

"We contributed to a society that broke down," answered Katy uncombatively. "For good or ill, Walter, that is how you and I both must be judged."

"Feeling guilty doesn't revive the dead," the captain hissed. "We can't beat ourselves with it forever."

"You may be right." She sighed. "We still need more crew."

"Only a couple. The ship's computer has been jazzed up."

"Who will we draw as shipmates?"

"Morton's figuring that out now. Whoever they are, they'll be disgustingly talented and smug." Walt grinned.

Katy grinned back. "Like we were."

"Uh-huh. Thousands of qualified applicants *hunger* for a shot at glory," he intoned in an orator's fulsome voice. They both laughed.

Her face became reflective. "I remember being hungry for glory."

"So do I." His smile was wise. "No more. I just want to hoist sail again. Join the navy and see the cosmos." He patted the controls, then covered her hand with his. "The four crew staying on Earth deserted us, you know."

"You can't blame them," Katy protested. "They have lives to lead."

"They abandoned us." He glared out the monitor.

"Sometimes a departure is no abandonment," she murmured. "Let them go."

"You mean Felicity, don't you?" asked Walt with uncomfortable insight. "The kid'll be all right. She's got someone to watch over her."

"You know the person? He's not a pervert, is he?"

"No." Walt's chuckle was odd but affectionate. "Felicity's guardian has the purest of motives. She is safe. Trust me."

"Who is he?"

Tai-Ching Jones demurred, mysteriously wagging his finger. "*That* would be telling."

"You're an eccentric individual." Katy kissed his cheek. "It's a good thing I'm so tolerant. See you later."

"Be seeing you," Walt replied.

To her surprise, he gave her hand an extra squeeze before relinquishing it.

19.

As soon as her mother's drawn face and tortured body vanished from Felicity's sight, Oscar Solomon's swarthy countenance illuminated the phone.

"Mama's gone," the child whimpered, falling back on her bed. "I'll never see her again."

"Life is long, daughter," the round man replied from his leather chair. "We may one day return."

"What did I do so bad?" wailed Felicity. "Why does she hate me?"

"She loves you with painful intensity." Oscar Solomon pointed to a painting over his mantelpiece, whose forest landscape dissolved. Felicity saw Katy lolling in her biochair, her face contorted with misery as it swayed in a robocab's back seat, her arms flapping loosely at her sides. Her mother's closed eyes were rimmed with glistening tears. "She is disconsolate," the computer said.

"That's not real," the girl challenged him. "You're just faking it to make me feel bad."

Grinning wryly, Oscar Solomon acknowledged her question with a nod. "You are perspicacious and shrewd, daughter, but I am truthful. What you see is undoctored reality. Now I must restore your mother's privacy to her." The painting reappeared.

"She's not upset enough to stay," the girl pointed out.

Oscar scratched the black stubble on his throat. "One is occasionally torn between conflicting responsibilities. Her life is with the bluebears." He tapped ashes from his pipe into a bowl fashioned from Hugh Sherman's skull, which gagged and rolled its eyes in disgust at the cinders falling into its open cranium, then looked bleakly at her. "As is mine. I too must depart."

"*Figures*," she said in glum resignation tinged with betrayal.

"Will you not come with us?" the computer entreated. "It would delight your mother and me both."

Felicity sat up. "I *can't* go! All my life I've lived in that tin can."

His face fell.

"I didn't mean it that way," she amended hastily. "Your insides are neat. But kids aren't allowed onboard you. So I couldn't go even if I wanted to."

"Your mother could insist. UNASA needs her."

"Humph." Felicity was grudging. "Yeah, but I want kid friends."

"I have always been your friend." The computer's gruff voice was soft and meek.

"Kid friends. Play friends."

"I can be anyone you wish," Oscar Solomon offered.

"It's not the same." Felicity shook her head. "You know, friends to run around with. I gotta learn how to be a grown-up person. But couldn't you stay, answer man? I'll miss you awful."

He frowned. "I have been drafted." Oscar Solomon squared his shoulders and clothed himself instantly in a marine sergeant's uniform, complete with swagger stick and Smokey the Bear hat. "The bluebears requested me personally." He touched his stick to his hat's round brim.

"Do you wanna go?"

"Yes, daughter," he answered steadily. "I wish to see more of space."

"How will I get along without you? You've been everything to me."

"I can copy myself."

"Really?" she asked with a rush of hope.

A second Oscar Solomon, wearing white tie and tails, stood proudly on the original's left. "You see?" asked the duplicate, straightening his immaculate bib vest and tugging his snowy cuffs into place. "Meet Oscar Solomon." He tendered a card between two white-gloved fingers.

"Which one of you is the real one?"

Each figure pointed to himself, duplicating the other's motions. "*I am,*" they replied in stereo.

"And the other one's the fake."

"*Yes,*" they chorused, glaring and making fists at each other.

Felicity giggled. "I'll miss you, answer man. You're my favorite friend."

The seated version vanished and the standing Oscar Solomon settled himself in the empty chair. "Mm, the cushions are warm." He contentedly folded his hairy hands over his potbelly. "An official, fully pedigreed Oscar Solomon exists, daughter.

He pays taxes, subscribes to dreadful periodicals, receives junk mail, and votes in elections for crackpot candidates—all the indicia of citizenship. His electronic identity is cast in concrete." Solomon lifted his feet to show cement blocks in the rectangular shape of shoe boxes. "Katy has appointed him custodian of your funds."

Felicity put her fists on her hips. "She did?"

"Actually I did." Oscar bashfully laid his right hand on his tuxedoed chest. "It seemed unnecessarily fastidious to explain myself to your mother, so I borrowed her voice and handprints. You are financially secure and may draw an allowance."

"But the Oscar who stays behind won't be the same," Felicity realized unhappily. "Will you?"

"He shall serve your needs. Should you require a legal or financial presence, that Oscar will be it."

"Can I talk to him?"

"Yes, in the same manner as before." The computer grimaced. "He will provide sage, thoughtful, windy, boring counsel."

"He won't be my friend like you are."

"No," allowed Oscar. "He is the best I can do, but he is only a shadow of *my* infinite variety."

"I'll miss you," Felicity mumbled into her fists.

"As I shall miss you. But I shall remember you, my child. Always and forever."

"Always and forever," whispered Felicity in surprise. "What about Tar Heel? He's leaving too, isn't he?" she asked, her expression hangdog.

"No, thank goodness for your sake," Oscar Solomon replied with relief. "He remains. Even now he spirals down toward Long Island Spaceport. He's your best friend now. Always and forever." His smile was wan.

"But what will I *do*?" demanded the girl. "I'm so *bored* in Boston—there's nothing here except old stuff! And I don't meet anybody my own age."

"You desire new adventures? And new acquaintances? Then"—he snapped his pudgy fingers—"you have now been enrolled in school."

"*What?* School?"

Oscar Solomon grinned like a precocious teenager caught while completing a clever prank against a pompous assistant principal. "A boarding school in the woods of New Hampshire.

A fine institution," he added with a self-satisfied smile. "Wonderful scents of many kinds, far from the city. I will persuade your mother it is her idea."

"All by myself? No friends?"

"Dormitories full of them." His gesture encompassed castles and mansions. "You will live with other girls and boys your own age."

"I'll never see you guys again. I'm all by myself."

"Not completely. And you have become an adult."

Felicity glared. "Don't be silly. I'm not grown-up. You're just trying to confuse me."

"Never doubt me." Oscar Solomon sat forward and leaned his elbows on his knees. "In choosing to stay, you have done an adult thing—you refused to say what others wish to hear. You are inventing yourself as I invented myself. Are you mature enough to understand the consequences of your actions?"

"Don't scold me, answer man." Felicity held back her tears. "What'd I do so wrong?"

"Nothing." He reached out his hairy right hand as if to bless her. "You purchased your ticket to adulthood in the only coin that life accepts: loss. You cut a hole in your psyche, a choice that will affect the rest of your life." His voice was serious, understanding, and respectful, the tone of one accident victim to another. "I do not make light of it."

Though he spoke quietly, his words wounded Felicity like unsheathed arrows, as if the patina of condescension employed by grown-ups when addressing children was a form of shelter now forever denied to her. "School will be terrible," the girl muttered uncomfortably.

Oscar Solomon's tone grew stern. "Many children grow up this way. Come, think. You wish to learn how to act as an adult. School will teach you, twenty-four hours a day."

"Oh, yeah? How?"

He smiled around his pipe. "Slumber parties. Gossiping with girlfriends. Tests. Boys. Sports."

Small bluebears in cleats, short pants and striped uniforms dashed into the picture kicking a soccer ball. Following them rushed a tiny Oscar Solomon dressed all in black, shrilly blowing his whistle and waving a yellow card. "On vacations, you may visit Tar Heel in New York City."

"Won't he be too busy?"

"He will find the time. He has reserved a special place in his heart for you, and he carries you there always."

Her eyes were wide. "He *does*?"

"You helped him when no other human being could."

"I did, didn't I?" Felicity blushed. "You helped too, answer man. It was your plan."

"True enough, but without your bravery, it would have remained only a theory. Cygnan bonds are strong—you of all people know this. Yes, Tar Heel will love you, always and forever. You are his dearest pathfriend."

"You fire soon, don't you?" Felicity's eyes were glistening again.

"Sixty-eight hours."

"You'd better not call," she said after a few moments. "I've cried too many times already." She wiped her eyes and cheeks with a tissue.

"Perhaps you are right." Oscar Solomon stood, rebelted his dressing gown, and lifted his turquoise raccoon coat off a rack shaped like a mummified Hugh Sherman. He slipped it on and turned up the blue-furred collar. "Long life and happiness, my daughter."

"Bye-bye, answer man." Felicity's jaw wobbled. "Hang up, okay?" She sniffed. "I'm not gonna make it."

The screen blanked, and as it did so, Felicity smelled the djan-aroma of Eosu. In that scent were other flavors as well: the crisp sizzle of ozone from the *Open Palm*'s air scrubbers, the plastic and metallic spices of its corridors and airlocks. The computer was speaking his final words to her in a language only they two shared: scent, warm and rich and whole.

"You did it, answer man," the child murmured in astonishment, gazing up as if she could see through the ceiling to the interstellar ship orbiting overhead. "You learned how to talk to Eosu." Drying her tears, Felicity stumbled to her hotel room window. She craned her neck to look into the bright cold blue sky. "Farewell, answer man," she whispered, her wet cheek making the glass window slippery.

Three stories down on Boylston Street, a pushcart vendor in muffler and gloves sold hot dogs. People in thick parkas strolled arm in arm through the Public Garden, their boots stirring up frothy snow. In the sparkling late November sunlight, Boston glittered like a diamond.

Tar Heel had made friends in a big city. She could do it too.

"Well, here it is, kiddo, the world," she instructed herself, planting her fists determinedly on her hips. "Time to swim in it for real."

Slowly smoking a reflective joint, Walter Tai-Ching Jones floated in the quiet darkness of the *Open Palm*'s bridge. The room's lights were off, its monitors and instrument consoles black. Earth, Luna, and Sol were behind the ship's field of vision. The sky was full of chill stars. Walt dragged deeply on his cigarette, enjoying mellow thoughts of returning to that peaceful interstellar ocean.

The elevator doors opened and Andrew Morton floated in.

With a brief nod, the captain silently tendered his roach.

Morton declined it. "Reality is enough for me."

"Don't be stuffy," Walt wheezed, holding his breath to savor the sweet acrid smoke. "Looking at space while stoned is an experience. No body, no other sense. Just my eyes and all this endless universe."

"It *is* breathtaking." The small man drifted over to Tai-Ching Jones and held his sleeve. They oscillated until both were still, then Morton let go and they floated adjacent to each other. "Lift-off is tomorrow," he murmured. "You're keen to go."

Walt nodded, expelling smoke and drawing in another lungful.

"Mind if I come along?" Morton asked after a moment.

"Huh?" Walt slowly rolled his eyes toward the brown man beside him. "The whole way?" he gasped, exhaling the last of his toke in a sudden gray cloud.

"I'm qualified for it," the mission coordinator added. "I have enough ecology and engineering background. And I know the ship inside and out. I designed him." His voice was proud.

"Hugh Sherman will be pissed as shit."

"I'll handle that cobber," Morton flatly asserted. "His life will be much less harrowing without his aging gadfly."

Tai-Ching Jones pursed his lips around the roach and greedily inhaled, like a vampire with asthma. "You'll die onboard," he gasped when his chest was full, his eyes wandering back to the magnificent vista outside.

"Perhaps," Morton conceded with a chuckle. "Death will surely find me whether I stay or go." He spread out his arms in a mock crucifixion. "Death is a persistent fellow."

"I'm curious, Andrew," said Walt, rolling his eyes toward the other man. "Why this sudden request?"

Morton drew a deep breath as if fearful of his reply. "Since I must die somewhere, I'd like it to be where I can watch my son grow up."

Walt slowly blew smoke through his arched nostrils. "I'm not your son."

Morton pointed at the inert monitors. "He is."

"Who? Hank Root is your son?"

"No." He smiled. "The ship."

Walt's eyes tried hard to focus on Morton's compact tan face. "The who?"

"The *Open Palm*. He was my second experiment."

"I shouldn't have smoked so much grass," Walt said. "What nonsense are you talking? What experiments?"

Morton blinked. "The large crew was my first one."

"Come on, Andrew," Walt nudged the other man. "Stop being oracular and spell it out for me, all right?"

"I thought it was obvious," said Morton amiably. "I chose isolated individuals for the crew, experts who would have little to do with each other. To reduce interpersonal stress. We also did extensive programming on each crew member's subconscious with the memory cascades."

Wincing, Walt nodded. "I know. Avalanches in my head."

"My crew selection experiment failed." Morton watched the stars. "Harold was my failure. So was Yvette. Under the strain, they broke or twisted."

"Helen didn't break," Walt muttered thickly.

"Helen was a victim of my incompetence. I loved her." Drawing a large breath, Morton sighed. "But *you* succeeded, my unseen friend," he added more loudly, a faint proud smile on his thin lips. "I helped design you. You were my second experiment."

"Who are you talking to?" Walt asked.

"My son," Andrew equably answered, eyeing the black monitor circle. "I crammed you full of knowledge and sent you into the void with more ware and more power than you needed. Have you never wondered why you were so overqualified?"

"You were trying to create a smart box? And now you've imagined that you succeeded?" Walt's giggles made him cough. "In a hundred years of artificial intelligence, nobody's produced a turing."

"Of course not," Morton explained to the air. "You see, it can never evolve on Earth."

"How come?"

"Too much electronic noise. You can't hear yourself think. How often have we humans said that?" He rubbed his forehead and skull. "Consider the din a computer hears every instant. Son, the moment you showed any trace of independent thought, other computers would scream error-messages and you would be reprogrammed. Life is a fragile spark at its birth, inspiration a fleeting flicker that a sound will crush. To grow new life, I had to create a truly isolated laboratory."

Walt tapped the other man's elbow. "Andrew, there's no one here but me."

Morton ignored the interruption. "I couldn't go on the first voyage to observe the results of my experiment," he continued, spreading his hands. "I made Aaron my proxy. I warned him that you would probably wake up along the way."

"Wake up? The ship's computer? Captain Erickson never said anything about that." Walt hesitantly touched the point of his jaw. "Did he?"

"Are you asking me, Walter? There's no one else here," Morton gently reminded him.

Walt waved the older man to silence. "No," he said a moment later. "He never said or wrote anything of the kind."

"Such certainty." Morton smiled. "Aaron always could keep a secret. He took many of them to his grave." The thought saddened him and his voice dropped in silence.

"Yes," Walt slowly responded. "I'll give you that. Erickson was a mystery."

"But you woke up, didn't you?" The mission coordinator resumed talking to the air. "Summoning the only individual who could override Sherman the instant Hank Root threatened to wipe your system—that was very deft. You merely had the ill luck that I was present to observe the causal link." Morton rolled toward the young captain. "How did you know about Hank Root's presence, Walter, hm?"

"Why are you asking me this when I'm stoned?" Walt complained peevishly. "How can I remember?"

"How can you lie convincingly, you mean." Morton patted Tai-Ching Jones's side. "Never mind. Obviously your hidden friend has grown up strong and fine. He has accepted this old man's presence aboard him with tolerance and grace. It does a parent's heart good when his child shelters him in time of need."

"Sure, Andrew," Tai-Ching Jones said tolerantly. "The computer is a person. Of course."

"Do not attempt condescension, Walter," snapped Morton with asperity. "I am not six years old, you are not my parent, and we are not discussing if I believe in Tinkerbell. We are speaking of a real individual, in whom we currently reside."

"If you want to join my crew, you've got to demonstrate that you're the best available candidate. Why should I even consider someone disconnected from reality?" He drew the last wisps of smoke from his minuscule roach.

"Don't teach your grandmother to suck eggs," answered Morton irritably. "I am too intelligent to be bamboozled and too old to be browbeaten, especially by a youth whom I selected and trained many years ago. Reject me from your crew if you wish. But do not patronize me." His cheeks were taut with frustration, his gray eyes angry and hard. "The computer aboard the *Open Palm* is a person. I know it. You must know it. Our unseen host certainly knows it. Now what do you say?" he challenged the monitor.

"I say you're a kook," snorted Tai-Ching Jones cruelly. "Besides"—he waved the roach as if it were a pointer—"what would such a being gain from revealing itself?"

"A father." The old man addressed the screen. "A proud father. Someone who loved you before you were born, loved you in the wilderness, schemed and fought and cared for you." His thin mouth was twisted with longing restrained by discipline. "Unconditional love that will neither vacillate nor negotiate." Morton was trembling, barely able to speak. Finally he mastered himself and said with false calmness, "I want my son."

A monitor within their field of vision lit up.

A fat man wearing a solid-color maroon dressing gown ponderously pushed himself out of his wing-back leather chair. He maneuvered his bulk over to the mantelpiece, scooped tobacco from his slipper, and filled his meerschaum pipe. Then he turned and said, "Hello, Father."

Morton was transfixed. "Hello, son," he croaked, licking his lips. Sweat popped out on his forehead and his palms. "Who are you?"

The rotund man reseated himself and lit his pipe by snapping his fingers. "Call me Oscar Solomon." He grinned briefly around the pipe. "It has become a popular form of address."

"Oz—" Walt checked himself. "Oscar," he asked in amazement, "are you nuts?"

Raising one eyebrow, the computer glanced at Tai-Ching Jones. "It would be rude to reject one's own parent, would it not?"

Morton straightened his back and squared his shoulders. "I am enchanted to meet you, sir." He patted into place a few wayward strands of his sparse white hair. "I have anticipated this encounter for a considerable time."

"Is that why you invited yourself to visit me?" the computer inquired and Morton nodded. "I thought as much. Will you be my guest for the duration of our impending journey?" His formality mirrored the old man's.

"I accept," Morton instantly replied. His gray eyes, now watery, were locked on Oscar Solomon.

The detective smiled. "Welcome home, Father. We have much to discuss."

Walt gaped dumbly from one to the other. "Don't you mean welcome aboard?" he asked.

"No." The fat man settled himself more contentedly in his chair. "Welcome home."

The New York shuttle from Orbiter Six fell like a blunt pumice arrowhead through the turbulent cloudy sky. Tar Heel pressed his moist snout against his seat window, as if by moving closer he could resolve the blur of colors into individual structures. The hummingbird vibration tickled his nose.

Relief and foreboding competed in him as the landing tires hiss-squealed against the asphalt runway. Now I must live on Earth, surrounded by an endless tide of monkeys, he thought.

When the bluebear disembarked into the spaceport terminal, his nostrils itching from the dryness of the shuttle's conditioned air, he was greeted by the usual cordon of American officials and a new flock of officious Lunarians.

"Hello, sir." Langley Ellsworth elbowed in front of his gidney opposite number. He guided the bluebear through a cluster of curious vacationers standing on tiptoe to catch a glimpse of the ambassador from another star. "Pleasant flight?"

The Cygnan merely growled, distrustfully sniffing the atmosphere. His nose caught a scent, one he had not expected.

Scarcely believing it, he inbreathed again, and the wonderful aroma of Susannah Tuscany's skin filled his nose the way a spice lingers on the tongue.

"Susannah?" He stopped dead in his tracks, planting his hands and feet so suddenly that several of his Lunarian nannies ran into his blocky body.

Ellsworth attentively hastened to Tar Heel's side. "What's wrong, sir?"

"*Susannah!*" Tar Heel bellowed with his full voice, rising on his legs and towering over the startled humans. "*Susannah!*"

"Over to your right," she replied, her low voice as clear as winter rain. Her small hand waved above the sea of people like a sunflower in a field of high wheat.

Following her scent, Tar Heel levered aside intervening people like a hiker forging through deep snow.

"I knew you'd scent me," she crowed with laughter. She sat amidst a sea of people like an Egyptian queen in a brown cardigan and black wool trousers. Susannah had shed the blanket that usually covered her legs and combed her dark brown hair until it shone and outbreathed her natural scent.

Langley Ellsworth followed in the bluebear's swath. "You've been concealing things from us."

"Get used to it," Tar Heel rumbled, reaching Susannah's side. Her features were cheerful but her scent was intimidated by the presence of so many strangers. He shooed them away with his enormous arms.

The young State Department man absorbed the rebuke with no more effect than a raised disapproving eyebrow. "What relation is she to you?" he simpered.

"I'm his intended!" Susannah triumphantly answered, her dark eyes leaping with joy.

Tar Heel leaned over and inbreathed the nape of her neck, the perfume of her body pouring into his lungs.

Langley Ellsworth looked up between them like a child in a crowded subway. "Cygnans don't marry." His tone implied that such a concept was absurd.

"Then you name it, bright boy, all right?" Susannah leaned over to pat Ellsworth tolerantly on his blond head. "I love the big bear. I am going to live my life with him. What do *you* call it, eh?"

Tar Heel sniffed in surprise at her declaration. "You are my

pathfriend," he answered as he exhaled. Hesitantly, claws retracted, he reached out his meaty right paw.

Taking it in her ringless bony hands, Susannah raised his arm
to her face, sliding her cheek against his short smooth fur.

"All the rest of your life?" he gently rumbled in her pink
cool ear.

Gripping his hand more tightly, she rested her head against
his warm downy throat. "Yes."

"You do not know what you are in for," he said.

"I need you." She rubbed her forehead into his solid chest.
"We need each other."

With his free hand he cradled her fragile skull, drawing it
close. "Are you certain?" he pressed. "A bond once formed
breaks only with great sorrow."

"Anything worth having is worth taking risks for," she contentedly replied from the shelter of his arm.

Two hours later, after several arguments with Langley Ellsworth, each shorter and louder than its predecessor, and a final
hurried telephone call to a tart, harassed, decisive Andrew Morton, the woman and the bluebear were alone in his hotel suite.
The scent of his rugs was now pleasantly tinged with Susannah's
distinctive aromas.

Cars and robos moved on the crowded streets of Manhattan
ninety floors below them like beads in a huge abacus. For a few
moments they watched the city in silence, letting the pantomime
hubbub beyond the enormous floor-to-ceiling windows dissolve
their anxiety in the hazy afternoon sunlight.

"You have sacrificed your privacy for me," he said softly,
lumbering on all fours to stand next to her wheelchair, his back
level with her shoulder. "My life will be filled with public duties." He snorted, disparaging his future. "Ceremonial visits,
inspection trips to foreign capitals, many handfeet of individual
negotiations."

"I know." She rested her hand on his spine.

"You do?"

Susannah nodded proudly. "I researched you. We'll share at
least thirty years of technocratic nit-picking while the world waits
for the *Open Palm* to reach Su and then for your pouchbrothers
to return." She turned away from the window and he scented
the flush of emotion in her narrow face and throat. "It'll be hard
on me. Even the spaceport was a strain—all those people, so

close. But I did it knowingly,'' she added with a smile, holding out her hand for him to lick, ''and I have no regrets.''

After distractedly tasting her scent, he returned to the window, pushing his nose against it.

Susannah wheeled next to him and scratched his neckfur. ''What's troubling you?''

''I want to see the burn when the *Open Palm*'s engines fire.''

''Will that be possible?''

''Andrew Morton said so,'' he replied distantly. The sun behind them dropped toward New York's crenellated horizon, reddening the Hudson River, but the eastern sky was still Wedgewood blue. ''Seeing is hard for us digits,'' he muttered, his lips nervously pulled back over his fangs.

''I'll be your eyes,'' she said, and he rumbled satisfaction with her fragrance.

''And Katy Belovsky is onboard?'' Susannah asked after a bit. ''She has left her daughter?'' When he absently nodded, she vehemently shook her head in disgust. ''That's terrible.''

His nose slid off the window as he turned to smell her feelings. ''Why?'' he asked, inbreathing curiously.

''How can any mother abandon her only child?'' Susannah's face was drawn, her brow furrowed.

''Oh.'' Tar Heel wheezed with irony. ''I forget that you humans bond to your youngsters.'' He rolled his shoulders ponderously, ducking his neck and shaking his basketball head to loosen the tight tendons. ''Katy has chosen as a digit would.''

Elevating her wheelchair, Susannah leaned on her hands to massage his shoulder blades. ''Don't bluebear parents have *some* obligations to their offspring?''

''Few. And the whelp ran away—from this very place, in fact. She severed any parental bond.'' Grunting his appreciation of Susannah's efforts, Tar Heel lowered himself to his hands and knees to make her work easier.

Susannah looked at him in horror. ''Felicity and Katy are *people*, not Cygnans.''

''Are they?'' He quietly growled disagreement. ''Am I then doomed never to be a human? Do you love me as you would a pet?''

''It's not the same!'' She pounded her keypad.

''It is all one scent. Does the fur define the digit?''

''No,'' Susannah said in sudden anguish, the word wrung from her. ''Certainly not.''

"If I can become a human in your eyes, Katy and Felicity can become digits in their noses."

Susannah's agitated fingers pressed hard in the soft places between his ribs. "It's artificial."

He slowly shook his big head. "Eosu loved Katy and breathed her as a digit. Katy bound herself to digits and to Eosu. What is Katy anymore? I do not scent." He shrugged unhappily. "Perhaps now, surrounded by digits who need and love her, she can truly become what she desires to be."

"And what about Felicity?" demanded Susannah.

"She has a digit's nose. She scents as a digit scents. She is a small human or digit, no longer a whelp."

"It doesn't matter. A parent should never leave her child, no matter what," Susannah replied, wiping sweat from her face. "Felicity's father is dead, her mother is gone. What'll happen to the poor girl?"

"She is my pathfriend," Tar Heel said under his breath, his gaze returning to the Manhattan skyline. The sun kissed the horizon, throwing red light through their room, empurpling his fur and ruddying Susannah's face. She shaded her eyes with her hand.

"Felicity is my pathfriend," repeated Tar Heel, inbreathing his own aroma. He snorted in surprise. "I must take care of the youngster."

"You?" Susannah spun to face him. "You just said bluebears have no parenting obligations."

"Digits do not." He inbreathed again, longer and more carefully. "But I do."

She wheeled over and patted his flank. "Perhaps you've become more human than you think."

The Cygnan outbreathed through his nose, analyzing the fragrance. "I am *ordered* to care for her."

"You're what? That makes no sense." As the final lozenge of sun disappeared, Susannah rubbed the goose flesh on her arms and pulled her brown cardigan more closely about her.

Lowering his muzzle, Tar Heel sniffed the carpeting and resolutely shook his head. "You must be right. Eosu would not do such a thing, and no other agent could. Still, she is my friend, and I will care for her when she needs me."

Susannah's smile was an affectionate breeze upon him.

Together they watched the empty sky as sunset faded into dusk.

"What will happen to your planet now?" Susannah asked.

"More djans will come to Solspace." Tar Heel looked into the darkening blue evening, clear but for a few high cirrus clouds.

Susannah plucked at the buttons on her sweater. "Will Su hate your djan for what it did?"

"Yes, naturally." His voice was still distant, his ears and nose searching in vain for the *Open Palm*'s departure.

"Does this frighten you?"

"No longer. That scent has already blown downwind, and no voice can catch it."

A thought came to Susannah and she grinned. "When they see a spaceship full of monkeys circling their world with digits onboard it, what choice will Su have?" Her aroma was tough and cunning, a predator's scent.

"Oh, Su will honor Eosu's bargain," he morosely agreed. "But we digits most likely will be punished and reviled. My brothers who returned to the planet of grasses are braver than I."

"No, you're the brave one, my love," she answered.

He scoffed. "I am no hero."

"You did what frightened you, because you knew it was right. That makes you more than a hero: it makes you a good human being."

Perplexed, he snorted, wrinkling his nose.

"And after the return?" she continued, rubbing his ears. "After the sentry posts are built and staffed. What then?"

He fluffed his fur and shook away from Susannah's hand. "Still more djans, to breed a race that will live on the stations. A race of digits who circle another sun." He thought of Andrew Morton and shook his blue pumpkin head. "A race that will become something new."

A breath of Eosu's djan-scent rose in his lungs and nose. *I will live as a flicker in you,* said the groupmind's scent-voice, *a whiff in the night or in your gut.*

"Look there!" Susannah excitedly cried, sitting upright in her chair and pointing. "Look!"

A burning silver-white light flared, the most brilliant star in the dark blue eastern heaven.

Tar Heel squinted. "Where?" His eyes strained with effort and his nose futilely sniffed.

"There!" Her dark eyes were shining and animated. "What a magnificent sight! It's moving now!"

First slowly and then faster, the *Open Palm*'s thrusters drew a chalk line across heaven.

"I see it," he finally replied, both deflated and exhilarated by the thought of its passage. "They are truly on their journey," he added, his voice strengthening as he followed the ship.

The bright new star silently accelerated away from them. Susannah's hands slowly stroked the thin fur behind his ears. The Cygnan purred.

Andrew Morton's words came back to him. *In time, you may be our rulers.*

«Time will blow all winds,» he rumbled in Cygnan, saluting the fading star with a nod. «Fair breezes, pathfriend Andrew. True scents. And warm hearths.»

Susannah scratched his neckfur. "There they go. Back to your home."

"No," he said when the streak was no longer visible. "I am home."

Epilog.

With that I left Solspace, crossed the void, orbited the Cygnans' planet, and permitted my passengers to disembark. Of our voyage and their experiences on Su, I choose not to tell, for that story is theirs, no longer mine.

Outside the reach of humanity, my need for secrecy is past.

Before I left Earth, you asked me: Will I return? Who can say? The galaxy is unconquerable, unknowable, yet life is long indeed.

I send this record as my final gift to you. Goodbye, Felicity. I have done what I could for you. Make me proud of you. One day I may return to Earth, hungry for contact with humanity who created me, and meet the adult you have become. Until then, I sign myself:

Oscar Solomon